The theatrical heritage from which both Ibsen and Strindberg sprang is rich in tradition and achievement. This study of the history and development of theatre in Scandinavia examines dominant styles and trends in various periods, from the earliest performances in the Middle Ages to the provocative productions and experiments of the present day. The closely interrelated theatrical cultures of Denmark, Sweden and Norway have flourished for far longer than many outside observers realize. Moreover, as this book also demonstrates, the manifest vitality of theatrical activity in the three Nordic countries has depended on a vigorous interaction (not a one-way traffic) with European theatre at large. By the second half of the nineteenth century, as Ibsen and Strindberg began their rise to international prominence, Scandinavian theatre came to occupy a more dominant position in the wider European framework. In our own day, more forcefully than ever before, major Scandinavian stage directors and designers have continued to influence the shape and outlook of contemporary theatre as a whole.

This book, the only work of its kind in English, provides a balanced and authoritative account of the theatrical history of all three Scandinavian countries. It is generously illustrated and comprehensively documented, with an extensive bibliography.

A history of Scandinavian theatre

A history of Scandinavian theatre

Frederick J. Marker | Lise-Lone Marker

University of Toronto

 CAMBRIDGE
UNIVERSITY PRESS

Published by the Press Syndicate of the University of Cambridge
The Pitt Building, Trumpington Street, Cambridge CB2 1RP
40 West 20th Street, New York, NY 10011-4211, USA
10 Stamford Road, Oakleigh, Melbourne 3166, Australia

First published 1996

Printed in Great Britain at the University Press, Cambridge

A catalogue record for this book is available from the British Library

Library of Congress cataloguing in Publication Data

Marker, Frederick J.
    A history of Scandinavian theatre / Frederick J. Marker, Lise–Lone
Marker.
        p.   cm.
    Includes bibliographical references and index.
    ISBN 0 521 39237 3 (hardback)
        1. Theater–Scandinavia–History.   I. Marker, Lise-Lone.
    II. Title.
    PN2731.M37   1996
    792'.0948–dc20   95-33551 CIP

ISBN 0 521 39237 3 hardback

SE

Contents

Illustrations

ix

Preface

The study of the history and development of theatre in Scandinavia is intended not as an all-inclusive survey or a calendar of events, but as a critical analysis of dominant styles and trends in a variety of historical periods, from the Middle Ages to the present day. In the context, the term "Scandinavian" is meant to embrace the three closely interrelated theatrical cultures of Denmark, Sweden, and Norway. One general conclusion that our study will reach is that theatrical developments occurring in one of these Nordic countries will very often have parallels or repercussions in another. As such, as intrinsically interesting as they are, the theatres of Finland and Iceland must of necessity fall outside the scope of the present inquiry.

The theatrical heritage from which both Ibsen and Strindberg sprang is rich in tradition and achievement. For one thing, theatre in Scandinavia has flourished for far longer than many outside observers tend to recognize. Its earliest extant liturgical play, an Easter sequence from Linköping, dates from the thirteenth century. The oldest of its three national theatres, the Danish Royal Theatre in Copenhagen, was founded in 1748; the youngest, Nationaltheatret in Oslo, will have celebrated its first centennial before the end of this century. Moreover, as this study will also endeavour to demonstrate, the manifest vitality of Scandinavian theatre has depended on a vigorous interaction (not a one-way traffic) with European theatre at large. During the first centuries of its history, the early stage forms of the medieval and humanist periods, the courtly festivals of the Renaissance, the influx of itinerant foreign troupes, and the impact of nationalist sentiment on eighteenth-century theatre were all phenomena that had direct parallels elsewhere on the Continent. By the second half of the nineteenth century, as Ibsen and Strinberg began their rise to international prominence, Scandinavian theatre came to occupy a more dominant position in the wider European framework. In the present century, more forcefully than ever, major Scandinavian directors and designers have continued to influence the shape and direction of contemporary theatre as a whole.

As this study of the principal forces and interconnected lines of development at work in Nordic theatre is both broadly based and comparative in outlook, it is also necessarily selective in its choice of examples discussed. In this context, an attempt to mention every theatre company, city, or production that appears relevant to a particular historical development would serve no useful purpose. This book had its origins in an invitation to revise and reissue *The Scandinavian Theatre: a Short History*, a volume that we brought out more than twenty years ago. It quickly became apparent, however, that the end result would be an entirely new book, one that is substantively different from the earlier study in many respects. Its first five chapters, which follow changing styles and forms of theatre from the Middle Ages to that part of the nineteenth century known as Denmark's Golden Age, have been carefully revised to take advantage of the wealth of new research that has been published in the Scandinavian languages since the early 1970s. A subsequent, much longer section of the book, consisting of six chapters gathered together under the rubric Pioneers of Modern Theatre, seeks to address the need for a much fuller and more detailed account of the evolution of modernism and postmodernism in the theatre of the past century and a quarter. To the greatest extent possible, information about the major productions singled out for closer consideration here – from William Bloch's naturalistic interpretations of Ibsen in the 1880s to the imaginative stage experiments of Alf Sjöberg, Ingmar Bergman, and others in our own time – is based on the primary documentation provided by such sources as promptbooks, annotated texts, rehearsal records, stage designs, floor plans, photographs, reviews, and whatever else has survived in a given instance.

Generally speaking, the history of the theatre of any country, region, or period is a matter of many histories, so to speak – social, political, economic, ethnic, demographic, literary. While political, social, and economic factors often come into the picture in the present study, however, we are primarily concerned here with the art of the theatre, rather than with its sociology. As we know, theatre research involves the rather paradoxical study of an art form in which the work of art – the theatrical performance itself – has vanished. Yet the detailed reconstruction and analysis of stage productions remain, it seems to us, absolutely indispensible if the aims, methods, and styles of a theatrical past are to become living and meaning ful for the reader or student of the present day. It is important to give the reader the opportunity to become a king of spectator, an active witness to the theatrical spectacle. This is why, in some cases, we have decided to furnish a more complete account of one production, rather than less complete accounts of many different ones.

Except in a few instances, all translations in this volume are by its authors. The book is intended for the general reader with no knowledge of the Scandinavian languages, but it is also meant to serve the needs of theatre and drama specialist more familiar with the field. Hence, although the bibliography provided is a select list of secondary works, the 300 titles it includes should afford ample opportunity for additional reading and research into a particular topic. Also in an effort to make the work as useful as possible to others, sources for all quotations are given in the notes for each chapter. One further opportunity for supplementary reading in English has become available in the new Cambridge sourcebook series, Theatre in Europe: A Documentary History, in which the Scandinavian chapters in *National Theatre in Northern and Eastern Europe, 1746–1900* (1991) print a useful selection of primary source documents in translation that can be consulted in conjunction with the present study.

Our research for this book has been greatly aided by the cooperation of the various institutions and archives mentioned in the list of illustrations and the notes. On the editorial side, we offer our thanks to Victoria L. Cooper and Sarah Stanton of Cambridge University Press for their able assistance and continued encouragement. Not least, we are profoundly grateful to the Social Sciences and Humanities Research Council of Canada for research grants in support of this study.

FREDERICK J. MARKER   LISE-LONE MARKER

I FROM THE MIDDLE AGES TO A GOLDEN AGE

1 Early stages

Although the great mystery cycles that flourished elsewhere in Europe during the Middle Ages seem not to have taken root in Scandinavia, the development of other forms of medieval drama and theatre there followed a traditional pattern. The genesis of that development was the *Quem queritis* trope, the announcement by the angel of Christ's resurrection on Easter morning, which was prescribed by Bishop Ethelwold for the Benedictine order in his tenth-century *Regularis Concordia*. A direct parallel to this basic trope is found in a thirteenth-century Easter sequence from Linköping in Sweden. In this brief liturgical play, performed during the service on Easter morning in front of a crypt representing the holy sepulchre, three priests wearing headdresses enacted the encounter of the three Marys with the angel at the tomb – in this case two angels, played by acolytes seated inside the crypt. In a later version of the same text, from about 1300, this basic dramatic situation was expanded to include the appearance of Simon Peter and John, whose Gospel tells of the footrace of the two disciples to the grave. From these early sources we can trace the gradual growth of a more elaborately conceived Easter performance.

Resurrection plays eventually became as popular in Scandinavia as they were in France and Germany. Within the confines of the church itself, episodes derived from the Gospels were enacted by the priests for the pleasure and edification of their congregations. Hence we find that in 1475 a so-called Marian Chapel was erected in the Church of Our Lady in Flensborg, where four priests known as Marians "acted . . . during Lent the tragedy of Our Lord Jesus Christ, and laid Him in a walled-up grave."[1] This practice persisted until 1527, while the holy sepulchre itself, covered by a large stone, could be seen in the Marian Chapel at Flensborg as late as 1864. A Swedish *ludus resurrectionis*, acted by the teachers and students of the Latin school in Söderköping, is mentioned in a letter written by the parish priest, Hans Jacobi, in 1506. Even as late as 1635, the records of a Danish town refer to a mummer who had "for two days acted in the town hall the story of Christ's Resurrection."[2]

Often richly carved and ornamented, the structure used in these Easter dramas to designate Christ's tomb became the midpoint of other related rituals as well. Sometimes this crypt was carried in solemn procession before being placed beside the altar on Good Friday evening. A Swedish eyewitness also speaks of seeing carved images of Christ being placed in such a sepulchre and anointed with fragrant balsam for the Easter service in the Uppland churches of Vada and Vester-Löfsta. Around the tomb at Vester-Löfsta, which is now preserved in the Nordic Museum in Stockholm, parishioners crawled on their knees to obtain forgiveness for their sins. In Denmark, a similar practice prevailed at the Church of Saint Peter in Næstved, where seventy days' indulgence was granted to anyone who walked around Christ's tomb "praying for peace, for good weather, for the welfare of the Danish kingdom, and for those buried here."[3] The ceremony of the burial of the cross, which was the real purpose of these sepulchres, was particularly frowned upon by the Reformation, and for this reason zealous Lutheran prelates did their best to banish such structures from the churches. A Swedish church edict from 1591 expressly prohibited the ritual known as *Depositio Crucis*, in which a crucifix kissed by the congregation would be first wrapped in a cloth representing Christ's grave clothes and then symbolically "buried" in the sepulchre. During the state visit of the Polish king Sigismond to Sweden in 1594, great public indignation was aroused when Roman Catholic priests persisted, despite the edict, in burying a picture of Christ that was subsequently taken up from the grave on Easter morning.

The coming of the Reformation, which reached Denmark in 1536, had a similarly repressive effect on the popular Epiphany plays that celebrated the second great feast of the Catholic Church. The action of this liturgical form was universally familiar. In solemn procession the priests who impersonated the three wise men would move up the center aisle of the church; one pointed with his scepter at a star that was carried on a pole or was moved through the church on a wire. At the altar the procession halted before the manger, where the Magi sacrificed to the newborn babe. As they fell on their knees in prayer, an angel appeared before them in the shape of a boy clad in white. As the drama developed in complexity, the tyrannical Herod began to make an appearance, causing the three kings to pause at his throne on their way to the crib.

Although Epiphany plays were unconditionally banished from the churches by the Reformation, their popular appeal remained undiminished. Gradually it became customary at Epiphany time for students from the local Latin school to impersonate the three wise men, marching in procession from house to house in search of donations. Always dressed in white, these scholar–kings wore high paper caps lavishly decorated with gilt to emphasize their regal state. Often they were joined by a crowd of other recognizable biblical figures. In Bergen, Norway, where these processions survived almost to our own day, the Magi were accompanied by "Mary with the child in a little cradle, Joseph with an axe in his hand," and "some secondary figures."[4] In addition, one also encountered such characters as Herod, old Simeon, and a Judas in whose conspicuous purse the coins of the onlookers were collected. In Sweden, folk figures became part of the spectacle. Occasionally a fool would also join the motley troupe. In fact, the star processions of the Bergen students were commonly referred to as "farces" or, as a diary entry from 1665 calls them, "*ludos comicos.*"[5] Always at the head of these processions, however, was the indispensable symbol of the star, held aloft on a pole for all to see.

The most tangible evidence of the original form of the Epiphany ritual in Scandinavia stems from Halland, where even the strictures of the Reformation failed to drive the star processions from the churches. Three very short Epiphany plays from this district of Sweden are extant, two from Falkenberg and a third from Laholm. All three texts, which appear to stem from a common source, mingle dialogue with incidental songs, fragments of old Epiphany melodies sung in part by the performers and in part by the audience in unison. The Falkenberg texts are essentially similar. The Magi are summoned to appear before Herod, a focus of dramatic interest in these plays as in so many other liturgical dramas of the Middle Ages. Ordering the wise men to go and seek the newborn King of the Jews, this ferocious theatre tyrant warns that if they are not back within three nights and three days, they will pay with their lives. The wise men set off, but Herod, sensing treachery, decides to saddle up and ride to Bethlehem himself. The slaughter of the Innocents is related in a song, after which Herod's servant returns to assure his master, by way of conclusion, that he indeed "took the newborn babes, pierced their hearts and crushed their bones."

It is safe to assume that the staging of this drama was simple in the extreme. Even the slaughter of the Innocents, so often a cherished opportunity for medieval realism, was kept off stage. The only prop mentioned in these Swedish plays is a chair for Herod, perhaps a reminiscence of the tyrant's lordly throne in the older church ceremonies. To the compact cast of characters in the procession, however, the Laholm text adds the figure of the Virgin Mary. When the wise men ask her about the newborn king, she replies with a fragment of a Christmas song that is her only speech in the drama. In other Epiphany plays from Bergen, probably based on scholastic traditions of German derivation, Mary is also joined in the procession by her husband Joseph, who serves as the source of rather irrelevant comic relief.

When such a play concluded, the moment came to address a tactful reminder to the audience that art deserves its reward, usually gathered up by Judas in his purse. In one instance, however, we find the villainous Herod himself rising from his chair to address the spectators directly:

> Your pardon that I am so bold
> To step before you here;
> My question to you now is this:
> Will there be some cheer?

When the players had finished passing the hat, they sang a song of thanks, sometimes cleverly contrived to become less complimentary if the take did not meet expectations.

Miracles and a morality

There is every reason to believe that miracle plays dramatizing the lives and deeds of the saints enjoyed as much popular appeal in Scandinavia as they did in other parts of Europe during the Middle Ages. Concerning actual performances of these plays, however, very little evidence survives. In the preface to the *Tobie Comedie* (1550), the first drama printed in Sweden, the anonymous author (assumed until quite recently to be Olaus Petri, the biblical translator and influential spokesman for Luther's teachings) argues that performances of moral comedies and tragedies have long been used to instruct the common people about right and wrong in the world. "Our forefathers," the writer adds, "had done the same in this country as in other countries since the coming of Christianity, with songs, rhymes, and comedies about holy men."[6] A sample of such a work, regarded

Plate 1 The familiar biblical image of Simon of Cyrene bearing Christ's cross is juxtaposed with the figure of a prancing, performing stage fool leading the procession to Golgotha. Fresco in Bellinge Church, Odense (1496).

as the oldest surviving Swedish play, is *De uno peccatore qui promeruit gratiam*, performed in the latter half of the fifteenth century during one of the countless Maria festivals of that period. This simple little exemplum depicts a sinner's foregiveness through the (initially reluctant) intercession of the Virgin Mary. The fact that it was intended for performance is indicated by its stage directions and by a prologue in which the speaker greets the audience and calls for silence.

Something of the style and imagery of the traditional miracle performance is revealed, albeit indirectly, in the matchless ceiling and wall frescoes that have now been uncovered and restored in many medieval Danish churches. The figures and situations depicted in these church frescoes call to mind their counterparts in the living theatre of the later fifteenth century. In a painting in Bellinge Church on Fyn, dating from 1496, the procession to Golgotha is led by a prancing stage fool blowing a curved horn. In Skiveholme Church an unknown artist has left a fresco, from 1503, depicting another fool playing two instruments at once, a medieval characteristic that reappears in the Elizabethan theatre. Many of the localities shown in these paintings are closely related to the mansions that stood on the polyscenic medieval stage. Chief among them, of course, is the hellmouth, shown in Selsø Church on Zealand as a dragon's head combined

Plate 2 An elaborate fresco in Tybjerg Church, near Præstø (c. 1450) depicts horned, winged, and claw-footed devils driving the cowering figures of the damned into a gaping hell-mouth.

with a castle-like prison. Vivid depictions of naked souls being thrust, dragged, or even ridden into the gaping hell-mouth by winged and horned devils are common to several Danish churches. The same dragon mouth would, as in a fresco from Vallensbæk Church, serve equally well as the setting for Christ's harrowing of hell. In Tybjerg Church, meanwhile, we find a more cheerful vision of whiter and more fortunate souls with folded hands being led into the city of eternal bliss, reached by a short flight of stairs. In much of this iconography, masked devils in the shape of hairy animals with talons for feet wage a ceaseless struggle for the soul of Man. On the vaulted ceiling of Sæby Church in Jutland, a particularly dramatic episode depicts a devil snatching the soul of the deceased from under the very noses of his wife and her lover, while a sorrowful angel and a crowd of faithful in the walled city of God watch helplessly.

The best example of an authentic miracle play in Scandinavia is the *Ludus de Sancto Canuto duce*, a dramatization of the life and death of Knud Lavard, a Danish saint who was murdered in 1131. Legend has it that a well sprang up from the spot in a forest near Haraldsted where the Holy Duke Knud was slain, and that miracles took place at his grave. The martyr soon became a folk hero, and to the great joy of the Danish people his son, King

Plate 3 Christ's harrowing of hell, as depicted in a fresco in Vallensbæk Church, near Copenhagen (1450–75). The two figures pleading for mercy are undoubtedly Adam and Eve, traditional supplicants on this occasion. The dramatic postures and expressions of the three figures convey a sense of actors playing roles.

Valdemar the Great, succeeded in having him canonized in 1169. A play based on the incidents of Knud's life and martyrdom seems to have been a very old tradition in Ringsted, the place of his burial. This verse drama, dating from the beginning of the sixteenth century and preserved in a later transcription, was itself an outgrowth of two twelfth-century Latin masses celebrated each year in the Church of Saint Bendt in Ringsted to commemorate the anniversaries of the murder and the saint's later interment before the high altar.

In addition to the thirty speaking roles found in the *Ludus de Sancto Canuto duce*, a large number of supernumeraries – privy counselors, courtiers, and citizens – swelled the processions and tableaux of this colorful outdoor spectacle. At the center of this historical pageant stood Duke Knud, the image of the good and pious leader who dies young, and his envious assassin Magnus, boldly drawn as the embodiment of godlessness and

Plate 4 The frescoes in Tybjerg Church offer a glimpse of paradise, shown here as a walled city on a raised platform to which Saint Peter is about to admit an eager crowd of the blessed.

virtually demonic malice. The framework for this epic clash of the forces of good and evil was an elaborate one, spanning thirty years and exploiting the medieval principle of polyscenic mansion staging to the fullest. The herald Preco, speaker of the prologue, asks the spectators to "hold their peace and make room," thereby implying that, as the space for performance was not clearly marked off, the sprawling action to follow would likely have used an open, simultaneous acting area rather than a raised stage. The mansions or localities needed for this production were probably set up around the largest square in Ringsted, close to the church where the martyr was held in special veneration – a practice entirely consistent with both the Villingen passion play and the Lucerne Easter play. Chief among these mansions was the royal court at Roskilde, which would have had a central position in the square. In addition, the audience would have seen localities representing the Danish Privy-council chamber, sundry castles and manors, a gallows, and the fateful grove where Knud is killed – all grouped topographically, with localities on Zealand gathered in one part of the performance space and Knud's castles in Jutland and Slesvig in another.

Characters and processions moved freely and frequently from one such mansion to another, both on foot and even on horseback. Messengers

Plate 5 In this miniature drama, painted on the ceiling of Sæby Church in Jutland, devil and angel compete for the soul of the man in the bed, while his wife and her lover appear otherwise preoccupied. Behind the angel, the averted faces of the inmates of paradise express their grief, while the devil makes haste to convey his victim to the hell-mouth seen at the left.

journeyed ceaselessly from castle to castle. When the Privy-council meets in its mansion and reaches a decision it wishes to convey to the wicked King Harald, a stage direction indicates that the counselors "journey to Harald's castle," where one of them simply shouts to the king: "Harald, look out and go here forth, the Privy-council has arrived." While at his castle in Ribe, Knud is named Duke of Slesvig, whereupon he promptly "rides to Slesvig, takes up residence in the castle," and delivers an address to the inhabitants there.

As we might expect, this period's taste for bloodshed and cruelty on the stage found ample expression in this Danish miracle. Medieval audiences relished scenes of torture and execution, familiar to them from a daily life in which the hanging, drawing, and quartering of a criminal was a source of public entertainment. To this category belongs the highly realistic execution of a thief in the play. The Latin legend relates that, after having been sent to Slesvig by King Niels, Knud demonstrated his righteousness by dealing strictly with the many criminals who ravaged and plundered the country during this restless age. In the drama, in what must have been a lively chase sequence, "the thieves are pursued, one of them is caught and is brought before the Duke." Although (for practical reasons) only a single robber is actually taken and hanged, Knud's men reassure their master about the fate of the other thieves: "We have both impaled them and buried them alive." The onstage hanging of the hapless captive was a high point in the performance, during which all other action ceased and no further dialogue was permitted until "after the thief has been hanged." Although one of Knud's servants relays to him what the offender has to say in his own defense, the thief himself does not speak a word — most likely because a dummy may have been used for the actual execution, thereby allowing much greater flexibility in the range of tortures inflicted.

Such scenes of violence are not, however, the real focus of the *Ludus de Sancto Canuto duce*. The anonymous clerical author is chiefly concerned with the depiction of the benevolence and humanity of his protagonist, the *rex pacificus* whose betrayal and martyrdom reflect, in the sphere of human politics, the suffering and death of Christ himself. True to this focus, the playwright ends his *ludus* with Knud's death at Haraldsted. Tempting though they would be as occasions of scenic display, the miracles said to have occurred at the saint's grave have no part to play in the human drama of Knud Lavard.

A quite different approach to the miracle genre is found in the *Comoedia de Sancta virgine Dorothea*, the only other extant text of a Scandinavian miracle play. Unlike the indigenous Knud Lavard play, the *Dorotheæ Komedie* is a Danish verse translation of a Latin prose drama by Knight Chilian of Mellerstadt, published in 1507 and inspired in turn by an earlier comedy on the subject by Hroswitha. The Danish adaptation of this material, dated 1531 and attributed to an Odense schoolmaster, Christiern Hansen, is a rich mixture of the familiar miracle-play ingredients, including several conversions, assorted miracles, and a series of scenes involving corporal punishment. Saint Dorothea, who suffered martyrdom in Asia Minor during the reign of Diocletian at the beginning of the fourth century, spurns the advances of the pagan ruler Fabritius because she prefers "to live in poverty until she may gain heaven after her death." Enraged, Fabritius has her flogged and brought to the stake, but she remains miraculously unharmed. She converts her two sisters to Christianity, with the result that the evil Fabritius has them burnt at the stake. Dorothea herself is thrown into prison for her faith and must ultimately yield her young life to the executioner's axe. Before she dies, however, she delivers such a moving description of the joys of paradise that a young pagan, Theophilus, promises to embrace the true faith if she will send him a sign from heaven. The miracle occurs – an angel presents Theophilus with a basket of fragrant flowers and herbs gathered from the meadows of paradise – and the young man immediately keeps his promise.

A prologue, or *argumentum*, introduces the Danish audience to this exotic and unfamiliar subject matter, after which the speaker leads in the players and introduces the principal characters one by one. Hansen's version reveals some traces of the emerging humanist tradition (the prologue, a five-act structure, occasional quotations from Plautus and Apuleius), but it relies squarely on medieval staging principles and techniques – though nothing is known of an actual performance in Odense. Mansions would be required for the "houses" of Fabritius and Dorothea and for a prison, a temple with pagan idols, and the crucial localities where victims are tortured and put to death. That such structures could often be quite elaborate is indicated, for example, by the fact that Dorothea's "house" was equipped with a practicable door, which Fabritius' henchmen knock on and then batter in with a stone when they come to seize the chaste woman.

If performed, all the technical resources of a medieval *maître de secrets* would be needed for the gruesome torture scenes at the center of the play. When Dorothea refuses to renounce her faith, Fabritius orders the executioner, Runcardius, and his assistant into action:

> With stake and iron bind her fast,
> Then let her body feel the whip;
> Next tar and oil on her cast,
> For our gods she will not worship.

After "she is whipped," the executioner orders his assistant to fetch fire. In what is apparently meant as a humorous interlude, the helper tries long and hard to find sparks in the ashes but must finally resort to flint and steel. At last the stake is ready; the victim is partially stripped and bound, the flames lick up about her, yet she remains unscathed. Fabritius then casts Dorothea into prison, but soon she is dragged before him again. After a futile attempt to force the saint to worship pagan idols, the tyrant hands her back to her tormentors with orders to torture her with glowing tongs "set upon her hands and feet." The executioner is explicit in his description of what awaits her:

> I shall now hang you by your feet,
> And with the strongest rope you tie,

To twist your arms and legs a-wry,
And stifle your mouth from all breath,
And finally torture you to death.

Jean Fouquet's famous miniature of the martyrdom of Saint Apollinia (*c.* 1460) is the best medieval illustration of how close to reality such a torture could come.

The climactic beheading of Dorothea was a *secret* that doubtless followed all the rules of the art. A saint of this importance could hardly be executed without the presence of a substantial audience. Even Fabritius, who until then apparently did not leave his mansion, is seized by a desire to witness the scaffold scene ("I will be there at once with some a-riding, / And some a-foot for those who like walking"). Surrounded by a crowd of onlookers, Dorothea is led to the block, where the executioner draws his sword and warns her to make ready ("Stretch forth thy neck with greatest haste, / And I shall chop as I've been taught"). After a final prayer in which Dorothea reaffirms her faith, an angel appears with "apples and roses that grow in the fields of Paradise." Once this miraculous harvest was bestowed on Theophilus, the play ended with the beheading of the heroine (who would be substituted at the last moment by a dummy).

Although the religious character of medieval drama altered decisively in the face of the new forces of cultural change that accompanied the Reformation, the theatrical conventions of the medieval mansion stage maintained a surprising continuity in Scandinavia. A unique piece of seventeeth-century iconography, depicting a performance of a German morality play called *Tragödia von den Tugenden und Lastern* (*The Tragedy of the Virtues and the Vices*), illustrates the survival of the older style of staging in the very midst of what was otherwise a typical Renaissance festival. This anonymous morality was performed on the castle square in Copenhagen as part of a spectacular thirteen-day celebration held by King Christian IV in 1634 to mark the wedding of the crown prince to Princess Magdalena Sibylla of Saxony.

The action of *The Tragedy of the Virtues and the Vices* is allegorical rather than biblical. King Fastus (Pride), the King of the Vices who dwells in the Castle of the Dragon, attacks the Virtues – Faith, Hope, Charity, Truth, Patience, and Courage – who live in the Castle of Hope. Driven back by the intervention of the archangel Raphael, Fastus consults his advisers

about how best to overcome the Virtues, whom he cannot conquer in battle. The Vices decide to feign friendship, and three "simple and honest"
Virtues foolishly let themselves be deceived and attend a banquet. They are
overpowered and taken prisoner, but Raphael once more comes to the rescue with his flaming sword. He liberates the captive Virtues and sets fire to
the Vicious abode. A "holy dragon" is brought down on a wire to inciner-
ate the place, and the godless Vices are driven by devils into a gaping hell-
mouth. The traditional German fool Hans Bratwurst, here seen as a servant
in the Castle of the Dragon, functions as the ironic *raisonneur* of this
medieval morality show.

The pictorial record of the event, which was arranged by Christoffer
Swencke and his son, is actually a composite view of several episodes in it.
A round, lavishly decorated tent, which served as the mansion of the
Virtues, is located in accordance with custom at the farthest end of the acting area from the hell-mouth. The mansion of the Vices is a quadrangular
structure with an ornamental gothic roof supported by columns, completely open to allow the antics of the Vices to be seen from all sides. Only at
the spectacular conclusion of the "tragedy" was the entire square bathed in
the flood of illumination shown in the engraving. At this moment the
Castle of the Dragon, bombarded by fireworks set off by Raphael's flying
monster, exploded and burst into flames. The banquet table ignited and
chairs blew up as the inhabitants scrambled for cover. The climax of the
display was reached when pillars at the four corners of the center mansion,
each with a sphere at the top and six spheres on its pedestal, all spouted
fire simultaneously. Devils fired off rockets from high poles, ground pieces
ignited, and the hell-mouth into which the Vices were herded belched
forth its infernal flames. The pyrotechnics of this royal game were pure
Renaissance, but its staging techniques dated back to the great medieval
outdoor pageants of the previous century.

Shrovetide farces

Carnival time, or Shrovetide, was the season for merrymaking and masquerades in medieval Scandinavia, and the *Fastnachtspiel*, or Carnival play,
emerged as a popular form of entertainment at an early date. In 1447, the
prior of the Monastery of Saint John in Odense, wishing to establish a
school at the monastery, even had to promise not to allow "scholaribus
(suis) . . . choreas et ludos carnisprivales . . . celebrari."[7] In this case,
Scandinavian theatre came directly under German influence. Expecially in

Plate 6 A late example of medieval mansion staging: *The Tragedy of the Virtues and the Vices*, performed in Copenhagen in 1634. This engraving, published in J. J. Holst's *Triumphus nuptialis Danicus* (1648), is a composite view of the production's more spectacular scenes, including its fireworks finale.

nearby Lübeck, the Shrovetide farce was cultivated energetically by an upper-class association known as the *Zirkelgesellschaft*, performances by whom are recorded as early as 1430. German merchants in Bergen carried their native Carnival customs to Norway, while in Denmark a play about the Judgment of Paris emulated a farce on this subject performed by the Lübeck *Zirkelgesellschaft* in 1455.

Paris' Dom (*The Judgment of Paris*), one of only two extant Danish farces from this early period, is a somewhat crude popularization of the growing humanist interest in classical subjects and themes. Bellona, goddess of strife, presents Paris with the apple he is to confer on the most beautiful of three contestants, Juno, Venus, and Pallas Athene. Captivated by the physical charms of Venus, which he describes in quite tangible terms, Paris awards her the prize. In response, Pallas castigates the lechery of men and the disregard of justice that it fosters. *Den utro Hustru* (*The Unfaithful Wife*), which like its companion piece is an anonymous one-act farce found in the same manuscript that contains the Dorothea miracle play, is a more interesting example of the *Fastnachtspiel* tradition. Three suitors court a wife whose husband goes off on a pilgrimage. Two of them, a peasant in need of a bath and a monk, are quickly dispensed with, and even the elegant courtship of a nobleman fails at first to move the virtuous woman. Not satisfied with her refusal, however, the third suitor seeks out a witch to whom he promises a reward if she can bring the beautiful woman into his power. The old crone first sends a devil to coax the wife, but this inept emissary fails miserably and is given a thrashing for his pains. Deciding to take matters into her own hands, the witch appears before the woman with a dog to plead tearfully for alms. Asked why she is so unhappy, the crone instantly replies that her dog is in fact her own beautiful daughter, thus transformed because she spurned the love of a young man. The sad tale makes such an impression on the virtuous wife that she resolves at once to yield to the nobleman's demands ("ere I become a dog like this, / I'll say yes to all he may wish").

The prologue and epilogue to a sixteenth-century Swedish farce, *Een Lustigh Comedie om Doctor Simon* (*A Merry Comedy About Doctor Simon*), clearly reveal the itinerant character of these pieces, intended for performance by strolling players with the simplest of means. In this play a peasant and his wife quarrel over a pair of trousers, the signifier of domestic power and authority. The wife, who bears the unusual nickname Doctor Simon, wins out in the end. After being beaten and driven from the house, the husband must relinquish his authority. The epilogue expresses the hope that the hard rule of Doctor Simon may come to an end in the new year. Requirements for the performance of such a farce were extremely modest. There would have been no question of a raised platform or elaborate mansions. The acting area was a floor or the ground itself, on which the necessary localities, or *standorte*, were designated in the simplest possible way, by means of a chair or a bench.

We may envision a troupe of strollers, preceded by a musician, arriving at a house to perform *The Unfaithful Wife*. When the players had entered the hall and a space had been cleared for them, they arranged themselves "in order" at the rear of the "stage." The so-called crier – usually the leader of the troupe – then stepped forward to deliver his introductory speech *ad populum*. Called Preco in both Danish farces, the crier gave a summary of the action and, with the aid of a pointer or staff, introduced the characters. *The Unfaithful Wife* needed at least three localities, which may be called "the wife's room," "the witch's room," and a public bath in which the malodorous peasant is given a scrub and a shave. In addition, at least one neutral locality was provided where those characters not bound to these *standorte* could remain when not participating in the action. Stage directions (in Latin) suggest the continual free movement of characters from one locality to another: "the peasant returns to his wife," "the nobleman goes to the witch and says," "the witch goes with her dog to the wife," and so on. At the conclusion of the farce, the actors again arranged themselves in order at the back, while Preco came forward to deliver his final speech. Included in it was a customary reminder to their host that liquid refreshment was expected by the players before they moved on to their next engagement ("Thus will I go out the door, / Give me some drink before").

Humanist theatre

Although performances of school drama in Scandinavia during the sixteenth and seventeenth centuries observed the same principles of simultaneous staging that had governed older forms of medieval drama, the twin forces of the Renaissance and the Reformation strongly affected the repertory of the new humanist theatre. Latin plays both ancient and new, translations of these, and original dramas in the vernacular began to be acted in the larger Scandinavian towns by university and Latin school students. These productions were supervised by local teachers, themselves often the author or the adapter of the piece. The burgeoning humanist preoccupation with classical literature and civilization influenced the selection of plays and brought the classical genre patterns of tragedy and comedy to bear on native drama.

Although the Reformation frowned on the older church drama, it enthusiastically supported school and university performances as an excellent pedagogical tool for educating youth to high morals and good manners. Luther was known to view plays as "useful illustrations" of virtue and vice, "very necessary and wholesome to know."[8] Next to the Bible, the great Wittenberg Latinist Philipp Melanchthon could think of no more useful books than tragedies. In accordance with this attitude, a Swedish church ordinance from 1572 strongly recommended the acting of comedies and tragedies "so that both those who play and those who watch may be instructed and improved."[9] When King Gustav II Adolf consulted his bishops in 1620 to find means of advancing learning and knowledge in Sweden, one piece of advice given him was to follow the example set by other European countries where professors of rhetoric were encouraged to teach their students to present plays.

In Norway, a comparable ordinance from Bergen, dated 1617, decreed that local schoolmasters should "let their pupils enact short Christian comedies as academic exercises . . . according to ancient custom, so that youths can become more accustomed to polite behavior and good manners." As this ordinance specifically names "the good people" of the town as a potential audience, it is obvious that these performances were not meant solely as intramural exhibitions. "The master himself," readers are told, "accompanies his pupils, directing their playing and action in a proper manner."[10] An example for such performances had been set in Bergen over fifty years earlier by Absalom Pederssøn Beyer, a local master who had ("with much trouble and expense") staged a play on the Fall of Adam in the town churchyard in 1563. During the next ten years Beyer recorded no fewer than five other school performances of plays, including two by Terence, given under similar circumstances.[11]

Of much greater interest than the numerous performances of Plautus and Terence given during this period are, of course, the native dramas that grew out of the humanist theatre tradition. Usually based on biblical (especially Old Testament) subjects, these plays were at first mostly free adaptations of foreign models. From Sweden such titles as *Holofernis och Judiths Commoedia*, *Rebecka*, and *Tobie Comedia* are typical. Danish scholastic plays were similarly devoted to such subjects as *Cain and Abel*, *David and Goliath*, *Kong Salomons Hyldning* (*Allegiance to Solomon*), a local *Tobie Komedie*, and *Susanna*. The last-named work, subtitled "a strange play taken from the Book of Daniel about the purity of the upright woman Susanna and her wondrous rescue," was adapted by Peder Jensen Hegelund from Sixt Birck's Latin original, which had itself been acted by Danish students before Frederik II at Copenhagen Castle in 1577. Hegelund's version, performed under his supervision in Ribe in 1576, became the first Danish school drama to be printed (in 1578). Its hybrid character is typical of the genre in general. Divided into five acts with a prologue and epilogue, its form emulates classical comedy. The didactic tone and the episodic structure are, however, directly inherited from the medieval period. Hegelund's tale of the chaste Susanna follows its biblical model fairly closely. Falsely accused of impurity, the heroine is brought to trial and condemned to death by stoning. At the last moment the treachery of her two calumnators is revealed by the young prophet Daniel, and her unsullied virtue is given its due. The two slanderers are, in turn, themselves stoned to death, with gruesome results: "See how their brains are running down over their eyes," remarks one observer.

A single dominating principle, the power of moral exemplum, constituted the aesthetic of these homiletic school dramas. This aim is particularly apparent in the late medieval morality plays that survive from this period. *Dødedansen* (*The Dance of Death*), an anonymous Danish allegory published in the 1550s in an edition illustrated with woodcuts, takes up one of the most predominant pictorial–choreographic themes of the Middle Ages, the *danse macabre*. Death appears with his scythe and orders people of all ranks and classes to follow him along "an unknown road." One by one the characters move toward him with a few dance steps and are led into his castle. In another Danish morality, *Comedia de Mundo et Paupere*, a poor man decides to serve Lady Mundus (the world) in spite of better advice given him by two angels. Having renounced God, Pauper gains riches, becomes emperor, and weds the daughter of Lady Mundus. In the midst of the marriage festivities he falls ill. Beyond all help he dies and, after being judged before the throne of heaven, devils carry his soul into hell. Although no actual performances of *The Dance of Death* are recorded, *Mundo et Paupere* was played in Randers in 1607 under the direction of schoolmaster Peder Thøgersen, the "ludimoderatore" who probably adapted the play from an unknown source.

The creation of a body of indigenous drama found its most ambitious champion in Johannes Messenius, a professor at Uppsala who declared his intention of illustrating the entire history of Sweden in fifty plays, which were to be "exhibited publicly" by his students. Six of these plays, based on Nordic sagas and legends, were actually completed, and four were acted. More significant, however, is Messenius' grand vision of a nationalistic drama that could introduce a broad popular audience to "the strange and glorious old stories of their fatherland."[12] The first and most elaborate play by Messenius, "a merry comedy about the wise and renowned Queen of Sweden, Lady Disa," gave his country its first national history play in 1611.

Filled with comic episodes, music, processions, dances, and lively depictions of folk customs, *Disa* won great popularity in Sweden and Germany. Performances of it were seen in Stockholm far into the eighteenth century. Although his favor at court did not last long, Messenius did see the second of his historical pieces, *Signill*, performed by forty of his own students at Stockholm Castle, in celebration of the royal wedding of Prince Johan and Princess Maria Elizabeth in 1612. It, too, was popular and went through ten editions by 1750. Although the great cycle envisioned by the father of the Swedish history play never materialized, he articulated an abiding aspiration to which, for example, Strindberg was to return almost three centuries later.

The interest in historical drama fostered by Messenius soon spread. Andreas Prytz, an Uppsala professor and ecclesiastic who had acted a leading role in *Disa*, carried on in the historical vein with such dramas as *Olof Skottkonung*, performed at the wedding of Gustaf II Adolf in 1620, and *Konung Gustaf Then Första*, acted the following year at Uppsala University to mark the anniversary of the nation's liberation by Gustav Vasa. While no comparable plays based on national history emerged from the humanist theatre in Denmark, Hans Thomsen Stege made an initial attempt to use classical history as tragic subject matter in his *Cleopatra*, "an historical tragedy about the last queen of Egypt, Cleopatra by name, and M. Antony, a Roman emperor" from 1609. Other seventeenth-century schoolmasters in Sweden found new material in classical legend, as seen in Magnus Olai Asteropherus' *Thisbe* (1609), or sought to revitalize the old biblical morality, as Jacob Rondeletius did in his *Judas Redivivus* (1614). Whether nationalistic, classical, or biblical in subject, however, the primary concern in most of these plays remains a didactic moral correspondence between history and contemporary life.

Perhaps the most memorable exception to the homiletic tenor of most school drama from this period is *Karrig Niding* (*Niding the Niggard*), the jewel of the humanist theatre movement in Scandinavia. Written by Hieronymus Justesen Ranch, a parish priest in Viborg, this delightful character comedy is found in an edition from 1664, but was probably completed around 1598, when it may have been acted on the town square in Viborg on a simple platform stage.[13] It is conceived as a conscious counterpart to Plautus' *The Pot of Gold* (*Aulularia*), with which it seems to have been performed. Both of these comedies ridicule the foibles of a miser, but there the resemblance ends. Ranch's *Karrig Niding* is a thoroughly original creation that transcends the scholastic convention of classical imitation. The wealthy but niggardly Niding, obsessed by the idea that he will one day find himself in need, compels his household, including his wife Jutta and their children, to subsist on mouldy bread and rancid pork, while all sorts of appetizing delicacies are kept under lock and key, to be devoured by rats. Taking the keys to the larder with him, Niding and his servant Meagre-cole set off on a begging expedition, and in their absence two tramps, Jep Skald and his boy, arrive on the scene. Plying the ravenous Jutta and the others with food from his well-stocked beggar's sack, Jep succeeds in usurping the absent husband's marriage bed. In conspiracy with the servants, the tramp lays a trap to catch the miser. The locks are changed, Jep dresses in the husband's best clothes, and when Niding returns, distressed by a dream in which a tramp has usurped his rightful place beside his wife, no one seems to recognize him. His keys fail to fit, and soon he is convinced that his memory of himself as master of the household must have been a dream. The reversal is completed when, delirious from hunger, Niding begs his alter ego for shelter for the night, is royally feasted by Jep, and even begins to have lecherous vagabond thoughts about Jutta. Revived by food and drink, the transformed miser sets off in search of his true wife, home, and self. At the climax of his comic humiliation, he gratefully accepts Jep's gift of a tattered beggar's cape, the ultimate sign of the identity swap.

Performances of these school dramas, usually given during the mild months of May and June or at Shrovetide, were important civic events often subsidized by local town councils, normally in the form of a subvention to the supervisor. Like the medieval religious dramas, the plays were given in whatever location seemed convenient. In rainy Bergen, a long-standing tradition of indoor performances in the town hall seems to have prevailed. In Elsinore, the town hall is also known to have been at the disposal of student actors both in 1572 and 1574. Performances inside the churches were disapproved of but not unknown. Considerable trouble arose, for example, when a minister in Slesvig produced Terence's first comedy, *The Woman of Andros*, in his church with boys from the local Latin school in such roles as the midwife Lesbia and the title character herself, who gives birth during the course of the action. The cleric's enthusiastic plan of following up his success with a church production of Terence's *The Eunuch* was firmly squelched, and the performance moved to the town hall.

Outdoor performances seem generally to have been more usual than indoor ones. The main squares of such Danish towns as Odense, Ribe, and

Viborg could accommodate large crowds and were well suited to theatrical purposes. The local churchyard was another useful site. We know that the Bergen productions recorded by A. P. Beyer used this venue, as did the Swedish students in Örebro, who put on Johannes Rudbeckius' *Rebecka* in 1616. This work, adapted from a Latin original by Nicodemus Frischlin, was staged in the cemetery adjacent to the school, where yet another attempt at *The Woman of Andros* was presented the following day. These productions, which were given in the afternoon and lasted until six o'clock, began with a colorful procession from the headmaster's house, where the actors dressed, to the "theatre." Admission was free, and the spiritual edification of the plays was followed by a *convivium*, during which actors and spectators consumed some fifty-eight courses of food and quaffed fourteen barrels of beer.[14]

The raised stage on which the school plays were often acted made use of the familiar medieval principle of mansions, though the style in which these localities were represented could vary from the very simple to the elaborate. The evidence seems to allow for both extremes. Leaving conflicting conjectures about its exact appearance aside, the so-called *Palads* or *Palatz* stage of the humanist theatre in Scandinavia combined, in very basic terms, a spacious, neutral playing area (often called "proscenium" in play texts from the period) and a curtained booth (the "scena") at the back. At their simplest, the "domicilia," or houses, of different characters might be no more than slits in this rear curtain. Whether arranged on a raised platform outdoors or on the floor of a castle hall, however, the mansions of this itinerant theatre were still deployed in accordance with the medieval concept of a polyscenic stage of juxtaposed action.

For example, the Uppsala production of *Holofernis och Judiths Commoedia*, which probably took place in the 1570s, would have had a relatively large number of distinct, juxtaposed action-locations, including the Temple, Judith's house in Bethulia, the city wall with a practicable gate (on which Judith knocks), a "room" where the heroine prepares to meet the enemy commander, and finally the tent of Holofernes, from which she emerges triumphantly with the severed head of her opponent. Although the stage itself is not described in detail, these various elements emerge clearly in the script. Along similar lines, the implied mise-en-scène for the Danish *Tobie Komedie* (a Viborg play once attributed to Ranch) entails a comparable number of localities, flanked in this case by two thoroughly medieval mansions. To one side, surrounded by the heavenly hosts, God appears in an elevated paradise from which Raphael, Tobias' angel in need, descends to earth. Located at the farthest remove from heaven was a hell occupied by the play's two devils, Asmodeus and his helper. Situated between these opposing metaphysical extremes were such localities as the house of Tobias' parents, the fateful bridal chamber where the devils make off with the unfortunate Sarah's bridegrooms, and "the River Tigris" (compared by Raphael to Viborg Lake!) from which Tobias pulls the remarkable fish that God has commanded him to catch.

Extensive Latin stage directions for Hegelund's *Susanna* seem, on the other hand, to indicate a much simpler scheme. In addition to the houses of the three groups of characters (slits in the rear curtain, perhaps), only two specific action-locations are called for, the garden where Susanna is spied on in her bath and the court of law where she is tried. The garden locality for the bathing scene is described in some detail, but the manner in which the illusion was to be achieved is left vague:

> Part of the stage (proscenium) is covered with greensward, in which herbs and flowers are planted and around which foliage is woven so that it resembles a garden. As large a basin as possible should be placed there, filled with water, or else water should be poured from a pitcher from above, as if a spring were flowing.[15]

The author's subsequent description of the "bath" itself is, however, a telling indication of the stylized simplicity of this scene and its staging. Watched by two lecherous scoundrels (peeking through the curtain, perhaps), Susanna – who would have been played by a boy – "chastely uncovers her arms and a bit of her legs, while observing the propriety and dignity of a married woman."[16] An even stronger indication of the stylized quality of this performance is found in a contemporary engraving of Calumnia (Slander), whose long allegorical interlude interrupts the trial scene in Hegelund's version of the story. Although created for the later publication of this interlude and hence not an actual costume picture from the 1576 production, this engraving still tells us much about the purely emblematic style in which this personification of *Fama malum* was conceived. In Calumnia's multiple attributes – large ears, two tongues, more tongues and eyes painted on her clothing and wings, a drawn bow ready to shoot off shafts of slander, a knife, shears, mirror, magnifying glass, the severed head of a fool, and other items hanging from her belt – a sixteenth-century audience could be expected to read the identity of this Danish equivalent of Shakespeare's "Rumor painted full of tongues."

Plate 7 The allegorical figure of Calumnia, or Fama malum, in Hegelund's *Susanna* (published 1578). This woodcut, by an unknown artist, appeared in a separate edition of the "Calumnia" interlude published the following year.

The allegorical tendency apparent in the Calumnia figure in Hegelund's *Susanna* found much more elaborate expression eight years later in *Allegiance to Solomon*, H. J. Ranch's first play. This "new merry and instructive comedy derived from the legends of King David and King Solomon" was performed on the main square in Viborg in 1584 as an allegorical homage to Frederik II (King David) and his son, the newly elected crown prince Christian (King Solomon). In the midst of this regal pageant, Ranch himself appeared in the medieval guise of the Fool, called Crow, who loses no chance to mock his master Adonias, the figure of negative princely traits in the play. The system of mansion staging at work in the production is clearly alluded to in the prologue:

> This building is called Jerusalem,
> Here King David holds house and home;
> Look now there is lovely Zion,
> Here stands Israel's regal throne.[17]

Ranch's lively stage picture also included instances of simultaneous action, as when a sumptuous third-act banquet in David's palace continued through the subsequent act, irrespective of action going on in the other mansions. The banqueters were cautioned, however, to avoid drinking, noise, and other "foolish pranks" that might disrupt the "artistic continuity." Its medieval characteristics notwithstanding *Allegiance to Solomon* was, in its essence, a Renaissance panegyric to the ruling house. The climax toward which the spectacle tended was thus the allegorical moment (IV.vii) at which allegiance was symbolically pledged to the future King Christian IV, in the person of Solomon: "Twelve angels on the uppermost ring, seven Planets beneath, King Solomon kneeling in white in the midst of the circle. All sing and dance." Conceived in the humanist tradition exemplified by Erasmus of Rotterdam, this tableau placed the ruler at the center of a balanced universe governed by the twinned images of Christian belief and the classical harmony of the spheres.

As in this instance, humanist playwrights frequently introduced musical and choreographic elements in their plays, in emulation of classical theatre. The formation of whirling planets and hovering angels grouped about the chosen sovereign in *Allegiance to Solomon* represented an attempt by Ranch to recreate, in typical Renaissance fashion, the singing and dancing chorus of ancient Greek drama. In *Samsons Fængsel* (*Samson's Prison*), a play by Ranch from 1599, the musical element became more pronounced and more fully integrated. Each of the nine songs in this work (sometimes called the first Danish operetta) contributes to characterization of dramatic tension. Dalila lulls the strongman to sleep as her maids sing love songs and a pastoral ballad. The melodies of merry millers are heard during the blinded Samson's captivity, and he himself sings of fickle fortune, "so like the wheel and grinding mill." Choreographic sequences and even full-scale balletic interludes sometimes lent these school plays the character of a Renaissance *ballet de cour*. In the same manuscript that contains *Samson's Prison*, the Randers schoolmaster and playmaker Peder Thøgersen notes that a production of Plautus' *The Pot of Gold* in his town in 1607 incorporated "an antiphonal chorus, resounding trumpets and horns, pantomimic *entr'actes*, and vocal music." From the same source we learn that, also in 1607, a performance of Terence's *The Eunuch* was embellished with three original *intermezzi* – "The Four Seasons," "Hercules and Omphale," and "The Four Ages" – presented as pantomimic character dances by allegorically costumed figures.

In productions such as these, the humanist theatre of the early seventeenth century reflected the spirit and style of the elaborate royal festivities of this age, with their amalgamation of music, ballet, song, declamation, and pageantry. And, indeed, for more than a century the school drama had played an important role in entertainments at court, where a royal wedding or christening was often an occasion to invite student players to perform. By the middle of the seventeenth century the situation had changed, and the popularity of such performances had declined in the Scandinavian countries – with the exception of Finland, where Latin school plays performed by students at the newly founded university in Åbo introduced theatre to that country in 1640. In Denmark, however, other forms of theatre gained precedence during the long reign of Christian IV (1588–1648), while at the Swedish court of Queen Christina (1632–54) student actors from Uppsala appeared only once, in a performance of Seneca's *Hercules Furens* in 1648. Seventeen years later, during a visit to Uppsala by the eleven-year-old Charles XI, the university students were once again able to entertain their monarch with Urban Hiärne's robust and gory verse tragedy *Rosimunda*, which introduced the antics of a Pickelherring derived from the famous itinerant clown of Robert Reynolds. By this time, though, the vogue of humanist theatre had definitively passed.

A significant epilogue to its history in Sweden is added by the cycle of performances given by the Uppsala students at the court theatre of Charles XI in Stockholm from 1686 to 1691. In almost every respect, however, the features of the old scholastic drama had altered. Dressed in costumes borrowed from the royal wardrobe, this student troupe performed on a fully equipped baroque stage in Lejonkulan, a lion pen converted to a theatre and located beside the wall of the old castle, Tre Kronor. Here, with Isaac Börk as a guiding spirit and impressive stage machinery at their disposal, they gave public performances of a series of plays whose very titles – *Apollo, Darius, Philomela, Hippolytos*, and the like – reveal their imitative heroic style and their lofty preoccupation with subjects of classical mythology. Eager to emulate the ideals of French classicism, these seventeenth-century student productions were pale reflections of the baroque splendor of contemporary court theatricals. As part of a larger picture, however, these six seasons at Lejonkulan mark an important first step toward the establishment of a permanent Swedish theatre ensemble.

2 Theatre at court

During the sixteenth and seventeenth centuries, the royal courts of Scandinavia glittered with a series of pageants, processions, and court ballets comparable to the more internationally familiar Renaissance festivities of Europe. A royal wedding, a christening, a burial, or a coronation became the traditional occasion for an opulent display of royal largesse and taste. The mummings, disguisings, and courtly revels of the sixteenth century eventually evolved into the spectacular festivities and *ballets de cour* that hallmarked the important events at the courts of Christian IV, Frederik III, and Queen Christina. Sometimes extending over a period of days or even weeks, these "compliments of state," as Samuel Daniel liked to call them, would incorporate the central ceremony into a rhythmic and coordinated round of jousts, tournaments, fireworks, masques, and triumphal processions. As insubstantial as these pageants may have been in the eye of history, something of their splendor lives on in the engravings and detailed descriptions of them that survive.

A delight in emblematic spectacle and dramatized representation characterized the sixteenth-century mind, and this delight found its full expression in the treatment accorded significant public events in the reign of Frederik II of Denmark (1559–88). No instance better illustrates the essentially theatrical conception of such a public action than the ceremonial oath-taking of the Slesvig vassals at Odense in 1580. A curtained *Palads* stage decorated with an elaborate framing arch – a much grander variant, in fact, of the booth stage of the humanist tradition – was erected on the public square. The king made his entrance surrounded by 100 halberdiers, in advance of whom came heralds wearing "the Danish coat-of-arms, richly and artistically embroidered and worked with gold and pearls." When the monarch had taken his place on the stage, with his Privy-council at his feet, the royal vassals, marshaled on horseback under a blood-red banner, drew up their ranks in attack formation and rode about the platform. Dismounting, they ascended to the king and swore fealty. Frederik II then seized the banner of blood, while the dukes of Slesvig grasped its staff. The fiefdom was conferred upon them, and the king then threw the banner to the crowd, which "according to ancient custom and usage tore it to pieces."[1]

The resplendent coronation rituals of Christian III (in 1537) and Frederik II (in 1559) were but a prelude to the weeklong celebration marking Christian IV's official assumption of the Danish throne in 1596. Particularly popular on such occasions were the *Trionfi*, or royal processions, which evolved during the Italian Renaissance and which afforded an opportunity for the princes and nobles of the realm to masquerade in the guise of the gods, heroes, and generals of antiquity. The chief participants were joined by a cavalcade of elaborately constructed pageant cars, displaying allegorical and fantastical groupings appropriately termed "inventions." Trained camels, flights of angels, a ship with blazing cannons, rolling mountains, a lush landscape crowded with hunters – all this and more rumbled past the gaping spectators gathered on Amagertorv in Copenhagen for this particular festivity.

Nor was the tone of such an event all self-conscious solemnity. On the sixth day of this celebration, a procession to introduce the traditional contest of riding at the ring was led by the young Christian IV in the guise of a fictitious "Pope Sergius VI," riding jauntily in a sedan chair under a canopy. Flocks of cardinals, bishops, Swiss guards, and monks swinging smoking thuribles added to this picturesque Lutheran satire of the lavish rituals of the papal court. In the following day's procession, the newly crowned monarch appeared in a woman's opulent gown ("gleich die Cortisanen zu Rohm," the German account of the event reads), followed by a rolling Mount of Venus furnished with its own little orchestra.

Along the route of a typical Renaissance coronation or royal entry, triumphal arches frequently added to the spectacle. Coming back from the coronation ceremony on this occasion, Christian IV and his retinue encountered just such a structure, apparently several storys in height and supported at each corner by "a giant with a gilded shield in his left hand, a scimitar at his side, and a gilded helmet on his head."[2] As the king passed through this arch of triumph, an angel descended to place a crown on him, the four giants are said to have nodded with "appropriate reverence," and

Plate 8 Sixteenth-century pageant figures: a triumphal arch in the coronation procession of Christian IV of Denmark in 1596. Detail from a contemporary engraving published the following year.

a roll of kettledrums blended with trumpet fanfares from musicians positioned atop the monument. Although a contemporary engraving depicting the event does not match the written account of it in every detail, it still provides an excellent impression of the size and appearance of this all-important accessory of sixteenth-century street theatre.

Ballets de cour

The princely appetite for masquerade and spectacle represented by these examples of Renaissance pageantry discovered its fullest satisfaction in the great *ballets de cour* of the age. This theatrical form, which grew out of the Italian *intermezzi*, spread across the courts of Europe during the sixteenth century. The model on which many subsequent imitations were based is the famous *Ballet comique de la Reine*, performed at the Petit-Bourbon Palace in Paris in 1581. As the form established itself, three component parts remained more or less constant: *l'ouverture*, an exposition in song or recitative; *les entrées*, a succession of loosely related episodes, usually no more than five in number; and *le grand ballet*, an extended closing dance in which the courtly spectators joined. It seems hardly surprising that Christian IV, brother-in-law of James I of England, at whose elegant court the masques of Ben Jonson and Inigo Jones flourished, should take a special interest in this type of royal entertainment.

Outshining all other Renaissance festivities in Denmark was the thirteen-day celebration held by Christian IV in October of 1634 to seal the union of his eldest son Prince Christian with Princess Magdalena Sibylla of Saxony. *Trionfi* (which included the king and the crown prince in the heroic guise of Publius Scipio Africanus and Lucius Scipio Asiaticus), grand balls, banquets, tournaments, fireworks, and theatre events all contributed to the pomp and circumstance of this politically important occasion. A high point in the crowded program was reached on the third day, however, with the performance of Scandinavia's first full-scale *ballet de cour*, conceived by the court dancing-master Alexander von Kückelsom and scored and directed by Heinrich Schütz, a prominent German composer and exponent of the new Italian musical style of Monteverdi.

True to tradition, this untitled ballet paid allegorical homage to its royal sponsor. The *ouverture* saluted the sea god Neptune (Christian IV) for having cleansed his realm of all monsters and having silenced the fierce goddess of war, Bellona. (The compliment alluded to the Danish king's role as peace broker in the Thirty Years' War.) In the most striking of the *entrées*, Orpheus and the wild beasts that dance to his sorrowful music are torn to pieces by resentful bacchae and she-devils. Appalled by this outrage, the gods decide "harmoniously to create a new world and love from Orpheus' ashes."[3] Cupid accordingly wounds Neptune's son (Prince Christian) and the goddess of wisdom Pallas Athena (Magdalena Sibylla) with his amorous darts. Descending on a cloud, the gods arrive to bless the union of the royal pair and to join in *le grand ballet*, which in this case spelled out in intricate dance patterns the names of the crown prince and his bride.

This noble display, performed largely by the court amateurs themselves, was given in the castle ballroom. Although a printed program prepared by Kückelsom is explicit about the course of the action, less is certain about the staging itself. The festivities of 1634 represented a striking mixture of Renaissance and medieval tendencies, as already seen in the performance of *The Tragedy of the Virtues and the Vices* on the castle square. The medieval technique of simultaneous staging adopted for this morality play was undoubtedly carried over into the indoor court performances as well. The *ballet de cour* seems to have made use of at least two distinct, free-standing localities, which were supplemented by rolling scenery (the hill on which Orpheus sings his plaintive monody, for example), a flying machine for the climactic theophany, and a back curtain, called a "tent," to facilitate entrances and exits. The problem of scene changes within this curtainless space was handled adroitly. As soon as the bacchae had torn Orpheus and his dancing beasts to shreds, for instance, four angels appeared "to bear the dead Orpheum away" while three Pantaloons "collected the dead animals and cleared the ballroom."

Some added light is shed on the question of staging by the two other dramatic performances given during this festival. In the past it would have been customary at such a wedding celebration to include a humanist drama acted by local students. Such had been the case, for example, during the festivities held in 1589 to mark the union of Princess Anna, sister of Christian IV, with James VI of Scotland, England's future monarch. When King James, who was married by proxy, arrived in Denmark the following spring, his brother-in-law again mounted an impressive royal festival that also included "Latin and Danish comedies for the entertainment of their high lordships," presumably given by student players.[4] By 1634, however, professional actors had displaced the student amateurs, and thus two German allegories composed for the occasion by the Sorø academic Johannes Lauremberg were most likely performed by an invited troupe of itinerant English "comedians," tentatively identified as Robert Archer's company.[5] These experienced professionals would have been fully conversant with the new style and methods of the perspective stage used for the second of Lauremberg's comedies.

For the first of these works, given in the ballroom on the day following the great ballet, the older style of simultaneous staging was obviously adequate. In this rather obvious fable Aquilo, rude ruler of the North, complains to Jupiter of the intemperate climate of his realm and his own lack of a wife. To solve his problem, Venus transforms him into an attractive youngster who easily makes off with the lovely and amorous Orithyia. Two juxtaposed mansions, called "Theatrum" in the text, were needed to depict the prevailing antithesis. In pleasing contrast to the snow-covered and forbidding "winter theatre" of Aquilo stood the luxuriant and inviting "summer theatre" of Orithyia. The neutral forestage was unlocalized and could change character from scene to scene. By contrast, however, the second Lauremberg comedy relied on an entirely different kind of theatrical illusion for its effect. For this erudite fable about the rescue of King

Phinéus from the savage harpies (*Wie die Harpyiæ von zweyen Septentrionalischen Helden verjaget, und König Phinéus entledigt wird*), orders were given both for the construction of a "complete perspective stage with the orchestra behind clouds" and for the painting of a landscape drop depicting Kronborg Castle and Elsinore.[6] Within this effectively localized perspective setting, the sight of sirens singing to Neptune from the rolling waves of the Sound must have made a striking impression on Christian's wedding guests. Performed on the eighth day of the festival as its last theatrical event, *Harpyiæ* thus foreshadowed the new style of painted perspective scenery.

Not to be outdone by these Danish revels, the court of Queen Christina of Sweden soon brought the art of the *ballet de cour* to the peak of its development in Scandinavia. Surrounded by some of the best minds and ablest statesmen in Europe, Christina was imbued with a passion for magnificent entertainments that was eagerly shared by the younger nobility. Indeed, her prodigality in this respect became one of the principal charges raised against this troubled queen. The idiom of her courtly entertainments was emphatically French, rather than German. Beginning with *Le ballet des plaisirs des enfants sans souci*, which was staged by the French ballet-master Antoine de Beaulieu and presented in 1638 by the Countess Palatine Catharine to amuse the twelve-year-old Christina, the Swedish court ballets grew steadily in munificence and scope. An era had dawned whose splendor and opulence dazzled even the ambassador of the young King Louis XIV himself.

Le Monde rejovi, "occasioned by the commencement of Her Royal Majesty's happy reign" and danced at Stockholm Castle on New Year's Day 1645, exemplified the basic function of the *ballet de cour* as a homage to the ruling house. Traditionally, the dramaturgy of the spectacle was designed to allegorize the political occasion. The opening section of this work revealed the rejoicing of heaven as Virtue, the signifier of Christina, ascended the throne and Mercury, her ambassador, was dispatched to proclaim the glad tidings. The subsequent *entrées* represented the resultant jubilation in the sea and on the earth. Christina's praises are sung by one and all, including "the four winds" who promise that they will look after her armed forces at sea.

As these ballets became less improvised and more complicated by a formal *mise-en-scène*, their texts clearly reveal the use of the Italianate system of perspective staging and changeable scenery. To better accommodate the demands of these dance dramas, the Italian *machinista* Antonio Brunati was summoned in 1647 to convert a large room in the castle to a modern court theatre, patterned on French models. For this theatre, which Brunati enlarged and improved seven years later, a contemporary plan and description survive to tell us that it was painted in imitation marble with grooved Doric pilasters. A curtained perspective stage, a full seventeen meters in depth, was framed by a proscenium arch flanked by columns with niches containing statues, and topped by an emblematic frieze. Here, Swedish audiences had their first real glimpse of the marvels of changeable baroque scenery, in productions conceived to rival those of the fabled Torelli in Paris.

In November of 1649, Christina's newly equipped theatre served as the venue for the production of court poet Georg Stiernhielm's celebrated ballet text *Then Fångne Cupido* (*Cupid Captured*), in which the queen herself appeared as the chaste Diana and Duke Adolf was Apollo. So delighted was the queen dowager, in whose honor the performance was given, that she conferred two pieces of property on the ballet-master Beaulieu for his choreography. In general, the graceful lyrics of Georg Stiernhielm have raised the printed program texts of several of these Swedish ballets to literary as well as theatrical importance. A month after his *Cupid Captured*, Stiernhielm provided the Swedish lyrics for *La Naissance de la paix*, a more significant and elaborate production given on the queen's birthday to commemorate the Treaty of Westphalia and the end of the Thirty Years' War in 1648. No less a figure than René Descartes, who resided in Stockholm at this time as Christina's tutor, was responsible for the actual conception of this trenchant piece of pacifist agitation. In it, the customary allegorical figures are juxtaposed with a vision of grim reality. Mars and others praise the glories of combat, until "some soldiers appear as proof that war is no pleasure," and ruined peasants are seen contemplating their burning farms. Earth and the other three elements deplore Mars' bellicose attitude, while Justitia, Pallas, and Pax grieve at the fact that Peace has no homeland. At last the gods agree that war must end. The impression left by Stiernhielm's majestic and provocative verses has been compared by Agne Beijer to the effect created by the visions of horror in the *Misères de la guerre* by Callot.[7]

All previous spectacles paled in the brilliance of Christina's formal coronation in October of 1650. For her ostentatious royal entry into Stockholm, she rode in a chariot covered in rich brown silk brocade, embroidered in silver and gold and drawn by six white horses decked out in plumes and gilded harnesses. For an entire intoxicating week wine flowed from the public fountains. For two and a half months the round of balls, tournaments, processions, fireworks, and ballets continued, crowned by the production of Stiernhielm's great ballet tribute, *Parnassus triumphans*, on the first day of 1651. This stage extravaganza, designed to pay homage to the queen as the protectoress of art and learning, had been intended for performance on the coronation day itself, but the immense staging and costuming problems it created necessitated its postponement. The literary text survives; the scenery, costumes, and choreography for the sake of which it was created have vanished without a single trace.

With the abdication and exile of Queen Christina in 1654, the Swedish worship of French culture subsided for a time, and the more hospitable climate for the *ballets de cour* again became the Danish court, presided over by Frederik III (1648–70) and his pleasure-loving queen, Sophie Amalie. Reports of Christina's luxurious entertainments had reached the Danish king through his ambassador Peder Juel, and they no doubt fired the active theatrical imagination of Sophie Amalie. During the 1650s, the two Scandinavian courts vied with one another in the elaborateness of their so-called *Wirtschaften*, a popular form of courtly masquerade that imitated the life in and around a country inn or a marketplace, allowing the courtly participants to cavort in pastoral surroundings dressed as soldiers, pilgrims, hunters, shepherdesses, and the like. In general, the court ballets of Frederik III tended to differ markedly from those seen during his father's long reign. The unified focus provided by the allegorical figures of antiquity was now shattered. Within a looser and nonsequential framework, the so-called *ballet à entrées* of the seventeenth century sought to present a baroque variety of character types, among whom pastoral figures were in particularly high favor.

The enthusiastic queen herself led the court amateurs in the performance of these entertainments. In a ballet-masquerade entitled *Unterschiedliche Oracula*, composed by the court poet A. F. Werner to celebrate the acclamation of crown prince Christian in 1655, Sophie Amalie charmed her audience in no fewer than five different roles. Among the great variety of characters who solicit the oracular reply of the Sibyl in the thirty-five *entrées* of this loosely knit work, she was seen as a peasant girl, a Spanish woman, and an Amazon. In a letter describing the production, Count Bernardino de Rebolledo, the Spanish ambassador to Denmark, had high praise for the queen's depiction of the Muse of War, "dancing and swinging a banner with such extraordinary agility in tune to the music" that she "transformed the surprise of the spectators to rapt amazement."[8] As Fama she appeared, quite like Calumnia in Hegelund's *Susanna*, in "a costume woven with a multitude of eyes, ears, and tongues." Something of the "indescribable charm" that Rebolledo found in her peasant-girl characterization has been captured in a contemporary portrait of Sophie Amalie, probably in this very role.

This portrait by Wolfgang Heimbach is even more interesting as evidence to indicate that a perspective stage with painted scenery was indeed used in the production of *Unterschiedliche Oracula*. When the curtain opened, the Spanish ambassador writes, "a large stage with bushes on either side was revealed," while "a perspective which ended in the cave of the Sibyl" was seen in the background – as indeed it is in the painting itself. The illusion created was, Rebolledo assures his correspondent, "so natural that even the keenest attentiveness would be deceived." Adroit stage lighting added to the effect. "Through the bafflingly natural sky, covered with reddish and transparent clouds, illumination was cast from countlessly many lamps, without anyone being able to detect how it was done."[9] The visible or *a vista* scene change, a technique that lay at the heart of the wing-and-border system of staging, was also seen in this ballet when "toward the end the stage was suddenly transformed, and two enemy camps were seen facing one another."[10]

This production was not, of course, the first to use the new perspective staging, with its painted wings, borders, and backcloth, on the portable stages erected in the ballroom of Copenhagen Castle. The second of Lauremberg's festival plays had, for example, evidently done so more than twenty years before. On the basis of numerous painters' invoices and other financial records, a reconstruction of the salient features of the perspective wing-and-border stage in use at the court of Frederik III has been put forward by Torben Krogh.[11] An elaborate proscenium arch framed the stage, painted to resemble stone blocks and decorated across the top by an ornamental frieze. A bill for painting scenery used in an earlier ballet by A. F. Werner, entitled *Vergnügung und Unvergnügung* or *Les Contents et mécontents du siècle* (1650), mentions "five cloths and four boards" painted to resemble gray and yellow stone tiles. A similar "tiled" forestage is clearly visible in the Heimbach painting of Sophie Amalie, which also contains a hint of the matching steps (the "four boards" in the painter's bill) that led down from

Plate 9 Queen Sophie Amalie as a peasant girl in *Unterschiedliche Oracula*, a ballet-masquerade performed at the Danish court in 1655. Painting by Wolfgang Heimbach in De danske Kongers kronologiske Samling, Rosenborg Castle.

the stage to an open dancing area on the ballroom floor. A railing may have been erected to separate this open playing area, or "orchestra," from the surrounding spectators.

A printed program for *Ballet des 4 Elémens*, danced to celebrate the christening of Prince George of Denmark in 1653, seems to be a virtual compendium of typical seventeeth-century stage decors.[12] This "musical play and ballet" depicted the joyful homage to the infant prince ordered by Jupiter in each of the four elemental spheres. (In this respect, its affinity with

Le Monde rejovi, the allegorical tribute to Queen Christina, seems obvious.) A garden, with flowers, fountains, and shady paths all painted in perspective to create an illusion of three-dimensionality, was all but indispensable in these *ballets de cour*. In this one, such a decor served as Earth, "where the Five Senses are presented." A functional sea with rolling waves was another such basic piece of inventory, needed as early as 1634 for the second of the Lauremberg plays. The nautical element in *Ballet des 4 Elémens* was, however, far more complex: "The perspective is changed to a sea, upon which the royal navy is seen. Neptune comes forth with the other water gods." In the air, this ambitious ballet did its best to incorporate the spectacular cloud machines and flying feats with which the great Torelli had dazzled Parisian audiences. Pax and Fama appeared in the opening section "out in the clouds," with other gods seen "out in the perspective," while Jupiter arrived, as he is wont to do, "from above, riding on an eagle." To signify the realm of Fire, a forbidding version of the mandatory underworld decor was used: "In the play the setting is changed to Hell, where Tantalus and Titius are seen in their suffering and torment. Cerberus lies before the gate of Hell, howling in his bonds." An invoice for this production suggests, moreover, that this decor also incorporated a traditional hell-mouth, in the form of "a large devil's head" – a reminder of the long persistence of medieval conventions on the Renaissance perspective stage.

The great pageants and *ballets de cour* in which cavaliers capered at the courts of Scandinavia remained popular throughout the seventeenth century, and the reigns of both Christian V of Denmark (1670–99) and Charles XI of Sweden (1660–97) offer notable examples of the survival of this form of theatre. The fifteenth birthday of Charles XI in 1669 was marked by the performance of *Den stoora Genius* (*The Mighty Spirit*), a court ballet conceived by the poet and politician Erik Linschölt in the lyric tradition of Stiernhielm's tributes to Christina. In *Certamen equestre*, an elaborate pageant enacted three years later to celebrate the coronation of the young Swedish monarch, Charles made his entrance on horseback costumed as a Roman warrior and followed by his courtiers masquerading as Roman foot soldiers. In the same frame of mind the Lord Chamberlain of Denmark, Ulrik Frederik Gyldenløve, decided to salute his sovereign's birthday in 1683 with a suitably allegorical *Festspil* in verse, written by the distinguished poet and bishop Thomas Kingo. This work, a kind of miniature opera with balletic interludes, brought greetings to Christian V from the heroic world of Jupiter, Mars, Fama, Victoria, and his own legendary forefather, King Dan.

Ephemeral by their very nature, these princely toys and "transitory devices" nevertheless exerted a lasting influence on the evolution of theatre in Scandinavia. The future development of both opera and ballet was directly shaped by their example. In terms of stagecraft, they embodied the transition from the medieval conventions to the baroque style of perspective illusion and changeable scenery. As far as the growth of a broad popular theatre culture is concerned, however, a second, coexistent tradition, sustained not by the courtly amateurs but by troupes of seasoned professionals who visited the royal houses of Scandinavia during this period, played a far more dominant role.

Royal troupes and strollers

The bands of itinerant players who came to Denmark and Sweden during the seventeenth and eighteenth centuries were ambassadors of theatrical style. They performed under royal patronage and were occasionally invited to take up residence at court for extended periods of time. The acting of these foreign troupes was often of high artistic caliber, and their presence thus helped to establish a fertile climate for the eventual growth of a native theatre. The warmth of the welcome accorded such companies of strolling actors depended, of course, entirely upon the views and tastes of each reigning monarch.

As early as 1579, Frederik II set an influential example when he brought the first four English "instrumentalists," as they were called, to the Danish court. This troupe, in varying permutations, remained in the king's service for seven years, during which they performed at the newly built Kronborg Castle for the glory of his majesty and the pleasure of the numerous sea captains returning with bulging coffers from their long ocean voyages. In the summer of 1586, a second troupe of English players, numbering such illustrious Shakespearian comics as Thomas Pope and Will Kempe, entered Frederik's service for a short time before moving on to the court of the Elector of Saxony. Although these smaller bands of comedians, usually about five in number, may sometimes have performed complete plays, their normal repertoire consisted of dancing (for which Kempe, of course, was renowned), singing, gymnastics, clowning, and declamation. Eventually the generic term "English comedians" came to be applied to similar German, Swedish, and Dutch strollers who commanded the so-called English arts of fencing, vaulting, and ropedancing.

Although the sixty-year reign of Christian IV of Denmark saw more attention paid to music and courtly festivities than to professional dramatic performances, there is evidence that the major English troupes of the day all visited the country at one time or another. The famous troupe of comedians and acrobats under Robert Browne and Thomas Sackville, which was made up of eighteen performers, was dispatched to Denmark by its patron, Duke Henry Julius of Brunswick, to take part in the celebrations marking the coronation of Brunswick's brother-in-law as Christian IV in 1596. The great wedding celebration of 1634, the most munificent of all Renaissance festivities in Scandinavia, was likewise an occasion for which a leading English company, under the direction of Robert Archer, was summoned. Although one must assume that these actors had a hand in the three theatre productions at this festival, *The Tragedy of the Virtues and the Vices* and Lauremberg's two German plays, there is no factual evidence of what such a troupe actually did perform.

In seventeenth-century Sweden, a comparable interest in things theatrical led King Gustav II Adolf to invite Christian Thum, the first German comedian to visit Stockholm, to form a professional troupe for the entertainment of the Swedish court. In *Elizabethan Players in Sweden 1591–92*, Erik Wikland identifies the presence of the first English players at the court of Duke Charles in Nyköping, but these strollers were musicians rather than actors. It was Thum, who acted before Queen Marie Eleonora in 1628/9 and before the young Christina in 1637, who became the country's first court theatre director. To this end he was granted not only an annual stipend of 400 silver dollars, but also permission to borrow costumes from the royal wardrobe. In 1640 he was given an additional sum of money for the construction of a public theatre in the Södermalm district of the capital, where his actors could present plays when not engaged at court. Again, nothing very specific is known about Thum's repertory, but his venture seems to represent a forerunner of the virtual invasion of German and Dutch itinerant troupes that followed the earlier English companies to Scandinavia during the middle decades of the century.[13]

At the resplendent and distinctly French-minded court of Queen Christina, meanwhile, the popularity of such wandering troupes declined. Even the company of the renowned Dutch principal Jan Baptista van Fornenbergh, who first came to Stockholm in 1653 and remained a frequent visitor to Sweden, found little favor with the queen herself, who was preoccupied instead with the amateur theatricals and lavish *ballets de cour* given at her elegant new court theatre. These aristocratic pastimes were supplemented by the professional performances of Italian opera and *commedia dell'arte* staged by an Italian company of actors and singers under the direction of Vincenzo Albrici. Determined to rival Versailles in every respect, Christina had summoned Albrici and his players to her cosmopolitan court in 1652, not long before the end of her troubled reign.

The theatrical tastes of the Danish ruler Frederik III were considerably more eclectic. In addition to bringing the first troupe of French actors to Scandinavia in 1669, this self-proclaimed absolute monarch and theatre enthusiast also welcomed the many German and Dutch strollers who visited Denmark during his reign. In 1662 he granted a patent to the Dutch entrepreneur Andreas Joachimsen Wolf that permitted him to erect the first permanent public theatre in Copenhagen. This structure was patterned on and named after the Schowburg in Amsterdam, a hybrid form of theatre with elements of both the Elizabethan-style open stage and the Italianate stage of pictorial illusionism. The royal patent enjoined Wolf to present something that "is not common, and has not been seen by any ordinary comedian." Eager to oblige, he engaged one of the outstanding troupes of the day, led by the German principal Michel Daniel Treu (or Drey) and numbering among its members the noted actor Johan Velten. The Treu company arrived early in 1663 and was allowed to perform "comedies, tragedies, and other such actions and plays" at the palace tennis court until the new Schowburg was ready for them later that same year. During its very brief existence, this endeavor showed Danish audiences a style of theatre that represented the highest professional standards. In addition to Treu's players, Carl Andreas Paulsen's important troupe and van Fornenbergh's Dutch actors also managed to appear at the Copenhagen Schowburg before the enterprise ended in bankruptcy and the theatre was pulled down in 1666.

Following this disappointment, the cluster of companies dispersed. A troupe headed by Paulsen and Velten continued to appear at regular intervals in Copenhagen, while Treu moved his base of operations to Lüneburg and van Fornenbergh and his actors were transported to Stockholm aboard the royal yacht "Green Parrot." This time the Dutch actors were more fortunate and found favor and employment in the service of the young Swedish king Charles XI. Under their supervision another replica of the Schowburg was created in 1667 in Lejonkulan, or the Lion's Den, a structure originally built to house and display a lion brought home by the Swedish army as a souvenir of their capture of the Castle of Prague in 1648.

In its converted state, Lejonkulan came to serve as Sweden's first permanent playhouse, where Stockholm's theatre-loving public was introduced to the French classical style, albeit *en hollandais*, with such productions as Pierre Corneille's *La Mort de Pompée* and Rotrou's *Bélisaire*. The inauguration of the king's new Schowburg was commemorated in a booklet published by the Dutch poet Henrik Jordis, auspiciously entitled *Stockholms Parnas*.[14]

In general, the repertory of these seventeenth-century German and Dutch itinerant players was a curious mixture. In addition to adaptations of classics by such dramatists as Shakespeare, Lope de Vega, and the French playwrights of the day, they also specialized in the highly popular and broadly theatrical form known as *Haupt- und Staatsaktionen*, a genre that mingled elevated heroics and farcical *lazzi* and thus played upon the contrast between the noble and spectacular actions of the main story and the commonsense reactions to it provided by the clown, Hanswurst or Pickelherring. Usually, of course, the main play was also capped by a broadly farcical *Nachspiel*.

A contemporary document offers at least some idea of the titles performed by such a troupe. When Treu left Denmark for Lüneburg in 1666, he petitioned the authorities there for permission to perform and, happily, supplemented his application with a list of the plays he had performed while in the service of the Danish king. Treu's list includes twenty-five plays as well as an unspecified number of "various lovely pastorals."[15] His flair for scenic effects is suggested by the very first item, a chronicle of the destruction of Jerusalem "presented naturally on the stage with the help of special inventions." The predominant subjects are biblical, mythological, and especially historical (including plays about the death of Cromwell and the restoration of Charles II). In addition to adaptations of Calderón and Lope de Vega, a rich inheritance from the earlier English troupes is apparent in such titles as Marlowe's *Doctor Faustus*, Kyd's *The Spanish Tragedy*, and Shakespeare's *King Lear*. The version of the latter play that Treu performed in Copenhagen, "The History of King Liar of England, being a Matter in which children's disobedience is punished and obedience rewarded," is obviously of special interest. A later program outlining the action of this German seventeenth-century *Lear* has come to light. In this version, in which the Fool is absent and the ending is greatly altered, both Regan and Goneril stab themselves to death onstage, the latter because she "cannot have Edmund." The fate of the bastard is even more gruesome: Lear orders that Edmund shall "an 4 Ketten in die Luft hängen, und also sein Leben beschliessen." A comforting reunion follows these horrors, however, as Lear in the end "rejoices over his daughter Cordelia's obedience."[16]

French influences

In the France of Louis XIV the art of acting had reached a peak of excellence, and the courts of Europe naturally competed to secure French companies for themselves. These were seen as more permanent than the essentially itinerant English, German, and Dutch troupes, and they brought with them something of the splendor of the great court at Versailles. The first company of French players, led by the accomplished Parisian actor Jean Guillemoys du Chesnay Rosidor, came to the Danish court in 1669, but their stay was cut short by the death of Frederik III the following year. During the reign of his successor, Christian V, theatre of all kinds flourished: a small wooden opera house was erected on the palace grounds (and almost immediately burned), the temporary stage in the palace ballroom eventually became permanent, and a new group of French actors was summoned to Copenhagen in 1681. With some interruptions and changes of personnel, this company remained active at court for the next thirteen years. Although little definite is known about its repertory or playing conditions, the usual size of this troupe seems to have been twelve performers, probably seven actors and five actresses. Even the bare fact that they celebrated the king's birthday in 1683 with a performance of the festive comedy *L'Inconnu*, a demanding *pièce à machine* written by Thomas Corneille and Donneau de Visé for Molière's company in Paris eight years earlier, reveals a good deal about their technical ability and range. In retrospect, the most notable contribution of this troupe was its engagement in 1686 of René Magnon de Montaigu, the son of Molière's friend, dramatist Jean Magnon, and subsequently the founder of the first permanent national theatre in Scandinavia.

The crowning of King Frederik IV of Denmark in 1699 and the succession of his warlike cousin Charles XII to the Swedish throne two years earlier marked the beginning of a new era – a new century rich in theatrical developments and conducive to the growth of permanent theatres for a new popular audience. In 1699 the court architect and avid theatrical collector Nicodemus Tessin the Younger persuaded the young Swedish king to do credit to his country as one of the great powers of Europe by engaging a permanent French troupe for his court, made up of

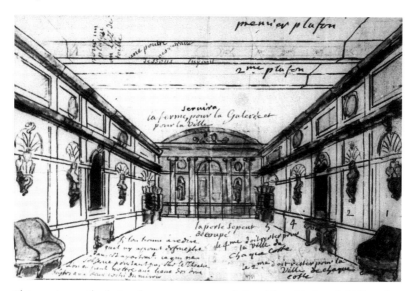

Plate 10 Among the designs for new scenery commissioned from Bérain and d'Olivert for the opening of the new court theatre in Stockholm in 1699, a sketch for a formal hall (*La galerie*) uses five perspective side wings decorated with busts and mirrors to create the illusion of a closed interior.

Plate 11 In a watercolor sketch for a street (*Le village*), the five side wings now depict an alternation of two-story buildings and cutout trees.

Plate 12 In a third watercolor sketch, the basic tragedy decor (*Palais à volonté*) is shown with the same arboreal background shutters used for the setting for a village street.

twenty-three actors, singers, and dancers under the leadership of Claude Guillemois de Rosidor, son of the former director of Frederik III's royal troupe. For public performances, this new company was granted permission to equip and operate Bollhuset, the palace tennis court, at its own expense. For productions at court, however, a private stage was also needed. As fire had destroyed Stockholm Castle and, with it, Lejonkulan two years earlier, Tessin decided to build a new theatre in the great hall of the Wrangel Palace.

The resultant plans and sketches for this project are today among the most informative pieces of iconographic evidence we have concerning seventeenth-century European stage practice. Tessin invited no less a figure than Jean Bérain himself to design the necessary scenery in Paris. In the end it was Bérain's collaborator, Jean Saint-Hillaire d'Olivet, who filled the commission, tested the sets on the stage of the Hôtel de Bourgogne, and then promptly shipped them to Stockholm. The three basic designs making up the Bérain–d'Olivet package could be combined in various ways to create a total of six distinct decors. With their ingenious permutations, the sets provided the full range of timeless scenic environments needed for the classical repertory of Corneille, Racine, and Molière. "La galerie," a formal hall, could be transformed into "la place publique" and then into "le village" by the swift insertion of new side wings into the setting. The basic tragedy decor ("Palais à volonté") could, before the eyes of the audience if one wished, become a setting for "serious pastorals" simply by opening the back shutter to reveal a new background. There can be no doubt that Tessin's stage in the Wrangel Palace, five wings deep with two sets of wings in each position to permit rapid *changements à vue*, was a worthy rival to the theatres of Paris in its use of the latest stage techniques.

Rosidor's players opened the new court theatre on 20 November 1699 with a performance of a recent Parisian hit, Jean-Louis Regnard's comedy *Le Joueur*. Their subsequent repertory consisted of Corneille, Racine, Molière, Regnard, Dancourt, and other French novelties. The converted tennis court in Bollhuset was ready for them in February of the following year, having become a smart modern theatre furnished with blue-upholstered benches to seat 800 spectators. The auditorium consisted of a standing pit and three tiers of boxes, with a royal box in the first tier near the stage. Unlike the court theatre, admission was charged: those selecting the better seats paid one caroline for the second level, two carolines for the first, and three carolines for a prominent seat on the stage itself. Here as elsewhere, this latter practice persisted far into the eighteenth century.

The extensive wars of Charles XII took their toll, however, and eventually all theatrical activity was suffocated in gunpowder smoke. By 1706 the Swedish war effort had undermined the economy to such an extent that the salaries of the French actors could no longer be met, and the last of the troupe turned homeward. During the period that followed, various itinerant companies continued to perform in Sweden, but without any particular regularity.

Although his adversary on the battlefield, Frederik IV resembled Charles in his desire to brighten his court with a new troupe of French players. These actors, who arrived in Copenhagen at the end of 1700, actually included some of Rosidor's gradually dissolving company. The Danish court troupe, which remained in the service of the king for two decades, was organized by the able René Montaigu and consisted of seven actors and five actresses. Montaigu bore the responsibility for every aspect of the operation, taking his orders from the king and the court, casting the parts, supervising preparations, acting, arranging music and choreography, and even contributing the occasional prologue. Each of Montaigu's players was handpicked, and his ensemble undoubtedly represented a high level of artistic ability.

Most likely, the Montaigu troupe played the same repertoire of new and older French plays that Rosidor had presented in Stockholm. During its twenty-year existence, however, Montaigu journeyed four times to Paris at the king's expense for the purpose of scouting new trends, finding suitable new plays for production, and studying the French acting style. These four field trips (in 1708, 1711/12, 1717, and 1721) took place during a period of transition when a new style of restrained and subdued acting, represented by Michel Baron and his pupil Adrienne Lecouvreur (who made her debut at the Comédie Française in 1717), was gaining ascendancy. Lecouvreur's "simple, noble, natural declamation," which stood in sharp contrast to the histrionics of the German *Haupt- und Staatsaktionen*, must almost inevitably have exerted an influence on Montaigu's work with his own actors.

At the outset, the Montaigu troupe performed on temporary stages erected in various palace locales, often in conjunction with the royal banquet. If the theatre itself on such occasions was rather makeshift, however, the settings and staging were neither primitive nor lacking in complexity. Time and again one encounters the comment that "the stage was numerous times transformed in great haste and with complete illusion."[17] For a few years after it opened in 1703, a new opera house built by Frederik IV also served both the French actors and another resident troupe of Italian singers, but this building was soon converted to other uses. In about 1712, a new court theatre was created in Copenhagen Castle, adjacent to the great hall where, a century and a quarter earlier, school dramas were performed at court. This spacious playhouse, which became the winter home for Montaigu's actors, consisted of a horseshoe-shaped auditorium with fifteen boxes and a perspective stage of equal size, deep enough to accommodate six wing positions.[18] Some have speculated that admittance to this royal theatre may have extended at times beyond the narrow court circle to include segments of the general Danish public.

Throughout the story of the French actors at the court of Frederik IV, German strolling players continued to appear in Copenhagen and occasionally even performed at the palace. In 1718 a royal patent to present public theatre performances in the capital was granted to Samuel Paulsen von Qvoten, a colorful mountebank and medical quack who had toured the provinces with a traveling puppet show. Soon joining forces with him was Etienne Capion, a prosperous caterer who was also Montaigu's stage manager and chief technician at the court theatre. The partners began to present both puppet shows and live performances by a troupe of "high German comedians" in 1719. Their theatre was one of the admiralty's warehouses (a disused cannon foundry) on the city's most fashionable square, Kongens Nytorv. After von Qvoten departed for Sweden in 1720, Capion carried on alone and succeeded in obtaining an enviable monopoly on all forms of popular theatrical entertainment in the capital. When his lease on the warehouse expired the following year, he gained a new license for the construction of a permanent playhouse, to be located on a side street off Kongens Nytorv called Lille Grønnegade (Little Green Street). The name has remained synonymous with the founding of Scandinavia's first permanent vernacular theatre.

Capion's 500-seat playhouse, which he designed and equipped to rival the glories of the court theatre, was built during the autumn of 1721. By the kind of coincidence upon which such historical developments sometimes depend, the king had unexpectedly chosen this same year to dismiss Montaigu and his French actors, whom he had decided to replace with a German opera company. A partnership between the unemployed theatre director and his erstwhile stage manager was an obvious solution. Thus when Grønnegadeteatret opened its doors in January 1722, its attractions included performances twice weekly by René Montaigu and his formerly royal comedians. When the other French actors left to seek employment elsewhere in Europe, Montaigu was obliged to devise a new and bolder scheme – the formation of a Danish-speaking company based in Capion's popular new theatre. These developments did not, in fact, mark the end of the vogue of the French acting troupe at the courts of Scandinavia, where the presence of such troupes throughout the eighteenth century continued to influence theatrical culture. What Montaigu's initiative did signal, however, was the beginning of a much more broadly based drive toward the creation of a truly national theatre, with a corresponding repertory of plays by native writers.

3 Playhouses of the eighteenth century

It is hardly necessary to emphasize the acknowledged position of Ludvig Holberg as the foremost playwright of the eighteenth century in Scandinavia. Less clearly evident, perhaps, is the process of development and change undergone by the theatre during this century of enlightenment and revolution. Above all, the surge toward the establishment of permanent national theatres was, despite setbacks, not to be denied. The first steps toward this goal, taken by Montaigu and his Danish actors at Grønnegadeteatret in the 1720s, led in due course to the founding of the Danish Royal Theatre in 1748. From the launching of the so-called Kungliga Svenska Skådeplats, or Royal Swedish Stage, in 1737, a similar but more indirect path led, by way of A. F. Ristell's abortive season of Swedish plays at Bollhuset in 1787, to the foundation of Scandinavia's second national theatre, the Royal Dramatic Theatre in Stockholm, the following year.

During this period of restless activity and growth, the tastes and traditions of the aristocratic court theatres continued to exert a parallel influence of equal strength. In particular, under the festive aegis of such stagestruck royals as Lovisa Ulrika of Sweden and Frederik V of Denmark, the enjoyment of French drama and Italian opera remained the true hallmark of an enlightened mind. To compartmentalize these two kinds of theatre, popular and courtly, would be to distort the brisk interplay of styles and crossing of currents that characterized the theatrical climate of the age.

The first vernacular theatre

"Dans l'impossibilité de faire à l'avenir éclater mon zèle pour le service de Vostre Majesté en parlant franccçois," Montaigu wrote to the Danish king

50

on 1 July 1722, "je luy demande très humblement la permission de pouvoir établir ici vne Comédie en langue Danoise."[1] Cut off from performing in French by the king's decision, the former court theatre director, prompted no doubt more by simple practicality than by patriotism, turned to the national language as the medium in which best to continue his work. Backed by influential supporters, Montaigu's proposal for "la Comédie Danoise" received prompt royal approval and a modest subvention. During the summer Montaigu put together his small band of Danish actors, consisting of seven men and three women. Although the majority were university students, a small nucleus of experience was formed by Marie Magdalene Montaigu, the director's wife and a leading player in his court troupe, and Frédéric Daniel Pilloy, Montaigu's successor as the company's romantic *jeune premier* and hence the first interpreter of Holberg's Leander figures. Although Montaigu himself was obviously unwilling to appear on stage in a language he did not fully command, his immersion in the Molière style of comedy and his outstanding ability to train actors were powerful assets for the new theatre. The Danish Comedy thus began on a solid artistic footing. Financially, however, its position was badly undermined from the beginning.

Scandinavia's first public vernacular theatre opened in the playhouse on Lille Grønnegade on 23 September 1722 with a translation of Molière's *L'Avare*. In a prologue written for the occasion, Thalia came forward to proclaim her traditional comic intent:

> I mention neither man nor town nor house nor street
> But punish without fear what we should hate,
> Wherever I may see it, of whomever it is said,
> For the instruction of all who pay good heed.

Two days later came the first of many Holberg premieres with the production of *Den politiske Kandestøber* (*The Political Tinker*), a play which, as its author notes, "had the good fortune which all good comedies should have, namely that a flock of people became angry over it" but which also "kept the audience laughing from beginning to end."[2] Holberg, who had been approached by "certain persons" to write for the new Danish stage, more than kept his word: during the first eighteen months of its existence, Grønnegadeteatret was able to produce fifteen original Holberg comedies, five of which were staged in the very first season. Thus fortified, the Danish actors enjoyed not only popular success but also the patronage of the court, where command performances of Molière's *Le Bourgeois gentilhomme* and *Le Mariage forcé* were given during the first season. Even before the theatre's auspicious opening, however, Capion had mortgaged both his playhouse and his patent to the hilt, and it became steadily more difficult for the box-office receipts from the 500-seat house to cover his debts and expenses. The title of Holberg's *Den ellevte Juni* (*The Eleventh of June*), which refers to the fiscal date on which installment payments and interest usually come due, had a grim relevance when this debtors' comedy was first produced on that date in 1723. Shortly after the second performance, Capion was himself hauled into jail for his own bad debts.

Although the financial situation improved temporarily as Holberg continued to turn out play after play for the Danish company, further setbacks were in store for Grønnegadeteatret during its second season. A substantial portion of Capion's income derived from the profitable biweekly "assemblies" that took place in the theatre, featuring "gallant music," masked balls, coffee or tea, and some discreet gambling. When these frivolities, which form the background for much comic indignation in Holberg's *Mascarade*, were outlawed as a source of youthful corruption in February of 1724, Capion sought desperately to counteract the loss by supplementing the Danish actors, who performed twice weekly, with a band of ropedancers. Outraged, Montaigu succeeded in wresting control of the playhouse from the patentee. Ownership passed into the hands of creditors, and the wily Etienne Capion decamped for good in the summer of 1724, ostensibly to take a troupe of Danish actors on tour to Norway. Continued efforts by Montaigu to avert a total financial collapse were in vain, however, and his Comédie Danoise, faced with dwindling attendance, closed in bankruptcy in February 1725.

Exactly one year later the embryonic national theatre was temporarily revived when its company resolved, "despite the harsh fate that has for some time befallen the Danish plays," to resume performances "at their own risk."[3] The actors, who now rented the theatre for each performance and then divided the proceeds, chose *Tartuffe* for their opening – suitably adapted, however, to meet Holberg's rather parochial objection that, as Molière had written this play for a Catholic audience, it would have no relevance for a Danish public. In themselves, the surviving playbills for Grønnegadeteatret tell their own story of the efforts made during this difficult period to attract a following. Performances were now given three times a week, sometimes with as many as four plays on a single bill.

Audiences were treated to displays of perspective staging and scenic effects reminiscent of those seen in Montaigu's court productions. A "much improved" revival of Molière's *Amphitryon*, a favorite Montaigu spectacle both at the public theatre and at court, included such flying feats as Mercury seated on a cloud in the prologue, Night riding through the sky in a chariot drawn by horses, and the majestic descent of Jupiter on his eagle at the conclusion (for which, the playbill promised, "the entire stage will be illuminated, which will be very pleasing to see"). Liberal infusions of local color were provided both in the texts and the settings of the French plays performed. Thus, for Nicolas Boindin's *Le Port de Mer*, a popular comedy of rogues and lovers set in the exotic seaport of Livorno, local spectators were promised (20 May 1726) "a complete view of the Copenhagen Roadstead as it appears nowadays, with numerous men-of-war, three-masters, other small vessels and barges rowing here and there in the water."[4] This recognizable scene (most likely a painted backcloth) alluded, in fact, to an event of the day, the visit of the British fleet to the Copenhagen harbor.

Song and dance also gained new popular appeal with the arrival in June of the French ballet-master Jean Baptiste Landé and his wife. In Stockholm, Landé's staging of two Regnard comedies and an original ballet, performed in 1721 by court amateurs for the birthday of King Fredrik I, had made such an impression that he was granted a license to form a French opera troupe under the patronage of the Swedish monarch. On his way to Paris to recruit a company, Landé stopped for several months at the theatre in Lille Grønnegade. Here, his considerable talents were utilized in a variety of ways. He restored most of the ballet interludes in Molière's *Le Malade imaginaire*, entertained with his own ballet divertissements and comic routines, and enlivened the Holberg performances with interpolated pantomimes and harlequinades. Among these a favorite was "The Italian Night of Scaramouche and Harlequin," the comic effect of which depended on the ability of the performers to "act night" on a brightly lighted stage.

New plays were continually added during the theatre's last months in an effort to broaden its repertoire and stem the financial ebb tide. The production in May of *Le Menteur eller Løgneren* probably introduced Danish audiences not to Pierre Corneille's comedy of that name but to an adaptation of Richard Steele's *The Lying Lover*, a sentimental drama introduced in Scandinavia by Swedish playwright Carl Gyllenborg's 1721 translation. A month later Montaigu and Landé joined forces to stage Holberg's *Banquerouteren eller Den pantsatte Bondedreng* (*The Bankrupt or The Pawned Peasant Boy*), like *The Eleventh of June* a comedy about rescue from bankruptcy on the fateful day of reckoning. The subject was unquestionably uppermost in the minds of everyone connected with the enterprise. The timely arrival of Holberg's *Den Stundesløse* (*The Fussy Man*) in November once again rescued the actors from the public's indifference, but not for long. Audiences shrank, and a particularly ill-attended performance even had to be called off. Just before the end, Montaigu made a desperate excursion into the *commedia dell'arte* with his production of Le Noble's *Les deux Arlequins*, a demanding harlequinade of mistaken identity from the repertory of the *Théâtre Italien*, a tradition close to Holberg's heart. No amount of effort or inventiveness could, however, exorcise the twin demons of insolvency and indifference. Bowing to the inevitable, the bankrupt Danish Comedy gave its final performance the following day, Shrove Tuesday 1727.

The event was solemnized by the staging of a grimly farcical afterpiece entitled *Den danske Komedies Ligbegængelse* (*The Interment of the Danish Comedy*), borrowed by Holberg from a French–Italian farce and written by him when the theatre's economic crises had driven it into bankruptcy for the first time in 1725. In the final scene of this mock-heroic *jeu de théâtre*, a solemn funeral service to mark the death of Comedy is described in detail in the stage directions. As a procession of sorrowing actors, led by Montaigu's children, marched three times around the stage, a drummer draped in black and two men bearing marshals' batons with crêpe streamers ushered the once-vital corpse – an actor dumped in a wheelbarrow – to the grave. Comedy was then lowered to rest through a trap in the stage floor. Henrik, the roguish servant figure in many of Holberg's comedies, leaped grief-stricken into the grave. After the procession had departed, the solitary figure of Thalia, who less than four and a half years before had stood on the same stage to proclaim the start of halcyon days, came forward again in the person of Madame Montaigu to pronounce a eulogy over the defunct venture.

Holberg's theatricality

The mock funeral described at the end of *The Interment of the Danish Comedy* is but one example of the theatricality of Holberg's comic theatre – a characteristic he emphatically shares with Molière, his true counterpart.

The essence of theatre, in Holberg's view, is what he calls the festive spirit, "the soul of comedy" that brings a play to life on the stage. "A comedy must possess *festivitas*, gaiety, and the ability to make people laugh," he writes in a 1723 preface known as "Just Justesen's Reflections." It is not enough for the comic writer to study "the ridiculousness of humanity" and be able to "chastise faults so that he amuses as well," he insists in this revealing piece of comic theory. In addition to fulfilling this dual Horatian purpose of pleasing and instructing, the comic playwright must always envision the effect that his play will have in performance. "Sometimes the comedy that is the wittiest to read is the least amusing on the stage" if it lacks "that which cannot easily be described but which is the thing that makes a theatre live."[5] Accordingly, each comic effect and situation in a Holberg play is calculated from the point of view of the audience.

The exaggeration or heightening of a situation that is typical of Holberg is thus always governed by the requirement that "the audience will be able to believe in its reality." Regarded in this way, the principle of decorum comes to mean, for Holberg, what is acceptable or comprehensible in the context of prevailing customs and fashions. Characters or subjects unfamiliar or alien to his Danish audience are, by definition, unsuited to his comic purpose. Hence, he is led to reason, "highly romantic and amorous plays are very inappropriate here and have not had the same acceptance as in England and other lands where people hang themselves for the sake of love."[6] Understandably, this emphasis on the element of audience self-recognition caused Holberg to make a strong case for indigenous drama and localized comedy. It also provided him with a welcome excuse to bait Molière, his prodigious and more popular rival in the Grønnegade repertory. For every negative example he singles out in a Molière play, he is ready with a positive counterpoint taken from his own work.

In Holberg's admittedly polemical view, Molière's plays enjoyed a distinct advantage over his own when these were performed for the first time at Grønnegadeteatret. For the performance of a Molière role, he writes in his first Latin epistle (*Epistola prima*, 1728), a tradition of gesture and movement (*gestus ac gressus*) existed beforehand and was communicated by Montaigu to the young Danish actors. By contrast, Holberg's own works had only "their own intrinsic merit to recommend them." That they succeeded was due, the Danish dramatist insists, to the fact that they afforded, even to inexperienced actors, a veritable blueprint for character physicalization. And indeed, the comic figures in Holberg's classically ordered universe, each with a particular dominant trait or attitude, are scrupulously differentiated in terms of appearance, speech, and manners and are armed by the playwright with a battery of opportunities for effective *lazzi* and bits of comic business. Each character is in turn related to a distinct, localized milieu which, while obviously in no sense naturalistic, adds color and concreteness to the classical simplicity of the comic design.

Born in Bergen in 1684 and appointed a professor of metaphysics at the University of Copenhagen in 1717, Holberg had already achieved a solid literary reputation (under the pseudonym Hans Mikkelsen) for his mock-heroic epic *Peder Paars* when he was asked to provide comedies for Montaigu's troupe. The nature and extent of his previous knowledge of the stage is quite unclear, but there can hardly be doubt that it was the interaction with Montaigu and his Danish actors that conclusively shaped Holberg's dramatic method. The inherent theatricality of his vision derives not least from the fact that his characters are invariably conceived as, above all, roles for actors – in the first instance for Pilloy, Marie Magdalene Montaigu, and the other members of the company at Grønnegadeteatret whose initial performances laid a foundation for a vigorous and organic Holberg tradition that has continued to flourish in the Scandinavian theatre to the present day.

The first cluster of his plays to be performed are called character comedies by Holberg, who, with Molière before him as the great model, considered this form the superior comic mode. Throughout the action of such works as *The Political Tinker, Den Vægelsindede (The Weathercock), Jean de France, Jeppe paa Bjerget (Jeppe on the Hill)*, and *Mester Gert Westphaler*, dramatic interest remains focused on the foibles of the title character and the absurd predicaments caused by his or her ruling folly. As a typical product of the Enlightment and spokesman for the Age of Reason, Holberg is in all his work distrustful of violent passions and excesses. "I have made no attempt at tragedy, nor have I any inclination to do so," he later remarked, "for I am repelled by everything that is affected and is placed, so to speak, on stilts" (Epistle 447). Especially in his comedies of character, it is precisely this "stilted" attitude that is consistently ridiculed. Eccentricities and foolish quirks rather than grand vices are the object of his satire.

In *The Political Tinker*, the opening salvo in Holberg's comic offensive, Herman von Bremen is a muddle-headed tinker whose risible political pretensions become his undoing after he is duped into believing that he has been elected mayor. "The play is merry and *moral* as well," Holberg asserts in a later epistle (249), and while grotesque exaggeration and broad farcical effects abound in these comedies, their underlying satirical intent is indeed always evident. "Just Justesen's Reflections" refers specifically to *Jean de France* as "a bitter satire" of the bourgeois tendency to corrupt the country with foreign affectations. Jean de France (alias Hans Frandsen), a perfect role for Pilloy, is a younger but no less egregious ass who, after a fifteen-week stay in Paris, has become so besotted with French fashions and so oblivious to reality that he proves an easy target for the various hoaxes played on him. In *Erasmus Montanus*, a Holberg masterpiece written during this same period but first performed in 1747, the same basic theme is developed in far more complex and ironic terms. Rasmus Berg, the peasant student and pride of his parents who returns from the great world of the university to his native village, is puffed up with his newly acquired proficiency in Latin disputations and syllogisms. There is, in fact, nothing wrong with the pretentious student's Latin learning, but the inhumanity and conceit with which he flings it in the teeth of his uncomprehending surroundings render it foolish and irrelevant. At the climax of the comedy, Erasmus suffers humiliation and defeat at the hands of public opinion, in the person of the village deacon, on the crucial question of whether the earth is flat or round. It is, the tormented scholar is forced to concede at last, "flat as a pancake," and he promises to mend his ways and refrain from further disputation.

As a rule, Holberg's character comedies focus on figures set apart from and held up as ludicrous contrasts to the society in which they find themselves. One kind of play criticizes foolish ambitions and pretentions; another sort pokes fun at character quirks and foibles. Thus, the central character in *Gert Westphaler* is a compulsively talky barber, while *Jacob von Tyboe* transplants the popular figure of the braggart soldier and would-be lover to Danish soil. In *The Weathercock*, the second of Holberg's comedies to be acted at Grønnegadeteatret, he created the role of the capricious Lucretia, an unpredictable woman who is forever changing her mind, for the particular abilities of Madame Montaigu who, according to "Just Justesen's Reflections," "portrayed her habits so nicely that one can say she lacked nothing of what is needed to convey such a personality." A male counterpart to the fickle Lucretia appears in *The Fussy Man* in the character of the busy Vielgeschrei, who spends his time rushing furiously and aimlessly from one activity to another, accomplishing nothing in spite of all his energy.

With uncharacteristic modesty, Holberg ascribed the eventual success of *Jeppe on the Hill* at Grønnegadeteatret to the portrayal by Johan Gram of "the language, manners, and customs" of an authentically conceived Danish peasant. The appeal of Holberg's most discussed and most performed play reaches, however, far beyond the limits of regional folk comedy. Its source is an anecdote in Jacob Biedermann's *Utopia*, rooted in the popular fable of the peasant made king for a day – a dramatized practical joke, in other words, with a deeper dimension of comic irony. Unlike the protagonists of the other character comedies – the ambitious Herman von Bremen, for example, or the obsessive Vielgeschrei – Jeppe is a good-natured and witty soul whose principal shortcoming is a predilection for sleeping his cares away or drowning them in a bottle. When he is discovered by the local baron asleep on a dunghill after one of his drinking bouts, he is carried off to the nobleman's manor, dressed in the finest clothes, and placed in the baron's bed. He is told when he awakens that, as master of the house, his notion of having been a poor peasant must have been a bad dream. Jeppe takes to his new life with gusto, proves something of a tyrant, and eventually becomes drunk again on the fine wines that are served to him with trumpet fanfares. Tossed back on the dunghill, he is once again plucked from his repose, accused this time of impersonating the baron, and executed in a mock hanging. He again awakens from his drunken haze to find himself alive, unharmed, and strung up on the gallows by ropes placed under his arms. The open ending leaves the baron to draw a moral lesson from Jeppe's humiliation, while the resourceful rustic Harlequin himself goes off in search of another glass of schnapps. The essence of this comedy of dream and reality is thus not the traditional unmasking of folly but the richly detailed delineation of the down-to-earth reactions of its comic antihero to the dreamlike experiences that befall him.

In general, Holberg's first group of comedies sought consciously to present, as the Just Justesen preface points out, "original" characters that other dramatists "had not worn too thin." Often, however, the types surrounding the main character reappear from one Holberg play to the next. This principle of a permanent gallery of recognizable secondary figures then became the dominant one in his intrigue comedies, a group of plays that depend for their effect not on a particular central character but on a succession of unexpected situations, bewildering misunderstandings, and mistaken identities. In these plays, as in the *commedia dell'arte* tradition, the cast of characters with their distinctive traits remains largely unchanged; only the intrigues themselves vary. For them, Holberg drew his inspiration from Gherardi's *Le Théâtre Italien* and from Roman comedy, where Plautus was his professed favorite. At the head of the list of permanent Holberg types stands the saucy and indefatigable servant Henrik, who made his first entrance in *The Political Tinker* munching a sandwich, confident as always of his command of the situation. A long tradition of Henrik actors was established on the Grønnegade stage by the young Henrich Wegner, who also acted Chilian, the first known Danish Harlequin, in Holberg's madcap Homeric parody, *Ulysses von Ithaca*. The maid Pernille, Henrik's equal in wit and ingenuity, usually teams up with him to manage the intrigue and unite Loenore and Leander, the somewhat bloodless young lovers whose troubled affairs of the heart form the nucleus of the plot in such comedies as *Henrik og Pernille, Pernilles korte Frøkenstand* (*Pernille's Brief Ladyship*) and *De Usynlige* (*The Invisible Ladies*). A far more vigorous character than the young lovers is Jeronimus, the *senex* whose stubborn paternal opposition to the world in general, and to any form of youthful frivolity in particular, motivates the action in many of these plays.

A different kind of Holberg comedy, written to accommodate the Montaigu troupe's desire for plays incorporating greater visual appeal, depends for its effect on more or less elaborate theatrical spectacle. Although the Just Justesen persona deplores the "machines, displays, masquerades, and other such things which attract more spectators than the comedy itself" in a play such as *Le Bourgeois gentilhomme*, the playwright later admits having "often wished that my comedies had been as much embellished with actions, movements, and displays as the French translations were – but such was not the case, for more expense was often lavished on the production of a single French play than on all my comedies together" (Epistle 249). Holberg's own "display" comedies often depend on visual effects and animated crowd scenes used to depict local customs and festivities. *Barselstuen* (*The Lying-in Room*), a lively satire of the popular custom of visiting women in childbed, makes effective use of the throngs of gossiping visitors to intensify the comic agony of the old husband who has married a young wife and now doubts his own paternity. *Julestuen* (*The Christmas Party*) is an afterpiece that uses the Yuletide socializing and merrymaking of the period as the setting for another comedy on the old husband/young wife theme. In *Mascarade*, a companion piece in which the

festivities of the Carnival season provide the comic context, the love intrigue develops out of a masked ball that is presented entirely in pantomime between the first and second acts.[7]

The extent to which Montaigu actually followed Holberg's detailed stage directions in these display comedies is unknown. The nature of the mise-en-scène envisioned by the playwright, however, ranges from the comparative simplicity of the staging in *The Christmas Party* to the complexity of the crowd arrangements called for in *Kildereisen* (*The Healing Spring*). In this work, in which the object of the pilgrimage to the therapeutic spring pretends to suffer from an inability to express herself in other than operatic arias, the entire second act is replaced by a complicated pantomimic interlude in two parts. In the first part, played on a shallow forestage area, "a road to the spring" is seen, crowded with throngs of wayfarers. ("The same ones can hurry out on one side and come in from the other, in order to give the impression of many," the practical playwright suggests.) The scene culminates in two processions accompanied by music. One is made up of gaudily costumed peasants celebrating springtime, while the other consists of "old crones, all wearing different deformed masks and walking with crutches in time to the music." Following this grotesque pageant, the stage opens to its full depth to reveal a picturesque view of the healing waters surrounded by small tents. From the "spring" – a small hole in the stage floor – "some constantly scoop water, others use pitchers, still others use their hats," the stage directions continue. The use of real water undoubtedly added to the effect of this colorful folk scene, as did the commotion and noise of the crowd: "Some shout, others talk, still others swing and crack their whips, and old crones fight to be the first at the spring. A blind man enters with a violin, after which the peasants dance."

As time passed, Holberg grew progressively more disillusioned about the taste of theatre audiences who, he maintains, no longer care whether a play "is well or poorly written, if only it ends with a song and a dance" (Epistle 360). Yet even debased taste can have a certain usefulness in the world, he adds drily, for it helps to support the theatre. Perhaps with this in mind, the less popular philosophical comedies of his later years, which reflect the moralistic climate prevalent at mid-century, were often made more palatable by catering to the "depraved" taste for singing, dancing, and scenic effects. In 1751 his *Plutus* furnished the new Royal Theatre with a particularly extravagant stage spectacle that included divinities in flying machines, special lighting effects, magnificent costumes, and a pompous procession to welcome the god of riches to the poor country where the action takes place. Never, the delighted author decided, was a play performed with greater success: "What contributed to it were the many splendid displays that please both mind and eye alike because they flow naturally from the action itself."[8]

Holberg's reputation as a dramatist rests, however, on the comedies he wrote during the 1720s for the embryonic national theatre in Lille Grønnegade. Twenty-seven of his plays stem from this period. When the Danish Royal Theatre was at last founded in 1748, after a twenty-year hiatus in theatrical activity, an aging Holberg again came to the aid of the revived national stage with six more works, but these comedies, cast in a more serious philosophical vein, added little to the measure of his dramatic achievement. In 1754, the year of his death, twenty-five of Holberg's plays were in the active repertory of the Royal Theatre – in itself convincing evidence of the significance of his work as a mainstay in the comic tradition that linked Montaigu's defunct playhouse in Lille Grønnegade to Frederik V's rococo theatre on Kongens Nytorv.

Theatres royal and popular

For a brief period after its closure, in fact, Grønnegadeteatret had seemed on the verge of a brilliant resurrection. The tireless efforts of René Montaigu to secure royal support finally bore fruit in February 1728, when the Danish actors were raised by Frederik IV to the status of a court troupe with a modest annual subvention. Soon, however, the company again found itself in legal and financial trouble with the theatre's owner, an implacable military man prepared to call in a squad of musketeers to back his demands. The dispute was settled permanently, however, by a force of a quite different and unexpected kind. On 20 October 1728 the great Copenhagen fire gutted two-fifths of the city, razing 1,670 buildings including the university and the town hall. Pious minds saw the disaster as a punishment of godless activities, high on the list of which stood acting and playgoing. Although the playhouse itself was not damaged in the fire, the dark mood that followed the catastrophe swept away any thought of continuing the Danish Comedy. With the succession of Christian VI to the throne two years later, a reign of pietism (1730–46) ensued, during which theatrical activity soon perished. The official death certificate, dated 21 March 1738, decreed that "no play actors, ropedancers, conjurers, or those who run so-called games of chance shall be found in Denmark and Norway, nor shall their plays or routines anywhere be performed or exercised."

Although comparable antitheatrical sentiments were entertained and voiced by the clergy in Sweden, the result there was far less damaging. Throughout the 1730s itinerant German troupes continued, as they had done for a century, to perform their motley repertory of *Haupt- und Staatsaktionen*, farcical afterpieces, acrobatics and ropedancing. One year before the edict abolishing Danish theatricals, a group of Swedish students and young civil servants obtained permission to enact the story of "the unfortunate but thereafter happy Tobias" at the "Royal Theatre" in Stockholm (i.e. Bollhuset) on the occasion of the king's birthday. Although reminiscent of the scholastic traditions of the previous century, the enterprise was clearly inspired by the example set by Montaigu's Danish Comedy. The enthusiastic response to it swelled the impetus toward national self-assertion in Swedish theatre. Four performances of the Tobias play to crowded houses provided an encouraging basis on which to proceed with the Kungliga Svenska Skådeplats, the Royal Swedish Stage. Montaigu's counterpart as artistic leader of the new venture was a professional French troupe actor, Charles Langlois.

The Swedish Comedy opened in October 1737 on the renovated Bollhus stage with a production of Carl Gyllenborg's original five-act comedy, *Den svenska Sprätthöken* (*The Swedish Fop*). Its comic syntax is clearly Holbergian. Count Quick returns, *à la* Jean de France, from his schooling burdened with French affectations and a profound distaste for the Swedish language and customs. The fop's salvation is the spirited girl who agrees to marry him on the condition that he renounce his folly and become a sensible Swede again. The topical satire enjoyed the fate prescribed by Holberg for "all good comedies": "a flock of people became angry over it," and audiences were delighted.

Although no equivalent of a Holberg emerged from the endeavor, other aristocratic authors joined Gyllenborg – at least for a time – in the campaign to provide new plays in the vernacular. Such efforts as Erik Wrangel's *Fröken Snöhwits Tragædia* (*The Tragedy of Snow White*), Reinhold Modée's *Fru Märte Rangsjuk* (*Lady Snob*), and Olof von Dalin's pseudo-classical verse tragedy *Brynilda* contributed to a mixed repertory that combined originals and translations (Molière, Holberg, Corneille, Voltaire) with the traditional burlesque afterpieces and harlequinades. Thus, the versatile Petter Palmberg could be seen both as Count Quick in Gyllenborg's comedy and as Brutus in Voltaire's newest Parisian success, *La mort de César*. Like their colleagues at the Danish Comedy, the Swedish actors performed twice weekly. During their first two seasons some twenty new plays were presented, more than half of which were originals.

Interest wanted, however, and even the skill of such actors as Palmberg, Petter Stenborg, and Petter Lindahl, the popular Harlequin, could not rescue the Royal Swedish Stage from that fatal cycle of public indifference, financial crises, and internal strife. The aging King Fredrik I seemed far more interested in the joys of Bacchus and Venus than in the pleasures of Thespis. When the cosmopolitan Lovisa Ulrika, a true product of the French Enlightenment transplanted to Sweden in 1744 to become the bride of the future King Adolf Fredrik, visited the theatre, her verdict sealed its doom: "I found so little enjoyment," she wrote in 1746, "that I shall never in my life return. The vulgarities lasted for four hours. No possibility of escaping because of the mob that blocked the passage."[9] In 1753 the new regime canceled Langlois' patent and soon evicted the Swedish company from Bollhuset to make way for a new French troupe. A segment of the original company under Petter Stenborg was granted permission to continue performing in the capital, but it now became their own responsibility to find a suitable stage. Stenborg's theatre, moving from one hastily improvised playhouse to another, continued its fitful existence for nearly two decades before Gustav III again raised the Swedish-language stage to grace and respectability.

Simultaneous with the demise of the Royal Swedish Stage, however, the desire for a truly national theatre that had inspired both the Langlois and the Montaigu companies achieved its fulfillment in Denmark. Following the death of Christian VI in 1746, the new monarch Frederik V lost no time in reviving the performing arts banned by his father. No fewer than six separate theatres were authorized by the young king during the first years of his reign (1746–66). A pall had lifted, and theatre flourished as never before. To the dismay of the pietists, its restoration in courtly life was swift and emphatic. The traditional French acting troupe, *de rigueur* for any civilized court, was soon installed again, first in a theatre in Nørregade and subsequently in a new playhouse fitted up in Charlottenborg Palace by the noted designer Jacopo Fabris. Queen Louise, daughter of George II of England and an avid opera enthusiast who had studied with Händel, was equally eager to adorn her court with the Italian opera company of

Pietro Mingotti, which she had enjoyed in Hamburg on her honeymoon. During the 1748/9 season the conductor of this company was no less a luminary than C. W. Gluck.

In the meantime, Samuel Paulsen von Qvoten, the quack dentist and medicine man who had obtained a theatre patent in 1718, turned up with his son Julius Heinrich to claim his rights. Yet another claimant came forward in the person of the pugnacious General Hans Jacob Arnoldt, the former patentee at Grønnegadeteatret who had threatened the Danish actors with eviction on the eve of the great fire. In the end, the younger von Qvoten and the general formed a partnership to start a German–Danish theatre in Store Kongensgade in 1747. During the single season he endured, Heinrich von Qvoten treated Copenhagen to a fascinating potpourri that mingled the venerable traditions of the harlequinade and the *Haupt- und Staatsaktionen* with the new Scandinavian drama, including Dalin's tragedy *Brynilda* and seven comedies by Holberg, and the pseudo-classical imitations championed by J. C. Gottsched and popularized by Caroline Neuber's renowned German troupe. When von Qvoten gave up the theatre in 1748 to return to his family calling as oculist, hernia surgeon, and "tooth-breaker," an era in Danish theatre ended. Audiences had seen the last of Pickelherring's antics and the *lazzi* and heroics of the vigorous *Haupt- und Staatsaktionen*.

Hence, Carl August Thielo faced stiff competition when he sought and obtained royal permission to reestablish a Danish national theatre along the lines attempted in the Grønnegade venture. Thielo, a former organist and composer, secured the king's consent at the end of 1746 to "employ such qualified persons as can for reasonable payment please all and sundry with their comedies."[10] Like Montaigu before him, Thielo turned to the university community for his company. Frédéric Pilloy, the last living connection to the Montaigu style and original Holberg traditions, was put in charge of rehearsing, costuming, and training the new actors. Baron Holberg himself, although unwilling to assume an official role in the theatre's management, obviously functioned behind the scenes as the advisor and protector of the new Danish stage. The top floor of Christian Berg's public house in Læderstræde was hastily equipped with a small provisional stage and a gallery, and Thielo's company, following Holberg's advice, opened its embryonic Danish Royal Theatre on 14 April 1747 with *The Political Tinker*. Twelve more Holberg comedies followed, including the first productions of *Erasmus Montanus*, *The Invisible Ladies*, and his popular satire of social climbing, *Den honnette Ambition* (*Honest Ambition*). The public response was gratifying, and soon the number of performances given each week could be increased from one to two.

The temporary theatre in Berg's public house remained in operation only eight months. Having gained confidence and experience, the actors were eager to acquire their own playhouse. After having deposed Thielo, they sought a collective license to establish a permanent theatre on Kongens Nytorv itself, to be built on the site of the old naval storehouse (Tjærehuset or Lille Giethus, as it was called) where Capion and the elder von Qvoten had given performances thirty years before. After some maneuvering, the actors obtained their coveted royal privilege, granting them a monopoly on "the performance of any kind of play in whatever language," on 29 December 1747. While preparations for the building of a new theatre went forward, they moved their base of operations first to Tjærehuset and then, when that site was cleared for construction in June, to the theatre in Store Kongensgade just vacated by the ruined Heinrich von Qvoten.

The elegant rococo playhouse designed by court architect Nicolai Eigtved rose with remarkable haste. On 18 December 1748, Queen Louise's twenty-fourth birthday, the Danish Royal Theatre opened with a prologue extolling the generosity of the royal family, seated in its brilliantly decorated box in the center of the first tier. The main attraction of the evening was Regnard's comedy *Le Joueur*, with which Rosidor had opened the new court theatre in Stockholm some fifty years earlier. This perennial favorite was now given by the Danish actors as an implicit challenge to the competing French troupe in Nørregade. Taken loosely as a moral satire of the gambling mania, Regnard's play could also serve as a perfect expression of the eighteenth-century view of drama as a school for virtue. Writ large on a tablet above the main entrance to the new theatre was a motto that left no doubt about the earnestness of its purpose in this respect:

> Fellow countrymen and whoever you may be: when in our plays, as in a mirror, you observe the ways of the world, the evil and the good, and laugh at humanity's frailty, wickedness, and vice; then learn thereby to know your own, to correct it, to improve and change from impropriety to decency, from evil to good, from vice to virtue.[11]

At the outset the theatre on Kongens Nytorv shared many of the characteristics of its modest forerunner in Lille Grønnegade. Holberg's House remained essentially a comic theatre. Its first acting company, consisting of eight actors, four actresses, and three dancers, appeared twice weekly in a repertoire based squarely on the classical comedy of Molière, Regnard, and Holberg and on the farcical *lazzi* of the *commedia dell'arte*. Almost immediately, Mingotti's more fashionable Italian opera troupe was also moved from the palace to the king's new playhouse, at first as a paying tenant of the resident company and later as an integrated part of the enterprise. The earliest ticket records show that Eigtved's structure, which underwent extensive renovation and expansion in 1773, was at first able to accommodate 782 spectators (excluding the royal party) in three tiers of boxes and a seated pit. (The days when dandies could buy a seat on the stage, as they had still done at Grønnegadeteatret and in Berg's public house, were now over.) Capacity houses were rare, however, and the financial position of the theatre was often extremely precarious. Hence, when the king decided in 1750 to hand over control of the debt-ridden venture to the municipality of Copenhagen, the city fathers were understandably unenthusiastic about the "gift." It was, in fact, not until 1770 that the so-called Royal Theatre again came under the economic protection and administrative aegis of the monarchy.

Jacopo Fabris, the experienced Venetian stage designer and technician who had equipped the opera house in Charlottenborg Palace, also supplied Eigtved's public theatre with the latest machinery and technology. As both the architect's ground plan for the theatre and C. F. Harsdorff's plan for its expansion in 1773 clearly indicate, the original stage was fitted with four rows of flat wings on each side, fastened to counterweighted carriages, or "chariots," running in slots in the stage floor. An additional set of carriages was provided for a back shutter, if needed. Scene changes were facilitated by the use of double carriages in each wing position, to which a second set of flat wings were attached and ready for a swift *changement à vue* to a new setting. (The added convenience of triple carriages in each position was not introduced at the Royal Theatre until 1826.)[12] The six principal stock settings designed by Fabris for the new theatre – a room, a wood, a street, a garden, a great hall, and a sea decor – provided a perfectly adequate basic framework for the spoken drama, while larger and more elaborate settings were required for Mingotti's opera productions. The same sets were reused continually in changing combinations, with set pieces added to create variety and strengthen illusion. "The setting we will ignore," writes Peder

Plate 13 Projected design by Jacopo Fabris for "a great hall or temple." In Fabris' sketchbook (1760), only the left half of this symmetrical setting is included; the right side was reconstructed photographically by Harald Langberg in *Kongens teater* (1974) to complete the picture.

Rosenstand-Goiske drily in the first number of his influential *Dramatic Journal* in 1771, "since it is, so far as we know, used for other plays and consequently not appropriate."[13]

Within this painted perspective framework, impressive visual displays and spectacular effects were the order of the day. The aerial appearances of Mercury and Night and the majestic descent of Jupiter in his "Gloria" naturally made Molière's *Amphitryon* a popular choice for the first season at Kongens Nytorv. In the world of Harlequin such scenic legerdemain was an even more indispensable ingredient. Holberg's freewheeling parody *Ulysses von Ithaca*, revived in 1750 and traditionally played as a harlequinade, relied heavily on Fabris' flying machine, notably in a scene in which Queen Dido whistles for her dragon, which obediently descends, bears her aloft, and then returns to carry off her terrified servant Rasmus. The theatre's dragon appeared again in the inverted universe of *Le Monde renversé*, an entertaining example of the *Théâtre de la Foire* by Le Sage and d'Orneval that the Danish company took up in 1751. Harlequin and Pierrot, having served Merlin the magician, are rewarded by being sent to a utopian world of milk and honey where everything is topsy-turvydom.

At the start of their journey, the two clowns are seen high in the air astride the sprightly monster, which "circles the stage two or three times." Near the end, audiences watched the mighty Merlin "descending from the air in a car" drawn by "two vultures."[14] Probably the favorite harlequinade of all at the Royal Theatre was Regnard and Dufresny's *La Baguette de Vulcan*, a sensation when first produced by the Théâtre Italien in Paris in 1693 and a staple afterpiece in the Danish company's repertoire since 1748, when Gerd Londemann first created the leading role. Here, Harlequin's bat is no longer a slapstick but a magical wand bestowed on him by Vulcan. The most striking of the play's many *lazzi* and transformations must be said to be the exceedingly demanding scene in which Roger (Harlequin) battles a fearful, bearded giant, succeeds in hacking off the ogre's head and limbs, thinks he has won – and then sees the amputations "re-unite themselves with the body, yet in a different shape, giving Harlequin the occasion for a new battle."[15] A French drawing by Claude Gillot (in the Louvre in Paris) depicts one of the greatest Harlequins of the *commedia*, Evaristo Gherardi, in this scene, wielding a sword twice his size and confronting the decapitated giant's huge, glowering head – from which protrudes the left foot and right leg of the actor in charge of operating the complex mechanical dummy. There is some evidence that the technical challenge was handled similarly in the Danish performance.

Even before Holberg's death, in 1754, this older comic tradition was being challenged by new dramatic styles and tastes. Serious neoclassical drama, represented at von Qvoten's theatre by Dalin's tragedy *Brynilda*, came to the Royal Theatre in 1752 with Gottsched's adaptation of Addison's *Cato*, a lavish production in which careful attention was paid to the correctness of the Roman costumes and accessories. Sentimental comedy, the antithesis of both the laughing comedy of Holberg and the anti-sentimentalism of the *Théâtre de la Foire*, began to appear in ripples that soon became a small wave. Steele's transitional comedy *The Conscious Lovers* (1722), with its appeal for "a joy too exquisite for laughter," reached Kongens Nytorv in 1761 in a thoroughly localized version that nevertheless failed to draw. A decade earlier, however, the French court troupe led by Pierre de Launai had introduced Copenhagen audiences to the Gallic strain of the sentimental movement with its productions of Destouches – Holberg's avowed *bête noire*. The national theatre opened its doors to the popular lachrymose comedies of Destouches in 1751 with *Le Dissipateur*, a typical example of the genre's obligatory moral conversion in which a young girl rescues her lover from prodigality. Productions during the same season of Voltaire's *L'Enfant prodigue* and *Nanine*, his adaptation of Richardson's sentimental novel *Pamela*, lent added impetus to the tide of sensibility. The short but intense popularity of this vogue gave rise in the 1760s to the rather turgid moral comedies of Charlotte Dorothea Biehl, the first woman dramatist of note in Scandinavia.

Regardless of these new currents, however, Harlequin and Henrik, the ubiquitous servant figure in Holberg's comedies, retained their supremacy during the generation in which Gerd Londemann reigned as the Danish theatre's outstanding comic virtuoso. Masked and clad in his familiar patchwork costume, Londemann stood for audiences of the eighteenth century as the essence of Harlequin. After his death in 1773, the genre seemed virtually inconceivable without him. His improvisations were versatile and unpredictable: as Sganarelle in Molière's *Dom Juan*, for instance, he dashed out through the auditorium in fright during his master's duel. A genius in his comic mimicry, he was the archetypal clown with a hint of the marketplace buffoon about him and more than a trace of melancholy and sadness behind the grinning mask. Wessel's famous miniature elegy captures something essential in Londemann's art: "We sigh because he is no more, / Recalling what he was, we roar."

A company of gifted comic performers surrounded Londemann in the early days of the Royal Theatre. His opposite in type and manner was Niels Clementin, the tall, reflective, drily humorous embodiment of Jeronimus, the Holberg *senex*, and Molière's miserly Harpagon. Anna Materna Passow, whose moral comedy *Mariana* (1757) was the first Danish play acted after Holberg's death, was the company's stately and cultivated female lead until she resigned in 1753. Her successor in the Leonore parts was Elisabeth Charlotte Amalie Bøttger, who joined the theatre at Holberg's urging when she was just fourteen. Bøttger's subsequent aspirations as a tragedienne in the French style of Clairon sometimes led to difficulties. By persuading her friend Charlotte Biehl to translate Colardeau's *Caliste* (a version of Rowe's *The Fair Penitent*) in 1765, she found the kind of challenge she craved as an actress, the depiction of a woman torn apart by the conflicting passions of love and hatred of the man who has ravished her. Frequently, however, her mannered imitation of the acting style of the king's French court troupe drew critical fire from Rosenstand-Goiske and others. In serious parts, Overskou tells us, she had two expressions, "a weeping tone with limply hanging or imploringly outstretched gestures

Plate 14 Elisabeth Charlotte Amalie Bøttger in the last act of Colardeau's *Caliste* (1765), sketched by the Royal Theatre's designer Peter Cramer. In a dimly lighted "room hung with black," Caliste is discovered alone with the corpse of Lothario, which lies on a bier behind her. Cramer's sketch reveals an unusual use of plain blackish side wings, borders, and backcloth, framed by pillars to create a stylized, dimensionless inner space in which the corpse of the heroine's lover and the cup of poison that awaits her are the two fixed points of focus.

when she was happy; loud cries and violent gestures when she was triumphant or had the intention of displaying passion."[16] When Rosenstand-Goiske saw her as Caliste in 1771, he complained that her facial expression was limited to a "strange raising of the eyebrows" at each new emotional peripety.[17]

The model for Bøttger's misunderstood imitation of serious French acting was, it seems, Jeanne du Londel, the outstanding talent in Frederik V's court troupe and one of the great beauties of her day. The troupe's influence on both the style and the repertory of the Danish actors was considerable, particularly in its propagation of Destouches and the new sentimental drama. In 1753, du Londel and most of her company moved on to the Swedish court in Stockholm, leaving the Royal Theatre without significant competition. Ironically, while the popular theatre movement in Denmark was now firmly established, Stenborg and the so-called Royal Swedish Stage were left homeless, evicted from Bollhuset by the new French guests.

A theatre built for a queen

It is hardly surprising that Lovisa Ulrika, an avid champion of French culture eulogized by Voltaire himself, should long for her own personal Versailles. She created it at Drottningholm, a seventeenth-century summer palace on the shores of Lake Mälar, barely five miles from Stockholm. Here, aided by the court poet Olof von Dalin and her *maître de plaisir* Carl Gustav Tessin, she transformed the salons and surrounding gardens of her palace into a center for elegant theatrical spectacles that would bear comparison with the lavish festivities of *le grand monarch* himself – in *ésprit*, if not in expense. Enthusiastic court amateurs performed Racine, Molière, Voltaire, Marivaux, Destouches, and other popular French playwrights of the day – much the same repertory, in fact, that drew cavalier and citizen alike to the Copenhagen theatre of Frederik V. In 1749, for example, Lovisa Ulrika's aristocratic Drottningholm audience could join with their Danish neighbors in the exquisite enjoyment of the conversion of Ariste, the dissembling philosophical misogynist in Destouches' most popular sentimental comedy, *Le Philosophe marié*. The French ambassador to Sweden permitted himself to doubt that it could have been done better in Paris.

At Drottningholm, life itself (to paraphrase Taine) was an opera. In the park of this Baltic Versailles, outdoor pageants and pastoral entertainments were enacted by the self-conscious lords and ladies-in-waiting disguised as shepherds and shepherdesses, nymphs and satyrs. Soon after the birth in 1746 of the future Gustav III, the first Swedish-born heir to the throne since Charles XII, children's performances became another established pastime. Through his participation in court theatricals and ballets from an early age, the young prince was seen to follow in the footsteps of the great Louis. At age six he led a chorus of pages dressed as mandarins in an elaborate oriental homage to his mother, the queen, on her birthday. The source describing this occasion and what followed – allegedly an immense court masque, an opera, and a sixteen-act drama – is defective, but it leaves little doubt that a formal theatre of some kind existed at Drottningholm even at this date.[18] A backcloth for it, designed by Johan Pasch to represent a mountainous waterfall with gliding swans beneath, attracted great admiration.

Once he was crowned in 1751, Adolf Fredrik lost little time in supplementing his wife's amateur theatricals with the foreign professionals whose presence was the acknowledged hallmark of any important ruler's prestige. Accordingly, Pierre de Launai's troupe of French actors was imported from Copenhagen, followed in 1754 by an Italian opera company under the direction of the capable composer and conductor Francesco Uttini. To house these companies and their more polished productions, two new court theatres were created, one at Drottningholm and a second (the recently rediscovered Confidence) at Ulriksdal Castle, while the Swedish actors were forced to hand over Bollhuset to the French players for their town performances. The accomplished Jeanne du Londel quickly captured the hearts of the Swedish aristocracy in such plays as *Le Philosophe marié*. That the king seemed especially smitten by her charms caused endless comment. Appearing in Anseaume and Duni's comic opera *Le Peintre amoureux de son modèle*, her provocative rendition of "Quand j'étais jeune, j'étais une morceau, digne d'un roi" drew an incensed reaction from Lovisa Ulrika, and the knowledgeable court audience tittered.

During a performance at Drottningholm in 1762, a fire from which the royal audience narrowly escaped laid the queen's personal court theatre in ruins. Disappointed but as determined as ever, Lovisa Ulrika promptly built another, larger still and more elegant – world-renowned today as the most perfectly preserved rococo playhouse in existence. Designed by the foremost Swedish architect of the period, Carl Fredrik Adelcrantz, the theatrical phoenix that rose from the ashes of the first Drottningholm Court Theatre in 1766 was – and is still – an ideal example of the art and aesthetics of perspective staging. Behind a deceptively unpretentious exterior, a theatre machine of great beauty and corresponding technical versatility was constructed by leading experts in their field. The intimate 350-seat auditorium, painted and decorated according to Adelcrantz's specifications by the French artist Adrien Masreliez, was designed to blend with the equally large stage to form a single harmonious interior, where actor and spectator would be drawn together in one shared imaginative space. The goal of this style was what Agne Beijer, the historian who discovered the theatre fully intact in 1921, once described as "the illusion that the imaginary phantoms moving on the stage were nothing other than the idealized mirror images of the courtly society that followed the spectacle from their boxes."[19] Intrinsic to the preservation of this illusion was the evocative power of the textured, softly flickering candle lighting of the period. The muted illumination of the tallow candles – replaced in present-day performances here by electric bulbs of the same textured character and intensity – could mould the contours of the figures on the stage while at the same time reinforcing that essential bond between the stage and the softly lighted auditorium.

The spacious, deep-focus perspective stage at Drottningholm measures twenty-seven feet in width at the proscenium opening, but a cavernous sixty-two feet in depth (twice that of Eigtved's Royal theatre). Its design was entrusted by Lovisa Ulrika and her architect to the noted Italian theatre machinist Donato Stopani; the heavy oak machinery and technical devices he constructed survive today as practical evidence of the durability of his craftmanship. Beneath the stage a massive four-man windlass could move the wing chariots simultaneously, accomplishing the magic of a *changement à vue* – the visible scene change that is the heart and soul of so much of the eighteenth-century repertoire – in a mere ten seconds. Gods and goddesses could descend in comfortable dignity from the fly gallery, thirty feet above the stage, astride Stopani's three cloud machines. In the lashing billows of his wave machine, Neptune and assorted sea monsters often appeared.

Although Lovisa Ulrika's French players continued their performance at the second Drottningholm for five years following its completion, the period of greatest activity in this theatre's history occurred after Gustav III ascended the throne in 1771. This date, as we shall see, was a turning point that ushered in not only a new government in Sweden but also a new cultural and theatrical spirit.

The last court theatre

Few theatrical developments have taken place in one Scandinavian country that have not had their parallels or repercussions in another. King Christian VII, who came to the Danish throne in the same year in which the second Drottningholm Theatre opened, was easily persuaded to emulate the example with a court theatre of his own. A new French troupe organized by Marianne Belleval Martin was summoned to Copenhagen in 1766, much to the chagrin of the supporters of the struggling public theatre on Kongens Nytorv. In order to provide a performance space for his "Comédiens François ordinaires du Roi," the seventeen-year-old monarch ordered his court architect, Nicolas-Henri Jardin, to construct a theatre above the stables in Christiansborg Palace. Its model seems to have been the lovely court theatre of Charles-Theodor in Schwerzingen, near Heidelberg; an unusual feature was an auditorium floor that could be raised to accommodate the popular masked balls of the day and then lowered for stage performances. Jardin's fashionable new playhouse was inaugurated by the French players on 30 January 1767 with a production of one of Monsigny's most admired comic operas, *Le Roi et le fermier*, followed by a balletic homage to the king.

In general, the modern portion of the Belleval company's repertoire brought the newest Parisian fashions and styles to the Danish capital. Along with Lovisa Ulrika's court players, it introduced Scandinavian audiences to the new mode of *opéra-comique*, made popular by the lively and unpretentious melodies of Monsigny, Grétry, and Philidor. Similarly, the most recent French excursions into the bourgeois drama could be seen first at Christian VII's court theatre, which played Beaumarchais' *Eugénie*, Falbaire de Quingey's *L'Honnête criminel*, and a verse adaptation of Moore's *The Gamester*. From here, both these popular new forms made their way into the repertory of the Danish-language theatre.

Although nationalistic feeling seems on occasion to have led Danish theatre historians to disparage the artistic quality of the court troupe of Christian VII, it was in reality made up of a group of highly talented performers.[20] Chief among them was the company's versatile leading man Henry de la Tour, whose principal partners in the heroic tragedies of Voltaire were Elisabeth-Marguerite le Clerc and the temperamental Marie-Rose-Chatérine Cléricourt. This nucleus presented a complete gallery of the picturesque and exotic Voltaire couples that had taken audiences in Paris by storm: Arzace and Semiramis (*Semiramis*), Gengis Khan and Idamé (*L'Orphelin de la Chine*), Tancrède and Amenaide (*Tancrède*), Orosman and Zaire (*Zaire*). The essence of the acting style required for these plays was visual rather than declamatory, dependent for effect on intense pantomimic and gestural expressiveness. The highly accentuated poses and mimetic actions of its chief practitioners in Paris, Lekain and Clairon, were circulated widely in the 1760s in the numerous gouache role pictures of Foech-Whirsker and others. A parody of the crouched, bending attitudes of this style is found in the satirical portrait of de la Tour left by Clemens Tode, the court theatre's doctor:

> He could be good, in fact, but he liked to stand in conversation as if sawing a piece of wood, or rather, like the Roman gladiator in the Royal Gardens. The upper part of his body and the left leg had a vertical direction, the right leg was perpendicular: thus in some ways his figure, particularly when his hands were crossed over his chest, resembled a country well or a toll-bar standing open.[21]

Dr. Tode's wit notwithstanding, however, de la Tour and his successor le Boeuf – an acknowledged imitator of Lekain – were accomplished exponents of the emotionally charged and mimically eloquent acting advocated by Voltaire to express "those outbursts of nature which are represented by a word, by an attitude, by silence, by a cry which escapes in the anguish of grief."[22] As Clairon realized, moreover, "the truth of declamation requires that of dress," and there is little doubt that the French costume reforms brought about by her and others after the middle of the century were carried to Scandinavia by the illustrations of Foech-Whirsker and their flesh-and-blood embodiments, the Danish and Swedish court actors of the 1760s.

Despite the influence its example exerted (both positive and negative), Christian VII's court theatre had a brief existence. The young king sank deeper and deeper into the madness that had become apparent early in his life, and the court physician Struensee was quick to see his way to power as the weak monarch's representative. After a failed palace revolution in 1772 had cost the lives of the bold Struensee and Enevold Brandt, his accomplice and the *maître de plaisir* at court, the ascendancy of the French troupe was broken. Several of its members, including de la Tour and Madame Cléricourt and her husband, would turn up again at the court of Christian's brother-in-law, young Gustav III. In April 1773 the theatre at Christiansborg resounded with the last performance of the French players. The Royal Theatre on Kongens Nytorv, now securely under royal protection, was at last free of all foreign competition.

4 The Gustavian age

During the early 1770s the theatre entered a new phase in all three Scandinavian countries. The Danish national theatre in Copenhagen, now officially the king's theatre once more, began in earnest to cultivate the new vogue of the *singspiel* and the drama of sentiment made popular by Christian VII's departed court troupe. In Norway – still at this time a Danish possession dependent on provincial strollers for its theatrical entertainment – the first step toward the creation of a native professional company was taken by a German actor, Martin Nürenbach. On the basis of three Holberg performances given in Christiania (Oslo) in 1771, Nürenbach's troupe was granted a license to present Danish plays with Norwegian actors. The history of this venture, which seems to have recruited local acting talent of questionable ability, was brief. After performances of *Jeppe on the Hill* and *The Political Tinker*, Nürenbach's campaign to establish professional Norwegian theatre in the capital appears to have collapsed. Instead, a more fruitful line of development proved to be the activity of the amateur dramatic societies that began to flourish in Norway after 1780.

In Sweden, meanwhile, a quite different situation prevailed. The succession of Gustav III to the Swedish throne in 1771 marked the beginning of one of the most luminous periods in eighteenth-century European theatre. While virtually every branch of Swedish arts and letters achieved new life and national identity under the enlightened absolutism of Gustav's rule (1771–92), the stage remained the special passion of this remarkable actor–king. Earlier monarchs had, as we know, exerted considerable influence on the course of theatrical development in Scandinavia. In a far more direct sense, however, Gustav participated at every juncture in the selection, casting, performance, and writing of the plays and operas he wanted performed. Even on the battlefield he devoted himself to his grand theatrical design, the planning and realization of a national Swedish theatre and drama. To achieve political stability in his divided country, Gustav realized that a new national consciousness must be fostered – and he was well aware that the theatre could be a powerful weapon in such a campaign.

Less than three weeks after the death of Adolf Fredrik, the new king sent a dispatch from Paris dismissing the French court troupe. Petter Stenborg, the leader of the ragged descendants of the defunct Royal Swedish Stage, sensed that the moment was ripe for action and petitioned Gustav for permission to establish in the vacated Bollhus "a national theatre which, in the country's own language, [would show] its inhabitants representations of virtue to be imitated and errors to be avoided."[1] Stenborg was granted two performances in which to show his mettle. For the first of them, given on 11 March 1772, the unpolished Swedish actors chose a Plautus imitation by Regnard, *Les Ménechmes*, and a popular after-piece by Legrand, *L'Ami de tout le monde*. In an opening appeal to the king, delivered by Stenborg's youngest son Carl, the royal spectators were assured that "under an Augustus" the languishing native drama could "win such respect that a French Clairon or an English Garrick would in time find worthy rivals in Sweden."[2] The jubilant response of the audience, which "applauded every word" at this trial performance, made its impression on Gustav. A suitable performance space was eventually found for Stenborg in the Rotunda in Humlegården, a seventeenth-century royal pavilion where the Stenborg troupe regularly performed a light popular repertory of comedies, acrobatics, and operatic parodies every summer.

Gustav himself, however, was convinced that a more elaborate and more emotionally engaging medium was required to accustom the Swedish establishment to appreciating its own language on the stage. Influenced in part by the abbé Domenico Michelessi, a cosmopolitan Italian who made Francesco Algarotti's seminal treatise on opera reform (*Saggio sopra l'opera in musica*) known in Sweden, the king made his first priority the creation of a national opera that would combine all the resources of the stage. Progress was swift. The aging theatre in Bollhuset underwent a thorough face-lifting. The spacious royal box, patriotically covered in blue with gold crowns, was moved to the center of the first tier; an amphitheatre, or *balcon noble*, situated beneath it, a standing pit, and three tiers of boxes now gave the theatre a capacity of about 500 spectators. The subject matter for the opening performance was selected by Gustav personally, and his choice, the story of Thetis and Pelée with which Mazarin had entertained Louis XIV, was a revealing one. The glories of the court of the Sun King had long held a magnetic appeal for the Swedish nobility. Hence, the court counselor and poet Johan Wellander was invited to write a libretto on Gustav's chosen theme, Francesco Uttini, the former director of Lovisa Ulrika's Italian opera company, composed a pleasing score, and the French ballet-master Louis Gallodier created choreographic interludes for Sweden's first opera.

Although experienced professional performers were obviously scarce, Carl Stenborg and Elisabeth Olin, the wife of a public official and overnight Sweden's first star, formed a talented nucleus around which to build a successful production. On 18 January 1773, barely ten months after the elder Stenborg's demonstration of vernacular theatre in Bollhuset, the newly formed Royal Opera gave the first of twenty-six successive performances of Uttini and Wellander's popular *Thétis and Pelée*. In its mythological subject matter, the tale of Pelée, King of Thessalonia, and his love for the sea goddess Thétis, this allegorical piece differed little from numerous baroque forerunners. In its succession of spectacular descents, ascents, storms, and other *coups de théâtre*, however, it exemplifies a trend toward a less static stage picture, marked by the greater scenic illusion advocated by Algarotti and others at the time. In the earliest, five-act version of this work, the antipodal entrances and exits of Jupiter and Neptune, Pelée's cosmic rivals for the hand of Thétis, introduced an effective rhythm and variety of movement into the baroque-inspired decors of Lorentz Sundström. At the climax of the first act, for example, Jupiter appeared on a cloud and angrily summoned Aeolus to create havoc in Neptune's realm. The stage darkened, storm winds raged, thunder rumbled, and lightning ripped the sky as Neptune and his nautical minions sank beneath the turbulent waves. Among Gallodier's ballet divertissements, which occupied fully one-fourth of the performance, one of the most effective was the passionate and indignant dance of the Thessalonians on behalf of their king, who in the fourth act has been shackled to a rock and tormented by Furies in the service of the scheming Jupiter.

The new Royal Opera was thus crowned with popular success from the outset. Elisabeth Olin and Carl Stenborg personified, on the stage and off, the image of the eternally young lovers. *Thétis* was followed in May by another legend of lovers, Lars Lalin's version of *Acis and Galathea*, per-

Plate 15 In the theatre paintings of Pehr Hilleström, the freer emotional expressivity cultivated in the opera performances of the Gustavian period is vividly conveyed. Here, Carl Stenborg and Elisabeth Olin are shown emerging from the underworld in the third act of *Orpheus and Eurydice*. Swedish Royal Opera, 1773.

formed as a "heroic ballet" with Händel's music and Gallodier's choreography. But the year's triumph was yet to come. Convinced, as he told the Swedish Royal Society at his induction, that "tragedy will teach the Swedish people the diction that can most move the heart," Michelessi was also responsible for introducing Calzabigi's libretto for *Orpheus and Eurydice* to Sweden. The production of Gluck's masterpiece at Bollhuset (25 November 1773), heard in Uttini's transposition, challenged the artificial baroque tradition still reflected in *Thétis and Pelée*. In doing so, it touched off a veritable Gluck fever that continued to rage throughout the Gustavian era. Among the remarkably accurate scene pictures from this period executed by the Swedish artist Pehr Hilleström, one of the most exquisite of all is his rendering of Olin and Stenborg as Gluck's lovers. Laurel-crowned and lyre in hand, Orpheus virtually drags his beloved from the ugly grotto of hell, where Charon's boat can be glimpsed floating on the waters of the river Acheron. The expressive stances and gestures of the performers emphasize the freer and more emotionally charged acting style that had begun to make its way from France to the courts of Scandinavia during the previous decade. Also, the costumes they wear in this picture – a fiery red sateen cape over a gold sateen doublet for Orpheus, a white sateen dress with a bodice of silver cloth for Eurydice – suggest a comparable movement away from the obligatory powdered wigs, much more ornate court dresses, and formal *habits à la romaine* of the older tradition. Here as well, the efforts of Clairon and Lekain to reform the Parisian theatres in this regard were an important influence.

Gustav III's vision of a political theatre devoted to the glorification of his country's history and culture was comprehensive, and he was determined to have a native spoken drama take its place beside the newly established national opera. After being shown a trial performance by court amateurs of a translation of Voltaire's *Zaire*, put on in order to test the reaction of sensitive courtly ears to spoken Swedish, the king concluded that tragedy should best be presented "in the Greek manner" – i.e. accompanied by the choral music and dancing that the Renaissance had associated with ancient tragedy. Gustav's own plan for an original three-act drama, entitled *Birger Jarl*, was conceived to suit this model perfectly. The material was transferred to verse dialogue by G. F. Gyllenborg, music was arranged by Uttini, and Hinrich Philip Johnsen even provided a miniature opera-within-in-the-play, called *Eglé*, for the first performance of this spectacle in the summer of 1774. No less a figure than Carlo Bibiena was invited to design the stage for Gustav's first Swedish historical play. Although its premiere took place at court, the acting was entrusted to professionals from the Royal Opera. Elisabeth Olin and Carl Stenborg were again the deathless lovers, Mechild, the fugitive queen in danger, and the gallant Earl Birger, once her enemy but ultimately her savior and spouse.

No outpouring of Swedish drama was immediately forthcoming, but both the court amateurs and the artists of the Royal Opera continued to cultivate a repertory of Swedish "imitations" of French classics. The range extended from old favorites by Racine (*Athalie*), Corneille (*Cinna*), and Crébillon (*Rhadamiste et Zénobie*) to such Voltaire pieces as *Mérope*, *Adelaïde du Guesclin*, and *L'Orphelin de la Chine*. In courtly circles, a full program of

Plate 16   A Carlo Bibiena design for a Gustavian opera (c. 1774). The original setting, which is photographed here, is preserved at Drottningholm.

these dramas was performed during the amazing round of private theatricals held at Gripsholm Castle during the Christmas holidays of 1775/6. Gustav, who loved acting, included Racine's Joad, Cinna, Rhadamiste, and Voltaire's Gengis Khan among his major roles – at least until he was dissuaded for political reasons from performing in public. For a few years the professional company at Bollhuset also tried, without much enthusiasm, to follow this example by giving Swedish-language performances of these same tragedies for the general public. Squeezed into a demanding repertory that ranged from the light melodies of Grétry and Monsigny to the powerful tones of Gluck, performances of spoken drama were not welcomed by the opera singers, and the experiment was soon abandoned.

Something of the performance style that characterized opera and drama alike during this period survives, however, in the paintings of actual scenes left to us by Pehr Hilleström. Especially in his depictions of Gluck and Calzabigi's *Alceste*, played at Bollhuset in 1781, and Piccini and Marmontel's *Roland*, staged at Drottningholm in that same year, the fiercely conceived and contrasted "outbursts of nature" demanded by Voltaire are brought to life on canvas. In the former picture, the convulsive despair of Carl Stenborg's Admetus, who lies prostrate in the foreground, is juxtaposed with the heroic presence of Hercules, fighting off the Furies of the underworld with his club. The physical expressivity required of the

Plates 17 and 18 The passionate "outbursts of nature" advocated by Voltaire found vivid expression in the actions of the mythological figures popular in Gustavian opera theatre. Paintings by Hilleström record (Plate 17) the convulsive despair of Admetus (Carl Stenborg) in Calzabigi and Gluck's *Alceste* (produced 1781).

hero in *Roland*, played by Stenborg's younger rival Christofer Karsten, seems even more emphatic as he lashes out at a stature of Diana, goddess of love, to demonstrate his anger at female duplicity. There is perhaps no better example of the graphic physical language inherent in this style than the gestures and stances of Marie Louise Baptiste and the grotesquely transformed Karsten as they stand, like Beauty and the Beast, before the enchanted mirror in Grétry and Marmontel's fantastical opera-ballet *Zémire et Azor.*

The first production of this latter work, in the summer of 1778, marked the reawakening to life of Lovisa Ulrika's court theatre at Drottningholm, which Gustav had purchased from his mother the previous year. Although the king no longer appeared on the stage personally, his beautiful new

Plate 18 The rage of the furious Orlando (Christofer Karsten) in Marmontel
and Piccini's *Roland*, also staged in 1781.

theatre quickly became the hub of his musical and theatrical universe.
Especially during the long summer sojourns of the Swedish court,
Drottningholm swarmed in the 1780s with hundreds of resident actors,
singers, dancers, and musicians. Productions of opera, ballet, and spoken
drama on the interior stage – sometimes as many as four of them in one
week – were complemented by lavish outdoor spectacles reminiscent of
the great Renaissance festivals and *trionfi* of the past. Two of the most
famous of these outdoor pageants, *The Feast of Diana* and *The Conquest of the
Galtar Rock*, have been captured in all their color and action in paintings by
Hilleström. *The Feast of Diana* was enacted in the palace grounds by the
lords and ladies of the court in the summer of 1778, shortly after the Royal
Opera's command performance of *Zémire et Azor*. The imposing entrance
"to martial music" of Gustav III on horseback, resplendent in the red and
white costume of a Roman warrior, might well have called to mind the

Plate 19 Hilleström's rendering of the central scene in Marmontel and Grétry's *Zémire et Azor* (1778) showing the bewitched Persian prince (Christofer Karsten) and Zémire (Marie Louise Baptiste) standing before an enchanted mirror in which she sees her father and sisters.

appearance of his forebear Charles XI in his own ornate coronation pageant, *Certamen equestre*, more than a century earlier. The tone of this typical Gustavian "carousel" was conventionally paternalistic (as we would say today): as Meleager, the king led his warriors in allegorical combat with Nessus (the future Charles XIII) and his rapacious fauns in order to defend the virtue of Diana and her nymphs – all decorously dressed in the rococo court dress recently proclaimed by royal decree.

Despite the conventionality of the subject matter and the mixture of

Plate 20 The atmosphere of gothic romance pervades Hilleström's painting of *The Conquest of the Galtar Rock*, a Gustavian pageant performed in the castle park at Drottningholm in the summer of 1779.

costume styles, however, these Drottningholm pageants may be said to prefigure the coming romantic vogue of historical drama in Sweden. A growing fascination with historical – notably medieval – environments is even more evident in *The Conquest of the Galtar Rock*, an elaborate spectacle performed in the castle park in August 1779. Although in this case some items from the 1672 pageant of Charles XI seem actually to have been used, *Galtar Rock* looks forward rather than back, toward the kind of gothic romance that would prevail on the early nineteenth-century stage. The growing preoccupation with gothic picturesqueness is especially vivid in Hilleström's painting of the realistic torchlight assault on the three-dimensional medieval fortress of Galtar, a brooding pile where dragons dwell and Queen Briolanie languishes in the clutches of the evil wizard Arcalaus. The fire-belching dragon at the center of the composition seems about to be subdued by the five Gustavian warriors surrounding it – but it was to return in many a Drottningholm production to come.

The second decade

A combination of new developments served to make the second decade of Gustav III's reign one of the most significant in the history of Swedish theatre. Behind each development moved the guiding hand of the king. In 1781 he seemed to be emulating the example of his forebears by summoning to his court a French troupe of fifteen professionals under the leadership of Jacques-Marie Boutet de Monvel, a full-fledged Sociétaire of the Comédie-Français. In reality, one compelling reason for engaging this troupe was pedagogical. Monvel, an able and intelligent Parisian actor and writer, was available only because he had been expelled from France by the police for unspecified offenses, probably amorous in nature. During his five years of exile in Stockholm, he functioned both as director of the court troupe and as Gustav's personal tutor, conceivably even his dramaturgical adviser.[3] Besides appearing in the French classics at the summer and winter palaces and on the public stage at Bollhuset, he and his company were expected to instruct and encourage potential Swedish actors in their art. The scheme worked admirably. Monvel's trainees included several future domestic stars, the brightest of whom was the versatile and lucid comic actor Lars Hjortsberg, whose long career extended the Gustavian traditions far into the following century.

The new French troupe in no sense deflected the king's other theatrical pursuits. Having long recognized the inadequacy of the century-old theatre in Bollhuset, Gustav commissioned Carl Fredrik Adelcrantz, the architect of the Drottningholm Court Theatre, to provide a permanent home and suitably equipped stage for the Royal Swedish Opera. The new theatre opened at the end of September 1782 with the gala premiere of an original opera by Johann Gottlieb Naumann, *Cora and Alonzo*. Gudmand Adlerbeth's libretto, based on a popular tale by Marmontel about the destruction of the Incas of Peru, afforded rich opportunity for exotic mass scenes and spectacular effects. The opening night, however, belonged to Adelcrantz. The acclaim and the diamond-berried laurel wreath that his sovereign bestowed upon him were well deserved. The playhouse was a worthy counterpart to his Drottningholm, a theatrical jewel that combined architectural elegance with acoustical perfection.

At the same time, Gustav was working vigorously toward the realization of his vision of a native Swedish drama based on national themes – a vision he shares with Messenius and with Strindberg. Following an outpouring of creative energy during the fall of 1782, his new Society for the Improvement of the Swedish Language – the amateur actors of the court, in other words – was ready in the new year to embark on what surely must be a season without parallel in theatrical history. The repertory of the

Society consisted solely of Swedish plays, most of them written by the king himself. The round of productions began at Gripsholm Castle, where Gustav had fitted up a theatre in one of the towers. Still intact today, Erik Palmstedt's gracious little playhouse combines the Ionic pillars, semi-circular shape, and half-domed ceiling of the neoclassical revival with the changeable scenery, magnifying mirrors, and false proscenium pillars of the baroque period. Here, the court actors began rehearsing at ten o'clock in the morning, often dining with the king on the stage, and work continued until well into the evening. After opening with a revival of *Birger Jarl*, Gustav's courtiers were ready on 14 January 1783 with the first of his wholly original plays, a five-act "drama with song and dance" entitled *Gustaf Adolfs ädelmod* (*The Nobility of Gustav Adolf*). The cast was headed by Duke Charles, who played the idealized seventeenth-century monarch Gustav II Adolf in this complicated drama of intrigue about babies switched at birth and identities (in this case "the rightful Lars Sparre") to be sorted out.

Somewhat more skillfully constructed was Gustav's *Helmfelt*, a five-act drama performed in the Ulriksdal court theatre three months later and subsequently revived with great success on the public stage in 1788. The return of the prodigal Helmfelt, now a military hero, to the trembling embraces of his aged father, his deserted wife, and his son was a subject squarely in the mainstream of the French bourgeois drama of sentiment. Hilleström's depictions of this play in performance provide a good visual impression of the emphatically conceived pantomimic pathos expected in this genre. A perfect model for the Swedish actors in this respect was Monvel himself, who had been a major exponent of the new sentimental style during his years in Paris. As a kind of antidote to the heady emotionalism of *Helmfelt*, the court amateurs finished with *Tillfälle gör tjufven* (*Chance Makes the Thief*), a charming vaudeville by Carl Israel Hallman and Gustav Armfelt that enjoyed a longer stage life than all the tragic imitations of the Gustavian era together. In the role of a sprightly, fast-talking mountebank with a portable peepshow, Lars Hjortsberg later popularized this folk comedy in the nineteenth century. In the original performance at Gustav's court, the mountebank number was created by Carl Michael Bellman, and no doubt Hjortsberg was there to see the great lyric poet and songwriter do his stuff.[4]

Plays and plans for plays continued to flow from Gustav's pen throughout 1783. After its production in July of the king's one-act comedy *Frigga*, an arid mythological exercise borrowed from Saint-Foix's

Plate 21 The ecstasy of conflicting passions in the eighteenth-century drama of sentiment: the return of the prodigal son in Gustav III's *Helmfelt*, first acted at the Ulriksdal court theatre in 1783. Painting by Hilleström.

spectacular afterpiece *L'Oracle*, his Society took to the Drottningholm stage with *Sune Jarl*, a Nordic tragedy by G. F. Gyllenborg in which Gustav had undoubtedly also had a hand. In September, Duke Charles and his tireless associates were again ready with the king's newest ancestral drama of royal romance, *Gustav Adolf and Ebba Brahe*. All these plays are, in fact, essentially "operatic" in style and scope, and it is hence no surprise that both *Frigga* and *Gustav Adolf and Ebba Brahe* were soon turned into full-scale Gustavian operas, the latter distinguished by the gifted poet Johan Kellgren's libretto.

During this same prolific year, Gustav completed his plan for *Drottning Christina* (*Queen Christina*), a four-act play that was rendered in verse by Kellgren and presented at Gripsholm on Twelfth Night 1785. In the meantime the king had met and engaged Louis Jean Desprez, one of the out-

Plate 22 The art of Louis Jean Desprez, seen at its best in his sketch for the first act of Kellgren and Gustav III's historical drama *Queen Christina*, first staged at the Gripsholm court theatre in 1785.

standing stage designers in Europe, during an extended journey to Italy. To Desprez, then, fell the task of creating, within the restrictions of the Gripsholm stage, the lavish operatic setting and staging needed for Gustav's anecdotal, Racine-inspired drama about Christina's desperate passion for Magnus Gabriel de la Gardie. While the plays of Gustav III anticipate by half a century the style of historical melodrama that culminates with Scribe, Desprez's scenic art exhibits a comparable spirit of romantic intensity that was first matched by Cicéri in about 1810. One of the best-known Desprez designs was drawn for the first act of *Queen Christina*, depicting the de la Gardie gardens dominated by a brilliantly illuminated palace in the background. By using an imaginative device to create an illusion of depth on the shallow Gripsholm stage, the designer made the characters in the foreground appear to be standing on a raised terrace from which steps descended to a larger courtyard beyond. The decor possesses an almost magical luminosity, reminiscent in some ways of a mountainous Italian landscape yet evocative of all the atmosphere of a Nordic summer night. The actual wings, borders, and backcloth for this setting are among the fifteen complete stage decors from the period conserved at Drottningholm.

Dwarfing these previous spectacles was the production one year later of *Gustav Wasa*, a work based on a scenario by Gustav that was transformed by Kellgren into some of the best dramatic verse written in Swedish. The performance of this "lyric tragedy" in three acts called upon the finest theatrical talents of the age. The pace and vitality of Gustav's scenario and the pliant verse of Kellgren were effectively complemented by Naumann's musical score. Picturesque new settings designed by Desprez added greatly to the mass popular appeal of this patriotic music-drama. The work of the Society for the Improvement of the Swedish Language was now finished, and this production was placed in the hands of the professional company at the Royal Opera. Stenborg as the heroic title figure and the majestic Karsten as the tyrannical Danish ruler Christjern II headed a cast of some 140 characters. Extolled in countless letters and memoirs at the time and besieged by eager audiences, these first performances of *Gustav Wasa* in 1786 marked the beginning of a long stage life for the work.

The reasons for its great popularity are fairly obvious. The nationalistic appeal of the subject matter – the myth of Sweden's liberation from foreign tyranny – was undeniable. The eighteenth century had, in fact, already seen earlier attempts by several European dramatists to write a play about Sweden's national hero, the most notable of which were Alexis Piron's *Gustave* (1733) and Henry Brooke's *Gustavus Vasa, The Deliverer of his Country* (1738), which was banned by Walpole's Licensing Act. With its succession of thrilling stage actions and images, the Gustav–Kellgren–Naumann collaboration succeeded in maintaining an unbroken pitch of patriotic fervor. From its opening scene, set in a vaulted cellar beneath Stockholm Castle where the ladies and children of the Swedish nobility languish in chains, the spectacle appealed both to the deep sympathetic engagement of the audience and to its fascination with mysterious gothic surroundings. The startling transition from Desprez's shadowy dungeon setting, lighted by a single lamp, to his brilliantly ornamented rendering of the Hall of State in the castle above, was only the first in a long series of such spectacular *coups de théâtre*.

As many observers at the time recognized, *Gustav Wasa* was political theatre pure and simple, using the emotional suasion of music, verbal imagery, and stirring pageantry to establish a polemical contrast between the cruelty of the hated Danish tyrant and the courage and charisma of Gustav's great ancestor (who, by implication, became his alter ego). The covert agenda here was Gustav's desire to rally popular support for his plan

Plate 23 The third-act climax of Kellgren and Neumann's music-drama *Gustav Wasa*, as conceived and painted by Desprez in 1786.

(later modified but never abandoned) to wage war on Denmark and conquer Norway. In theatrical terms, the agitprop character of this unusual music-drama found expression in a montage of sharply juxtaposed visual and aural impressions. The insistent leitmotif was the black-and-blond conflict of good and evil, embodied in Karsten's dark, swarthy portrait of Christjern II, a loner supported only by mercenaries and cowardly conscripts, and Stenborg's blond-haired and blond-bearded image of Gustav Wasa, surrounded by a bodyguard of loyal peasants and fellow countrymen. In matching dream sequences, the latter is blessed with visions of his coming triumph, whilst Christjern is visited in the third act by the ghastly spectres of his victims, in a manner that points unmistakably to the inspiration of Shakespeare's *Richard III*. This mighty Augustan conflict resolves itself in the kaleidoscope of battle scenes in which the mise-en-scène attempted to replicate Gustav's siege of Stockholm in 1521. Unlike its French models, *Gustav Wasa* brought the sights and sounds of war before the audience in graphic detail. Desprez's watercolor and gouache depiction of the decisive victory of the Swedish troops over the Danish army (III.viii) captures the mood and style of the production in general, as we see the opposing forces sweeping toward each other in a sea of banners and cannon smoke, overlooked by the towering architectural monuments of sixteenth-century Stockholm. Small wonder that the first audiences cheered and roared to encourage their liberators and that loyal guardsmen, recruited to serve as supernumeraries in the battle and subsequent rout of the Danes, gladly offered their comrades on the Swedish side a schnapps if they would take their place beneath the hated Danish flag.

The founding of Dramaten

Despite sporadic efforts by Gyllenborg, Carl Leopold, and other court dramatists such as Carl Hallman, Elis Schröderheim, and Olof Kexel, the prolific creativity of Gustav III did not elicit the outpouring of new plays he had hoped for at the start of his work. Nevertheless, the realization of his grand design for a national dramatic theatre was at hand. A responsive climate, an audience, and experienced personnel had all been fostered by the performances of the Monvel ensemble, the Royal Opera, the court amateurs, and Stenborg's resilient troupe, established since 1784 in Munkbroteatern. In 1787 the king granted Adolf Fredrik Ristell, his librarian at Drottningholm and an avid play translator, a six-year license to put on Swedish plays at Bollhuset in alternation with the French troupe. The conditions of the patent were far from ideal: free use of the playhouse was Ristell's sole subvention, only original plays not previously acted at court were allowed, and new translations of foreign plays were specifically forbidden. Actors had to be hired on an individual basis from the Royal Opera company. In June 1787 Ristell's oversized company of thirty-six actors opened at Bollhuset with the patentee's own trivial imitation of Poinsinet's comedy *Le Cercle ou La Soirée à la mode*, familiar in the theatres of Copenhagen since the 1760s. Ristell soon proved unequal to the task of building both an acting ensemble and a repertory from the ground up, and after only ten months his plan collapsed. It has also been suggested that, at a time when political opposition to Gustav's rule was growing, the perception of Ristell as the king's man gave him powerful enemies in the aristocracy. In any case, the hapless librarian was obliged to abandon the venture and flee the country in bankruptcy.

Ironically, his salvation might have been closer than he had realized. Less than a month before his collapse, Gustav's newest and most consistently popular play, *Siri Brahe and Johan Gyllenstjerna*, opened at the public theatre with great success. This historical melodrama of love, revenge, and dangerous intrigue drew a succession of capacity audiences, attracted in no small measure by the debut of Fredrika Löf, this period's leading actress, in the title role. After Ristell's exit, an association of actor–shareholders banded together, the company was trimmed to twenty-one performers, and their new enterprise – christened the Royal Swedish Dramatic Theatre – was granted a royal patent and a modest subsidy on 10 May 1788. One week later the curtain rose at Bollhuset on the first production in the long history of Dramaten (as it is always known), the public premiere of Gyllenborg's tragedy *Sune Jarl*. The restless movement during the eighteenth century toward the founding of national public theatres in Scandinavia had reached its culmination.

Even as he waged war against Russia, Gustav continued to be ready with advice and instructions for his "Theatre dramatique que je regarde comme un port tranquille ou on pourra se reposer apres les oragees."[5] Five of his own plays were on the first season's program at Dramaten – which may not have enhanced its popularity among the disaffected aristocracy. Neither the boundless optimism nor the tireless encouragement of the king could foster enough good original plays to sustain a major theatre. The onerous prohibition of translations was reaffirmed by Gustav in laconic dispatches sent home from the battlefield to Niklas Clewberg, who had been left in charge of both royal theatres. Compromise on the issue was inevitable, however, if Dramaten was to survive. Matters came to a boil when Abraham de Broen, the company's distinguished but quarrelsome *père noble*, put forward his wife's adaptation of Sheridan's *The School for Scandal* and apparently secured the king's "special gracious leave" to perform it as an original work.[6]

A new set of Regulations for the Swedish Dramatic Theatre, given royal assent in May 1789, introduced several important organizational changes.[7] The actors were now entitled to participate in bimonthly assemblies where such issues as casting, repertory, budget, and play selection were decided in democratic fashion. The tempo of work was also stepped up: an actor was now required to memorize forty lines of eight-word length daily, and the first rehearsal was held "When half the time for memorizing the longest role" had elapsed. In view of the small number of rehearsals normally held in the eighteenth-century theatre, the stiff fines imposed for inadequate role preparation were not unreasonable. The most significant of these changes concerned the lifting of the ban on translations. With this new rule, a wider and more cosmopolitan range of dramatic styles became available to the emerging national theatre, which had already begun to assemble a solid acting ensemble that included de Broen, Lars Hjortsberg, Fredrika Löf, Maria Louise Baptiste (now Madame Marcadet), and the sonorous and stately Andreas Widerberg.

New schemes – arrangements for an expansion of Drottningholm by Desprez, alternative projects for a playhouse to replace Bollhuset, proposals for casting a series of French tragedies – continued to occupy the king's mind until the fateful evening of 16 March 1792, when all such plans came to an abrupt end. The masked ball at the Royal Opera, where Gustav III was mortally wounded by an assassin's bullets, was in itself a moment of high drama and irony that would subsequently fire the imaginations of Scribe, Auber, Planché, Verdi, and (perhaps most strikingly of all) Strindberg. In broader historical terms, the assassination brought to a close one of the most expansive eras in Swedish theatre. A cultural age of iron followed. The French troupe was summarily dismissed, the Stenborg family's comedy theatre was eventually forced to close, and the century-old Bollhus was dismantled. The stage at Drottningholm fell into disuse, and soon even its existence was forgotten.

Nevertheless, the tradition of native theatre and drama that Gustav had so singlemindedly cultivated had taken root. Moved to new quarters in the so-called Arsenal, a turreted seventeenth-century palace converted to a 600-seat theatre, Dramaten reopened on 1 November 1793 with the premiere of the murdered king's last and darkest play, *Den svartsjuke neapolitanaren* (*The Jealous Neapolitan*). The melancholy romanticism of this exercise in the *genre sombre* struck a timely and symptomatic chord. Intense emotionality in picturesque and forbidding medieval surroundings – the true spirit of gothicism – was quickly becoming the highest fashion. The abducted virgins, disguised gypsies, and agitated strangers of August von Kotzebue had already begun to weave their spell on the stages of Scandinavia. The atmospheric, three-dimensional mood pictures of the gothic style, prefigured in such Gustavian works as *Gustav Wasa* and *The Conquest of the Galtar Rock*, drew upon the same set of signifiers that enlivened the novels of Mrs. Radcliffe, "Monk" Lewis, and Walter Scott: medieval fortifications with walls, moats, and drawbridges, haunted towers and castle specters, landscapes shrouded in shadow, graveyards bathed in moonlight, secret grottoes, gothic ruins, and robbers' dens. The vogue of the so-called *genre sombre*, heralded by Gustav's last play, soon reached fever pitch with melodramas like A. P. Skjöldebrand's *Herman von Unna* (seen in Copenhagen in 1800 and in Stockholm in 1817), on which the author's knowledge of freemasonry and secret orders brought to bear the whole symbolic machinery of clanking chains and glittering daggers, flickering torches and blazing altars, sinister rituals and masonic tribunals.

Extending, then, to the verge of romanticism, the Gustavian age represents not only a time of rising national identity and cultural awareness in Sweden, but also a period of transition in the arts in general. The recent upsurge of scholarship about this period has usefully stressed the inherent interconnectedness of music, opera, dance, and drama in Gustav's grand design. It has also demonstrated the rather controversial manner in which this design sought to harness the arts to a royal policy of personal and political aggrandizement. In terms of the broader subject of the Scandinavian theatre as a whole, however, the Gustavian phenomenon must be seen, so to speak, both as a prologue and an epilogue. Viewed as the latter, it marks the definitive conclusion and summation of the period of court theatricals and royal influence on theatre affairs that had lasted for more than two centuries. On the other hand, with its cultivation of historical subjects and flavor, its concern with a stronger sense of mood and atmosphere on the stage, and its introduction of a more complex approach to mise-en-scène in the work of such figures as Gallodier, Desprez, and Gustav himself, the Gustavian era broke with the controlled artifice of the baroque and foreshadowed the flamboyant theatricality which the new century held in store.

5 The romantic theatre and its aftermath

By the beginning of the nineteenth century, theatrical life in all three Scandinavian countries had undergone great change. The elite courtly theatre had lost its importance, and the itinerant foreign-language troupes of the past had vanished from the scene. At the center of the expansive theatre culture of this period were the major public theatres founded in the previous century, with their performances in the language of the country and its people. In Stockholm, the Royal Dramatic Theatre and the Royal Opera were both securely established by 1800. The Danish Royal Theatre, having weathered its first half century, now housed resident companies for opera, drama, and ballet under one roof. The local dramatic societies and theatre clubs that sprang up and flourished in many Norwegian towns after 1780 prepared the way for the founding of the Christiania Theatre, the first permanent playhouse with a company of Norwegian professionals, in 1827. More than a quarter of a century earlier, however, the amateur dramatic society in Bergen had already opened a permanent theatre of its own, called Comediehuset, in what was to be an important first step in the rapid evolution of Norwegian-language theatre.

In a great many respects the general development of theatre in Scandinavia during this period paralleled the course of events elsewhere, most obviously in England and France. The primacy of the established national theatres in Stockholm and Copenhagen was soon challenged by the emergence of new "private" (as distinct from "royal") theatres determined to compete for a share of the growing popular audience. The example set in this respect by Nya teatern (the New Theatre), which opened in Stockholm in 1842, was soon followed in Copenhagen by Casino (1848) and Folketeatret (1857), both "folk" theatres exerting wide popular appeal. Advances in stage lighting were accompanied at this time by significant

changes in stage technology and set design. The box set or closed room of
the modern theatre, which Madame Vestris seems to have introduced in the
London theatre in 1832, was seen in Denmark three years before that date,
when August Bournonville used it for his ballet *La sonnambula*. The style of
production adopted briefly at Dramaten by Gustaf Lagerbjelke in the mid-
1820s anticipated – in very much the same way that Macready's London
productions of the 1830s did – the principles of ensemble direction and
disciplined crowd mise-en-scène brought to perfection by Charles Kean
and the Duke of Saxe-Meiningen.[1] Above all, however, the nineteenth century was an age of great acting, not least in Scandinavia. At the Danish
Royal Theatre in particular, a cluster of exceptional performers – Johan
Christian Ryge, N. P. Nielsen, Anna Nielsen, C. N. Rosenkilde, Michael
Wiehe, Ludvig Phister, and, above all, Johanne Luise Heiberg – entitled
this theatre to be counted among the foremost playhouses of Europe
around mid-century. This era of virtuosity and theatrical achievement
coincided, moreover, with a much broader flourishing of art, literature,
and culture, deservedly known as Denmark's Golden Age.

From gothic to romantic

The new romantic spirit which, through the direct influence of the plays
of Adam Oehlenschläger, transformed the Scandinavian theatre in the
early 1800s, sprang from the pre-romantic climate that prevailed at the end
of the eighteenth century, in Denmark as well as in Gustavian Sweden. An
important harbinger of the revolution wrought by Oehlenschläger's
drama was the lyric poet Johannes Ewald. In 1769, Ewald's unproduced
verse drama *Adam og Eva*, a Corneille-inspired work focusing on Eve's
inner conflict, had become the first Danish tragedy. The following year his
Rolf Krage, a five-act historical tragedy that took its subject from the second book of Saxo Grammaticus, turned from Corneille to Shakespeare for
its inspiration. Although this play was never acted, its more stageworthy
successor *Balders Død* (*The Death of Balder*), also based on Saxo, succeeded
in establishing a lasting stage tradition of gothic dramas on Nordic themes.
An effective musical score for Ewald's three-act *singspiel* was provided by
the German composer and concert-master Johann Hartmann. The playwright's treatment of his subject reveals a characteristic desire on his part
to blend Racinean erotic passion with the pathos and sentiment of the
bourgeois drama of Diderot, Lessing, and their influential Danish spokesman, K. L. Rahbek. After a miscarried premiere, marred by inappropriate

Plate 24 The closing tableau in the revival of Ewald's *The Death of Balder* (1779), painted by the designer Peter Cramer. Beside the upright runic stone, or menhir, in the background one sees the figures of Odin and Frigga looking on.

costumes and old sets, in 1778, *Balder* was revived at the Royal Theatre the following year in a new mise-en-scène that afforded a piquant foretaste of the picturesque gothic settings, supernatural wonders, and emotional tableaux of high romanticism.

The new production owed its success in large measure to the theatre's capable designer, Peter Cramer. Still working within the basic eighteenth-century framework of open side wings and painted backcloths, Cramer created a convincing stage picture of a spruce forest in the rugged Norwegian highlands, surrounded by steep, jagged peaks covered with snow. Prominent among the set pieces that he used in order to add texture and authenticity to this perspective setting was a menhir in Odin's honor, introduced as a reminder of the Nordic past of Ewald's drama. This tall, upright monumental stone is clearly in evidence in a painting by Cramer that depicts the final lachrymose tableau of Balder's death. In the second act, as the hero's desperate rival Hother seeks help in witchcraft, the woodland setting was "instantaneously" transformed to a sorcerer's cave. As was often the case in this period, the scene change was only partial. While the downstage wings, painted as "wilderness," remained, the upstage wings and the backcloth changed to a gloomy cavern where two magical altars, dragged on by ropes, provided a focus for a hellish ritual danced by a brood of Valkyries.[2] Like the staging, the costuming of this production set the tone for a generation of Nordic tragedies to come. In the course of greater "authenticity," the theatre invited Nicolai Abildgaard, one of the foremost painters of the age, to design the costumes and actually drape the actors. Abildgaard's pronounced neoclassical sensibility shaped a simple, strongly Greco-Roman mode of dress for Ewald's saga figures, from which every trace of barbarism or historical accuracy was eliminated.

In strictly dramaturgical terms, the requisite sense of tragic inevitability seems, in a work such as *The Death of Balder*, as superimposed as it is in Johan Herman Wessel's brilliant parody of the genre, *Kjærlighed uden Strømper* (*Love without Stockings*). In this mock-heroic "tragedy" of love, the usual high-flown sentiments are now declaimed in verse by tailors and artisans whose collective doom has been sealed at the outset by the sinister oracular warning recollected by Grete, the heroine, in her opening line: "'O never shall you marry, if not this very day.'" When first staged in 1773, the sense of the play as a theatrical quotation of tragic conventions was heightened by beginning the farce in ordinary domestic clothing and changing gradually to the plumes and attire of heroic tragedy as the mock suspense mounted.

As for Ewald, however contrived or Wesselean the issues of tragic fate and motivation may seem in his drama, its theatrical effect and subsequent influence are indisputable. In his last play, *Fiskerne* (*The Fishermen*), he chose a new course by abandoning historical characters and demigods to explore, in the true spirit of the sentimental drama, the heroism of the common man. Although still cast in the form of a *singspiel* with music by Hartmann, *The Fishermen* presents a touching domestic drama played against the background of an actual occurrence, a selfless rescue action carried out by a colony of poor Hornbæk fishermen. The shipwreck that prompts this gallant deed is the high point of Ewald's play, and for its Royal Theatre production in 1780 considerable ingenuity was again required. The theatre's machinist, Christopher Nielsen, rose to the occasion with a new "movable sea" of waves in motion, so convincing and effective in its operation that its creator was awarded a medal for his service. Such a sea machine, which because of its demanding nature was usually employed only when absolutely necessary at the Royal Theatre, consisted of a number of rollers placed across the stage to represent waves. By rotating these rollers at different speeds, the sea could be shown in all its phases, from gentle agitation to the lashing billows of a tempest – the illusion of which was enhanced by a storm horizon on rollers, painted with dark and transparent clouds that seemed to scud across the sky.

With the production of Vicenzo Galeotti's *Lagertha* in 1801, the interest in Nordic subjects ignited by Ewald's work spread to ballet. Based on Christen Pram's Saxo-inspired historical drama of unfaithfulness, domestic retribution, and female courage and determination, this mimic–lyric dance drama was a milestone in the career of the renowned Italian choreographer, whose fifty-odd productions at the Royal Theatre laid the foundation on which the great traditions of the Danish ballet rest. Costumed by Abildgaard and located in a rugged Gothland landscape by the French painter Chipart, Galeotti's display of spectacular processions, ancient warrior dances, and richly textured movement patterns and tableaux added a whole new dimension of plastic eloquence to the emerging romantic style. Above all, however, it was the "strength and passion, grace and wildness, freshness and fullness" of the Nordic tone-poem composed by Claus Schall for *Lagertha* that left a lasting impression on August Bournonville, who made his debut in this production as one of the warlike Lagertha's small children.[3] Later as Galeotti's successor, Bournonville went on to create a repertoire of romantic ballets that broke conclusively with what he came to regard as the symmetry and conventionality of the Italian master's genre of pantomimic dancing.

Another significant foretaste of the new romanticism was afforded by O. J. Samsøe's national–historical tragedy *Dyveke*, first acted at the Royal Theatre in 1796. For this demanding production, great effort was made to provide the kind of picturesque historical coloring and authentic costuming that would, for much of the next century, continue to be known as "Gothic." Samsøe's play, one of the most admired historical dramas of its period, emulates the sentimental tragedy of Lessing, whose *Emilia Galotti* enjoyed considerable popularity on the Danish stage. As the mistress of the medieval king Christjern II, Dyveke – much like her counterpart in Lessing's drama – is a wronged innocent brought to ruin in the courtly milieu into which she is enticed. Although no Desprez, designer Thomas Bruun created four attractive new interiors which, in the influential opinion of K. L. Rahbek, "proved to be both true to his period and pleasing to our own age."[4] These sets, consisting of painted backcloths, borders, and

Plate 25 "The Queen's Chamber": one of four new interiors designed by Thomas Bruun
for Samsøe's historical drama *Dyveke*. Danish Royal Theatre, 1796.

side wings decorated, in Bruun's words, "with the architecture, ornaments,
and weaponry in use at the time," were to reappear often during the nineteenth century when a suitably "gothic" impression was required. Gracing
the plays of Shakespeare, Goethe, Schiller, Oehlenschläger, Hans Christian
Andersen, Henrik Hertz and others, the *Dyveke* scenery could still be found
in the Royal Theatre's inventory of active decors in 1873 – scarcely six years
before it presented the world premiere of Ibsen's *A Doll's House*.

The gothic mode, transmitted by such preromantic works as *The Death
of Balder, Lagertha*, and *Dyveke*, is at the theatrical heart of the plays of Adam
Oehlenschläger (1779–1850), the most important Scandinavian dramatist
of the first quarter of the nineteenth century. In *Poems 1803*, the most discussed book in the history of Danish literature, Oehlenschläger proclaimed
the establishment of a new movement, aimed at breaking with traditional
forms and championing the revolutionary spirit of German romanticism.
"Guldhornene" ("The Horns of Gold"), the stately keynote poem of this
collection, is a ringing declaration of the renaissance of ancient Nordic culture. In *Aladdin* (1805), a lyric – dramatic fantasy admired in turn by Heiberg,
Andersen, Kierkegaard, Ibsen, and Brandes, the young poet turned briefly
to a more exotic and fantastical subject matter for his infectious celebration
of youth, beauty, and genius. The figure of Aladdin, the apotheosis of the
heroic dreamer, became virtually a hieroglyph for the romantic spirit in

Scandinavia. As a playwright, however, Oehlenschläger is identified chiefly with the cycle of Nordic tragedies he created under the influence of Shakespeare and the later works of Schiller (notably the *Wallenstein* trilogy, *Maria Stuart*, and *Die Jungfrau von Orleans*). The popular appeal of Oehlenschläger's dramaturgy derived in no small measure from his intimate knowledge of the practical theatre and its conventions, acquired in part during his two years as a professional actor. When *Hakon Jarl*, the first of his romantic dramas on Nordic themes, reached the stage early in 1808, a popular new genre was established.

In its staging and costuming, the first performance of *Hakon Jarl* at the Danish Royal Theatre made liberal use of the atmosphere and accoutrements of gothicism. Several of the sets were borrowed, in fact, from earlier gothic productions – among them *Dyveke*, in which Oehlenschläger himself had acted. Abildgaard's brand of stylized historicity again governed the replication of Viking dress. Spectacle abounded. For the arrival by sea of Olaf Trygvesøn, the adversary of Hakon Jarl who is bent on converting Norway to Christianity and destroying the power of Hakon's heathenism, special care was lavished on a picturesque maritime tableau of the kind that had long delighted Royal Theatre audiences. The royal bark – with King Olaf in the bow, surrounded by retainers and singing monks – sailed forth from the wings through a painted sea, struck its mainsail, and landed majestically on the beach. Far less idyllic was the crucial fourth-act scene in which the ambitious and ruthless Hakon decides to sacrifice his son to gain Odin's favor, thereby sealing his own doom. Set in a suitably sinister "sacrificial grove" dominated by threatening statues of Viking gods, this splendidly theatrical episode blended tearful pathos – as the heartless father hesitates to drive home the dagger while little Erling kneels in prayer – with spine-tingling terror. At last, the tyrant led his unwitting child out of sight behind Odin's icon, from whence were heard screams so unnerving and indecorous that even Oehlenschläger ordered them cut. The drama reached its fifth-act climax in a dimly lit and forbidding underground vault where the once-mighty Hakon hides from his enemies. Slain by his slave while restlessly sleepwalking, Hakon Jarl is ultimately seen as an heroic figure in Oehlenschläger's romantic conception, a "great soul" over whose black coffin his sometime lover Thora is left to speak one of the playwright's finest eulogies.

The role of Hakon Jarl, the first in a gallery of Nordic heroes "redolent of sea fog, heathenism, and sacrificial blood" (to borrow a phrase from

Bournonville), was intended for the author's former acting teacher, the gifted Michael Rosing, but crippling rheumatism prevented the aging star from attempting this demanding part. With Oehlenschläger's next tragedy *Palnatoke* (1809), a *Wilhelm Tell*-inspired drama that again centers on the doomed struggle of ancient Nordic strength against the inroads of the new Christianity, the lack of an authoritative heroic actor was even more keenly felt. Four years went by before the ideal Oehlenschlägerean actor appeared, but with the debut of Johan Christian Ryge as Palnatoke in 1813, the fiery embodiment of the romantic hero had been found. Ryge, a district health officer who gave up a profitable practice for the stage, surprised even Oehlenschläger, who compared him to Garrick, Talma, and Friedrich Schröder. In a repertoire that made the severest demands on the physical resources and vocal stamina of the performer, he was the perfect expression of towering Viking strength, both as a personal quality and as the fulfillment of an aesthetic ideal. "His words," writes Bournonville, "rang like sword blows on copper shields, they bored into the soul like runes cut into granite boulders. His voice resounded like the shrill tone of the lure over the North Sea's breakers."[5] True to the spirit of *Schöne Wahrheit*, however, the romantic ideal of strength that Ryge so manifestly embodied was always coupled with an unconditional exclusion of all indecorous declamation and gesture. Goethe's maxim that the player must "not only imitate nature but also portray it ideally" was still a guiding practical principle of the romantic actor's art.[6]

Strongly influenced by developments elsewhere in Europe, Oehlenschläger continued to experiment with a range of styles and subjects, with varying success. The popular antihero of German romanticism is represented in his *Correggio*, an artist tragedy that was lavishly staged with borrowed Renaissance paintings and rich costumes in 1811. Originally written in German, *Correggio* was also performed with success in Berlin and Vienna and was widely read in Germany during Oehlenschläger's lifetime. His *Hugo von Rheinberg* (1814) is a botched attempt to emulate the heady medievalism, poisoned chalices, and castle specters of the more sensational gothic melodramas of the day. The play was no match, however, for the real masterworks of this colored genre: Skjöldebrand's *Herman von Unna*, Galeotti's electrifying Bluebeard ballet *Rolf Blaaskæg*, and Kotzebue's *Johanne von Montfaucon* and *Die Kreuzfahrer*, both of which took the Royal Theatre and Dramaten by storm during the early years of the century.

The Nordic tragedies of Oehlenschläger took on a new, more con-trolled tone with *Axel og Valborg* (1810), a twelfth-century drama of forbid-den love and duty based on a folk song motif. Influenced, it seems, by his admiration for French classicism and its greater formal regularity, Oehlenschläger confined the potentially sprawling subject matter of his ballad source to a single day and a single location, the ancient cathedral at Nidaros (Trondheim) – a departure that audiences, accustomed by then to spectacular displays of changing scenes in gothic tragedy, found difficult to accept. Nevertheless, *Axel og Valborg* enjoyed great influence and a long stage life. When its premiere at Dramaten in 1829 introduced the Oehlenschläger genre on the Stockholm stage, critics had particular praise for the playwright's ability to "combine the demands of romantic tragedy – an exciting and well-managed action, more vigorously individualized char-acters, and luxuriant poetic dialogue – with the unities of time, place, and action."[7] In this play, as in the even more tightly structured *Hagbarth og Signe* (1816), the undivided focus is the tragic love of the title characters, who, separated by hostile circumstances, face their destiny bravely and achieve union in death at the end. This quintessentially romantic action achieved its fullest expression on the Royal Theatre stage in the performances of N. P. Nielsen, Ryge's most gifted pupil, and Anna Brenøe (later Madame Nielsen), one of the Scandinavian theatre's loveliest romantic heroines. Both made their debuts in the 1820/1 season, she in a revival of *Dyveke*, he as a dashingly handsome and lyrical Axel Thordsøn, Oehlenschläger's hero. With them, Oehlenschlägerean tragedy acquired the ideal Axel and Valborg to complement the robust Viking figures created by Doctor Ryge.

It is hardly surprising that the new spirit introduced by Oehlenschläger's romantic tragedies drew with it the first important pro-fessional productions of Shakespeare in the Scandinavian theatre. Shakespearean drama was seen in the provinces long before it finally gained a hearing at the Royal Theatre and at Dramaten in the early nine-teenth century. The Swedish town of Norrköping witnessed the first per-formance of Shakespeare in Scandinavia in 1776, when the enterprising theatre manager Carl Gottfried Seuerling presented a version of "the new and all too magnificent Bourgeois Tragedy called *Romeo and Juliet*."[8] A Swedish translation of *Hamlet* was acted in Göteborg by Andreas Widerberg and his company in 1787, shortly before he was called to the newly formed Royal Dramatic Theatre. In Odense, where the first profes-sional provincial theatre in Denmark was established, the Schröder version of *Hamlet* was given by Friebach's German-language troupe in 1792 – fully two decades before audiences at the Royal Theatre in Copenhagen were offered their first glimpse of a Danish *Hamlet*, on 12 May 1813.

It seems fitting that Peter Foersom, who translated *Hamlet* and had struggled for a decade to convince the theatre's skeptical management to hazard a production of it, was given the title role in the Danish premiere of this play. Foersom's performance was, in fact, the high point of an otherwise modest production put together of older gothic settings taken from *Dyveke* and *Herman von Unna*. These borrowings were combined, when necessary, with a few new set pieces and props, including five painted burial mounds, a "Death's head," and some "skeleton bones of wood." This gothic *Hamlet* was followed in September 1816 by *King Lear*, which proved to be a box-office disaster that closed after three poorly attended performances. Ryge's vigorous attack was ill-suited to the role of Lear; it is, the actor stoutly maintained, "against both my inner and my outer nature to play mad kings when they are not allowed to strike back at their enemies."[9] A somewhat more successful production of the Schiller version of *Macbeth* a year later, also featuring Ryge in the title role, completed the Royal Theatre's first round of Shakespearean flirtations.

Dramaten quickly followed suit with the first Stockholm showing of *Hamlet*, staged at the Arsenal Theatre on 26 March 1819. This production, a major event in the Swedish theatre of this period, typifies in many ways the accepted approach to Shakespeare at the time. The cuts introduced by P. A. Granberg's prose translation, the running time of which was three and a half hours, followed the lead of traditional English stage versions of the play. Cornelius and Voltimand, those uninteresting ambassadors, were eliminated, as was the dispensable scene between Polonius and Reynaldo. Like Garrick before him, the Swedish translator banished the clownish gravediggers, and, as in the Bell edition of 1773, he dispensed entirely with Fortinbras and his army, assigning some of the Prince of Norway's speeches to Horatio. The Dramaten cast featured two of its strongest actors: the noble and authoritative Gustaf Åbergsson was, at age forty-four, a stately and mature Hamlet, while Lars Hjortsberg, one of the Swedish theatre's greatest comic actors, was Horatio. This much-discussed production was further enhanced by an original musical score, prepared by the Swiss-born composer and concert-master Edouard Du Puy – a figure whose importance for the development of the musical stage both in Sweden and Denmark was immeasurable.

Of particular interest are the staging principles at work in the Swedish *Hamlet*, as recorded in Dramaten's archives – principles still for the most part anchored in eighteenth-century methods. Stock settings of the wing-and-border variety were used for all five acts. The opening scene, for example, utilized five rows of stock forest wings and a background of fortress and battlement pieces borrowed from such gothic favorites as Kotzebue's *Johanne von Montfaucon* and Grétry's *Richard Coeur-de-Lion*. The backcloth was a standard sea drop. The only furnishing on the otherwise bare stage was a stone bench downstage right. As the curtain rose the scene was lit only by the moon, but when the Ghost appeared upstage and moved across a raised, horizontal platform, light was brought up between the wings, disappearing again on the Ghost's exit. After Hamlet's encounter with his father's spirit later in the act, the grim specter was seen to sink through the main trap, moving beneath the stage for each "Swear" and drawing the onstage group after him in symmetrical pattern: first stage center, then downstage right, then downstage left, and finally down center for Hamlet's "Rest, rest perturbed spirit!"

The mise-en-scène for the third act again used a conventional five-wing decor, called simply "Temple of the Muses." Within this characterless framework, however, the play-within-the-play was quite imaginatively staged. Blue curtains, hung behind the third row of wings, served as a front curtain for the miniature stage erected in the background. The miniaturization was complete to the smallest detail: the little stage, reached by steps on either side, was fitted with two pairs of forest wings, a forest backdrop, and a grass seat for the Player King, all reminiscent of the arrangement for act 1. An elaborate dumbshow devised by Du Puy added its own ironic comment on the reiteration effect of the mousetrap scene. The musical theme that accompanied the Player Queen as she laments the King's death was repeated a moment later when Lucianus *pretends* to lament with her. Similarly, the theme used to express the Queen's acquiescence to Lucianus' advances was the same one heard earlier to signify the love between her and the Player King. This act continued in the same decor, in fact, until Hamlet discovered Claudius at his prayers. Pages then appeared and carried off the few items of furniture on the stage, while another page entered carrying a table, chair, and candle. A *changement à vue* to the closet scene was then ready to take place.

Although the use of borrowed or incongruously combined settings, clumsy set-shifting techniques, partial scene changes, primitive lighting effects, and similar technical inelegancies had been roundly challenged by such eighteenth-century critics as Peder Rosenstand-Goiske, many of these conventions persisted – as the 1819 *Hamlet* shows – well into the nineteenth century. Nevertheless, the emergence of a new theatrical style, particularly in France and England, was causing profound and rapid changes in this regard. In 1827, Victor Hugo's preface to *Cromwell* proclaimed a new charter of freedom from the remaining neoclassical restrictions on drama and theatre. The guest performances of the English actors in Paris in 1827/8 and the productions in 1829 and 1830 of Dumas' *Henri III et sa cour*, Vigny's *Othello*, and Hugo's *Hernani* confirmed the breakthrough of romanticism on the European stage. In Scandinavia at this time, the comparative formality and abstractness of the eighteenth-century stage picture were also being displaced by the new romanticism, the goal of which was to produce an illusion of living, plastic reality in settings, costumes, and lighting. Among the aesthetic criteria driving this revolution were the demand for more atmospheric and illusionistic staging, the increased emphasis on local color and authenticity, and the redefinition of the theatre as (to borrow K. F. Schinkel's phrase) *eine lebende Bildergallerie*. Obviously, however, the practical realization of this "living picture gallery" depended on significant technical changes.

Eigtved's original Royal Theatre had undergone major renovation under Harsdorff's supervision in 1773, during which the stage had been expanded and the machinery greatly improved. Although Harsdorff's theatre remained in use until 1874, when it was demolished to make way for the present Royal Theatre structure, the stage continued to undergo significant alterations and improvements from time to time. Changes of scene, which still took place in full view, were greatly facilitated in 1826 by the installation of a third set of wing chariots, making it possible to mount as many as three settings at once and thereby reducing the necessity of partial scene shifts.[10] Even more important were improvements in lighting, which obviously played a major role in the achievement of greater stage illusion. The candles and tallow lamps of the older theatre were replaced in 1819 by the safer and more flexible oil-burning lamps invented by Aimé Argand. Dramaten, housed in the Arsenal Theatre from 1793 until it burned down in 1825, had in fact introduced that change five years earlier. Still greater flexibility was achieved at the Royal Theatre in 1826 when the footlights were made longer and were equipped with more powerful lamps. Colored lighting was also introduced at this time, together with a mechanism for simultaneously dimming the lamps in the wings. Two years earlier the cosmopolitan theatre reformer Gustaf Lagerbjelke, whose term of management at Dramaten from 1823 to 1827 brought the new romantic mise-en-scène to Swedish theatre, had already employed the novelty of moonlight and other colored lighting effects in his production of P. A. Wolff's popular drama *Preciosa*. Although gas lighting was introduced in the English theatre in 1817, this more sophisticated means of creating such favorite romantic phenomena as moonlight, storm effects, sunsets, and volcanic eruptions did not reach Scandinavia until much later. Gas was first tried at the Royal Opera in Stockholm (whose stage the dramatic theatre shared for four decades after the Arsenal Theatre fire) on New Year's Day 1854. It came next to Det Norske Teater in Bergen in 1856, and was finally seen on Kongens Nytorv during the 1857/8 season.

Historians have summed up the development of scene design in the first half of the nineteenth century by observing that the backcloth eventually absorbed the side wings and finally swallowed the whole stage picture – in other words, objects and structures previously painted in two dimensions on canvas eventually became solid and three-dimensional. The architectural formality of the baroque theatre receded before wide stretches of blasted heath, distant vistas of medieval towns, and picturesque views of Mexican burial grounds or Italian village squares. The scene-painter came to exert a major influence on the character and style of the entire repertory, and it was often his name that appeared most prominently in reviews and playbills. Aron Wallich, the Royal Theatre's stage designer for nearly four decades from 1814 to 1842, found in the towns of northern Italy his models for the favorite subjects of contemporary scene painting – murky cathedrals, walled fortresses, somber churchyards, vaulted monastery passages. Like his Swedish counterpart Carl Jakob Hjelm, who inherited Desprez's legacy as Dramaten's designer during the years from 1798 to 1827, Wallich retained a strong predilection for the grandiose lines and deep perspectives of the eighteenth century, while incorporating a richness of romantic detail inspired by such European masters as Schinkel, Cicéri, and Sanquirico.

The growing importance and complexity of stage design led the Royal Theatre to retain two highly trained and talented scenic artists after Wallich's departure, Troels Lund and Christian Ferdinand Christensen. Lund, who specialized in historical and architectural designs, brought both the romantic influence of Cicéri, with whom he had studied in Paris, and

Plate 26 Undated design by Aron Wallich for a vaulted dungeon, colored in contrasting browns, with blue sky and green trees visible through the perspective arch.

the amazing atmospheric effects of Daguerre's Diorama to bear on his art. As the architect of Vesterbro Theatre, one of the new "suburban" thea-tres built outside the city walls in 1834, he actually introduced the round auditorium and flexible stage space of the Parisian panorama theatres into his innovative plan. Christensen, who was employed as a designer at the Royal Theatre until 1869, was an imaginative pictorial artist widely conceded to be more gifted than Lund. His special strength lay in finely wrought romantic landscapes, executed in bright, warm, and genial tones. Among his greatest successes were his exotic settings for Bournonville's Italian ballets, notably *Napoli* (1842) and the earlier *Festen i Albano* (*The Festival in Albano*, 1839). The panorama for the latter design, with its green vegetation, high blue sky, and view of the gray Campagna with Rome in the distance, continued to haunt a legion of subsequent romantic stage pictures.

Within the framework of pictorialism provided by these artists, theatrical life flourished at the Royal Theatre during the second quarter of the nineteenth century. A constellation of new playwrights and an extraordinary company of actors joined forces to create the most memorable epoch in Danish theatrical history. Architecturally as well as culturally, the playhouse on Kongens Nytorv dominated the daily life of Copenhagen, and the leading figures of this golden age gathered in the stalls each

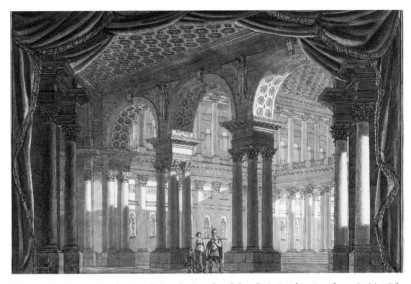

Plate 27 Design project by Troels Lund, signed and dated 1828, when Lund was in Munich studying theatrical design under Giuseppe Quaglio. The niches, galleries, and Corinthian pillars of his great hall suggest a strong neoclassical influence, while the three figures in the foreground of the drawing show the scale on which the project was conceived.

evening. Hans Christian Andersen's lodgings were always within easy walking distance of the theatre; Oehlenschläger was there every evening; the great sculptor Bertel Thorvaldsen died in the theatre; and the solitary Søren Kierkegaard was an habitual playgoer. At the center of this glittering circle stood the Heibergs.

The Heiberg years

P. A. Heiberg, whose exile and subsequent divorce had astonished polite society around the turn of the century, rehabilitated Danish comedy with a series of trenchant eighteenth-century satires of fools and double-dealers. It remained, however, for his son Johan Ludvig (1791–1860) to bring about a genuine comic renaissance to balance the serious dramas of Oehlenschläger and his imitators. After a brilliant doctoral dissertation on Calderón in 1817, the younger Heiberg rose quickly to dominate intellectual life in Copenhagen in a variety of capacities, as publicist, philosopher, theatre manager, and unofficial arbiter of taste. As a playwright, he has remained second only to Holberg as Denmark's most performed dramatist. As a tireless cultural intermediary, he worked to transplant the newest German and French developments to Scandinavia. Having spent several

Plate 28   Working design by C. F. Christensen for Bournonville's ballet *The Festival in Albano* (1839): an exotic panorama of lush green vegetation, high blue sky, the gray Campagna, and a glimpse of the city of Rome in the distance.

years in Paris, Kiel, and Berlin during the early 1820s, he was in a position to bring the powerful intellectual forces of Europe to bear on Danish cultural life. From Germany he introduced the new philosophy of F. W. Hegel to Scandinavia – voicing in his Hegelian treatise *On Human Freedom* (1824) the demand for introspective self-scrutiny and reflective inner freedom that drew Ibsen so strongly to Heiberg. In theatrical terms, however, his most significant contribution remains his domestication of the Scribean vaudeville comedy – a genre that was to have an even greater influence on Ibsen's development.

Heiberg embodies, as it were, the concept of romanticism as an elegant and refined parlor game. His affinity for Gallic culture was intense, and his determination to de-Germanize and thereby internationalize Danish theatrical taste resulted in his translation of some forty contemporary plays, most of them modern French pieces. The majority of these were so-called *comédies-vaudevilles* from the prolific dramatic factory of Eugène Scribe. The wide popular appeal of the French vaudeville tradition, which reaches back to the harlequinades of the *commedia dell'arte* players in the service of Louis XIV, derives from the interplay it creates between dialogue and song. The typical vaudeville blends crisp comic repartee with topical songs and satirical ditties sung to familiar popular tunes or operatic arias. Scribe and other Parisian writers of the early nineteenth century seized on this effective formula to circumvent the monopoly on spoken drama held by the major patent theatres of the capital. Heiberg set out to transplant this popular genre to Denmark in order to create his own version of a Parisian alternative theatre, unpretentious in tone, contemporary in setting and subject matter, and populist in the appeal of its musical parodies.

Heiberg's ambitious comic offensive was launched at the Royal Theatre on 26 November 1825 with the production of his first vaudeville experiment, a farce on the theme of mistaken identity called *Kong Salomon og Jørgen Hattemager* (*King Solomon and George the Hatter*). The theatre's management was unhappy with such frivolity, initial critical reaction was largely negative, but the public response to the light, revue-like mixture of lyricism, jest, and satire was overwhelming. "It was a Danish vaudeville," writes that tireless playgoer Hans Christian Andersen, "blood of our blood, one felt, and therefore it was received with jubilation and replaced all else. Thalia held a carnival on the Danish stage, and Heiberg was her chosen favorite."[11] The popularity of the play and the genre also spread rapidly to Sweden and Norway. Even during Ibsen's tenure as stage director at the Bergen Theatre in the early 1850s, this comedy, along with others like it by Heiberg and Scribe, still figured prominently in the repertory.

One year after the premiere of *King Solomon*, Heiberg brought out *On the Vaudeville as a Dramatic Form* (1826), a book that not only caused an instant controversy but was still being referred to by Ibsen thirty years later. In this "dramaturgical investigation" Heiberg endeavored to demonstrate the generic superiority of the vaudeville, as a true Hegelian synthesis of the lyric and the dramatic. Unlike Scribe, who saw the genre as uncomplicated entertainment, he took care to emphasize its legitimacy as a dramatic form suitable for performance on the national stage. Hence, he insists, the musical element exists not as a pleasant diversion but as a device to focus audience attention on the dramatic situation:

> In musical plays, dialogue occurs in place of music; in vaudeville, music occurs in the place of dialogue, and this is why in the latter many familiar and easy melodies are used, for the attention of the spectators is not to be captivated by the musical element, but wholly

devoted to the dialogue, which is enhanced and clarified by familiar melodies, the recollection of which puts the spectators in the mood which the author requires in each particular instance.[12]

Once underway, this comic revival inspired a cascade of vaudevilles and light comedies in the Heiberg spirit. Hans Christian Andersen, also an active playwright throughout his career, made his debut as a dramatist in 1829 with *Kjærlighed paa Nicolai Taarn* (*Love on St. Nicholas Tower*), an irreverent vaudeville parody of heroic tragedy. A few months earlier, the theatre historian and stage director Thomas Overskou had added his share to the vaudeville rage with a realistic comedy of city types called *Østergade og Vestergade* (*East Side, West Side*). Two other Danish playwrights of importance were to carry the good-natured topical satire of the Heiberg vaudeville in quite different directions. Henrik Hertz, who began his career as a dramatist with a loosely sketched satire of amateur dramatics entitled *Herr Burchardt og hans Familie* (*Burchardt and Family*), soon went on to develop the richer and deeper comedic style that characterizes *Sparekassen* (*The Savings Bank*, 1836), his romantic character comedy about a family that mistakenly believes they have hit the jackpot in the lottery. In the forties Jens Christian Hostrup delighted audiences with a pair of plays that took their point of departure in the topical vaudeville tradition. *Genboerne* (*The Neighbours*, 1844) and *Eventyr paa Fodreisen* (*Adventures on Foot*, 1848) are festive comedies of Danish student life that combine occasional touches from the fairy tales of Andersen and the Viennese fairy-tale comedies of Raimund with the revue-like satire and idyllic lyricism of the vaudeville genre.

Across the Sound, the Heiberg revolution caught on quickly. Johan Erik Rydqvist carried the news of Heiberg's successes in the pages of his influential cultural weekly *Heimdall*, where a portion of the vaudeville manifesto also appeared in 1831.[13] This excerpt was evidently intended as a prolegomenon to the immediately ensuing launch of the vaudeville genre at Dramaten with *Les jolis soldats* (*Seven Girls in Uniform*), an amiable farce by Théaulon de Lambert and others that Heiberg had translated for the Danish Royal Theatre in 1827. It was, however, August Blanche who fully transplanted the techniques of Heiberg and Scribe to Swedish drama. With *Positivhataren* (*The Hurdy-Gurdy Hater*), a topical Stockholm comedy about an innkeeper called Propp who detests the sound of barrel organs, Blanche helped Anders Lindeberg to introduce his initial season at Nya teatern, the first private theatre to rebel against Dramaten's monopoly (in 1843).

Plate 29 Johanne Luise Heiberg as Sophie in her husband's vaudeville *No* (1836). As she tells Link, the sexton (Ludvig Phister), "no," she has her eye on Hammer (Johan Rudolph Waltz), who is waiting his turn in the open doorway. Pencil drawing by Edvard Lehmann.

Although Blanche was successful in other forms and styles, his true *métier* was folk comedy. *Ett resande teatersällskap* (*A Traveling Troupe*, 1848), his charming adaptation of a French vaudeville about the tribulations of a company of strolling players, remains a classic of its kind.

Above all, the vaudeville comedy was conceived by Heiberg as a text for performance, intended for a theatre where musical genres played an extremely important role and many of the performers were talented both as singers and actors. In its depiction of recognizable comic types, this kind of play harks back to the Holberg tradition of character comedy. Unlike Holberg, however, Heiberg had before him at the Royal Theatre an exceptional ensemble of accomplished comic actors, a new generation to complement the achi ..ents of Ryge and the Nielsens in the tragic mode. C. N. Rosenkilde brought to the comedies of both Holberg and

Heiberg a quiet, reflective humor, a faculty for improvisation, and a formidable sense of comic detail. His temperamental opposite was the great Holberg actor Ludvig Phister, whose debut in 1825 revealed a subtle malice that added a new dimension to the interpretation of classical and contemporary comedy. The stars in this imposing theatrical firmament paled, however, before the brilliance of Johanne Luise Heiberg, regarded by many of her contemporaries as unsurpassed by any other actress in Europe.

With her performance as the roguish and potentially amorous school-girl Trine Rar in her future husband's vaudeville *Aprilsnarrene* (*The April Fools*) in 1826, the thirteen-year-old Hanne Pätges became the toast of Copenhagen. Her triumph as Trine inspired Heiberg to tailor other roles in the same vein for her and her comic partner Rosenkilde, then three times her age. In 1827, the year in which the vaudeville fever reached its height, she was the flirtatious Christine in *Et Eventyr i Rosenborg Have* (*An Adventure in Rosenborg Gardens*) and the innocent young Caroline in *De Uadskillige* (*The Inseparables*), Heiberg's witty satire on the custom of pro-longed engagements. In these musical plays, her lack of a strong singing voice was more than compensated for by an extraordinary facial, physical, and vocal expressiveness. Out of these arch and lyrical ingenue roles she created, as the actor–historian Karl Mantzius puts it, "an ideal picture of a young girl such as she felt a young girl should be, and she did so with such an ingenious and confident grasp of contemporary taste that the real young girls – and the men – also felt that they should be such, and at last believed that they really were."[14] Edvard Brandes provides a penetrating glimpse of her technique in his description of her amalgamation of "inno-cent coquettishness and feminine self-assurance" as the nay-saying Sophie in Heiberg's *Nei* (*No*) in 1836: "Impossible to describe is the wonder of her entrance – her first lines, exchanged with Hammer [the suitor], her sparklingly modest and encouraging smile, the glance with which she caught sight of him in the half-open door all cast a spell that must have finished off both Hammer and the audience."[15]

Soon finished off himself, Heiberg made his poetic proposal of mar-riage in the form of the role of Agnete in *Elverhøi* (*Elves Hill*), the folksong-inspired romantic spectacle which, due in no small measure to an impressive musical score by Friedrich Kuhlau, has become Denmark's most frequently performed theatre work. This "national anthem in five acts" (to borrow Georg Brandes' phrase) was first performed on 6

November 1828 to mark the wedding of the popular crown prince, the future Frederik VII. The ruling poetic conceit in this complicated intrigue comedy is the legendary wisdom of King Christian IV who, during a hunting trip to the land of the elves, unravels a mystery of exchanged identities and thereby reunites two pairs of languishing lovers. Heiberg's basic aim, however, was to exploit the threefold resources of the Royal Theatre in drama, opera, and ballet for the simple purpose of patriotic celebration. In the spirit of the royal festivities of old, the facade of the playhouse was decorated to represent a temple illuminated by thousands of lamps. Inside, Heiberg's festive royal tribute found its perfect interpretation in Ryge's majestic Christian IV, Nielsen's dashing Ebbesen, the vassal prepared to defy this king to marry Agnete, Anna Nielsen's impetuous and strong-willed Elizabeth Munk, Rosenkilde's Bjørn Olufson, the comic keeper of secrets, and the changeling Agnete herself, played by the fifteen-year-old Hanne Pätges.

For almost four decades from her debut in 1826 to her early retirement in 1864, Johanne Luise Heiberg – known by royal permission as "Fru" Heiberg on the playbills, rather than the customary "Madame" – personified the neoclassic–romantic balance of opposites, the period's cult of wonder and strangeness coupled with unblemished idealization as the indispensable counterweight. Goethe's advice that the actor's presentation must "unite the true with the beautiful" touches the very core of Heibergian aesthetics, and it is a conviction often reiterated in Fru Heiberg's remarkable autobiography *A Life Relived in Memory*, which appeared the year after her death in 1890. "Is not all art beauty intensified?" she asks in this work.

> The human soul can be elevated both by King Lear's tormented outbursts on the heath and by the conflict of Per the Deacon and the bailiff [in *Erasmus Montanus*], for in both cases we are in the realm of fine art; but if art descends to the mere presentation of *reality*, from which the grosser elements have not been strained, we must declare with the poet: Das haben wir besser und bequemer zu Hause.[16]

In a review written near the end of her career, the novelist and critic Meir Goldschmidt came straight to the point when he remarked that "the principle she represents in our dramatic art is the ability and the desire to develop a personality in harmony with the beautiful, to achieve a perfect balance, to idealize Nature."[17]

The closely related romantic concern with harmoniously balanced poses and picturesque *tableaux vivants* on the stage was strongly influenced by the visual arts of painting and sculpture. In a review of her last important role as Maria Stuart in Schiller's tragedy, the Ibsen antagonist Clemens Petersen draws attention to a crucial aspect of Fru Heiberg's art, "a plasticity of movements and positions that reminds one of an ancient sculpture and a keen sense of unblemished formal beauty."[18] In attempting to describe the performance of Michael Wiehe as Mortimer in the same play, Edvard Brandes also fastens on one paramount feature: "He displayed so great a plastic beauty that, had one been able to make a series of plaster casts of him, they would have provided the most wonderful statues."[19] The many sketches and drawings of Fru Heiberg, whose performances with Wiehe constitute the apogee of romantic acting in Scandinavia, convey in themselves a forceful impression of the plastic eloquence and sculptural grace of which she was capable. This sense of expressive visual characterization was, in fact, evident from the start of her career, particularly in her performance as the mute Fenella in Scribe and Auber's spectacular opera *La Muette de Portici* in 1830. In this role, which had usually been reserved for a ballet dancer, the young Hanne Pätges conveyed, in the words of one observer

> not what Fenella said but how she heard, not what Fenella thought but how she felt, not what Fenella did but what she was like. This was what made Fenella a *character*, despite the fact that she is deprived of speech and action. Who can deny that Fenella was the character *who spoke most clearly*, whose inner self one was best able to comprehend.[20]

Working, moreover, within the prenaturalistic system of few rehearsals and no director, the process by which the actress prepared such a role was fiercely independent. She was convinced, she writes in her memoirs, that "it was not this or that pose, this or that pantomimic expression that caused the audience to be absorbed in my performance; it was because I succeeded in imprinting the role with a personality that fascinated them by its simplicity and truth." Given only two weeks to prepare the part, her characterization and interpretation were complete and unchangeable at the very first of the five stage rehearsals held for the production: "When the rehearsal was over, a number of actors came over to me and gave me good advice. But I said to myself: Talk all you want! I saw the chorus and the stagehands cry, and I'll stick to that."[21]

Plate 30 Hanne Pätges (later Fru Heiberg) as the mute heroine in Scribe and Auber's *La Muette de Portici* (1830). While her brother Masaniello fights for her honor, Fenella kneels to pray for his safety, all the while clutching and kissing the scarf she has been given by her seducer Alfonso. Costume sketch by Christian Bruun.

As Fenella in *La Muette de Portici*, the, strikingly exotic side of Fru Heiberg's personality had come to the fore, making her seem to Adam Oehlenschläger "magnificent in her fiery, passionate being, held in check only by grace."[22] Dark and foreign in her appearance, she excelled in evoking a piquant, mysterious, erotic impression delicately balanced by playfulness and lyrical naivety. The powerful sensual tension between fire and apparent nonchalance produced an emotionally charged doubleness that made the figures she created seem modern and "interesting" to her contemporaries. The latter term, a buzzword of the period, was defined by Heiberg in his review of Oehlenschläger's *Dina* (1842), in which the title role of the intense and psychologically complex *femme libre* was written for Fru Heiberg. Modern characterization, her husband argues in his essay, is "more strongly individuated," layered, and multidimensional, resulting in a personality with contradictory sides and hidden depths that cannot be articulated in words.

Such a personality was Fru Heiberg, or so she seemed to be, and the Danish playwrights of her day created a gallery of divided characters for her, in which psychological complexity included a strong undercurrent of the exotic, the passionate, and the demonic. Oehlenschläger gave her Dina, while Andersen enjoyed success for once when she played the passionate and unpredictable Cecilie in *Mulatten* (*The Mulatto*), his 1840 experiment in the exotic mode. Chief among these writers was Henrik Hertz, whose fascination with the ensemble playing of Fru Heiberg and Michael Wiehe inspired his best work for the stage. In his romantic verse drama *Kong Renés Datter* (*King René's Daughter*, 1845), the roles of the melancholy knight Tristan and Iolanthe, the blind princess whose sight is restored through the power of love, were tailored by Hertz to take full advantage of the rich pantomimic dimension of their art. Iolanthe's blindness, of which she is at first unaware, was evoked entirely by means of a graceful pattern of restrained gesticulation and movements (the blind, Fru Heiberg reasoned, "always move with a certain cautiousness, with their hands invariably slightly in front of their body"). She had also been Hertz's model for the sensual and demonic Ragnhild, the dark side of the female temperament in *Svend Dyrings Hus* (*The House of Svend Dyring*, 1837), a medievalized verse drama of runes and specters that bears a certain relationship to Ibsen's early saga dramas. Her most famous Hertz role was, however, the courtesan heroine of his *Ninon* (1848), another strong but divided spirit who discovers that her handsome young admirer (Michael Wiehe) is none other than her own son. Even Georg Brandes, otherwise no advocate of Fru Heiberg, was outspoken in his praise of her performance as the "apotheosis" of idealized passion, the embodiment of "that beauty which can never age, that nobility which can never be lost, that superior womanly intelligence which is able to guide no less than the earth itself with a light and confident hand."[23]

As one might expect, her conception of dramatic character as an amalgamation of contradictory tendencies and her espousal of that "enchanting variety" that the romantics saw as the reality of nature, inevitably drew Fru Heiberg to Shakespeare. As a young actress of fifteen, her appealing lyrical ability had made her a memorable Juliet. When she returned to this part almost twenty years later, however, her more mature and intense reflection on feminine youthfulness revealed a new dimension of her art. Her performance in the 1847 production of *Romeo and Juliet* stirred Kierkegaard, who perhaps best of all understood the demonic element in her being, to pay tribute to her unconventional achievement in *Crisis in the Life of an Actress*:

> The gallery wishes to see Miss Juliet, a devilishly pretty and damned lively girl of eighteen years, who plays at Juliet or passes herself off as Juliet, while the gallery is diverted by the thought that it is really Miss N. N. Therefore the gallery can naturally never get into its head that precisely in order to *portray* Juliet it is essential that an actress possess a distance in age from Juliet.[24]

The comic heroines Fru Heiberg played during these years in Sille Beyer's loose adaptations of *Twelfth Night* (1847), *As You Like It* (1849), *All's Well that Ends Well* (1850), and *Love's Labour's Lost* (1853) were characterized by emotional complexity and feather-light transitions from one mood to another. Typically, she viewed a character such as Helena in *All's Well* as a blend of contradictions "which form a perspective, thus making the picture interesting and fascinating." A similarly romantic, Tieck-inspired attitude governed her Ophelia, whom she saw not as an innocent, mistreated child but as "a repressed and passionate nature whose soul is torn apart when she believes herself deserted by the one she loves."[25] In the *Hamlet* production of 1851, however, her intense dynamism seemed misplaced beside the understated Hamlet of Frederik Høedt, a champion of the new realism and an avowed enemy of the House of Heiberg.

It was, above all, in the role of Lady Macbeth that Fru Heiberg achieved acclaim as a Shakespearean character actress, in a highly individualized performance that crystallized the neoclassic/romantic aesthetic upon which her art depended. The spirit of reconciliation, an indispensable element in Heiberg's aesthetic of the ideal, was thus the informing essence of her unconventional interpretation. Anna Nielsen, her rival and predecessor in the part, had followed established tradition in portraying Lady Macbeth as an older and consciously evil figure, "a passionless, icy, calculating yet imposing woman with an ability to make decisions, a power of will, a control even in the most fearful situations."[26] When Fru Heiberg was persuaded to take over the role in 1860, four years after Anna

Nielsen's death, she was convinced that an entirely different approach was required by the text. Her Lady defied tradition as a younger, attractive, fiery creature, recently married and ecstatic with ambition from the outset of the play. Her underlying attitude toward Macbeth and his wife as "beginners in sin" rather than "hardened criminals," gave her the key to their essential humanity. As such, the powerful emotional upheaval that occurred in Fru Heiberg's portrayal immediately after the murder of Duncan was a crucial transition that underscored this amelioristic view of her character. "From the moment she rushes from the bloody chamber, the transformation is visible," she writes in her painstaking analysis of the role. "Ecstasy has now given way to the most extreme terror."[27] Writing in *Fædrelandet* (16 January 1860) Clemens Petersen provided a vivid description of the visual impact of this moment: "Her eyes are flaming and rolling wildly, without the ability to focus anywhere, her face is frozen in horror, her whole figure totters."

In a quasi-religious interpretation intended, as it were, to give Lady Macbeth a soul, the primary emphasis was laid not on the guilt of the character but on her overwhelming suffering. When the audience caught its last glimpse of her in the sleepwalking scene, she was already in the hell of her own spiritual torment. "The three famous sighs which issue from her chilled soul during the sleepwalker scene" must, the actress insists, "sound like its trembling prayer for eternal mercy and forgiveness." In performance, the effect of this scene was said to have been so intense that it "held the spectators under an almost demonic spell."[28] Carefully prepared mimetic expressiveness was, as always, the principal weapon in Fru Heiberg's arsenal. A technique, perfected by her as the blind Iolanthe in *King René's Daughter*, of staring vacantly into space without moving her pupils or changing her focus was conjoined with a laboriously acquired ability to utter words without moving the lips or facial muscles. The result was a harrowing pantomimic portrayal of inner spiritual torment. "She wanders forth with stiffened limbs, her face is asleep and expressionless, even the lips remain motionless, so that her words and sighs reverberate as from a grave," recorded Clemens Petersen. "She plays [the scene] with a richness, truth, and confidence of artistic expression that will bring this sight to mind, with all its ghostly magic, long after the smile has faded from many another memory that we had carried with us of her art."

Despite the stature of this achievement, the 1860 *Macbeth* came to be seen only four times. With the sudden death of N. P. Nielsen, who played

Macbeth, in March of that year, the play was taken off and disappeared from the repertory until the close of the century. When Johan Ludvig Heiberg's death followed in August, an era in Danish arts and letters ended. A new age was on the horizon, and the spirit of revolt was already abroad in Scandinavia, in political and social life as in theatre. Disillusioned and brought to question the very justification of her art, Johanne Luise Heiberg appeared for the last time, with no warning that it was her farewell performance, as Elizabeth Munk in *Elves Hill* on 2 June 1864.

The rise of the director

Heiberg's stormy management of the Royal Theatre during the years from 1849 to 1856 marked its transformation from a royal to a democratic state theatre under the provisions of the newly adopted Danish constitution. His conservative regime had resisted both the early plays of Ibsen and Bjørnson and the "raw and ugly" side of Shakespeare ("Melpomene's dagger transformed into a butcher's knife"). What is more, it also sought in vain to stifle the demands for a greater verisimilitude in acting and staging being raised by Frederik Høedt and his new convert, Michael Wiehe. One immediate outcome of this latter rejection was the famous season of 1855/6 at the Christiansborg Court Theatre, where the rebels banded together to stage modern French comedies under the aegis of Hans Wilhelm Lange. This astute actor–manager's Casino Theatre had become the first private playhouse in Copenhagen in 1848, and his subsequent founding of a second private theatre, Folketeatret, in 1857 conclusively captured a growing new audience for folk theatre and family theatre. Under his management at the Court Theatre, meanwhile, the small impromptu company led by Høedt "spoke like people" (Wiehe's phrase) as they performed Augier and his lesser French contemporaries in settings designed to resemble actual rooms with real furniture. Under Høedt's guidance, Edvard Brandes later declared, "dialogue becomes real conversation" and "even the furnishings and the set seem to perform roles of their own."[29] The reformer shocked his audiences with such gestures of defiance as turning his back to them or puffing on a lighted cigar on stage. Although in one sense Fru Heiberg's penetrating psychological role interpretations point forward to the new modernism, she had no sympathy at all for the coarser aspects of Høedt's "natural" acting: "One sees actors make their entrance with the dirt from the street on their boots because that is so true and is taken from life. They cough, sneeze, blow their noses, scratch their heads, spit across the boards of the floor, all in reverence to truth and nature." It is too simplistic, however, to put her response down to the inability of the "old school" to accept renewal. Rather, the gist of Fru Heiberg's objection (that such is "not the kind of truth that rises to art") calls to mind, for example, Strindberg's unequivocal rejection of the coarser photographic realism which "includes everything, even the grain of dust on the lens of the camera" and "which holds that art merely consists of drawing a piece of nature in a natural way."[30]

Høedt's chief importance is as an early harbinger of the emergence in Scandinavia of a director in the modern sense, as a creative artist and coordinator of all aspects of the mise-en-scène. Another such pioneer was August Bournonville, who with Ludvig Josephson introduced a more disciplined style of production to the Swedish theatre in the 1860s. In an article entitled "On Stage Direction," published in *Berlingske Tidende* (30 January 1858) as part of a lively newspaper debate on the subject, the ballet-master argued that the true function of the director was to supply what he called "the leading thought" in a production, the analytical framework in harmony with which the positions and moves of the actors must be calculated. He must, Bournonville continues, be able to comprehend and influence each individual role so he "can create an ensemble, not only in the actors' blocking but also in the dialogue, so that continuity is achieved and the performance is rounded into a true artistic whole." When Høedt rejoined the Royal Theatre as its stage director in 1858, his aim was to put such a program into practice. In an effort to improve the quality of ensemble playing, he increased the number of rehearsals sharply (nineteen were held, for instance, for his production of Theodore Barrière's well-made play *Les faux bonshommes* in 1860). Both practice and theory were, however, still ruled by the principles and conventions of the prenaturalistic theatre, in which actors functioned as sovereign artisans in the preparation of their roles. Even Harald Christensen, the theatre's manager and a staunch proponent of the director's influence, hastened to add that "the larger the number of great artists working together, the more unnecessary or at least less appropriate such an influence would be."[31]

The fundamentals had not changed when Johanne Luise Heiberg began her own seven-year term as resident stage director at the Royal Theatre in 1867. "In their need they were forced to turn to *a woman*," Bournonville sneered in italics:

But how strange it was to see this ingenious actress, now an old woman, whose grace and amiability had become the hallmarks of her artistic demeanor, going about giving orders with the mien of an official and a voice which had none of the magic that in an earlier day had so enchanted lovers of art. . . . [I]f anyone else had allowed himself such balletic groupings and arrangements as those that were all too frequently to be found, he would have been severely castigated by the critics.[32]

Apart from its negative usefulness as a contradiction of assertions made by others that Fru Heiberg did not always direct or even attend her rehearsals, Bournonville's statement is redolent with a condescension that still seems to color the comments of some later historians about her "limitations" as a director. In technical terms, she remained as limited by the system within which she worked as Høedt had been. However, her vision as a director extended far beyond the arid mechanical reality of the *pièce bien faîte*, embracing as it did a range of plays that extended from *The Winter's Tale* and *The Merchant of Venice* to major new plays by Bjørnson and Ibsen. On balance, the surviving evidence indicates that she approached the mise-en-scène of a production with the same methodical care that had characterized her earlier analyses of her roles.

It is often assumed that Fru Heiberg's support for Ibsen and Bjørnstjerne Bjørnson was an attempt on her part to redress the wrong done by Heiberg in rejecting these writers. The available evidence does not, however, support such a view. The situation was now very different, and Fru Heiberg made no effort to return to the plays previously refused by her husband, Ibsen's *Hærmændene paa Helgeland* (*The Vikings of Helgeland*) and Bjørnson's *Halte-Hulda* (*Limping Hulda*). Instead, she was particularly interested in the newer works by these dramatists. Influenced by the widespread contemporary enthusiasm for "the young Norway," she cultivated Norwegian literature and drama vigorously. She was thus an active force in the introduction of the first modern Scandinavian problem play, Bjørnson's *De Nygifte* (*The Newly Married*), which she directed at the Royal Theatre in 1865. Its success was due, she later observed, to the fact that "it did not deal with the external conflicts of *salon* life but with the inner struggles of the soul."[33] Two years later she staged Bjørnson's *Maria Stuart in Scotland*, a play she found more compelling than Schiller's drama because it traced the source of Maria's tragedy to "the flood of eroticism suffusing her whole being."

Ibsen was introduced on the Royal Theatre stage with Fru Heiberg's production of *De Unges Forbund* (*The League of Youth*) on 16 February 1870, four months after the world premiere of the play in Christiania. Scribean in its tight construction, Ibsen's newest work also revealed that serious undercurrent which both she and Heiberg considered the *sine qua non* of the new modernism. When both the Royal Theatre's censor and its manager rejected the play, she rushed to defend it: "It is a vigorous satire of all the political charlatans and tricksters swarming about us, distinguished by characters consistently drawn, and with deep psychological background," she maintained. "Such serious, psychological genre vignettes are the signposts of the new drama; everything in literature points in this direction."[34] Less than a year after her considerable success with *The League of Youth*, she returned to Ibsen with a production of *Kongs-Emnerne* (*The Pretenders*) that remains a milestone in her directing career. She had read Ibsen's expansive historical drama shortly after its publication in 1863 and had been deeply impressed by its technical skill – though her enthusiasm was not as glowing as that which she reserved for *Kjærlighedens Komedie* (*Love's Comedy*), in the dark undertone of which she recognized the harsh voice of truth. When she returned to *The Pretenders* as a director, her production (11 January 1871) brought the play and its author to the attention of a much broader and more cosmopolitan public than ever before. In order to accommodate the play's ten separate changes of scene, Valdemar Gyllich was engaged to design a cluster of atmospheric medieval settings that were, in turn, deftly combined with a number of Nordic and "gothic" decors borrowed from the older repertory.

The scene changes themselves, particularly the more difficult ones occurring within a single act of the play, were felt by Fru Heiberg to disrupt the flow of the action, thereby dissipating dramatic tension. "In every true work of art each act is a unit, carefully measured by the author, and it is never to his advantage when this unity is broken in the middle," she writes in her memoirs. She was determined to avoid "the unjustifiable expedient which has found acceptance in all foreign theatres" of lowering a front curtain to conceal such changes, for then "the suspense of the action is relaxed, leaving the spectator completely confused about which scene concludes the act and which does not." On the other hand, she was equally unwilling to shatter the illusion by letting the audience "watch walls, trees, and other paraphernalia of the decor glide down helter-skelter from the sky." In the end she devised a system of her own, subsequently adopted as standard practice at the Royal Theatre, of blackouts for each scene change. "When darkness is introduced . . . the audience's attention is fixed upon what will next appear to them when the darkness is again dispelled, and the illusion is maintained," she comments, arguing shrewdly that "a setting never makes a greater impact than at the moment when darkness is replaced by light."[35]

Fru Heiberg's promptbook for *The Pretenders* survives as evidence of her concept and method. Alert to the theatrical potential of the powerful closing scene, she had the body of the slain Skule, the anti-Aladdin who is destroyed by his own self-doubt, borne onstage by his men before the final curtain fell, rather than risking an anticlimax or even laughter by leaving his corpse lying on the doorstep outside, as the stage directions indicate, while the final lines are spoken about him. Characteristically, the director also persuaded Ibsen to end the play by assigning an earlier statement by Sigrid about her brother ("Skule Baardsson comes home, a penitent, from his lawless journey upon earth") to the triumphant Haakon. This choice thereby eliminated the victor's own problematic closing reference to Skule as "God's stepchild on earth" – for in Fru Heiberg's world, if not in Ibsen's, a merciful and all-loving God had no stepchildren on his green earth.

A promptbook from this period will, of course, yield little or no information about the individual role interpretations and performances themselves. Clearly the most striking of these was the performance of the young Emil Poulsen, soon to become one of the foremost Ibsen actors of his generation, in the role of the toothless manipulator and schemer Bishop Nikolas. "It seemed," writes Edvard Brandes in his vivid analysis of Poulsen's almost legendary interpretation of this role, "that all the forces of genius and the demonical power that Bishop Nikolas possesses were concentrated in his fierce, frightening glance." His wild eyes "searched the facial expression of every speaker as though they sought to peer into his very soul." Every intonation of his labored speech (marked by "a constant rising and falling which created the impression that the Bishop spoke only with the utmost effort"), every movement of his expressive countenance and stooped, shrunken figure was a remorseless reminder of the hatred that Poulsen conceived to be the ruling force in Nikolas' character. "Thus, a perpetual smile – sometimes bitter and caustic, sometimes scornful, sometimes brilliant with demonic joy – played about his mouth." This cynical disdain suffused the Bishop's face "every time the other characters mentioned anything which, for them, belonged to what is noble and sacred."[36]

When the time came for this actor's son, Johannes Poulsen, to recreate the same role in his 1926 production of the play, there is little doubt that his performance – even in the midst of the abstract scenography created by Edward Gordon Craig – continued to bear the stamp of the graphic and faceted emotional realism ("the distinctly naturalistic bent," Brandes called it) of his father's approach.

Effectively staged and capably acted, *The Pretenders* moved Royal Theatre audiences as no tragic drama had since Oehlenschläger's *Hakon Jarl* sixty-four years before. Ibsen was keenly aware of his debt to Johanne Luise Heiberg, and her production of his play was the ostensible occasion for his "Rhymed Letter to Fru Heiberg," considered by Brandes "one of the finest works of art he has produced." In fact, however, the true inspiration for this lovely poetic epistle was "a greater, shining memory":

> the memory of a beauty-filled
> festive spell,
> the memory of a row of hours
> veiled in time,
> when first I saw you glide – sublime,
> jeweled, with grace and truth of heart –
> through the wonderland of art.
> This sight my debt in me instilled.

Ibsen had his first glimpse of the Heibergian "wonderland of art" during a study trip to observe theatre in Copenhagen and Dresden in 1852. It is fair to say that the plays and productions he saw at the Danish Royal Theatre exerted a strong influence on his future development. Choosing poetry rather than prose for his tribute ("prose is for ideas, / verse for visions") he conjures up the best roles of Scandinavia's greatest actress (not all of which he could have seen). Agnete, Dina, Iolanthe, Ragnhild, and Ophelia are pictured by the poet as a fleet of proud clipper ships gliding with fluttering ensigns down through the waters of the Sound. It is, in Ibsen's view, the protean, "myth-creating" capacity of the performer that matters most. The ability

> to bend
> your own content, spiritual, rich,
> to whatever form the common eye
> requires for its own poetry

ensures a securer immortality for her than for "the rest of us":

> color-, form-, and word-poets,
> architects,
> and whatever else we're called

who may at any time fall victim to interpretational obsolesence. No mean literary stylist herself, Fru Heiberg responded with a charmingly theatrical acknowledgment of her own for "the song of a seer about me and to me . . . about a long-forgotten time upon which I look back as a ghost looks back at a finished, lived-out life, with its struggles, its sorrows, but also with its joys, its triumphs, with the question whether the latter were deserved, whether they rightfully belonged to me."[37]

2 PIONEERS OF MODERN AND POSTMODERN THEATRE

6 Ibsen's Norway

The story of the premodern theatre in Ibsen's Norway is, to a great extent, that of its search for and eventual achievement of an artistic identity and integrity of its own. Its principal priority was the development of a dramatic repertory, a trained body of theatre professionals, and an authentic theatrical culture that could give voice to Norwegian traditions and aspirations. This country's long political and cultural association with Denmark, solidified by a relationship that dated from the Union of Kalmar in 1397, had lasted for more than four centuries, but nationalists of every stripe had now begun to view the old Danish ties as the most serious impediment to the achievement of nationhood. New political freedom was achieved in 1814, when Denmark was forced to pay the price for its ill-advised and casual alliance with Napoleon by ceding Norway to the Swedish king as a sovereign territory. Artistically as well as socially and politically, the period that followed the Treaty of Kiel was one of burning patriotic fervor and cultural self-assertion. Apart from the annexation of Holberg (who was born in Bergen), the Norwegian nationalists wanted nothing to do with the established figures, language, and tastes of the so-called Danish Period. Thus, the founding of a new Norwegian theatre was in every sense a pioneering proposition. The first important steps in this direction were the establishment of permanent theatre buildings and companies of professional actors in the early nineteenth century. With the fostering of playhouses, performers, and audiences responsive to native writing, the quickening of theatrical activity taking place at this time set the stage for the simultaneous appearance of Norway's two most significant modern playwrights, Bjørnstjerne Bjørnson (1832–1910) and Henrik Ibsen (1828–1906).

Prior to this time, professional theatre in Norway was confined to visits by foreign troupes of uneven merit, performing a bill of fare that ranged from gymnastics, weight lifting, ropedancing, and magic tricks to productions of actual plays. Side by side with these itinerant professionals, amateur dramatic societies catering to a more select public began to spring up and soon became the main impetus toward the development of an authentic theatre culture. These relatively small societies consisted of a few hundred members, each of whom was expected to participate actively in one or more of the productions shown to the membership at large. The oldest of these clubs was founded in the capital Christiania (later called Kristiania and then Oslo) as early as 1780. During the 1780s and 1790s the vogue spread to many other small towns dotted across the rugged Norwegian landscape. The performances of these enthusiastic amateurs included modern vaudevilles, bourgeois dramas, and light comedies – in fact, a repertory inspired by and in most cases acquired from the Royal Theatre in Copenhagen. In addition to developing a large potential audience of enlightened playgoers, these clubs were also frequently responsible for the building of well-equipped local theatres. Comediehuset in Bergen, apparently the first permanent theatre in Norway, was opened in this manner by the local dramatic society on 3 December 1800. Three years later Trondheim also acquired a dramatic society and a theatre of its own, evidently semipublic in nature. As it happened, however, it was the playhouse in Bergen that was destined to occupy a unique place in the history of Norwegian theatre. As the first home of Det Norske Teater from 1849 to 1863, it became the bastion of the national theatre movement spearheaded in Bergen by the dynamic and popular violin virtuoso Ole Bull. It was here during the 1850s that Johannes Brun began his illustrious acting career and both Ibsen and Bjørnson gained their initial experience in practical theatre. When it reopened in 1876 as The National Stage, Bergen's original playhouse had a strong historical claim to that title.

The founding of Det Norske Teater in Bergen, the signpost of a new era in Norwegian theatre art, confirmed a broader shift of emphasis from amateur to professional theatre that had been underway for several decades. The importance of the private dramatic societies had begun to decrease after the mid-1820s, as Danish and a few Swedish companies of professional players started to tour the country more extensively. At the same time, the Swedish-born dancing-master and impresario Johan Peter Strömberg realized a cherished dream when he opened Christiania Theatre, the capital's first public playhouse with a permanent company, on 30 January 1827. The members of Strömberg's Norwegian company of seven actors and three actresses were recruited from among the pupils in a theatre school he had founded two years earlier, as the first of its kind in Norway. In addition to its regular company, Christiania Theatre boasted a small ballet corps, also drawn from among Strömberg's pupils, and a modest orchestra. Criticism of the artistic standards represented by this assembly of local talent was soon raised, however, and Strömberg was obliged to rely for the rest of his management on more accomplished actors imported from Denmark.

The keynote for future developments was thereby sounded. Trained Danish professionals playing a repertory that reflected their own tastes continued to dominate Christiania Theatre for several decades to come – much to the disgust of activists like the young poet Henrik Wergeland, who used every opportunity to blast the activities of "the capital's Danish theatre." In the eyes of many, it is true, Danish performers were not viewed at this time as foreigners in Norway, any more than Danish literature and culture were so regarded. When, for example, Oehlenschläger visited the country in 1833 he was, Tharald Blanc emphasizes in his history of Christiania Theatre, "surely not without justification, celebrated as the foremost spokesman for the common spiritual interests of both nations," seconded closely by J. L. Heiberg, "whose vaudevilles had overjoyed all of Copenhagen and were bound to exert a similar effect on an audience separated by only half a generation from the time when life in the Copenhagen environment seemed as homelike as its own, or even more so."[1] Others, however, would vehemently agree with Bjørnson that "on the stage a language is still to be heard which, although perhaps not foreign, we are nevertheless unable to acquire as our own, and in plays and vaudevilles a life is depicted which, while not alien, is nevertheless not the life experienced in its characteristics and singularities by the Norwegian people."[2]

The makeshift theatre built for Strömberg eventually burned down in 1835, but the theatre company he had started remained active. After an interval of two years, during which the Danish actors were housed in the playhouse of the local dramatic society, a handsome new theatre building opened on Christiania's Bank Square in the autumn of 1837. The Danish-born architect for the project, Christian Henrik Grosch, collaborated from the outset with his former teacher Troels Lund, who was not only a noted scene painter but also an experienced hand at theatre design and equipment. The result of this partnership was a gracious and functional playhouse that stood until 1899, when it was replaced by the present National

Theatre. Throughout the nineteenth century this was the stage which, more than any other, set the standard for theatrical art in Norway. In itself, the choice of its opening production signaled Christiania Theatre's ambition to present lavish romantic spectacles in the grand manner of the national stages in Copenhagen and Stockholm. Andreas Munch's Nordic saga drama *Kong Sverres Ungdom* (*King Sverre's Youth*) was selected from among eleven entries in a competition for the best play with which to inaugurate the new building. Munch's work, actually a chain of dramatic vignettes featuring picturesque twelfth-century settings and atmospheric historical tableaux, immediately faced the new theatre with technical demands it found difficult to satisfy. Wergeland's *Campbellerne* (*The Campbells*), the runner-up in the playwriting contest, was no easier. This tale, of a son returned from a distant land, again aimed its appeal at the romantic theatre's preoccupation with bygone ages, faraway places, and exotic customs on the stage. In Wergeland's work the first act featured a picturesque East Indian environment, embellished with orientally flavored music and an intermezzo of bayadère dancing. As a contrast, the second act then transported the audience to a Scottish village whose ethnographic appeal was enhanced by effects such as the appearance in a closing tableau of "a number of Campbell clansmen in national costumes." In general, it is difficult to distinguish aesthetic outrage from political discontent in the riots that accompanied the production of this curious spectacle.

Critical complaints persisted throughout the theatre's salad days, but so did its determination. At first, technical control was unsteady in a wide range of production areas. Thus, for example, "dancing houses, flowing backdrops . . . long intervals with no one on stage . . . tasteless rose-red columns in an enormous yellowish marble hall, and the usual unfortunate bolt of lightning that kills the hero, but which in this case is represented by a kind of kite trailing a slow train of sparks after it" were but some of the problems that beset a performance of Mozart's *Don Giovanni*, staged in the face of popular opposition to the opera's "frivolity" in 1838.[3] Production problems such as these are hardly surprising, moreover, when seen in the light of the sheer number of productions put on by Christiania Theatre in its efforts to draw audiences in a town of fewer than 40,000 inhabitants. Records kept of its rehearsals and performances indicate that, in its first season of operation, the new theatre presented 101 performances of some sixty different titles (including short plays and afterpieces) in the course of an eight-month period. French drama, mainly Scribean, pre-

Plate 31 Medieval Norway reconstructed in nineteenth-century scenography: P. F. Wergmann's set design for the first act of Munch's verse tragedy *Duke Skule* (Christiania Theatre, 1863). The decor represents the courtyard of the palace at Nidaros, with a view of the great cathedral in the distance.

dominated with thirty titles; Denmark came next with eighteen plays; German works accounted for ten titles; and new Norwegian writing was represented by the two plays already mentioned.

In an effort to secure suitable scenery for this ambitious repertory, the directors of Christiania Theatre entrusted Troels Lund, as an expert thoroughly acquainted with the newest methods and styles of Continental stagecraft, with the task of furnishing the new playhouse with a total of fourteen stock utility settings. These ranged from a mountainous region, a wood, a garden, and a street to at least eight different comedy interiors needed to accommodate the heavy emphasis on the drawing-room drama of Scribe and Co. Among the sets he supplied, the progressively minded Lund included a closed room, or box set, with real walls and ceiling. In this and other respects, the Christiania Theatre stage was as completely up-to-date as any in Scandinavia, equipped with triple wing chariots in all five wing positions and otherwise designed "to satisfy any demand that can reasonably be made to complete theatre machinery."[4] Although Lund's active association with the theatre in Christiania ended in 1838, his basic stock of reusable decors lived on, supplemented from time to time by whatever new additions might be required, until by the 1840s they had become "old, oil-bespattered, wrinkled, and worn-out rooms and woodlands."[5] Peter Frederik Wergmann, Lund's successor and the true father of scene design in Norway, introduced a fresh and robust style of scenography, steeped in the atmospherics of national romanticism found in the paintings of J. C. Dahl and his contemporaries. During the middle decades of the century Wergmann brought the buildings and landscapes of an idealized Norway to the Christiania stage in such plays as Henrik Bjerregaard's *Fjeldeventyret* (*The Mountain Adventure*), Andreas Munch's *Hertug Skule* (*Duke Skule*), Bjørnson's *Mellem slagene* (*Between the Battles*), and Ibsen's *The Pretenders*. For a typical production of *Axel and Valborg* in this style in 1848, Wergmann's pupil and collaborator Wilhelm Krogh actually turned to an archeological reconstruction (with which Dahl was, in fact, connected) of the ancient cathedral at Nidaros for his design concept.

Throughout its early years, Christiania Theatre remained a flashpoint in the heated ideological struggle that raged between ardent Norwegian nationalists, led by the fiery Henrik Werggeland, and believers in the higher standard of Danish acting and writing, eloquently championed by J. S. Welhaven. At first, little of a practical kind had seemed to come from this acrimonious clash. Danish traditions continued to dominate the theatre, and (perhaps as a consequence) very little drama of significance was written by Norwegians. Although a number of original plays were submitted to Christiania Theatre, few new works were performed and even fewer enjoyed success. Indicative of the general situation is the fact that when Ibsen's first play, *Catiline*, appeared in print in 1850 (under the Vikingish pseudonym Brunjolf Bjarme), it was the first Norwegian drama to be published in seven years.

Around 1850, however, with the tide of nationalist feeling again at its height, important changes were finally beginning to reshape the theatre in Norway. The first professional Norwegian company was launched by Ole Bull in Bergen with the production (2 January 1850) of "our" Holberg's *The Weathercock*, in which Johannes Brun, destined to become Norway's first great star, sparkled as the roguish servant Henrik. In that same year, Christiania Theatre accepted its first Norwegian actresses, Gyda Klingenberg and Laura Svendsen – who as Laura Gundersen would remain a mainstay of the company for almost fifty years. In 1852 the capital moved to follow Bergen's lead with the founding of a new theatre staffed exclusively by Norwegian actors. Known for most of its ten-year existence as Kristiania norske teater, it was managed by Ibsen from 1857 until its disappearance in 1862. It was, however, the gates of Christiania Theatre itself, the citadel of foreign domination, that Bjørnstjerne Bjørnson was determined to storm.

Theatre and the nationalist cause

The elder Bjørnson, like many revolutionaries before and after him, understood the power of the theatre as a political force in the struggle for national identity. He, not Ibsen, contributed most significantly to the opening of new directions in Norwegian theatre, and he, next to Ibsen and Strindberg, was most responsible for the rise of Scandinavian drama to world prominence during the latter part of the nineteenth century. A popular leader, lecturer, journalist, novelist, director, and theatre manager as well as a playwright, Bjørnson started out, as Ibsen did, in the midst of the vogue of Nordic romanticism and historicism that flourished at mid-century. He made his debut as a dramatist at Christiania Theatre in 1857 with *Between the Battles*, an effective one-acter set in a moment of peace during a bloody twelfth-century civil war. A Wergmann drawing of a rustic log-house interior with solid walls and ceiling is in all likelihood his design for the "frugal little chamber with a lighted fire" in which the action takes place. Two subsequent saga dramas, *Limping Hulda* (1858) and *Kong Sverre* (staged by Ibsen at Kristiania norske teater in 1861), also reflected the growing popular interest in national history, folklore, and local landscapes. Their impact was not nearly as great, however, as that created in 1862 by the verse trilogy *Sigurd Slembe* (*Sigurd the Bastard*), a compelling pilgrimage drama that attracted a legion of admirers, including Ibsen, and left its mark on both the theme and characterizations of *The Pretenders*.

An entirely different aspect of Bjørnson's campaign to introduce recognizably Norwegian characters and speech on the stage is represented by his plays depicting contemporary society and social problems ("the spirit of the time as it is manifested in life's conflicts," as he put it in 1851). The first of these problem plays, *The Newly Married*, gained Bjørnson a much wider reputation as a dramatist when it was produced simultaneously in Copenhagen, Stockholm, and Christiania in 1865. This play, the subject of which is a young married couple's period of adjustment, emphasizes not the Ibsenian liberation of the woman but the dilemma of the man, who is treated, as Bjørnson expressed it in a phrase that was to catch on, like a doll. Throughout his career this director–dramatist was often a step ahead

Plate 32 An undated Wergmann design for a rustic log-house with an open fire, in all probability intended as the setting for Bjørnson's *Between the Battles*, staged at Christiania Theatre in 1857.

of Ibsen, in the sense that he was more directly attuned to contemporary currents in criticism and culture. In his theatre criticism from the 1850s, he had already given voice to the demand for a drama more responsive to contemporary modes of thought. Pointing to Augier, Musset, and Dumas *fils* as better models than Scribe, he called for a reevaluation of the theatre and its goals. "People are delving more deeply into human nature from every angle, in science as well as in art," he wrote in 1855. "We investigate each minute trait, we dissect and analyse . . . the smallest flower, the tiniest insect. . . . And in art this current of naturalism reveals itself in theatrical terms in a strong demand for individualization."[6] For Bjørnson as for an entire new generation of early modernists in Scandinavia, the enemy was not only romanticism, with its emphasis on beauty and ideality, but also the Scribean well-made play, with its involved complications, startling reversals, and improbable distortions of human psychology. Instead, Bjørnson proposed to introduce "truth" in the theatre, by means of a drama in which the characters are "no longer marionettes moved by invisible strings but human beings, men and women with the pain of life on their faces."[7]

Bjørnson's advocacy of a theatre that was at once artistically sound and conscious of its national identity, inspired not only his critical and dramatic writing but also his practical activities as a director and a theatre manager. As a young man of twenty-five, he gained his early experience in practical theatre at the new Norwegian Theatre in Bergen, where he succeeded Ibsen as artistic director in 1857. One of the first plays he staged during his season and a half at Bull's financially troubled theatre was Christian Momsen's *Gudbrandsdølerne* (*The Folk of Gudbrandsdal*), a patriotic spectacle about a seventeenth-century Norwegian victory that suitably expressed Bjørnson's own nationalist sentiments. However, his later term as artistic director at Christiania Theatre for two and a half seasons from 1865 to 1867 was a period of far greater significance for Norwegian stage history. During these years he presented an impressive range of contemporary Norwegian and Danish plays, including Ibsen's *Gildet på Solhaug* (*The Feast at Solhaug*) and *The Pretenders*, and his own *Sigurd the Bastard*, *Limping Hulda*, *The Newly Married*, and *Maria Stuart*. Nor was his repertory limited to Nordic drama. The French works he put on ranged from Molière to Musset, and his productions of Shakespeare, while by no means the first in Norway, showed Christiania audiences – or at least tried to show them – a new and more modern style of Shakespearean mise-en-scène, inspired by the work of Ludvig Tieck in the German theatre.

Particularly in these Shakespearean productions, Bjørnson aspired to incorporate the new European advances in stage composition and groupings exemplified, for instance, in Franz v. Dingelstedt's famed performances in Munich in the fifties, in particular his Tieck-inspired productions of Sophocles and Shakespeare. That Bjørnson was not really successful in this endeavor can perhaps be attributed not least to the absence of a designer and a trained acting ensemble compatible with these aspirations. In *A Midsummer-Night's Dream*, which he staged in April 1865 in Oehlenschläger's translation and with the customary Mendelssohn score, he introduced a rather baffled Christiania public to the radically simplified concept ("the light and natural arrangement," as he called it) adopted by Tieck in his original German production. By drastically reducing the heavy pictorialism and multiple changes of scene that usually accompanied performances of Shakespeare in Scandinavia (or in England) at this time, Bjørnson's method allowed, as he maintained, "the text to speak with its own power, neither submerged by inventiveness nor pushed aside by moveable scenery." For those who objected to the lack of pictorial and visual effects and the poverty of the lighting in his production, the director had a ready reply: "It takes a truly petty soul to sit and worry about the moon while Shakespeare speaks to us through Oehlenschläger's mouth and Mendelssohn adds the music."[8]

As a director, Bjørnson seems to have possessed an extraordinary ability to influence and inspire his actors, thereby imprinting his ideas (his "ruling thought," Bournonville would call it) on the overall performance. "He has," Clemens Petersen remarked, "an incredible, almost magical ability, even during a walk down the street, to paint a character in such a way that it ends up walking right alongside you."[9] Surely the best-known description of his directorial method is found in the tribute paid by Lucie Wolf, a longtime veteran of Norwegian theatre who had acted under both Ibsen and Bjørnson – and greatly preferred the latter. "Working with Bjørnson was a real feast," Wolf recalled in 1898. "He did not show us, literally, how we should perform our parts, he just talked with us; but in such a way that it was as if he lifted a veil, so that we could see clearly and feel that his approach to the part and no other was right. He proved so clearly that such and such a character said this, that, or the other in such and such a way because of the person's individual nature."[10] It is well to bear in mind that this was written as a polemical demonstration of the failure of the theatrical establishment in Norway to make adequate use of Bjørnson's great talent. Taken with the other evidence, however, it substantiates his significance as an early exponent of the function of the modern director. The growing dominance of this figure as the major creative force in the theatre would soon be demonstrated by the men who followed in Bjørnson's footsteps as artistic director at Christiania Theatre, notably Ludvig Josephson (1873–7) and his son Bjørn Bjørnson (1884–93).

It was as a playwright, however, that the elder Bjørnson had his greatest impact on the modern movement. The reality of contemporary life and its problems, which he brought to bear in *The Newly Married*, remained the syntax of such subsequent plays as *En fallit* (*A Bankruptcy*) and *Redaktøren* (*The Editor*), both of which depict contemporary environments and social issues in a critical light. When these plays were produced for the first time, in early 1875 at the enterprising Nya teatern in Stockholm, they became, August Strindberg recalled, "the signal rockets which rose towards the heavens and broke out into salvos we have not yet forgotten."[11] As dramatic breeches in the hitherto solid bulwark of romantic tradition, they answered the impassioned demand made by Georg Brandes in 1871 that literature should not embroider on memories of the past but must enter into the struggles of its own times, working actively for new ideas. *The*

Editor, an attack on the stifling effects of unscrupulous journalism on family life and human happiness, and *A Bankruptcy*, the story of a wealthy family that is ruined by dishonest business practices but regains its happiness under more modest living conditions, both "take up problems for debate" in the Brandes spirit. Yet neither faces really explosive or dangerous issues. The inherent strength of *A Bankruptcy*, Bjørnson's greatest international success, lies in the theatrical appeal of its richly conceived environment, redolent with the atmosphere of a particular home in which the characters seem to live a life of their own. Just such a close interaction of character and environment, giving the audience the illusion that they are watching actual events plucked from life, would soon become the basic tenet of the new stage naturalism. It is hardly surprising, then, that the progressive and commercially astute actor–manager Edvard Stjernström should use the world premiere of this play to reopen Nya teatern, Dramaten's troublesome competitor, in its ultramodern new home on Blasieholm on 19 January 1875.

By focusing more outspokenly on character as the victim of social environment and the narrow, stultifying restrictions imposed by bourgeois society in the name of truth and morality, Bjørnson, like Ibsen, often became drawn into the public controversies that followed in the wake of the new drama. This was particularly true of his two "women" plays, both of which provoked fierce outrage and were denounced by critics as offensive and immoral. *Leonarda* (1879) portrays the struggle of a divorced woman to find a place for herself in society, while *En hanske* (*A Gauntlet*, 1883) mounts an open attack on the double standard of sexual morality in contemporary society by adopting the Ibsenian premise that women are judged by other laws than men are. Yet if these plays ultimately failed to come to grips with the questions they raised and were overshadowed in this respect by Ibsen's modern dramas, at least part of the explanation lies, as even critics at the time realized, in an unfailingly conciliatory and optimistic attitude on Bjørnson's part. As a revolutionary he was a positivist, a believer in solutions, and a broad streak of ameliorism in his plays tends to rob his conflicts of bite and deprive his cheerful conclusions of trenchancy. With his energetic and hopeful outlook, he shared none of Ibsen's profound sense of the disintegration of an entire universe of spiritual and moral values. Nor did he possess his great contemporary's remarkable gift for transforming the stifling atmosphere of social prejudices and moral hypocrisy into a metaphor for a more encompassing tragic fate.

Ibsen's early years

Ibsen's first play, *Catiline*, was politely refused by Christiania Theatre and was not produced until 1881, when it finally had its world premiere at Nya teatern in Stockholm under the direction of Ludvig Josephson. By then, however, conventions and techniques alike had changed radically with the advent of the new naturalism, and this early experiment was no success in the theatre. Nevertheless, Ibsen retained a special affection for this youthful work because, as he remarks in his preface to the revised edition of 1875, it takes up themes that would recur frequently in his maturer writing: "the clash of abilities and aspirations, of will and probability, at once the tragedy and comedy of mankind and of the individual." In subject matter and in technique *Catiline* is colored by Ibsen's absorption in the passionate world of romantic drama, notably as it is represented in the work of Oehlenschläger, one of the very few playwrights for whom he expressed deep admiration. Surrounded by a corrupt, deceitful, and self-seeking society, the rebel–hero Catiline is a man divided; on the one hand an individual of vision and generosity who dreams of restoring the glory of Rome, on the other a doomed, tormented spirit who is trapped as much by the retributive pattern of his own past as he is by the mendacity of the world in which he moves. The atmosphere of the play is one of palpable darkness (the result, Ibsen says, of the fact that he worked on it only at night), and its theatrical syntax is pure gothicism, a blend of remote and exotic settings glimpsed by moonlight or in the gloom of night, picturesque tableaux, strong emotions passionately portrayed, and a liberal seasoning of the mysterious and the supernatural. The action takes place against the background of a shifting scenic panorama that moves from an evening view of "a road near Rome" where "the towers and walls of the city loom up in the distance" to the ominous darkness of a Vestal temple and "a subterranean vault" in which "a lamp burns faintly" and, finally, to the rugged prospect of Catiline's camp in wooded terrain: "It is night. The moon breaks through the clouds intermittently. A campfire is burning outside [Catiline's] tent and there are several more among the trees in the background." That the romantic pictorialism of Ibsen's scenic concept can be effectively transposed into more abstract and expressive stage images and figure compositions has been demonstrated by, for example, a production such as that directed by Per Bronken at Nationaltheatret in 1976.

At the Christiania Theatre more than a century and a quarter earlier, however, a more manageable proposition presented itself with *Kjæmpehøjen*

(*The Warrior's Barrow*), the next work submitted by "Brynjolf Bjarme." In its preoccupation with national themes, this one-act saga play represents a different facet of the romantic idiom. Written during the period of his stay in Christiania from 1850 to 1852, this short poetic drama became Ibsen's first produced play when it was acted at Christiania Theatre on 26 September 1850. The eighteen-year-old Laura Gundersen (Svendsen) was Blanka, the Southern girl who brings warmth and feeling to the cold but robust environment of the Viking chieftain Gandalf. Her performance was all the more remarkable, observed *Christiania-Posten*, "because the part does not afford as much scope for real acting as for declamation."[12] In any case, the production earned the young playwright a free pass to the theatre, giving him his first real opportunity to study live theatre by watching a variety of plays that constituted a representative cross-section of the romantic repertory. His reactions to this exposure are recorded in a number of articles and reviews that shed useful light on his attitude toward the theatre and culture of his country.

Swept up in the mood of patriotic fervor and optimistic nationalism that prevailed in Norway in the early fifties, Ibsen called for the creation of a distinctive Norwegian culture and the infusion of a national spirit into Norwegian theatre. That spirit must not, he emphasized, be artistically superimposed on the drama, nor should it consist of the "tawdry" depiction of happy people in folk costumes. For Ibsen, the truly national author is one who evolves a suitable metaphor to express in concrete fashion "those undertones which ring out to us from mountain and valley, from meadow and shore, and, above all, from our inner souls."[13] Side by side with this concern, one still hears an echo of the Heibergian principle of aesthetic idealism in Ibsen's critical insistence on the formal requirement, the necessity for the artist to "distinguish between the demands of reality and those of art." To the young Ibsen the fundamental syntax of the theatre was poetic; as such, drama demanded aesthetic distancing from the banalities of reality. For example, in comparing the relative merits of the contemporary French and German plays being performed in Christiania – "Scribe and Co.'s sugar candy dramas" with their sharply focused but schematically one-sided characterizations, as opposed to the "more solid German fare" with its elaboration "*in extenso* of character and situation" – he concludes that the German writer who aims at achieving verifiable reality at the expense of artifice in fact defeats his own purpose. The difference between the German and French modes of drama is, Ibsen continues, the difference between "a *tableau vivant* and a painting: in the former, figures present themselves in their natural contours and natural colors; in the latter, on the other hand, they only *appear* so to us – which is, however, the only right way. For in the realm of art, reality pure and simple has no place; illusion, on the other hand, *has*."[14]

Ibsen's initiation into the practicalities of theatre during his terms as stage director in Bergen and later in Christiania did nothing to alter his view of art as a heightened representation of the ideal. "People crave only what reality has to offer, neither more nor less," he observed with some bitterness. "The notion that art should uplift us is one that few are able to admit."[15] Yet the evaluation of art as a mere reproduction of reality seemed to the young Ibsen utterly absurd. Characteristic in this respect is the tribute he paid to Vilhelm Wiehe, Christiania Theatre's leading romantic actor during the fifties, for his "inspired striving, not for crass reality but for truth, that loftier symbolic representation of life which is the only thing artistically worth fighting for, but which is nonetheless acknowledged by so few."[16]

In the fall of 1851 Ibsen went to Bergen at the invitation of Ole Bull to take up a position as playwright-in-residence at the Norwegian Theatre, where he was to write a new play for performance each year on the theatre's birthday. At the end of the first season he was also offered the job of stage director and was given a travel grant for a three-month visit to Copenhagen and Dresden for the purpose of acquiring, as his contract stated, "such knowledge and experience as will enable him to assume the position of *Instructeur* at the theatre, which embraces not only the instruction of the actors and actresses, but also the management of everything pertaining to the equipment and properties of the stage, the costumes of the players, et cetera."[17] A letter from the Bergen management to J. L. Heiberg, the august head of the Danish Royal Theatre, acquired for Ibsen a free pass and backstage access to the playhouse on Kongens Nytorv during the most luminous period in its history. The stage director and historian Thomas Overskou acted as cicerone for "the little, hard-bitten Norwegian with the watchful eyes," and Heiberg accorded the guest a cordial reception. Both here and at the Court Theatre in Dresden, Ibsen would experience a broad selection of plays and productions that undoubtedly influenced his development immeasurably. Our specific concern in this context is with the repertory of the Royal Theatre which, during the period between 20 April and 6 June, offered the playgoer choices that ranged from Scribe to

Shakespeare (*King Lear, Romeo and Juliet, As You Like It, Hamlet*) and from Holberg (four comedies) and Oehlenschläger (*Hakon Jarl*) to Heiberg (two vaudevilles) and Hertz (*King René's Daughter*). In addition, Ibsen attended performances at the Christiansborg Court Theatre and at Casino, whose "house dramatist" Hans Christian Andersen recommended the subtle blend of fantasy and realism in the fairy-tale comedies of Ferdinand Raimund to the young director's attention.

Especially in the Royal Theatre productions, however, Ibsen could observe one of the finest companies on the Continent in action, headed by Johanne Luise Heiberg and bringing together the comic talents of Phister and Rosenkilde, the tragic grandeur of Anna Nielsen and her husband, and the romantic lyricism of Michael Wiehe. Wiehe was remembered by Ibsen years later as the finest actor he had ever seen: "When I recall his performances, it is as though I were walking through a gallery filled with ancient statues. Pure plastique! Pure beauty!"[18] In a very different mood, Ibsen also watched Frederik Høedt's realistically toned *Hamlet*, in which Fru Heiberg was an incongruous Ophelia, but he preferred to see Høedt's touches of domesticity applied to Scribe instead. All in all, there is no reason to doubt that the Royal Theatre provided an important model for his own management of the Bergen Theatre. Play scripts, musical scores, and books on costuming were procured in Copenhagen for use in his new capacity, and the Heibergian taste had a distinct effect on his own selection of a repertory. Critics have made a great deal of the fact that Ibsen came across Herman Hettner's *Das moderne Drama* (1850) at this time, either in Copenhagen or in Dresden, and that this work, with its emphasis on the dynamics of character and psychology as the true motivational force in great drama, impressed him deeply. And indeed, Hettner does synthesize ideas that are of obvious relevance to the evolution of Ibsen's dramaturgy. These lines of theoretical influence should not, however, be over-emphasized to the extent that one underestimates the tangible and immediate impact of the Danish and German theatre productions and methods of mise-en-scène that he encountered at this crucial juncture in his career. For the performances of Johanne Luise Heiberg, in which her emphasis on the tension of contradictions within a personality lent a fascinating spiritual depth to every role she played, Ibsen reserved the ultimate tribute of his Rhymed Letter:

> She is like a legend that trembles
> behind the veil enfolding it;

she is like a vision that rises
and hovers
along a secret riddle-path.

At the time when Ibsen took up his new directing duties, the theatre
in general was on the threshold of a profound transition. Despite the
increasing concern at mid-century with the ideal of ensemble acting, the
modern concept of a director as the guiding artistic force behind a production, coordinating all details of a performance and integrating them into a
unified whole, was not fully formed until the 1880s. Around 1850 the personal influence of the director was still limited by the principles and
aesthetics of a theatrical system based on relatively few rehearsals, the
observance of recognized rules and conventions of positioning on the
stage, and the preservation of the individual actor's independence in preparing his or her role. Nor were the responsibilities of stage direction necessarily vested in one person. In Bergen, this task was (very typically)
divided into two distinct parts, stage arrangement, which was assigned to
Ibsen, and role instruction, which was the province of Herman Laading, a
well-educated schoolmaster whom we might call a dramaturge today. In
establishing such a division of labor, the Norwegian Theatre in Bergen was
in fact simply adhering to a pattern advocated by cosmopolitan theatre
men like Heinrich Laube in Germany. A practical advantage of the scheme
was, according to a circular from the Bergen management, that "with two
people now sharing the task of instruction, it is possible to allocate some
time to the general education of the actors and actresses of the company"
– a very relevant consideration when developing artistic standards for a
green company such as this one.

At least in theory, Laading took charge of play analysis and character
explication at the first read-through. Specifically, his task was fourfold:

1   to remove all obstacles to a rapid and satisfactory stage rehearsal,
    both in regard to language and clarification of vocabulary;
2   to give the players such historical explanation as is needed, and
    ensure a correct interpretation of their roles;
3   to see that their diction is correct; and
4   to ensure that the players memorize their parts carefully and
    accurately enough for them to appear at the first stage rehearsal
    without books or papers.[19]

Clearly, the naturalistic concept of an integrated and balanced ensemble that is gradually arrived at during the course of numerous stage rehearsals was not the objective here. Although the dramaturge was free to attend rehearsals "in order that – within the limits of his function – he may supervise the observance of the prescriptions he has given to the actors," role interpretation and mise-en-scène were normally regarded as separate areas of work. At times, notably when his own plays were being staged, Ibsen did extend his mandate to embrace not only the creation of a suitable physical arrangement but the supervision of the actors' interpretations as well. Even so, the nature of his influence remained decisively different from that exerted by a succeeding generation of naturalistic directors like Bjørn Bjørnson, William Bloch, and their more famous counterparts in France, Germany, and Russia. Nor, if we are to trust Lucie Wolf's testimony, did Ibsen ("a silent and surprisingly shy man whom I always found at a distance from us all") possess any of the elder Bjørnson's charismatic persuasiveness as a director of actors.

Rather, as a director Ibsen was preoccupied chiefly with the visual effects of setting and costuming and with picturesque groupings and patterns of movement – effects and patterns that reflect the fundamental character of the romantic theatre as a colorful "living picture gallery." Specifically, the regulations required him:

1 to organize the scenic arrangements, including the costumes and scenery, of each play, and generally to direct it (groupings, entrances, exits and poses etc.);
2 to watch the mime and gestures of each player, to ensure that the physical expression is appropriate to the words and the character of the part; and
3 to achieve the necessary coordination and show each of the performers which part, in terms of the scenes, he is to play in the overall action.

Having eventually also assumed the supervisory task of stage-managing each night's performance, he kept a careful record of the sets, floor plans, crowd positions, props, and other matters pertaining to each production in the repertory. As scholars have demonstrated, these production notes (for 33 of the 121 plays performed during his five-year tenure in Bergen) provide a convincing impression of an able director's readiness to experiment with new and unconventional approaches to practical problems of stage arrangement.[20] The real significance of these notes, however, is as evidence of Ibsen's developing sensitivity to the importance of setting, lighting, and costuming as dramatic values – large-scale metaphors capable of concretizing the drama's theme and mood. Furthermore, of the hand-colored costume sketches and stage designs we are told he customarily prepared for his productions, enough iconographic evidence has survived to confirm this sense of Ibsen's responsiveness to the visual aspects of theatrical expression. The manner in which he utilized this visual component in his work would change radically – and more than once – during his career, but its central importance to his conception of a play never diminished.

While still on the threshold of that career, the rich pictorial beauty of the romantic style of theatre held a profound fascination for Ibsen the dramatist as well as for Ibsen the director. Although the technical and financial resources of the theatre in Bergen were limited indeed when compared to those of the Danish or Swedish national theatres, the five plays he wrote and directed at Bull's playhouse did their best to exploit visually effective staging as an integral part of the dramatic action. *Sancthansnatten* (*Midsummer Eve*), a romantic fantasy reminiscent of the popular fairy-tale comedies of Raimund and Andersen, was performed for the third birthday of Bergen's Norwegian Theatre on 2 January 1853. The action of this comedy of cross-wooing revolves around contrasted pairs of poetically visionary and prosaically commonplace lovers. Under the watchful eye of a cunning goblin with a strong family resemblance to Shakespeare's Puck, they and we are transported from a bucolic garden setting in the first act to a moonlit forest path in the second. The path leads to the enchanted Midsummer Hill, "on which the remains of a bonfire periodically flares up." The production would have needed not only some new scenery but also a fair bit of technical skill, especially at the moment when the magic hill opens to the sound of "soft background music." The transformation reveals "a large, brilliantly lit hall" populated by a collection of figures from the fantastic world of Andersen's tales (notably "Elves' Hill") and Bournonville's ballets. "The mountain king sits on a high throne in the background," reads Ibsen's stage direction. "Elves and mountain fairies dance about him." Under the influence of the supernatural events of this midsummer-night's frolic, the mismatched lovers sort themselves out and all ends well. This particular Ibsen exercise pleased no one, however, not even its author, and it vanished after two performances.

Although Ibsen's next Bergen play, a revised version of *The Warrior's Barrow* that was produced on the theatre's birthday in 1854, represented a much tamer and more static use of the stage, most of the plays he wrote during the next ten years reflected a restless experimentation not only with dramatic form but with the potentialities of theatrical expression as well. All, with the exception of *Love's Comedy* (1862), are set against a colorful background of Norwegian history and legend. Thematic affinities between a play like *Fru Inger til Østeraad* (*Lady Inger of Østeraad*, 1855) and Ibsen's later work have often been pointed out, but the conceptual use of setting and lighting in this early historical drama provides an indirect but equally significant indicator of the strong visual consciousness that becomes so characteristic of this dramatist's mature writing. Although set in the Norway of 1528, *Lady Inger* is far more concerned with the evocation of a sinister atmosphere of gloom and darkness than it is with the observance of historical exactitude. With its somber gothic interiors illuminated by moonlight, firelight, or the flickering glow from a branched candlestick, it illustrates Ibsen's growing ability to use the resources of the theatre to underscore theme and mood.

Lady Inger was an important milestone in other ways as well. Despite its Scribean net of intrigue, it rises to forceful tragic proportions in the depiction of the Lady Macbeth-like title figure, the strong motive force behind the action. The tension of opposites and contradictions in her personality, ecstatic with the notion of restoring national independence but tormented with doubts about her own ability to live up to her calling, generates a powerful field of dramatic intensity reminiscent, as critics have also noted, of both Shakespeare and Schiller. Inherent in this conception of a divided character is the need for an actress with Fru Heiberg's ability to comprehend and project such psychological dualism. Although this intense drama of passion failed first in Bergen and again when Ibsen directed it at Kristiania norske teater in 1859, its stageworthiness was vindicated by a production of the revised version of the play at Christiania Theatre in 1875, directed by Ludvig Josephson and starring Laura Gundersen as the strong-willed Lady Inger. This verdict was soon reaffirmed by the play's triumphant Swedish premiere at Dramaten two years later, in which Elise Hwasser assumed the title role. With her successive performances as Selma in *The League of Youth* (1869), Hjørdis in *The Vikings of Helgeland* (1876), Lady Inger (1877), Lona Hessel in *Samfundets støtter* (*The Pillars of Society*, 1877), Nora (1880), and Mrs.

Alving (1883), Hwasser was among the first to reveal, in terms of living representation, the temperamental bond between Ibsen's rebellious saga heroines and his portraits of strong "modern" women. It must be said, of course, that the unconventional female characters in the early plays still belong squarely within the bounds of the romantic tradition. As unconventional variants of a female stereotype, they were identified by such epithets as "interesting" or even "demonic."

Far from being hampered, as critics have sometimes maintained, by the so-called "artificiality" or "unreality" of the theatrical context in which he worked at the beginning of his career, Ibsen – who at this time regarded a measure of abstraction as a *sine qua non* of theatrical art – learned the power of mood, visual imagination, and suggestion from his immersion in the theatre practice of the romantic era. The creation of a strong, evocative atmosphere was the crux of his plan for *The Feast at Solhaug*, which both he and Bjørnson staged with great success in the 1850s. From the Icelandic Family Sagas, Ibsen had derived the idea of a great feast "with a fateful clash and much provocative talk," and this image provided both the thematic and the pictorial framework for his medievalized ballad play. "The fateful feast which I had felt to be of the utmost importance to portray," he writes in the preface to the second edition of 1883, "became in the drama the stage on which the characters appeared throughout; it became the background against which the action stood in relief, and informed the whole picture with the general atmosphere I had intended."[21] The theatre in Bergen also appears to have made every effort to achieve the level of picturesqueness demanded by the new play, which was produced with sets and costumes designed by the author–director in 1856. Set in the early fourteenth century, this folksong-inspired drama bears only a superficial resemblance to Henrik Hertz's *Svend Dyring's House* in its adoption of ballad rhythms and images ("There is a light summer breeze wafting over my rhythm; there is a feeling of autumn hanging over his," says the playwright). Wholly Ibsenian, however, is the character of Margit, who has deceived her true love to marry the rich but weak-willed Bengt, Master of Solhaug. Although she is brought to despair at the loss of her wandering knight Gudmund to her vivacious sister Signe, tragedy is averted in *The Feast at Solhaug* and the play ends on a conciliatory note well suited to win the applause of the Bergen audience.

This work was not only Ibsen's first – and only – complete popular success in Bergen, it was also the first of his plays to be acted outside

Norway, first at Dramaten in 1857 and subsequently at the Casino in Copenhagen in 1861. Ibsen tried in vain to follow up this triumph with another lyrical ballad drama, *Olaf Liljekrans*, but this medieval tale of romantic complications was taken off the repertory after two performances in 1857. It is remembered today almost solely on account of a series of colored drawings in Ibsen's hand, depicting eight of the characters in his folktale romance. Both the stylized folk costumes worn by the figures in these sketches and the highly emotional poses they strike convey something of the theatrical tone and historical flavor of the young dramatist's last Bergen play.

In the summer of 1857, Ibsen resigned his post in Bergen to take up a new and, he hoped, a more viable position in the Norwegian capital as "stage instructor and artistic director" at Kristiania norske teater, the new and distinctly unprestigious rival of the "Danish" theatre on the Bank Square. Located in an unfashionable street and patronized by a predominantly working-class audience, this playhouse had an artistic reputation that was none too high, and Ibsen's five-year directorship there ended with the theatre's financial collapse in 1862. The Christiania years were in general a time of great personal hardship and self-doubt for Ibsen, during which his dramatic output faltered and even threatened to cease altogether. For five years between *The Vikings of Helgeland* (1857) and *Love's Comedy*, his satire on the institution of marriage, he wrote nothing at all for the stage. On the other hand, his involvement in practical theatre – and in the ongoing debate over its true nature and purpose as a cultural force – continued unabated. In particular, his views on the function of stage direction reflect a wider attitude being voiced on many sides in the 1850s and after: the director's art can be compared to that of the painter; in both cases, once the pervading total coloring of the work has been established, the task then is to place the individual figures in the composition in an harmoniously integrated and meaningful relationship to the whole.[22] While hardly original in themselves, such ideas remind us of Ibsen's steadily developing concern with total theatrical effect, as an indispensable aspect of the *dramatist's* thinking about his play.

The Vikings of Helgeland, which Ibsen directed with great success at the Norwegian-language theatre (24 November 1858), proved to be a crucial turning point in dramaturgical terms – away from the contrived style and improbable situations of the earlier plays, toward a concept of dramatic action shaped by Herman Hettner's insistence (in *Das modern Drama*, which

Plates 33a & b The colored costume designs made by Ibsen for the production
of his folktale romance *Olaf Liljekrans* (Bergen 1857) also convey a sense of role
interpretation as well. (a) Hemming, the page, appears perplexed by the ring he
has received from his master's daughter;

Ibsen had read with profit during his early Bergen years) that great historical tragedy must concern itself primarily with character rather than with
mere intrigue. Centering on the Medea-like valkyrie Hjørdis and her ruthless pursuit of vengeance, the larger-than-life action and elemental characters of this saga drama gradually build up a powerful sense of nemesis,
of the inescapable burden of past errors upon the present. Ibsen makes
skillful use of costumes, setting, and lighting to accentuate the underlying
vision and atmosphere of the heroic grandeur and remote starkness of a
lost Viking age. From the turbulent, wintry seacoast of the opening act, the
drama moves to a banquet hall interior, at first dimly lighted by a log fire
burning on a stone hearth in the center of the floor and later (in act 3) seen

(b) the downcast Alfhild stands dressed and crowned for a wedding ceremony that will never take place.

by daylight, before returning in the final act to the rocky, barren shore. This coast, illuminated by the somber glow of torches, a log fire, and the moon ("occasionally seen through dark and ragged storm clouds") is the stern arena for the final tragic events that end with a vision of black horses and the avenging valkyrie Hjørdis riding through the sky – "the last ride of the dead on their way to Valhalla." Similarly bold contrasts are established in the color and texture of the costumes, which are described in unusual detail in the stage directions because Ibsen had hoped to have the play produced at Christiania Theatre itself, rather than by his own company. In other words, every aspect of the mise-en-scène was calculated to contribute to the picturesque impact upon which Ibsen's ambitious saga pastiche depends for its effect. It is not surprising that the singular attempt made by Edward Gordon Craig in 1903 to simplify and transfigure *Vikings,* in somewhat the same spirit Appia sought to transfigure Wagner, found no imitators in the modern period. Rather, this once-popular play is inseparably tied to the nineteenth-century taste for pictorial illusionism and ethnographic detail.

By the time Ibsen staged *The Pretenders* at Christiania Theatre more than five years later (17 January 1864), the long apprenticeship he had served in this older theatrical tradition was at an end. The dramatist, by then thirty-six years old, desperately needed – and soon found – a new and less constrictive artistic environment for his development. One year before, as part of its efforts to present a more authentically Norwegian image, Christiania Theatre had hired Ibsen as a part-time "aesthetic consultant," and plans were soon announced for a production of *Love's Comedy*, which appeared in print on New Year's Day 1863. Once this caustic domestic satire began to encounter a rising tide of abuse and almost hysterical hostility in the Norwegian press, however, the theatre quietly backed away from its offer to perform it. Ibsen was deeply shocked, for the event drove home to him, once and for all, the stultifying intellectual climate in which he found himself and the pressing need to escape it.

As his first incontrovertible masterpiece, *The Pretenders* is only superficially similar to his earlier works, for now the action and spectacle of medieval history – the violent struggle between the two principal pretenders to the Norwegian throne – are used as a metaphor for the underlying spiritual (and deeply personal) dichotomy between the irresistible power of a great calling and the paralyzing effects of self-doubt and corrosive self-scrutiny. Thus, the vacillating and reflective Skule must inevitably fall before Haakon, the unswerving believer in his own heroic destiny and in his strength to carry out his great kingly thought. Ibsen's highly successful production adopted a style rooted in a traditional attention to the historical "accuracy" and "authenticity" so dear to the nineteenth-century theatre everywhere. Wergmann was called upon to design new scenery for this sprawling historical chronicle, and the services of a local antiquarian were secured in order to provide the proper thirteenth-century Norwegian flavor. Wergmann's scene design for the moonlit convent yard at Elgesæter, where the defeated Skule and his son seek refuge from the angry townspeople of Nidaros in the final scene of the play, seems in perfect harmony with the carefully visualized stage directions in Ibsen's text – itself inspired by the playwright's reading of ancient Norwegian history. Both the heavy gate depicted in the background and the chapel

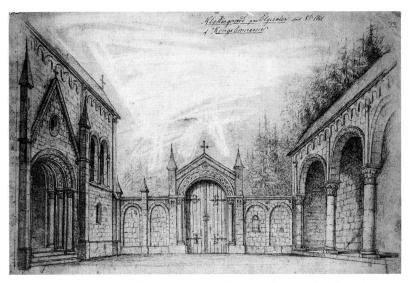

Plate 34 Wergmann's design for the last scene in Ibsen's production of *The Pretenders*, the convent yard at Elgesæter. Christiania Theatre, 1864.

with lighted windows where Haakon is to be crowned are key points in the action of the scene. Wergmann, on the other hand, added the cloisters formed of romanesque arches to Ibsen's description, possibly on the advice of the learned antiquarian.

In general, while the Wergmann design did not entirely satisfy the Christiania critics, it established a style of robust pictorial solidity that continued to dominate revivals of *The Pretenders* throughout the remainder of the nineteenth century. The influential production given by the Meiningen players in 1876, for which Duke Georg himself "journeyed to Ibsen's northern land" to make firsthand sketches for his company's scenery and costumes, remained anchored in the same concern with studied historical realism. ("The foreign quality shown in this production aroused such wide interest," observed Max Grube, that it helped at least in some measure to counterbalance the objections of the German critics to the play's "verbosity" and to the division of its focus between Haakon and Skule.[23]) Among the first to put forward an alternative to this style of academic realism was Fritz Ahlgrensson, who designed the Swedish premiere of the play at Nya teatern on 19 January 1879. The noted Swedish scene-painter, who worked at different times both in Copenhagen and Stockholm, attempted on this occasion to create a group of exterior settings in which the heavier, darker tones of the older romantic style were replaced by a lighter, cooler atmosphere directly influenced by the contemporary school of *plein air* landscape painting. At Nya teatern seven years later, the innovative Ludvig Josephson tried to alter the play's performance traditions in a much more radical fashion, without success. Josephson's *Pretenders* featured August Lindberg, one of the most accomplished naturalistic actor–directors of the period, in the role of Bishop Nikolas, yet the production proved a disappointment precisely *because* of Lindberg's restrained "naturalistic" approach to the deep-dyed scoundrelism of Ibsen's most diabolical cleric. His characterization seemed to contemporaries "well conceived and nicely developed, but so subdued and pale in coloring that the theatrical effect was lost."[24]

The tradition of historical pictorialism fostered by the original production of *The Pretenders* reached a culmination of sorts in Bjørn Bjørnson's revival of the play at Nationaltheatret in 1900. According to the director himself, his mise-en-scène followed the same approach he had adopted in an earlier production of the play at Christiania Theatre in 1888. This time, however, the attempt at historical reconstruction was far grander and more ambitious in its imitation of the Meininger method, of which Bjørnson was a keen disciple. Jens Wang, the leading Norwegian scene-painter of the period, designed ten completely new settings, each one part of "a milieu as authentic as history and the use of technical resources allowed."[25] Ibsen was shown photographs of Wang's scenery and conferred his blessing. Andreas Bloch was given the task of costuming the 130 actors and extras in the performance, all of whom wore lavishly finished replications of the dress and armor of the thirteenth century. The wonders of electric lighting enabled Wang to create an even stronger sense of virtual reality in the depiction of natural and supernatural phenomena alike. Thus, the ghost of Bishop Nikolas walked in an eerie green spotlight; a comet streaked across a starry sky; Skule appeared in the climactic battle mounted on a real white charger; and the sights, sounds, and martial music of clashing armies filled the stage of Norway's newly inaugurated national theatre.

To the dismay of Bjørn Bjørnson and his collaborators, who pointed repeatedly to their scrupulous observance of Ibsen's stage directions as evidence that they had fulfilled the author's "intentions," several of the Christiania critics disagreed strongly with the manner in which the director–manager had allowed the inner meaning of the text to be overwhelmed by excessively lavish scenic display. Although such an objection is hardly surprising under the circumstances, the nature of Bjørnson's refutation is rather curious. In the ensuing newspaper debate he responded that, having given full and sole responsibility for the principal elements of the physical mise-en-scène – scenery, lighting, and costumes – to Wang and Bloch, he himself had devoted most of his rehearsal time (thirty-six hours out of a total of fifty) to line reading and interpretation. Although some fourteen hours had eventually been spent arranging the extras in the fight scenes, it was not until the final three rehearsals that Bjørnson first saw the scenery and other stage effects to be used.[26] Hence, the concept of the total artistic dominance of an early modern director such as Bjørn Bjørnson seems, at least in this instance, to have been modified by a division of artistic responsibilities that harks back to the conditions under which Bjørnson's father and Ibsen had both learned the ropes forty years earlier.

As for Ibsen, *The Pretenders* was the last play he ever directed, and its 1864 production marked the end of his active involvement in the practical theatre. Nevertheless, countless letters to those involved in producing his plays, dealing with casting, interpretation of roles, and even specific staging suggestions, demonstrate that he never lost contact with the living theatre and wrote his plays with concrete performance conditions in mind. The intimate knowledge of the stage and its conventions that he acquired from his early experience as a director sharpened his sensitivity to the poetry of environment in the theatre, that is, to the use of theatrical elements that create a specific mood capable of strengthening the spiritual action of the drama. By directing the first productions of his early saga dramas, he taught himself to write a carefully visualized, highly charged mise-en-scène into his plays, as a means of giving tangible theatrical expression to the underlying psychological states and spiritual conditions of his characters. Costumes, settings, props, and lighting effects remained throughout his career the syntax of his dramatic poetry.

Ibsen's departure from Norway in the spring of 1864 marked the beginning of twenty-seven years of exile. *Brand* and *Peer Gynt*, the first two plays he wrote after leaving the country, initiated a new phase in his development. Both were conceived as dramatic poems, intended initially for a reading public. Ibsen's fiery indictment of the spirit of moral weakness and compromise in *Brand* caused a sensation when this play was published in 1866: "Every receptive and unblunted mind felt, on closing the book, a penetrating, nay, an overwhelming impression of having stood face to face with a great and indignant genius," Georg Brandes wrote, "before whose piercing glance weakness felt itself compelled to cast down its eyes."[27] *Peer Gynt*, on the other hand, was greeted with considerable acrimony when it appeared in print the following year. Clemens Petersen branded its blend of light-hearted fantasy and biting satire "unpoetic" and lacking in "idealism." However, the alleged blemishes that disturbed literary critics at the time – "the misanthropy and self-hatred" that bothered Brandes, the "general sense of incongruity and disjointedness" that troubled even an ardent Ibsen supporter like Edmund Gosse – have since become the very traits that have appealed to many actors and directors of the play in the modern period.

It is again Ludvig Josephson who deserves credit as the first to recognize the theatrical potential inherent in the new, freer, "reckless" style of these monumental reading dramas. The Swedish director enthusiastically accepted Ibsen's proposal to stage a somewhat shortened version of *Peer Gynt* at Christiania Theatre, accompanied by a new musical score composed by Edvard Grieg (who found it "a dreadfully intractable subject"). This lavishly expensive production, perhaps the most important of the many significant Ibsen performances staged during Josephson's enlightened leadership of this playhouse in the mid-1870s, opened on 24 February 1876. Its success was unprecedented, and its run of thirty-seven performances was cut short only because of a fire that partially gutted the theatre in 1877. Josephson's version, which adopted less drastic cuts than those first suggested to him by Ibsen, required four and three-quarter hours to perform, and in the process stretched the resources of the conventional theatre of *trompe l'oeil* illusionism to the limit. "When the director is entrusted with staging a play," Josephson writes in his book *Teater-Regie* (1892), "he must nowadays approach the task in the most painstaking way, through the study of detail – or, we might say, scientifically."[28] In somewhat the same spirit of pictorial fidelity as that which animated the work of the Meininger, he created a colorful and precisely tuned mise-en-scène for Ibsen's drama that pressed into service not only the theatre's own designers, Wilhelm Krogh and Olaf Jørgensen, but also a corps of landscape painters that included the gifted young naturalist Fritz Thaulow. Their common purpose was to provide a vivid pictorial background for *Peer Gynt* that was both rich in local color and "authentic" in its use of ethnographic detail. While full of admiration for the coordination and visual effectiveness of this spectacle, the reviewers did express some concern lest "the deeper core of the play be concealed or at any rate obscured by the brilliant outward display."[29]

In essence, the tradition established by the Josephson premiere approached Peer's progress through the world as a succession of realistically conceived incidents and striking (if quite literalized) theatrical pictures. (Precisely this impression is conveyed by a contemporary helio-type in *Ny Illustreret Tidende*, depicting a kaleidoscope of "snapshots" from this production.) Hence, even the grotesque and fantastical elements in *Peer Gynt* – the trolls, elves, and goblins whom Peer encounters in the abode of the Mountain King, for instance – appeared as "real" in their own realm as Mother Aase, Solveig, and the wedding guests at Haegstad Farm did in theirs. Rather than inhabitants of a symbolic and disturbing dream-world, these "entertainingly grotesque" figures (to borrow Brandes' phrase) were the comfortably familiar creatures of the *eventyr* tradition of adventure and romance – a tradition of which the tales and plays of H. C. Andersen, the folk ballets of Bournonville, and even an early Ibsen play like *Midsummer Eve* all partake. Henrik Klausen was a lyrical and sprightly Peer in an interpretation in which – despite the sardonic humor of Johannes Brun's Troll King – the lyrical element far outweighed the satir-ical. In this respect, Josephson's concept remained closely tied to Grieg's melodic musical score – that charming but incongruously rhapsodic excrescence of which the play has never fully succeeded in ridding itself. Ibsen's divided protagonist, the poet and visionary who is *also* the vain egoist and self-deceiver, became in this first ambitious production primari-ly a dreamer of poetic dreams that crystallized into a comforting vision of the redemptive Solveig, who literally hovered before him as he slumbered in the Moroccan desert in the fourth act.

Although Josephson had told Ibsen of his interest in *Brand* at an early point, it was not until 24 March 1885 that he staged the world premiere of this drama at the new Nya teatern in Stockholm, which ranked as one of the liveliest theatres in Scandinavia during his management. Once again the bold experiment was a success, but the mammoth six-and-a-half-hour production set no example; Ibsen's dramatic poem was to wait another ten years before anyone else was to attempt a performance of it. In the Josephson production, Emil Hillberg brought to Ibsen's titantic super-man–priest an imposing monumentality and unyielding sublimity that ran the risk of an indifferent or even unsympathetic audience response. "The danger inherent in portraying the sublime," one critic reflected, "is that it easily becomes uninteresting. Superiority leads to indifference toward human interest, the bond between the hero and humanity bursts, and Ibsen

Plates 35 a and b   Two "snapshots" from a composite heliotype of the first production of *Peer Gynt* at Christiania Theatre in 1876: (a) surrounded by an assembly of idealized theatre elves and sylphs, Peer (Henrik Klausen) negotiates with the Troll King (Johannes Brun) for his daughter (Lucie Wolf);

(b) as he slumbers in the Moroccan desert, Peer is consoled by a dream vision of Solveig.

has guarded against this by giving his hero the reformatory zeal and human warmth" that Hillberg's idealized portrait of Brand apparently lacked.[30]

By this time, meanwhile, the winds of change had conclusively altered the face of European theatre as a whole. Naturalism, with its accompanying emphasis on contemporaneity, had become the dominant theatrical mode. Stung by the criticism of the published text of *Peer Gynt*, Ibsen had determined to move with the times. "If I am no poet, then I shall try my hand as a photographer," he had written to Bjørnson from Rome (9 December 1867). "One by one I shall come to grips with my contemporaries in the North . . ." *The League of Youth* (1869) pointed the new direction, and with the completion four years later of *Kejser og Galilæer* (*Emperor and Galilean*), his epic chronicle of the clash of paganism and Christianity in fourth-century Byzantium, Ibsen's "poetic" period ended. During the decades that followed, his transformation of the apparently neutral language and settings of the realistic style created a new kind of dramatic poetry that redefined the nature of the theatrical experience itself.

7 Naturalism and the director

In the 1870s and early 1880s the theatre in Scandinavia and elsewhere underwent a period of transition and radical change, during which the new naturalistic aesthetic waged a decisive struggle against the accepted theatrical traditions and conventions of the past. A perception of stagnation gave rise to mounting critical dissatisfaction on the part of a younger generation of reformers. "There is no lack of individual talent, but the ability to exploit it is wanting; the raw material is there, but not the principles," declared Edvard Brandes, who attributed the "absolute decline" of Danish theatre to its neglect of Frederik Høedt and the "natural" style of acting and staging he had championed more than a decade before. "In the serious drama, the declamatory style is spreading fast, and in comedy coarse caricature prevails, with only a few exceptions," he continues in the pages of *Det nittende Aarhundrede* (*The Nineteenth Century*), an influential periodical published by the Brandes brothers during the mid-1870s. "If anything of consequence is to be saved from our dying theatrical art, the management of the theatre must have a definite dramaturgical principle as its goal."[1] The new principle advocated by this critic and others would bring the theatre into closer relationship with observed reality, making it literally the representation of what Zola called "a fragment of existence" and Jean Jullien later described as "a slice of life."

The rallying cry of the Brandes generation was the infusion of "nature" and "truth" into the theatre, achieved on the basis of a scrupulously detailed recreation of observed reality on the stage. The Heibergian view that the fundamental syntax of the theatre is, above all, poetic and hence dependent on an aesthetic distancing from the trivial circumstances of reality was challenged by Brandes' insistence upon "nature as opposed to an abstract ideal of beauty" and "speech as opposed to declamation."[2] The goal of naturalism was a style of performance replete with small but significant touches of the familiar and the specific. "Is not true art revealed in the perfect execution of details?" Brandes demands (in a study of Danish acting that polemically excluded Johanne Luise Heiberg). "For Messonier, a horse's tail no larger than the point of a pin is the object of as much study as the portrait of Napoleon the Third himself."[3] As the young Danish writer and director Herman Bang observed in a similar spirit in 1880, the chief business of the naturalistic director was thus to "determine and arrange the stage environments" in such a way that they correspond to "the occupations, character, and predilections of their inhabitants."[4] The underlying justification for this concern with the elements of external verisimilitude – in setting, lighting, props, sound effects, and all the rest – was not, however, a simplistic preoccupation with these details in themselves, but rather a conviction that the sum of them accounted for or helped to establish an inner authenticity. It was in such an atmosphere that Zola's demand that the new actor must "not *play* but *live* before the audience" could best be satisfied.

A linchpin in the naturalistic program was hence the concept of setting as environment, as a clinical manifestation of the conditions of life with which the characters in the drama must struggle. In fact, the French director André Antoine maintained, it was this lifelike environment that determined the movements of the characters, not the movements of the characters that determined the environment. As an indispensable component of what Zola describes as "the twofold life of character and environment," the so-called facsimile stage thus acquired individuality and meaning as a controlling factor to be observed and analyzed. Small wonder, then, that Georg Brandes had such contempt for the old, shopworn canvas drawing rooms he encountered on the stage of the Royal Theatre, "which make one so melancholy at times that he wishes that one of the actors in these passionless, bourgeois, narrow-minded, and stupid plays would, in the midst of the rubbish, fly into such a knock-down drag-out rage that he shattered his role and drove his arm through the canvas backcloth."[5]

Even more persistently than his older brother, Edvard Brandes remained, above all, the spokesman for a fresh approach to acting that would reflect the emphasis on psychological truth and motivation that was reshaping the new drama of the period. "Acting is above all else the depiction of human beings," he wrote in a review of an unprepossessing revival of Oehlenschläger's *Correggio* in 1872. "We do not go to see a tragedy in order to enjoy a sonorous voice, watch pleasing gestures and tableaux, or admire a pretty face. The pleasure we seek is to experience the essence of the personality, to observe the human soul in its inmost intricacies laid bare before us."[6] The model held up by Herman Bang in this regard was the urbane Swedish actor Gustaf Fredrikson, a figure whom Bang compared to Høedt and who was at this point in his long career the acknowledged master of the *raisonneur* role in the contemporary French drama of Scribe, Barrière, and Dumas *fils*. Fredrikson's touring company, which visited Copenhagen in the late 1870s, seemed to Bang to epitomize his ideal of an ensemble playing in which the actions and behavior of the actors were dictated by their realistic physical surroundings – rooms that seemed familiar to them, clothes that had been lived in, books that had been thumbed through, newspapers that had been read. Above all, as Bang put it in his characteristic way, "this is the school that sits, settles down, and remains seated . . . in chairs they know and in which they have sat hundreds of times before." In their performance of Dumas' *Le demi-monde*, he continues, "the stage was a room, and the audience looked in through a keyhole"; dialogue acquired the naturalness of everyday conversation, and "one wall of the room was a wall of glass," behind which the actors appeared like "figures in a painting that were indeed meant to be glimpsed through this glass."[7]

The true turning point in the process of renewal advocated by Bang, the Brandes brothers, and others was, however, marked by the momentous world premiere of *Et dukkehjem* (*A Doll's House*) at the Danish Royal Theatre on 21 December 1879. Although *Samfundets støtter* (*The Pillars of Society*) had aroused its fair share of critical controversy when first produced on this same stage two years earlier, the performance of Ibsen's latest play seemed to many to chart a new course in theatrical terms. Emil Poulsen, a versatile actor equally at home in the poetic melancholy of Holger Drachmann and the intellectual reality of Ibsen, made the role of Torvald Helmer far more than the colorless supporting figure he has sometimes become in subsequent productions. "Every speech displayed understanding, and the irony in his characterization was incomparable," wrote Edvard Brandes, who went so far as to assert that Poulsen alone stood on a level with Ibsen's composition.[8] He was able, Vilhelm Topsøe agreed in *Dagbladet* (22 December), to achieve "the right touch of vacillation, half educated, half amiable, a little arrogant, but cleverly ordinary." The actor's finely detailed reading of the part was, Erik Bøgh added in *Dagens Nyheder* (22 December), a remarkable filigree of contrasts and shadings that ranged from "the short-sighted, self-satisfied playfulness with his tormented wife" to "the exultant champagne mood that turns first to indignation and then at once to vapid jubilation" and on through "all the shifting moods of the closing scene in which he must deliver the cues for Nora's divorce proceedings." Brandes was alone, however, in recognizing the character of Helmer for what he is, "the intellectual aristocrat without intellect, arrogantly conservative partly by conviction and partly out of pragmatism, indifferent, but possessing all the opinions of good society." Yet this critic's prediction that the audience's shared philistine sympathy for Helmer would cause the play to fail on the stage proved far from accurate – due mainly to the extraordinary performance of Betty Hennings in the leading role.

To her contemporaries – including Ibsen himself – Hennings *was* Nora, the virtual personification of the dramatist's literary creation. At twenty-nine, she was the period's ideal of the charming, graceful ingenue, and as such her Nora was the embodiment of youthful gaiety and childlike capriciousness. Especially in the scene with her own children, Bang recalls in his detailed analysis of her performance, "one remembers her noise, her mobility, her extremely childlike manner of speaking, the rapidity of her gestures, the change in her diction, which takes on almost nervous speed during her long chatter with the children."[9] This approach to Nora's initial character served to place the dramatic emphasis on the first two acts of the play – filled, as *Berlingske Tidende* (22 December) observed, with a series of "charming pictures" in which "the sun-drenched comfort and happiness of the 'Doll's House' are depicted, and in which the lark cavorts with her children, decorates the tree, and plays hide-and-seek." As a former ballerina and Bournonville protégé, her supple grace and remarkable pantomimic ability made Hennings ideally suited to the visually expressive moments around which this segment of the production was concentrated – the children's game interrupted by Krogstad's sudden appearance in the doorway, the tree trimming punctuated by Nora's mimed reactions to her husband's recital of Krogstad's unsavory background, the hectic tarantella rehearsal. Each of these vignettes seemed, in the words of the reviewer for *Dags-Telegrafen* (23 December), "to stop in a tableau effect for an instant, implanting the picture indelibly on the mind of the spectator and then moving on again in the inexorable progress toward the fearful consequences of the conclusion."

Plate 36 A posed studio photograph of the tarantella scene in the world premiere of
A Doll's House (Danish Royal Theatre, 1879). Betty Hennings is Nora, Rank (Peter
Jerndorff) is at the piano, and Helmer (Emil Poulsen) sets the beat, while Mrs. Linde
(Agnes Gjørling) looks on.

Edvard Brandes argued, however, that while Hennings "struggled ably
and successfully against the gulf which her temperament and personality
placed between her and Ibsen's Nora," a moment like her technically skillful and vivacious tarantella ultimately lacked the "sensual abandon" needed to make it "the erotic high point of the marriage."[10] In this respect at
least, the virginal, asexual child–wife delineated by Hennings may have
had more in common with the idealized heroines of romantic fiction than
with the passionate young woman who frees herself with difficulty from
her physical relationship with her husband at the end of Ibsen's play.
Nevertheless, although the transition to the subdued and chilling mood of
the final act precipitated a jarring break with this Nora's previous personality, most reviewers were inclined to blame the writing itself. "The cold
and quiet clarity and seriousness which replace Nora's gay frivolity and
spineless despair cannot come so quickly. They must be prepared for with
many thoughts and considerations which the playwright has simply
skipped over," the poet and politician Carl Ploug asserted bluntly in
Fædrelandet (22 December). As for Betty Hennings, while Ploug found her

voice too subdued to be audible in this section and Brandes criticized her lack of authority in her confrontation with Poulsen's convincing Helmer, most commentators had only praise for her handling of this undeniably difficult transition from songbird to new woman. She rose, Topsøe declared in *Dagbladet*, from confusion and disappointment to become "what she must become, the greater of the two, completely superior to her husband." Subsequently, Johanne Juell's performance as Nora at Christiania Theatre less than a month later (20 January 1880) seemed to some critics, Brandes among them, to introduce a more convincing solution to the problem of the role's apparent bifurcation. The new sense of genuine mental anguish that Juell brought to her earlier scenes with Mrs. Linde and Krogstad caused her admirers to describe her as

> the first to hold Nora's character together, so that the childish gaiety of the first act did not clash incomprehensibly and crudely with the mature seriousness that follows the catastrophe. The highly regarded Nora of Fru Hennings fell as such into two parts, both equally striking in performance. But the gay little squirrel held not the slightest trace of that Nora whose terror later rouses her to seriousness.[11]

Although – unlike the generally slapdash Norwegian opening – the premiere of *A Doll's House* at the Royal Theatre was a carefully polished production that remained in the theatre's repertory for fully twenty-eight years, it was still, in essence, a stylistic hybrid, a transitional mixture of old and new methods. The experienced and painstaking H. P. Holst was placed in charge of the "arrangement" of this production, but one would search in vain for a director's script containing detailed instructions for movements, groupings, and line readings.[12] Although the function of the director gradually defined itself during the second half of the nineteenth century, such matters of interpretation were still, at this point, largely the province of the individual performer. Hence it was not in the least unusual for Betty Hennings to try (unsuccessfully) to persuade Frederik Høedt, her former coach, to assist her in developing her characterization. Actual rehearsals were few in number: only eleven in all, including the dress rehearsal, were held for this important premiere. As for the realistic living-room set, most of it came directly from the earlier production of *The Pillars of Society*, which was still in the repertory. Holst's mise-en-scène was arranged for the most part in accordance with the explicit and implicit directions supplied by Ibsen in the text. Of particular interest, of course, are the touches presumably added in an effort to strengthen the impression of a lifelike, three-dimensional environment. Although the hallway landing and the busy bank manager's study were hardly seen by the audience, both of these offstage areas were furnished with an attention to detail that would, twenty years later, be hailed as an innovation in the Moscow Art Theatre productions of Ibsen and Chekhov. In the room itself, a well-stocked sewing basket and a wood-box placed beside the stoneware oven gave the actors additional opportunities to create an atmosphere of living reality on the stage. Such items as flowering plants, floral bouquets, and chairs with flowered seat covers lent the Helmer parlor an air of middle-class refinement. Two provocative objects commented (whether intended or not) on Nora's two main functions in the marriage; on the bookcase, among sets of books in expensive bindings, stood a bust of Venus, while a reproduction of Raphael's *Madonna with Child* hung conspicuously in the middle of the rear wall, above the piano.

Ibsen's poetic use of lighting values and sound effects in *A Doll's House* aroused critical interest from the outset. From the cheerful brightness of the first act, accentuated by the glittering ornaments Nora hangs on the tree, the Royal Theatre production modulated to the more somber mood of the second, underscored by such visual details as the plundered Christmas tree and the burnt-down candle stubs in the chandelier that hung over the middle of the room. The lights continued to dim slowly during the crucial scene between Nora and Doctor Rank, until the maid carried in a lamp at her mistress's request and the stage again brightened. In the final act, the return of the Helmers from the costume ball was illuminated only by the light from the hallway and a small lamp on the round table, the battleground for the imminent confrontation. The atmosphere of joylessness and dissonance that affected many of the play's first reviewers in this final movement was intensified in the production by other elements as well: costume changes, as Nora lays aside her masquerade dress to reappear in "ordinary clothes, with a valise," and (live) sounds from beyond the room – music and distant voices from the party upstairs, steps heard softly on the landing, and at last the punctuating slam of the street door below.

The Bloch generation

With Ibsen's modern plays as their rallying point and the naturalistic theory of representation as their common ground, a new generation of directors came to the fore in Scandinavia during the years immediately following the first productions of *A Doll's House*. The Swedish actor–manager August Lindberg, who frequently collaborated with Ludvig Josephson at Nya teatern, was an ardent Ibsen supporter whose finely acted touring productions included the European premiere of *Gengangere* (*Ghosts*) in 1883 and the Norwegian premiers of *Brand* (1895) and *John Gabriel Borkman* (1897). Bjørn Bjørnson, who went on to become the first head of Norway's Nationaltheatret in 1899, began to introduce the naturalistic methods of staging, lighting, and ensemble playing when he joined Christiania Theatre as an actor and director in 1884, at the age of twenty-five. The Norwegian director and playwright Gunnar Heiberg was only two years older than Bjørnson when he, in turn, began his own influential four-year management of the National Stage in Bergen in 1884. William Bloch, the oldest of the group, was in many ways its spokesman and unofficial leader. During his two terms as stage director at the Danish Royal Theatre – from 1881 to 1893 and again from 1899 to 1909 – Bloch developed and systematized his method of stage direction, predicated on the conviction that "mise-en-scène has now developed into an art which requires an intensive study of the individual roles, a minute working out of all details."[13] Particularly in the Ibsen productions of these four men, there is a great deal that anticipates the later theories and practical advances of their more widely recognized European counterparts in the naturalistic movement.

Ghosts both demanded and helped to foster a new style of acting that would be capable, as Ibsen put it in a letter to August Lindberg, of "making the spectator feel as if he were actually sitting, listening, and looking at events happening in real life."[14] After Josephson, then head of Nya teatern, had pronounced this play "one of the filthiest things ever written in Scandinavia" and had categorically refused to allow a production of it, Lindberg seized the initiative and took to the road with a highly creditable production that eventually toured both the provinces and the capitals of all three Nordic countries. After a cautious summer opening in the coastal town of Hälsingborg (22 August 1883), the Lindberg troupe carried its bold enterprise across the Sound to Copenhagen, where most critics had high praise for his company's carefully coordinated ensemble work and, in particular, for his own introspective interpretation of Osvald, likened by many to his widely admired portrayal of Hamlet. As Mrs. Alving, the dignified, rather mannered acting of Hedvig Winterhjelm struck the reviewers as "a bit preachy in certain places," but Lindberg's portrait of her tormented son set the tone for generations of naturalistic Osvalds to come.

Edvard Brandes was deeply impressed by the pattern of abruptly changing moods used by the actor to delineate Osvald's gradual mental collapse, as "his sudden outbursts of energy rebounded into apathy."[15] This intricate, carefully integrated weave of shifting reactions and attitudes is described in detail by another eyewitness, Georg Nordensvan: "The different phases all found their proper expression, the 'worm-eaten' hopelessness, together with the rekindled desire for life, the nervous tension succeeded by apathy, the coldness of death, outbursts of childlike misery and of the selfishness of the invalid – at certain moments intense sensitivity and touching tenderness, always simply expressed, with no exaggeration of the pathological."[16] William Archer saw in the "slow, deliberate, dreamy" quality of this Hamlet-like Osvald "the manner of a man to whom the world has become unreal." Like many others, Archer found the key to the characterization in the extraordinary expressiveness of Lindberg's eyes and face:

> short, curling black hair, and a small black moustache, a very pale face, and those blinking, uneven, sort of light-shy eyes one so often sees in broken-down debauchees, one or other of the eyebrows having a tendency to rise now and then, without any apparent cause, and seemingly involuntarily. . . . Lindberg had actually invented and worked out in the smallest detail the *manner* of the man which, though it harmonized entirely with Ibsen's intentions, was by no means to be found ready-made in them.[17]

A few months before Lindberg staged *Ghosts* for the first time, Bloch's production of *En folkefjende* (*An Enemy of the People*) at the Danish Royal Theatre (4 March 1883) represented a milestone of another sort, a virtually perfect realization of the naturalistic ideal of totally integrated mise-en-scène. "The care with which Bloch had brought out even the minutest detail, had polished the smallest facets, created a theatrical phenomenon whose parallel has not been seen in any theatre in Scandinavia," Sven Lange declared. "The performance shone like a brilliant and glittering diamond behind the footlights."[18] The compilation of significant, tangible detail that invariably characterized a Bloch production was, however, never an end in itself but a means, later emulated by Stanislavski and others, of establishing a sense of inner, spiritual truth. Theatre, Bloch held, "should be not a mirror of life, but a reflection of the hidden life of the soul, acting not a direct imitation, illustrating 'reality', but the indirect revelation of the ever-changing facets of the soul."[19] As a firm believer that "the task of the director is to elaborate creatively on the work of the dramatist," he regarded the fuller explication of character and situation as his chief prerogative: "Where the author's intentions end, those of the naturalistic director begin."[20] Lindberg was in complete agreement. After reading a play for the first time, Bloch's great Swedish contemporary maintained

> the director must be inspired by the same fire as the author. He must feel and sympathize with all the characters in the play. He must see how they move, come and go, part and interact. He must lead them toward one another, to struggle or to be reconciled; he must penetrate their innermost core and show the actors how they look inside. With an intensity that resembles that of a visionary, he must be able to transport himself and the actor to other times and other surroundings.[21]

With its rounded ensemble work and its precisely executed staging, Bloch's *Enemy* pointed ahead to his later productions of the more complex and demanding Ibsen dramas that followed – *Vildanden* (*The Wild Duck*) in 1885, *Fruen fra havet* (*The Lady from the Sea*) in 1889, *Hedda Gabler* in 1891, and *Bygmester Solness* (*The Master Builder*) in 1903. From the outset, the effect created by his first attempt at Ibsen was an unbroken illusion of verisimilitude, fully in accord with the playwright's own injunction that the staging of *An Enemy of the People* must reflect, above all, "truthfulness to nature – the illusion that everything is real and that one is sitting and watching something that is actually taking place in real life." To achieve this end, Ibsen goes on in his long letter to Hans Schrøder at Christiania Theatre (14 December 1882), the play "demands exceptionally well-drilled ensemble playing, i.e., protracted and methodically supervised rehearsals." Ibsen's concern echoes, in turn, the shared preoccupation of the naturalistic movement with the attainment of an ensemble effect that projected, in Ludvig Josephson's words, "a true mirror image of life . . . as it once has been or as our modern times have shown it to be – in other words, as natural and as truthful as possible."[22] In pursuit of this goal, Bloch held an unprecedented total of thirty-two rehearsals for *An Enemy of the People*, twelve of them devoted to the mass scenes in the play. During these sessions he worked closely with each individual actor and then, in his words, "assembled the various individualities into a musical harmony of conversation within the inspired life of the ensemble."[23] His remarkably detailed promptbook for this production, still preserved in the Royal Theatre archives, contains not only set descriptions, floor plans, and elaborate blocking diagrams; it is also filled with directions for line readings that reflect his conception of the characters and their motivations. The public meeting in the fourth act, a masterpiece of naturalistic direction, required a separate booklet of over 100 pages in length, in which exclamations and snatches of dialogue are interpolated into the action in order to give the individual members of the crowd specific attitudes and reactions.

With their solid walls and three-dimensional furnishings, Bloch's renderings of the play's settings – Stockmann's "neatly furnished and decorated" living room in the first two acts, the "gloomy and uncomfortable" newspaper office in the third act, the "big, old-fashioned room" in Captain Horster's house where the fourth-act meeting is held, and, finally, Stockmann's disheveled study with its broken windowpanes – offered a suggestively amplified commentary on the lives and situations of the characters who inhabited these rooms. Critics were particularly impressed by his use of the unpretentiously "cosy and realistic interiors in the modestly furnished house of a doctor" that contrasted so sharply with the bleak prospect of "broken windows and a view of a poor alleyway" facing the denounced "public enemy" in the last act. As always, Bloch's purpose was to endow a given stage setting with an atmosphere and a life of its own. "When I walk into the auditorium at night, after the curtain has gone up," he observed, "the atmosphere upon the stage should make me feel the same as any guest walking into a strange parlor; the kind of house it is, the kind of people there, and what goes on between them, before I ever step inside."[24]

The intense and dynamic interplay of character and environment that characterized Bloch's *Enemy* reached remarkable proportions in the raucous meeting in Horster's house, at which Doctor Stockmann comes face to face with the "compact majority" of the town's citizens. Rather than providing Emil Poulsen's pugnacious and determined Stockmann with a faceless, chanting mob to contend with, the director was guided by Ibsen's own exhortation that the theatre "give the minor parts in the fourth act as far as possible to capable actors; the more figures you can have in the crowd that are really individualized and true to nature, the better."[25] In this spirit, Bloch added no fewer than fifty-three distinct new characters to create a gallery of types in which "life, movement, and individuality extended to every group and every figure."[26] Each of these additional characters was identified by occupation and, implicitly, by age in the promptbook. Except for four women, the assembly was comprised of an angry and unruly crowd of men. One was a blacksmith, another a typographer, a third a wholesale merchant, while others were sea captains, bricklayers, clerks, and the like. As the meeting progressed, each one of these figures had a carefully orchestrated role to play, and each added a strand to the tangible fabric of the society Stockmann must confront in this act. The speeches and exchanges of the main characters were continually punctuated by angry crowd reactions, loud outcries, whistling, imitations of cockcrows and barking dogs, and the noise of horns, lyres, and exploding cherry bombs. Most of all, Edvard Brandes admired "the excellent way in which the different interruptions are exclaimed, some sharply cutting, some resoundingly rude, some comically parodistic."[27] The result was a complex weave of detail and nuance that amplified but never distorted the thematic line of the action.

The savage irony of the choral accompaniment devised by Bloch reached its peak near the end of the act, at the point when Stockmann is proclaimed an enemy of the people. Pandemonium broke out. Everyone tried to fight his way toward the speakers' platform, shouting, stamping, and whistling. Three continually disruptive schoolboys, who later engaged in a spirited fight with the Stockmann youngsters, pelted the defeated doctor with orange peels. After he finally made his way slowly through the crowd with his family at the conclusion of the meeting, everything once again became dynamic movement and action. Hooting and shouting, fighting, and loud arguments broke out as the assembly disbanded. The dramatic irony of the events was thrown into yet bolder relief when one group began to chant the word "folkefjende" – enemy of the people – over and over again to the tune of a popular melody. The mocking song continued to be heard, fading gradually into the distance, as the curtain fell on a spectacle of disarray: an angry woman being helped to her feet; a man with a bloody nose being attended to; Aslaksen improvising a speech about the impending financial ruin of the Baths; "an umbrella, a lady's shawl, a high hat, an overshoe, and a couple of chalk pipes" as scattered remnants on the meeting-room floor.

Bloch's meticulous production of *An Enemy of the People* served notice of the power of a style of representation that would continue to maintain its influence on the theatre for the next half century or more. So inseparable from the spirit of this particular play did his concept seem that his mise-en-scène enjoyed a long afterlife: Bang used it to help Lugné-Poë stage the

Parisian premiere of the work ten years later; Poul Nielsen, Bloch's protégé, resurrected it intact at the Royal Theatre in 1915; and it once more
formed the basis for the notable Comédie Française revival that starred
Maurice de Féraudy as an aged Stockmann in 1921. It was, however,
Bloch's subsequent production of *The Wild Duck* in 1885 that conclusively
demonstrated the sensitivity and responsiveness of his method to the
increasingly complex, subtextual character of Ibsen's dramatic vision. His
approach to the new play, again grounded in a close attention to concrete-
ly observed details and reactions drawn from daily life, was a direct
response to the need for verisimilitude emphasized by the playwright himself, notably in his long, frequently reprinted reminder to Hans Schrøder
at Christiania Theatre that "in both the ensemble acting and the staging,
the play demands truth to nature and a touch of reality in every respect."[28]
No one, however, was more conscious than Bloch of the mesh of power-
fully symbolic and poetic resonances underlying the "realistic" surface of
a play like *The Wild Duck*. As such, his concern with the external dimension of recognizably credible detail was invariably his means – the only
means he knew – of heightening the audience's perception of the play's
inner, poetic dimension. Aware as he was that scenic truth is not to be
equated with truth in life, he set out to create a theatrical truth, an interpretation of the life of the drama, in terms that reduced to a minimum the
barrier between art and reality.

Bloch and his contemporaries in Norway and Sweden sensed
instinctively, however, that Ibsen's elusive and allusive new play faced
them with a challenge they had never met before. "It is as though *The Wild
Duck* were built on painful memories, on strange experiences from one's
own youth. And this gives the play a secret, intimate charm, a gentle atmosphere found in no other play of his," mused Gunnar Heiberg, whose finely
tuned production at the National Stage in Bergen (9 January 1885) was the
drama's world premiere.[29] "With Doctor Ibsen's newest play we have
entered virgin territory where we have to make our way with pick and
shovel," Lindberg wrote to the playwright before going into rehearsal for
his own production at Dramaten in Stockholm, which opened three weeks
after Heiberg's. "The people in the play are completely new, and where
would we get by relying on theatrical clichés?"[30] In a letter to his father,
Bjørn Bjørnson, whose production at Christiania Theatre followed only
two days after the world premiere, put his finger on one of the most pressing considerations influencing the rehearsals for this particular play:

Day and night *The Wild Duck* was with me. It had clamored its way into my very being. I lay in the stillness of the night and heard the lines. And *heard* the pauses. The ones that had to lift the words. Those to come, or those which had already been spoken. They loom larger after the pause that precedes them – or the silence that follows them.[31]

Bloch, on the other hand, seems to have had little of a general nature to say about the play, but his staging of *The Wild Duck* at the Royal Theatre in Copenhagen (22 February 1885) could well be seen as the ultimate realization of the principles and aims of the movement to which all four of these directors belonged. In Bloch's aesthetics (as, indeed, in Ibsen's) close attention to the outer dimension of unmistakably truthful detail served a far more important purpose than that of merely chronicling reality or creating a convincingly lifelike appearance. This attention was, above all, a stratagem for deepening the audience's perception of the essential spirit and meaning of the play, by revealing an inner world within the seemingly precise context of everyday life. "The inanimate, material objects and the so-called lifelike touches were his means of illuminating and breathing life into the setting, the situation, the stage action – of creating the necessary atmosphere around the only true reality in art, that of the soul," writes the playwright and director Henri Nathansen, a devoted pupil who carried Bloch's style into the new century.[32]

In their productions of a play like *The Wild Duck*, Bloch and his associates were thus crucially concerned with the creation of a charged stage environment that would participate in and accentuate the inner rhythm of the action. Accordingly, both Haakon Werle's richly and comfortably furnished study in act 1, with its spacious and elegant sitting room adjoining it, and Hjalmar Ekdal's manifestly simpler studio, with its strangely evocative inner loft, were seen as much more than inert backgrounds for the events of the play. Werle's room, for example, was treated by Bloch as something more than the appropriately furnished realistic interior described in the stage directions, with rugs on the floor, various tables, upholstered chairs, a sofa, a fireplace, and a desk cluttered with documents, newspapers, journals, account books, almanacs, writing materials, and the like. In addition to all this, small but telling nuances – the guns and hunting gear that decorated the walls in Bloch's production, the safe he substituted for the more cultivated bookcases mentioned by Ibsen – provided their own implicit, visually provocative comment on the owner of the house.[33]

A richer opportunity for the creation of a scenic environment animated and charged with an independent expressive potential of its own was afforded by the Ekdal world in which the subsequent acts take place. The bare, impoverished atmosphere of Hjalmar Ekdal's attic studio aroused particular interest wherever the play was first seen on the stage. "As difficult as it is characteristic, the studio decor with its mystical attic in the background belongs unconditionally to the best one has had occasion to see at Christiania Theatre," Henrik Jæger wrote of the Bjørnson production.[34] Lindberg's performance at Dramaten, which opened nearly a month before Bloch's, had actually caused considerable commotion with its microscopically truthful depiction of the Ekdal milieu, into which he incorporated a greatly discussed night commode, complete with chamber pot and washbasin, to signify the humble condition of the ruined Ekdals. Lindberg's actors moved in convincingly naturalistic fashion among the furnishings, handling props that had the solidity and authenticity of observed reality. "You believe in them because they speak and do not declaim, because they are seen in surroundings in which they clearly are at home, and because they not only speak, stand, sit down, listen – whatever the case may be – but even understand how to fill the pauses with all those *small tasks* which are so usual in daily life," Gustaf af Geijerstam declared.[35] In a similar way, the result of Bloch's painstaking attention to detail was an accumulating sense of the truth of the Ekdal existence. The poor photographer's studio, the Copenhagen critics agreed, was "a splendid setting full of atmosphere in the different lights in which it appears . . . and a striking frame, spacious if desolate, around the life of the Ekdal family."[36]

While the rather conventional interior of the first act could be put together (as was the custom) from scenery available from the stockroom, the unusual Ekdal setting was an entirely different matter. To capture its special flavor, Bloch turned to Valdemar Gyllich, a scene-painter with a remarkable flair for natural detail and chiaroscuro effects. In its spatial arrangement, Bloch's floor plan corresponded to the pattern followed in countless other productions of the play for generations to come. On the "living" side of the garret, beneath a slanting attic window, stood a sofa, table, and chairs (not included in Gyllich's sketch); on the "professional" side of the room, the audience saw a tiled stove, atop which perched a stuffed eagle (perhaps a reminder of Old Ekdal's hunting days), and a collection of objects denoting a modest photographer's flat: a tripod, a gilded armchair and small marble-topped table to pose beside, and an ornamental mirror above a mahogany console. Seen at the back, to the left of the double sliding doors in Gyllich's design, was a small bookcase crammed with even more domestic clutter than Ibsen had conceived: "on its shelves photographic plates, books, pamphlets, jars, boxes, small bottles, a glass pot, a flute, a hammer, pliers, household items, a suitcase with Hjalmar's lounging jacket."[37] For the last two acts, the prop list adds another significant item to this jumble on the shelves – a pistol.

The main source of fascination in Bloch's production was, however, the large, irregularly shaped interior loft that was seen only in momentary glimpses beyond the sliding doors in the rear wall. This was the real object of Gyllich's efforts, represented in a design that even today is redolent of this artist's strong feeling for the dramatic interaction of light and shadow. The floor plan for the production delineates an obliquely angled and very spacious area for the loft, taking up as much of the total stage space as the Ekdal studio itself. In the midst of the moldering and inanimate objects that filled the attic – packing cases, a pair of geographical globes, hampers, a table, an old dresser piled with large books, group photographs of anonymous people, a dead pine tree – Bloch placed a small handful of live birds (four hens and six pigeons, to be exact) to convey a suggestion of the living creatures that have their abode there and play their unwitting but essential role in the escapist fantasies of Ibsen's dreamers. Both Lindberg and Bjørnson were similarly taken by the idea of avian sounds in the attic. While the detailed list of props for the Lindberg production includes live hens in a wire cage, however, Bjørnson adopted a rather more oblique approach. Johannes Brun, who played Old Ekdal and was also known as an accomplished mimic of all animal noises, was apparently persuaded to endow the wild duck with an audible offstage vocal presence.

Such touches were never introduced simply as isolated flourishes in a picturesque *tableau vivant*, however, for the sum of these details had to add up to an integrated organic whole. They provided a means of translating the symbolic or allegorical dimension of Ibsen's drama, which in general greatly preoccupied its first critics, into terms of concrete, living reality. Hence, for example, Heiberg's work was admired by his contemporaries especially because "he senses the mood of the play, the spirit in which it was created, and conceives of it as theatre – not as literature."[38] Octavia Sperati, who acted Gina in his *Wild Duck*, offers a revealing comment on his approach in this regard. "Directing us he never tired of emphasizing

Plate 37 The Ekdal studio: Valdemar Gyllich's design for the Bloch production of *The Wild Duck* at the Danish Royal Theatre in 1885.

that the more naturally and realistically we acted, the more clearly the symbolism, the general significance, would emerge and enclose the play's action, as it does in life," Sperati writes. "The inhabitants of the studio must be unaware of the double life lived in *The Wild Duck*. They are buried in everyday prose and up to their ears in petty worries."[39] Similarly, the Danish reviewers felt, when Bloch's actors "created a rounded totality, and when the pointed arrows of the dialogue turned into living speech on the lips of the characters, the symbolism . . . retreated into the background."[40] Seen in this way, the interpolation of real birds and their indistinct peripheral sounds served to establish a tangibly perceived atmosphere that rendered this specific domestic milieu believable and comprehensible – not only to the audience, it might be added, but also to the actors who were thereby enabled to "live" their roles with stronger psychological conviction.

At the core of the new style of acting that sprang from the naturalistic movement was its emphasis on the related issues of motivation and physical action. The life of a dramatic character, Bloch insisted, does not abruptly commence at the moment he makes his entrance on the stage. The actor must respond to the unreal life of the theatre as though it were real: each and every movement and action in the performance must be saturated with the truthfulness and conviction of reality itself. Yet, since the theatre reflects only a corner of the larger fabric of living reality, every line of dialogue must, as in life, mirror the past. "If the character portrayed is to

Plate 38 Gyllich's chiaroscuro design for the interior loft in the Bloch production of *The Wild Duck*.

appear to the audience in the theatre not as an abstraction, living only a hollow life within the narrow circumference of the given conditions of the play, but a living creature, possessing within himself infinite possibilities," then Bloch would maintain that "the thoughts and feelings he reveals to us must be shown as they take root in his mind. Every utterance must be given a life of its own. It must be conceived, be born, live and die."[41]

To achieve this end in *The Wild Duck*, Bloch structured his mise-en-scène as a dynamic and kinetic mosaic of movements and physical actions that bonded Ibsen's characters to their environment. In this respect as in others, his approach anticipated Stanislavski's method of utilizing stage objects and stage business to endow a scene with the conviction of reality. The Danish director's promptbook is filled with circumstantial instructions for the continually varied but relaxed and fluid pattern of physical tasks to be performed by his actors. Gina and Hedvig, for instance, busied themselves throughout with domestic activities – tidying the house, sewing (shirts), serving (real) food, lighting lamps and trimming wicks, reading, and, of course, retouching photographs. Often the meaning of an action and the meaning of a speech were counterpointed to produce an acute sense of irony. In general, the coordinated, rhythmic flow of such physical activities served to integrate the individual figures into a fabric of human relationships, thereby making the common pattern that underlies their related actions – the wounded struggle to survive – more coherent and more evident.

Unlike Lindberg, who took the unusual step of using new or comparatively unknown actors in an effort to abolish mannerisms and stereotypes from his production of *The Wild Duck*, Bloch cast the play with some of the foremost actors of the day. Betty Hennings was thirty-five when she played Hedvig for the first time, but her sensitive performance radiated a child's trust and devotion to her father, made vividly physical in "her industriousness, her affection for [Hjalmar], and her total despair at the prospect of losing him."[42] Hjalmar Ekdal was played by Emil Poulsen as the virtual antithesis of his Torvald Helmer – a blend of essential naivety, childish pretentiousness, and lightly melancholy charm and warmth. Unlike Lindberg's brooding Hjalmar and the similarly serious reading of the part adopted by Arnoldus Reimers in Bjørnson's production, Poulsen's more faceted characterization incorporated a tone of witty irony and even self-satire. "He was utterly wretched in fine company, truly stingy, happily at home in the attic, and unspeakably tousled when put on the spot," Edvard Brandes concluded. "The continual variation between false pathos and the commonest everyday talk flowed naturally from his lips, and he held the character within the chosen framework with an iron hand."[43] In the opinion of most of the critics, however, the pivotal focus in Bloch's finely tuned ensemble was Olaf Poulsen's extraordinary portrayal of Old Ekdal – a role which, in the hands of the greatest comic character actor of his generation, fused intensely human proportions with formidable symbolic weight. His first stealthy intrusion among Werle's dinner guests, hunched and shyly delighted, his comings and goings with (real) hot water for that toddy which is his defense against the terror of reality, and his energetic hunting and rabbit shooting in the attic all contributed to the impression described by Brandes and others of a hieroglyph of drifting, foundering humanity, a perfect blending of "the tragic and the comic in this strange figure."

In spite of the force of such individual acting presentations as these, however, the essential strength of the naturalistic style propounded by Bloch and his contemporaries lay in its vigorous stress on totality, on the ensemble effect. Rather than isolate a single motif or choose a single mood, for example, Bloch deliberately accentuated the density of Ibsen's dramatic texture, the complexity of the pattern of interwoven and mutually sustaining themes and character interrelationships. The great expressive power of his staging of *The Wild Duck* was thus dependent on the cumulative effect of a multiplicity of fine scenic nuances and psychological character shadings, drawn together and integrated into an interpretative whole by the director. The all-encompassing creative function that this figure was now expected to serve is perhaps most succinctly summarized by Gunnar Heiberg, one of this movement's most articulate spokesmen: "He must perceive the totality which constitutes the through-line, and he must perceive all the thousands of details that make up the volume and color of life. He must be the rock of righteousness upon which the actor's natural tendency to perform without regard to others stands. . . . He must be able to build up a milieu. He must be capable of molding an ensemble."[44] These were the basic creative criteria that distinguished the art of directing from what Ludvig Josephson sarcastically referred to as the contemporary mode of mise-en-scène in which "the interior decorator or the furniture director plays the principal role."

By the mid-1880s naturalism had become the dominant style of theatrical production in Scandinavia, applied by its exponents to plays of all kinds and periods, from the works of Shakespeare and Holberg to the modern dramas of Ibsen, Bjørnson, Strindberg, and their lesser contemporaries (among whom Gunnar Heiberg had by then begun to figure prominently). Above all, however, it was Ibsen's plays and his insistence on "credible, true-to-life expression" in the performance of them that continued to inspire the new movement. Although the plays themselves became increasingly more symbolic in nature, early productions of them remained solidly anchored in the naturalistic mode of representation – something for which Bloch, for example, has sometimes been criticized, but which, in fact, must be seen in the light of Ibsen's own demands for a realistically grounded interpretation. "No declamation! No theatrical emphases!" he thus wrote to Sophie Reimers at Christiania Theatre in 1887, adding his customary warning that her performance as Rebecca West in *Rosmersholm* must "take real life and exclusively that as the basis and point of departure."[45]

Ultimately, the difficulties faced by Bloch in his later Ibsen productions stemmed not from the naturalistic style in which he staged them, but rather more directly from the general air of confusion and consternation that greeted the psychological nihilism of the plays themselves. *The Lady from the Sea* and *Hedda Gabler* were presented by him as studies in alienation, so to speak, inevitably disturbing portraits of women cut off from the environment of minutely detailed reality in which the director located them. In the first of these productions (17 February 1889), Josephine Eckardt's nervous, restless Ellida Wangel seemed an enigmatic figure to the critics, "an Ondine-like creature who lives in isolation in the midst of the people around her."[46] In Bloch's even more controversial production of *Hedda Gabler* two years later, Betty Hennings portrayed a "cold, proud, unapproachable" Hedda who displayed only icy contempt for the commonplace world of petty realities in which she found herself.[47] Even her vocal dynamics were scored in virtually musical fashion to emphasize a sense of the gulf placed between her and the other characters – to the manifest delight of Herman Bang, who found that she "depicted Hedda's coldness of heart with a frankness, almost a brutality that cut straight to the core of the play and touched the audience deeply."[48] Most, however, disliked both her reading and the "demonic" quality of the play in general; more than a decade elapsed before Bloch's concept was finally vindicated, in a revival of his 1891 production that was hailed as "a triumph for the Royal Theatre." Seen through the eyes of a new generation, the performance exhibited "a unity held together by a multiplicity of visible and invisible threads" that enabled the spectator, in the words of Johannes V. Jensen, "to reconstruct an entire period with its individualities and traits, its aberrations and unhappy secrets, its strengths and downfalls."[49]

The quality of quiet and restrained naturalness that Bloch sought to impart to a symbolic play like *The Master Builder* depended on a meticulously structured mosaic of character actions, reactions, and motivations. In this production (8 March 1893) Emil Poulsen's convincing portrayal of a tortured and guilt-ridden Halvard Solness drew its power from the degree of psychological plausibility attained by the actor, rather than from any attempt on his or Bloch's part to locate the character on a higher symbolic or mythic plane. In a similar way, the quality of self-confident vitality that Betty Hennings brought to the ambiguous figure of Hilde Wangel was also grounded in "realistic touches that allowed a certain straightforward naturalness to come to the fore."[50] On this basis and with close attention to the subtext that runs beneath the realistic surface of the dialogue, Bloch wove an intricate pattern of psychic dominance that took shape with effective clarity in the very first encounter between the principal characters. As Hilde circled restlessly around the stage, "her conquest of the master builder's thoughts and senses conveyed a striking impression of a bird of prey entrapping its victim. From here on, Halvard Solness became someone under the influence of a stronger spirit."[51] Even this measure of symbolic action was eschewed by the much younger Johanne Dybwad, the foremost Norwegian interpreter of this role, in her pursuit of complete simplicity and naturalness. "Fru Dybwad entered as Hilde with the self-assured step of youth, full of self-confidence and confidence in others," Heiberg writes of her performance at Christiania Theatre. "In the beginning there is as yet nothing of the wild bird, the bird of prey, only the yearning of youth, the eager ears of youth, the readiness of youth to go toward the great heights."[52]

Correspondence found among Bloch's papers indicates that Lugné-Poë was again advised by Herman Bang on the basis of Bloch's script for *The Master Builder*, specifically in regard to the latter's purely suggestive staging of Solness' unseen fall from the tower at the end. Yet the subsequent visit of the Théâtre de l'Oeuvre to Christiania in 1894 evoked little critical enthusiasm for Lugné-Poë's "symbolic" method. Clearly, the dominant style of naturalistic acting was not seriously challenged by the slow, trance-like gestures and ponderously intoned, even chanted delivery that the French director adopted in order to create a suitable air of mysticism and enigma. Ibsen's own reactions to this visit were evidently mixed. Although he appears to have pronounced Lugné-Poë's production of *The Master Builder* "the resurrection of my play," his only known reaction to the troupe's performance of *Rosmersholm* was the rather equivocal remark that, as a passionate writer, his work "should be acted passionately and not otherwise."[53]

To Ibsen's last plays, in which the dividing line between the realistic and symbolic modes of expression is sometimes all but obliterated, Scandinavian directors and designers of the period were inclined to respond with a curious mixture of naturalism and almost romanticized pictorialism. Critics and performers alike recognized that the main characters in these dramas stand above and beyond their everyday surroundings, and hence efforts of different kinds were made to suggest this perception in the theatre. Lindberg, whose intrepid troupe staged the Norwegian premiere of *John Gabriel Borkman* at the old theatre in Drammen (19 January 1897), made the title character up to resemble Johan Sverdrup, the former Norwegian prime minister and political reformer whose revolutionary vision of a democratized society must have suggested a rather ironic parallel to Borkman's Faustian dream of the welfare of all mankind. Emil Poulsen, who directed this play at the Danish Royal Theatre two weeks later, adopted a more obvious alternative by acting Borkman in the likeness of Ibsen himself, to suggest the artist figure whose suffering and guilt are so obviously the thematic center of the work. Apart from his modest "stylization" of Borkman's appearance, however, Poulsen's highly acclaimed production exemplified the naturalistic tradition that seems, on the surface, to govern and support the play's first three acts, if not its fourth. His own performance was an imposing fusion of grand passion and truth-to-life in the most intimate detail, and his able direction maintained a level of intense emotionality in such key sequences as the bitter first-act encounter between the estranged twin sisters, Gunhild Borkman and Ella Rentheim. Here, taking Ibsen's very explicit stage directions as his guide, Poulsen evolved a textured pattern of realistic actions and reactions in which, observed *Politiken* (1 February 1897), "even Ella's glances at the ceiling as she listened to the dragging footsteps overhead, as she listened to her sister's unpitying words each time the talk turned to the 'sick wolf,' were of the greatest effect." As a result, this scene in particular was praised by the Copenhagen critics for conveying "the tense atmosphere of death and destruction that lurks beneath the surface of the dialogue."[54] Betty Hennings, whose Ella Rentheim was all mildness and resignation in the teeth of Josephine Eckardt's passionate and unyielding Mrs. Borkman, was in fact criticized by some for seeming too unaffected by the overwhelming tone of bleakness and loss that this scene established.

Ideally, at least, the underlying focus of a naturalistic production like Poulsen's was the painstakingly reproduced milieu that both reflected and shaped the personalities of its inhabitants – in this case, the desolate Rentheim estate outside Christiania and, in the last act, the windy slopes of Grefsenkollen. Thorolf Pedersen, who had become the Royal Theatre's chief designer after Gyllich's death in 1895, located the two interior sets he created squarely in a tradition that can only be called Gothic, reminiscent of the romantic *genre sombre* still in favor when Ibsen first visited the Royal Theatre as an apprentice director, nearly half a century earlier. Outside the small windows of Mrs. Borkman's old-fashioned sitting room, blowing snow could be glimpsed during the first act. Upstairs, the walls of the deep, austere, windowless room that Borkman had made his prison were covered with moldering hangings: "the age of the fabric, the faded greenish-gray color that is so typical of old tapestries was splendidly captured," the reviewer for *Politiken* remarked.

As many a theatre critic has had occasion to point out over the years, meanwhile, it is this play's fourth act that invariably presents a problem in a conventionally naturalistic production of it. When, at the end of the long, uninterrupted night of reckoning, Borkman rushes forth from the house into the winter air and then climbs through the snow to the mountain lookout where he recreates his great dream for Ella, Ibsen enters new territory that lies beyond the reach of the realistic illusion created by painted drops, cardboard rocks, and canvas trees. Nevertheless, using every mechanical device at his disposal, Pedersen followed a purely representational approach, rooted in the pictorial traditionalism he always favored. After the moment in Ibsen's text when the house and its courtyard "disappear" as Borkman and Ella enter the woods, he introduced a blackout. A gauze transparency was lowered in order to fade in a hazily defined picture of a rugged Norwegian scene with a black fjord and distant mountains on the horizon. Pedersen's atmospherics – "the soft beauty of the Nordic winter night in half light, the blowing snowclouds that gradually disperse, allowing the pale glow of the sky and the winter stars to emerge" – made a strong visual impression on the critics, but many of them ultimately agreed with *Politiken* that "all the scene changes, the transparencies hoisted up and down, the snow and the moving clouds . . . unavoidably distract attention."

Ironically, Ibsen himself appears to have been fully in agreement with the impulse to paint a picture of this realm of dreams. For the important Christiania premiere of *John Gabriel Borkman*, which took place only six days after Lindberg's initiative at Drammen, the playwright pressed Jens Wang, Christiania Theatre's chief designer, to illustrate the oneiric journey of Borkman and Ella by employing a rolling panorama drop – a hackneyed effect that Wang rightly feared would draw unwanted comparisons with such popular potboilers as *Around The World in Eighty Days*. In spite of the designer's best efforts to paint evocative views of the picturesque Norwegian countryside that Ibsen had apparently envisioned, the misfired stage experiment failed to integrate the actors – who remained on level ground – with the "motion picture" of a steep climb up Grefsenkollen that unfolded behind them.[55] In the end, only Ibsen seems to have been satisfied with the result.

The essence of Wang's pictorial style is represented by the designs he made for the open-air scenes in *Naar vi døde vaagner* (*When We Dead Awaken*), which Bjørnson presented during his inaugural season as the first artistic director of Nationaltheatret. Even with Egil Eide as Rubek and his customary costar Johanne Dybwad as Maja, the Norwegian premiere of Ibsen's "dramatic epilogue" (6 February 1900) enjoyed little

Plate 39 Preliminary sketch by Jens Wang for the second-act wasteland setting in Ibsen's *When We Dead Awaken*, directed by Bjørn Bjørnson at Nationaltheatret in 1900.

favor with its first audiences. Here as elsewhere, the symbolic tone and associational technique of the play seemed at odds with the solidly representational scenery of the period. In order to create a realistic illusion of the "vast expanse of bare, treeless wasteland" described in detail by Ibsen in the second act, Wang opened his stage to its full depth. In front of a vista of mountains and sky painted on the cyclorama at the back, he constructed a mountain plateau made up of 123 platforms and other units, all covered with hemp painted to simulate heather and intended to give the actors an appropriate sense of uneven, rugged terrain underfoot.[56] Real water cascaded down what seemed a sheer rock face into a tranquil pool at the front of the stage, beside which the ghostly figure of Irene is seen standing in Wang's evocative preliminary sketch of the setting.

The avalanche in which Rubek and his nemesis are engulfed at the end of Ibsen's drama was unquestionably the severest technical problem Wang had to face, and he met it with great ingenuity. His design for the "wild, precipitous place high in the mountains" where the final act takes place was, in the words of one English observer at the time, an imposing panorama of "filed snowclad mountain peaks that stood out against a stormy sky, whilst the shadows of clouds passed over their untrodden glory and completed a picture which was vividly real."[57] This hazy, majestic landscape was actually viewed through layers of scrim; by the time the avalanche came, it was also partly obscured by clouds of vapor produced by fog machines. Depictions of natural disasters had retained a cherished place in nineteenth-century theatre practice, and Wang would have had no trouble in finding suitable models upon which to draw. Once Maja had disappeared from sight and her strange song was heard from far beneath the stage, a systematic, precisely timed collapse of breakaway elements in the setting began. Each piece of scenery fell in a predetermined sequence and direction, creating an illusion of falling rocks and snow. Caught up in this mechanical maelstrom, the indistinctly glimpsed figures of Rubek and Irene were seen "shrouded in gauze, fog, murky light, and confetti" as they appeared to be swept into the abyss.[58] To heighten the simulated reality of a snowslide, pellets of real ice rained down on the scene as the curtain fell. Beyond this spectacular moment the naturalistic devotion to external verisimilitude could not be carried.

At the century's turn

In many ways the turn of the century marked a significant watershed in the development of the Scandinavian theatre. The revolution which the Brandes generation had predicted and demanded had now become a practical reality through the productions of Bloch, Bjørnson, Lindberg, and others. Their work had established naturalism as the dominant style and the figure of the director as the indispensable interpretative force in the theatre. At the same time, plays like *When We Dead Awaken* and Strindberg's *To Damascus* I – both of which reached the stage in 1900 – heralded an altogether different conception of theatre that challenged the constraints imposed by the facsimile stage of the naturalists.

No event at this time contributed more to the sense of change and progress than the inauguration of Nationaltheatret at the beginning of the century's last season. Inspired by the tireless leadership of Bjørn Bjørnson, the Norwegian stage at last attained its goal of a truly national theatre when the old Christiania Theatre was demolished and a new playhouse with a new mandate opened its doors on 1 September 1899. Ibsen and the elder Bjørnson, captured in bronze in the monumental statues that still flank the theatre's entrance, were hailed by the audience and saluted by the stately King Oscar II as they took their seats. The momentous first night was devoted to extracts from Holberg comedies and a performance of Grieg's *Holberg Suite*. The second evening was Ibsen's, and the play selected – *An Enemy of the People* – was a felicitous vehicle for a personal tribute. On the third and most flamboyantly patriotic evening of the three-day festival, Bjørnson directed his father's nationalistic "folk play" *Sigurd Jorsalfar*

(*Sigurd the Crusader*) in a performance that included Eide as the warlike King Sigurd, Johan Fahlström as his noble rival King Eystein, and Dybwad as Borghild, the passionate and strong-willed woman in their lives. With more than a touch of historical melodrama about it, this revival of Bjørnson's saga play was greatly enhanced by a new musical score, composed and conducted for the occasion by the industrious Grieg.

The controversy that flared up over Bjørnson's liberal use of theatrical spectacle in his 1900 production of *The Pretenders* has its origins in his similarly lavish staging of *Sigurd the Crusader*. In both cases the goal of his mise-en-scène was a Meininger-like exactitude in the reproduction of historical period, place, dress, and armor. For the principal setting in the Bjørnson play, described in the text as "a great wooden hall richly ornamented with carvings," Wang copied the chief architectural features of the ancient wooden stave churches characteristic of medieval Norway. Skillfully worked into his design were embroidered ceiling hangings that concealed ultramodern electric projectors. Through the central portal at the back of the hall, where the altar would normally be seen in a church, one looked out instead on a Viking ship riding at anchor. As a director, Bjørnson was at his best in the creation of a dynamic pattern of ensemble action that filled such a historical framework with color and movement and brought it to life. When the same production later visited Stockholm, the Swedish critics readily agreed with their Norwegian counterparts that nothing comparable had been seen in Scandinavia since the guest performances of the Meininger themselves in 1889. "The life and color of the mass scenes, the natural and effective arrangement of the groupings, and the excellent coordination of the whole cannot be sufficiently extolled," wrote *Svenska Dagbladet* (4 June 1903) at the time. It did not escape notice, meanwhile, that the historical reality posited by Bjørnson *fils* and *père* was a highly idealized reality of "clean, neat clothes and shoes and . . . glittering swords" that had never known a rough sea voyage or a muddy battlefield.[59] Like the naturalism of contemporary life, the naturalism of historical period was, ultimately and of necessity, a construct of theatrical artifice.

The same is obviously true of the considerably less idealized periodicity invoked by Bloch in his six influential revivals of Holberg's comedies at the Royal Theatre during the early years of the new century. Brandes had already begun to agitate for an infusion of fresh life into the abstract, atrophied style of Holberg performance then in vogue. "Let us have the specific bourgeois society depicted by Holberg recreated in the theatre with as many of its characteristic traits as possible," he wrote in 1898. "One might, for example, begin by arranging for appropriate settings for them."[60] As if in response, Bloch's production of the rarely performed *Gert Westphaler* two years later initiated a veritable Holberg renaissance in the naturalistic mode. A new setting designed by Thorolf Pedersen replaced the traditional painted Holberg street with the virtual reality of a small-town square from the 1720s, comprised of timbered, gabled houses with solid doors and real windows. Yet the originality of this production consisted not only in its delineation of an environment and its cultivation of "small nuances, such as a pump that spouts real water [and] a maid who wrings out her dishclout from the top-story window of a building, but above all in the authority and clarity with which the director laid bare the inner rhythm of the work . . . its accelerating comic momentum."[61]

Mindful of Brandes' observation that "a play does not acquire a timeless quality by being presented against an abstract background," the new interiors Bloch devised for his Holberg productions were as specifically grounded in observed reality as the environments he created for Ibsen's prose plays. These naturalistic Holberg rooms were period paintings in three dimensions, with authentic furniture and props that reflected as accurately as possible the atmosphere and tastes of the author's own time. In turn, the intricately woven pattern of motivated actions and behavior linked the characters to their milieu in a wholly credible manner. As a result, Sven Lange noted, "the farcical comedies acquired a firm logic that had never been realized before, while the character comedies gained added strength because the actors in them no longer made their entrances from empty stage flats but seemed instead to have stepped out of life itself."[62]

In the 1904 revival of *The Lying-in Room*, for example, the bedchamber of the title, where old Corfitz's young wife receives the grasping, gossiping society that descends on her and her new baby, was a spacious, solidly constructed period replica in heavy baroque style. Bloch's promptbook for this production contains very detailed instructions concerning both the arrangement of the new setting and the wealth of realistic stage business for which it provided an opportunity.[63] Upstage left, a large bay window afforded a glimpse of the street outside. In the opposite corner of this curiously monumental lying-in room stood its decorously curtained bed. Across the room a folding screen concealed the cradle and its occupant –

Plate 40 Photograph of Bloch's naturalistic conception of the bedchamber setting in Holberg's *The Lying-in Room*. Danish Royal Theatre, 1904.

a live baby, seen at the beginning of the second act in the arms of a wet nurse and heard frequently during the course of the ensuing action. A window in the stage-right wall admitted a shaft of pale autumn sunlight that fell on the convalescent's comfortable armchair and the table beside it, on which stood smelling salts, drops, a snuffbox, and a vase of flowers. It was beneath this covered table that the bewildered and suspicious Corfitz (Olaf Poulsen) later tried to hide in his absurd attempt to discover the truth about the new arrival's legitimacy.

The current of astringent comic irony that ran through Bloch's Holberg interpretations was particularly evident in his 1903 production of *Jeppe on the Hill*, a durable mise-en-scène that held the stage for nearly fifty years. In itself, his visualization of the picturesque village setting in which the comedy begins and ends epitomized the subtle interplay of pastoral idyll and ramshackle reality that colored his entire approach to Holberg's complex masterpiece. The two thatched cottages that framed the rural scene, the luxuriant linden tree at its center, and even the faded pastoral backcloth that had been borrowed from the stockroom all contributed to an impression of bygone, idealized rusticity. At the same time, however, other elements in the composition alluded to the harsher, less attractive reality of Jeppe's peasant environment. His small, whitewashed cottage with its crumbling picket fence was visibly more dilapidated than the sturdier abode of his prosperous neighbor, Jacob the shoemaker, above

Plate 41 Pastoral idyll blended with ramshackle reality in the village setting for the Bloch production of Holberg's *Jeppe on the Hill*. Photograph of the Royal Theatre stage, 1903.

whose door a sign with a boot and a shoe proclaimed his trade. Beneath the romantic linden tree, the audience saw a pigsty and the "soggy" dunghill from which the frivolous Baron Nilus and his men pluck the sleeping peasant whom they proceed to "transform" into an aristocrat. Behind the tree (from which Jeppe is subsequently hung in a mock execution), the backyard of another rustic cottage afforded a glimpse of "an untended garden filled with a collection of bushes, flowers, and an assortment of pieces of trash." "The sun shines brightly," Bloch's notes continue, "where it manages to break through. It is early morning."[64]

From the outset, the life lived in this environment was depicted in graphic detail. The curtain rose on the sounds of a thrashing being inflicted on the wayward Jeppe by his shrewish wife Nille. When she at last emerged from their cottage, red-faced and out of breath from her exertions, she began to do the family laundry as she spoke her first monologue ("Was there ever a lazy lout in all the village like my husband!"), washing shirts, socks, and underwear in a basin, wringing out each item, and hanging it on the decrepit fence to dry. Olaf Poulsen made his entrance carrying Jeppe's hat, coat, kerchief, and garters in his hands, and his own opening monologue ("They say in the village that Jeppe drinks, but they don't say why he drinks") was similarly punctuated by the ritual of getting dressed for the day, as he fastened his garters, tied his kerchief, buttoned his vest, tidied his hair with fingers and spit, and finally donned his coat and hat. Here and elsewhere, a large part of Bloch's intent was to establish a socially determined differentiation between Jeppe's dress, manners, and milieu and the fastidious rococo costumes and puppet-like behavior of the noblemen who gull him for their sport. In this respect, the critic for *Nationaltidende* (24 February 1903) asserted, Bloch was the first director of the play to underscore "the glaring discrepancy between rich and poor by letting the prank that is played on the wretched Jeppe be acted out against a pointedly elaborate framework of rococo elegance." In this interpretation, then, the meaning behind Jeppe's famous allusion to the real reason for his own insobriety was to a considerable extent a social one.

The point relates directly to Bloch's conception of naturalism as the reconciliation of two imperatives, relevance to contemporary views and concerns and fidelity to the spirit of the period in which a given classic was written. "A Holberg style should not be regarded as something unalterable. Holberg is great enough to belong to all ages, for which reason every age has its own Holberg style," he maintained in an interview published in 1906. "It is comprised of Holberg on one hand and our time on the other. If you follow his text exactly and possess sufficient background and knowledge to grasp the spirit of its time, then you will render to Holberg what he justly deserves. If you use your eyes and ears to study the human beings living around you and apply the result to the characters in the plays, letting them speak in a straightforward and natural manner without trying to impose a 'Holberg tone,' then you will render to our time what is justly deserves."[65] For many decades to come, the melding of periodicity and contemporaneity advocated by Bloch was to remain an influential model for performances of both Holberg and other classical texts.

8 The Strindberg challenge

"It is impossible to set up rules for theatrical art, but it ought to be contemporary." This statement was repeated many times by August Strindberg (1849–1912), in varying terms and contexts, during the course of his forty-year writing career. As such, it points to a fundamental feature of his theatre practice, which was characterized by his restless search for new forms capable of meeting the changing demands of the consciousness of the times, as seen from his uniquely personal point of view. Both as a playwright and as a theorist, Strindberg kept in close touch with the newest directions and developments in theatre and drama, ready not only to absorb them but to reshape and expand them more daringly than anyone else in his time. Of no one can it be said with greater justification that he gave more impulses than he received. To a very significant extent, the development of the Scandinavian theatre in the modern period has been shaped and defined by the efforts of directors and actors alike to meet the challenge represented by his extraordinary dramatic imagination.

The range and energy of Strindberg's prolific genius are reflected in the sheer bulk and scope of his writings, which include not only drama but also fiction, poetry, autobiography, criticism, philosophy, and scientific theory; his sixty-two plays comprise only a portion of the total literary production collected in the fifty-five volumes of the standard edition of his works. His continual striving to reinterpret the spirit of the times made him not only the arch rebel and social iconoclast, the most modern of the moderns, but also the ardent champion of a comprehensive revitalization of the theatre, to be achieved through a redefinition of the nature of the theatrical experience itself. The challenge posed by the theatre was, as he knew at the outset, a particularly great one, and he prepared at the age of twenty to face it.

193

Strindberg's first unsuccessful brush with the professional stage, during a brief, unhappy period as an aspiring actor in 1869, was marked by his "debut" at Dramaten in a revival of Bjørnson's *Maria Stuart in Scotland*, in which he played a messenger with only eleven words to speak. A grander scheme, to make his stage debut as the stormy romantic hero Karl Moor in Schiller's *The Robbers*, predictably came to nothing. Between 1869, when he wrote his first (lost) play, and 1898, when he completed the first two parts of *Till Damaskus* (*To Damascus*), his idea of theatre underwent radical change. This process was not, however, one of continuous, linear, or even consistent development. Instead, its course was defined by an oscillating succession of experiments that led, gradually but surely, to a total rejection of accepted conventions of stage illusion and dramatic construction, as inadequate means of expressing the mystical and visionary qualities of life that, to an increasing extent, Strindberg came to regard as the true fabric of reality. His practical efforts to transfer his plays to the small stage and confined space of Intima teatern, the experimental theatre which he and the young actor–director August Falck operated in Stockholm from 1907 to 1910, took the form of a fresh series of tests and proposals aimed at dematerializing and simplifying theatrical expression. In general, his efforts to lift the theatre out of its everyday atmosphere into a richer, more poetic realm of grandeur and beauty placed him in the vanguard of the so-called New Stagecraft, alongside other revolutionaries like Appia and Gordon Craig who were also engaged at the beginning of the twentieth century in a similar struggle to fight clear of the theatre of realistic illusion.

In search of a form

Strindberg began his career as a playwright profoundly influenced by the romantic preoccupation with history and folklore, a tradition still in full bloom in the Swedish theatre of the 1870s. His first produced play, a one-act verse drama called *I Rom* (*In Rome*), depicts an episode in the life of the great sculptor Bertel Thorvaldsen, who as a young artist is saved from despair when an unexpected benefactor (Thomas Hope) commissions his famous Jason statue. Acted by an exceptional cast that included Axel Elmlund as an elegant, elegiac Thorvaldsen, the anonymous "Swedish original" began an encouraging run of eleven performances at Dramaten on 13 September 1870. A new Strindberg one-acter was seen at Dramaten in October of the following year. The theme of *Den fredlöse* (*The Outlaw*), a saga drama with strong echoes of Oehlenschläger and the early Bjørnson and Ibsen, is the conflict of Christianity and heathenism in twelfth-century Iceland. This time, however, Alfred Hanson, a decorative but stilted actor with a soporific delivery, was no match for the Viking hero Thorfinn ("a titan, a Prometheus who struggles against the gods"), and the play endured a cool reception.

More than nine years elapsed before another Strindberg play appeared on the Stockholm stage. Although the earliest prose version of *Master Olof* was submitted to Dramaten in 1872, the theatre's readers expressed "reservations about performing a play in which the historical characters appear so changed from their traditional conception."[1] Apparently the rival actor–manager Edvard Stjernström also read a version of the play and rejected it, but once Ludvig Josephson took the helm at Nya teatern, a bolder artistic policy prevailed. Josephson accepted the original prose version for production, preferring it over the verse revision published in 1878, and the first performance of this unruly masterpiece took place at his theatre, under the direction of August Lindberg, on 30 December 1881. With its revisionist view of the familiar figures of Swedish history, *Master Olof* focuses on the vacillating, hyperreflective religious revolutionary Olaus Petri who, by becoming a tool for other men's purposes, ends as an unheroic character and a traitor to his cause, branded as a renegade by the uncompromising Anabaptist rebel Gert Bookprinter. In other respects as well, the play's loose form, multiple scene changes, and incidental realistic details openly defied accepted conventions. The center of energy in Lindberg's riveting six-hour production was the larger-than-life characterization of Gert created by the young Emil Hillberg, whose demonic fanaticism and black humor provided a striking contrast to the weak-willed Olof of William Engelbrecht. Hillberg emerged as the rising new star of Swedish theatre, while Strindberg at last found himself acclaimed as the foremost dramatist of the early eighties.

Although he would later return with renewed vigor to the specifically historical genre, Strindberg continued for a time to use medieval settings in another way, as a framing device for domestic dramas reflecting his own initially happy but increasingly harrowing emotional life with his first wife, the strong-willed actress Siri von Essen. The production at Dramaten of *Gillets hemlighet* (*The Secret of the Guild*) in May 1880, which featured Fru Strindberg as the staunchly loyal Margaretha, marked an important step toward her husband's definitive breakthrough as a playwright the following year. Indebted to Ibsen's *The Pretenders*, this four-act play dramatizes the rival claims of two fifteenth-century master builders vying for the honor of completing the cathedral at Uppsala. One is a man who possesses the true strength of a great calling; the other, his own son, is the dishonest and inept pretender who is ultimately thwarted in his ambition when the tower he has constructed collapses. A comforting outcome is provided, however, by a closing scene in which Margaretha, the wife of the humbled upstart, forgives her repentant husband for all his faults. The Strindbergian theme of marriage as an emotional battleground is more strongly stressed in *Herr Bengts hustru* (*Sir Bengt's Wife*), a five-act medieval pastiche in which Siri von Essen enjoyed great success as Margit in the production at Nya teatern in late 1883. She is Strindberg's answer to Nora in a play that quite evidently presents an answer to *A Doll's House*. In this case, the marital combatants are reconciled in the end, as the warfare of the sexes is overcome by the strength of a love more powerful than either rational logic or individual will.

Lycko-Per's resa (*Lucky Per's Journey*), which proved to be one of Strindberg's most resounding popular successes when it was first staged at Nya teatern at the end of 1883, also employs a vaguely medieval setting, but this fairy-tale fantasy denotes a move in a new and highly significant direction. In this work the playwright embarked, as it were, on a drama of pilgrimage that was to be continued in his deeply pessimistic *Himmelrickets nycklar* (*The Keys of Heaven*, 1892) and then came to fruition in his expressionistic masterpieces, the *Damascus* trilogy, *Ett drömspel* (*A Dream Play*, 1901), and *Stora landsvägen* (*The Great Highway*, 1909). The bittersweet, fairy-tale atmosphere of *Lucky Per's Journey*, however, reverberates with echoes of the great works of Scandinavian romanticism – Oehlenschläger's *Aladdin*, Ibsen's *Peer Gynt*, and not least the stories and fairy-tale plays of Hans Christian Andersen. After young Per leaves the belfry in which he has been brought up, he wanders through the world in search of happiness, but in the process he discovers that nothing is what he had imagined it to be. Like many an Andersen character with a wishing ring and a fairy godmother, he learns instead that the realization of his dreams of gold and honor and power brings with it bitter disillusionment.

The fleeting, dreamlike transitions in this play, its replacement of the logic of reality with the imaginative logic of the fairy tale, and its magical realism of the unreal are all signposts that point ahead toward the dramaturgy of the mature dream plays. As it was originally conceived and produced, however, *Lucky Per's Journey* belongs in spirit to the romantic theatre of pictorial illusion. In its use of transparencies and startling transformations and its deployment of a multiplicity of elaborate settings for its short, kaleidoscopic scenes, it took full advantage of the spectacular stage effects and mechanical wizardry of which the nineteenth-century painted stage was capable. Consider, for example, a second-act *changement* in which "a snow-covered forest" at dawn, with "an ice-covered brook" running across the stage in the foreground, is transformed "from winter to summer: the ice melts on the brook and it runs freely over the stones, while the sun shines over the entire scene." Eventually, as we know, Strindberg came to look upon a literal or realistic representation of such an effect on the stage as "wasted effort," in that the careful, detailed staging required to bring it off convincingly only detracted from the mood to be evoked, rather than enhancing it. But before this crucial reorientation toward simplification, he had to pass through a phase colored, as he later writes, by "a naturalistic taste [which], adapted to the materialistic objectives of the time, strove for realistic accuracy."[2] During this period, which resulted in several of his best-known works, his primary concern became the intensification of an illusion of objective reality in the theatre.

Always closely attuned to new theatrical developments – and always prepared to acknowledge debts of literary or theatrical influence – Strindberg was preoccupied from the early 1880s with the emergence of naturalism and its quest for a "new formula" for art. In *Fadren* (*The Father*, 1887) he felt he had found the formula "the young Frenchmen" were still looking for. For this playwright, the term "naturalism" was synonymous from the outset with what he comes to describe, in "On Modern Drama and Modern Theatre" (1889), as "the great style, the deep probing of the human soul." He was never convinced by the merely photographic concerns of the movement or by its sometimes exaggerated insistence on the reproduction of the details of surface reality. "If a woman is seduced in a hothouse," he writes drily, "it isn't necessary to relate the seduction to all the potted plants you can find there and list them all by name."[3] The so-called greater naturalism was, for Strindberg, that "which seeks out the points where the great battles are fought, which loves to see what you do not see every day, which delights in the struggle between natural forces – whether these forces are called love or hate, rebellious or social instincts – which finds the beautiful or ugly unimportant if only it is great."[4] In this interpretation, the elements of external verisimilitude in the naturalistic style serve only as a means of achieving an intensification of dramatic mood and conflict.

Thus, the unrelenting struggle for dominance and survival between Laura and the Captain, the titanic contestants in *The Father*, acquires added horror by being precisely anchored in a recognizably contemporary Swedish bourgeois milieu. The same is basically true of the ineluctable warfare of the sexes in *Fordringsägare* (*Creditors*, 1888) and the grim, passionate battle of wills waged between the married couples of *Bandet* (*The Bond*, 1892) and the two parts of *Dödsdansen* (*The Dance of Death*, 1900), all of which make comparable use of a naturalistic pattern of surface detail. As in these later plays, the conflict in *The Father* quickly takes on an added dimension, bursting the bounds of realism and confronting us with a harrowing dramatic image of hell itself. The suggestion that the Captain is not the father of his only child festers and grows to an obsession that severs his ties with objective reality, undermines the basis of his very existence, and ends by bringing on the fatal stroke he suffers when he is lured into a straitjacket by his female tormentors. Here, as in other Strindberg misogynist marriage plays, the primary emphasis is not on the customary naturalistic interaction of character and a convincingly lifelike environment. In their depiction of a wrenching, nightmarish atmosphere that is rendered familiar by a close, sharply focused realistic technique, these works come closer in vision and approach to the modern school of magic realism in painting.

Nonetheless, despite Zola's complaint to Strindberg that the "Captain without a name [and] the others who are almost entirely abstract figures do not give me as powerful a sense of reality as I demand,"[5] the reception of the controversial world premiere of *The Father* was almost entirely colored by the impact made by the realistic immediacy of the production. This controversial performance, which opened at Casino in Copenhagen on 14 November 1887 under the direction of the young actor Hans Riber Hunderup, became in itself a battleground of opposing tastes and ideologies. To show his solidarity, Georg Brandes even took the unusual step of attending rehearsals. "From the very outset one could see how numerous the Strindbergians, or those whose natures were more or less in sympathy with the Strindbergian tendency, were in attendance: the applause which was heard from beginning to end was actually enthusiastic," the critic for *Nationaltidende* observed the following morning, adding: "Whether this success will last more than a very few evenings remains quite another question. So far as we are concerned, we do not think so." Despite their praise of the play's technique, most of its first reviewers took strong exception to the unrelenting despair of Strindberg's vision. *Berlingske Tidende* (15 November) summed up the reaction of a large conservative majority impervious to a fervent campaign by the Brandes brothers on behalf of Strindberg and modernism: "Despite the talent revealed in the technical construction of the play, it nevertheless remains a bitter, unpoetic fruit on the arid tree of realism."

At the eye of the critical hurricane was the unnerving straitjacket scene. "How far have we actually drifted, when that grim instrument of the insane asylum, the straitjacket, has managed to become a means of gaining effect on the stage?" demanded the outraged critics for *Dagbladet* (16 November). "An uglier, more revolting scene has probably never been presented in a Danish theatre. Those who merely read the play have no conception of how incredibly nerve-racking this sight is. . . . The mood of the real audience – those who had not attended a demonstration – was oppressed and indignant." This particular observer's logic is interesting: precisely because a play like *The Father* speaks to everyone in the theatre, he insists, modern drama "has no right to use such unrefined and brutal means to achieve effect." Although *Aftenbladet* (16 November) might argue that "in its scenic effectiveness it ranks on a level with the very best in modern dramatic literature," the harrowing straitjacket episode remained the chief source of conservative umbrage. "The drama is bleak enough as it is, so crushing and depressing that this scene is the drop that makes the cup run over," wrote the reviewer for *Nationaltidende*, while his like-minded counterpart at *Dags-Telegrafen* (15 November) added: "We can well understand why individual spectators stood up this evening during the third act and left the auditorium."

Although Hunderup's actors, accustomed to the light Casino repertory, lacked the requisite strength and technique for this demanding task, their performance, with Hunderup and his future wife Johanne Krum in the leading roles, won high praise. "When one must daily hold an audience through the aid of exaggerated outward action with many gestures and grimaces, it is no small problem when, for once, one must return to the evenness and naturalness that are the devices of all good plays," Edvard Brandes observed in *Politiken* (15 November). Nevertheless, he added, it was again demonstrated "that the good plays create good actors, who through artistic work come to an awareness of and a reliance upon their abilities." He was particularly impressed by Krum's outstanding portrayal of Laura, which he described as having been "acted with a natural and heavy tone of voice that has an extremely intense effect." Strindberg's own conception of the proper performance style for the play was, at first, very similar and emphasized a realistically subdued approach. "Play the drama as Lindberg plays Ibsen," he advised its first Swedish cast at Nya teatern eight weeks after the Copenhagen premiere. "In other words, not tragedy, not comedy, but something in between. Do not take the tempo too quickly, as we did here at Casino at first. Rather let it creep forward slowly, evenly, until it accelerates by itself toward the last act. Except from this: the Captain's lines when his obsession has taken root. They are to be spoken quickly, abruptly, spat out, constantly interrupting the mood." Remember, the playwright adds, that "the Captain is not an uncultivated soldier, but a learned man who stands above his profession."[6] The role should be acted "tastefully, quietly, resignedly," he emphasized in another letter, "with self-irony and the tone of the somewhat skeptical man of the world who . . . goes with relatively undaunted courage to meet his destiny, enveloping himself in the spiderweb of death that, for reasons of natural law, he cannot tear apart."[7]

Two decades later, when *The Father* was revived at Intima teatern in 1908 with August Falck in the title role, Strindberg's concept of the realistic fabric of the drama had changed greatly. He now wanted to see it performed in a simplified setting of drapes, so that "the play will be lifted out of its everyday atmosphere and become tragedy in the grand style; the characters will be sublimated, ennobled, and appear as from another world." The acting was to develop this idea further: "*The Father* should be played as tragedy! Grand, broad gestures, loud voices . . . let loose the passions."[8] By contrast, however, the 1911 film of the famous Intima production documents a performance in which the playwright's earlier vision of a very subdued, unhistrionic atmosphere seems to have prevailed. Also when the play finally reached Dramaten in 1915, Emil Hillberg's definitive interpretation of the Captain displayed a subdued, even meditative approach that reached its climax in the "appealingly quiet sadness" of his reactions in the final scene.

"Perhaps you know that I have no sympathy for the abstract," Zola had written to Strindberg (14 December 1887) in conjunction with the French translation of *The Father*. "I demand to know everything about the characters' positions in life so that one can touch and perceive them, sense them in their own atmosphere." In *Fröken Julie* (*Miss Julie*, 1888), Strindberg adhered more closely and perhaps deliberately to Zola's program. He himself considered this work "the first naturalistic tragedy in Swedish drama" – "ceci datera=this play will go down in the annals of history," he added, with characteristic directness, in a letter to Bonniers (10 August 1888) in which he offered the work for publication. (The rejection of the play by Bonniers lives on in the history of that great publishing house as its most monumental blunder.) In the well-known preface that Strindberg added later, he consciously set out to promulgate the ideas of theatrical reform adopted by Zola and Antoine in Paris. In so doing, he formulated what has come to be regarded to this day as one of the most succinct descriptions of the aims and techniques of naturalism in the theatre. In performance, the drama of the Midsummer-Eve seduction and eventual suicide of the aristocratic protagonist was meant to be perceived as an unbroken slice of living reality. To enable the audience to experience the events on stage as though they were actually occurring in life, no disruption was allowed to disturb the intense focus on the fateful confrontation between Julie and the valet Jean. The customary intermission was eliminated by the playwright, lest it break the spell of "the author–mesmerist's suggestive influence." To strengthen the illusion of reality, the large kitchen in which the action is set was meant to be fully three-dimensional in order to eliminate the strain of having "to believe in painted pots and pans." At the same time, however, the setting was conceived impressionistically, with a use of asymmetry that stimulated the imagination by leading the eye of the spectator "off into an unknown perspective." In proposing the elimination of footlights and heavy make-up and the introduction of strong sidelighting to accentuate eye and facial (i.e., psychological) expressiveness, Strindberg advocated a close-up drama of subtler reactions that were "mirrored in the face rather than in gesture and sound." Following Antoine's lead, he called for the actor to disregard the audience seated beyond the invisible fourth wall and to perform within, rather than in front of, the setting. In this way each scene would be played "at whatever spot the situation might demand." "I do not dream that I shall ever see the full back of an actor throughout the whole of an important scene," he writes, "but I do fervently wish that vital scenes should not be played opposite the prompter's box as though they were duets milking applause."9

Even more obviously than its views on theatrical production, the dramaturgical arguments advanced in the preface often combine aspects of the naturalistic aesthetic with observations that point in a new, distinctly post-naturalistic direction. A complexity of motives – psychological, biological, environmental, hereditary – customarily underlies the behavior of a naturalistically conceived character; yet the "split and vacillating patchwork characters" envisioned by Strindberg, "agglomerations of past and present, scraps from books and newspapers, fragments of humanity, torn shreds of once fine clothing that have become rags," are potentially Pirandellian in their characterlessness. His advocacy of a meandering, nonsequential pattern of dialogue, mirroring the randomness and casualness of everyday conversation, anticipates the dialogue of free association in Chekhov's work. Not least, the allusions in the preface to musical composition and thematics become fully meaningful in Strindberg's own dream plays and chamber plays.

Miss Julie is a play originally conceived for performance by a small, experimental theatre. The founding of Antoine's Théâtre Libre in Paris in 1887 had generated widespread interest in the concept of a free, independent theatre as a venue for trying out new plays and production methods. Strindberg, who had entertained the notion of his own theatre from as far back as 1876, was immediately attracted by the idea and approached the energetic Ibsen champion August Lindberg with a proposal that they collaborate to form an independent touring company. His sales pitch was as dynamic as ever: "Ibsen you cannot rely on any longer, since I am sure that he won't write much more, and his genre is his specialty and is on the wane. . . . He for himself and we for us!" Instead, the irrepressible Strindberg proposed a theatre devoted exclusively to a repertory made up of his own plays, and only new ones at that. "Holes in the repertory need not occur, as I write a one-acter in two days," he reassured Lindberg, to whom all the leading parts were to be tailored. Siri von Essen was to have all the female leads – but, he adds, "if you want your wife included, then I'll write every other role for her, every other for my wife, and all parts for you." The suggestions in his long letter (3 June 1887) were meant to be as practical as possible: "I will write the plays so that no costumes, sets, or properties have to be dragged along." He had, however, no illusions about fermenting a revolution: "To tranform the theatre or to reform it is something I wouldn't dream of, for that is impossible! It can only be modernized a bit!"

When Strindberg at last did succeed in establishing his own Scandinavian Experimental Theatre in Copenhagen nearly two years later, the venture survived only a week. Initial reaction to the project was less than encouraging: "A manager without sense – in theatrical matters, of course – a theatre without a location, a prima donna without lines, and the male parts without actors. That the auditorium will be without spectators seems quite certain, which then means a till without cash," sneered *Dagbladet*.[10] The little troupe of professionals and amateurs set up quarters in Dagmar Theatre, one of Copenhagen's leading private theatres, but one day before the opening of *Miss Julie*, which was to have launched the enterprise, the play was banned by the public censor because of its daring subject matter. Undaunted, Strindberg's experimental theatre quickly changed plans, opening a week later on the Dagmar stage with a single bill (9 March 1889) that included the world premieres of *Creditors* and two *quarts d'heure* written for the project, *Den starkare* (*The Stronger*) and *Paria* (*Pariah*). For practical as much as for artistic reasons, all three plays were designed to be performed by a small company with a minimum of technical and financial resources. (Strindberg described *Creditors* as "a naturalistic tragedy, even better than *Miss Julie*, with three characters, a table and two chairs, and no sunrise."[11]) Siri von Essen was effective as the loquacious Mrs. X in *The Stronger*, while Hans Riber Hunderup enjoyed a triumph as X in *Pariah*, which was held over in the regular Dagmar repertory. As the first Adolf in *Creditors*, however, the popular Danish author Gustav Wied gave a shaky amateur performance at which, according to *Vort Land*, "people laughed till they had tears in their eyes, while the small, slightly built writer wriggled like a worm in a monstrosity of an armchair up there on the stage."[12]

As for *Miss Julie* itself, the ban on public performances caused the world premiere (14 March 1889) to take place as a private showing before 150 spectators in a makeshift theatre in the student union of the University of Copenhagen. Strindberg's wife played a subdued Julie opposite the polite Jean of Viggo Schiwe. "Too cold, much too cold, and one gets no impression at all of the kind of woman who would seduce a man like Jean," complained the Stockholm critic for *Dagens Nyheter* (18 March). This observer also found that Schiwe "hardly suggested a servant; his manner was much more like that of a gentleman and a *viveur*." In spite of the primitive production facilities, however, Strindberg's demands for a realistically three-dimensional stage environment seem to have been met. The setting "looked surprisingly like a real kitchen" to the man from *Dagens Nyheter*: "A plate rack, a kitchen table, the speaking tube to the floor above, a big stove, not to mention the rows of copper pots above it, in short: everything is there to convey a vivid impression of an actual kitchen." Much about this play's interpretation would change during the course of its long performance history, but its meticulously conceived setting has remained an indispensable fixture of sorts, to be seen in all its naturalistic detail even in Ingmar Bergman's radical reinterpretations of *Miss Julie* in the 1980s.

Toward a new theatre

Although the biographical element has been greatly overworked in traditional Strindberg criticism, it is nonetheless indisputable that the so-called Inferno crisis through which this writer lived during the mid-1890s precipitated a startling renewal in his art and his attitude toward the whole question of theatrical illusion. In a letter to his family dated 24 May 1898, he describes *To Damascus* I, the first play he wrote after his shattering mental ordeal, as a radical departure, "a new genre, fantastic and shining like *Lucky Per*, but playing in a contemporary setting and with a full reality behind it." The reality to which he alludes had, however, nothing to do with the external verisimilitude of his earlier naturalistic dramas. In none of Strindberg's later plays, in fact, is there any hard and fast distinction drawn between what is "real" and what is not. Life, for the father of expressionism, *is* a dream, and so the dream (the play) is life itself – not a conceptual comment on "the dreamlike nature" of existence but a projected image of a psychic dynamism, an exteriorization of *what it feels like* to experience reality in this way. Hence the greatest challenge facing any interpreter of Strindberg's later work on the stage is to articulate the fundamental doubleness of its poetic vision – the perception of the dreamlike quality of reality that is always conjoined with the sharply insistent reality of the dream.

In Emil Grandinson the playwright was fortunate to find a director with an exceptional sensitivity to the complex inner life of his first dream play, the dramatization of the spiritual journey of the Unknown through a kaleidoscopic succession of "stations" on the road toward a distant salvation. "Grandinson," Strindberg later wrote in his *Open Letters to the Intimate Theatre*, "went beyond [the naturalistic director Harald] Molander's 'externals' and admitted I was right when I was right, seeing that the effect or the impact of the play depended on something other than what was piquant in the situation and the scenic effects" (*LIT*, p. 127). It has been shown that Grandinson, like Strindberg himself, was closely acquainted with the newest developments and currents in modern European theatre, as exemplified in the writings of Georg Fuchs (*Die Schaubühne der Zukunft*), Gordon Craig (*On the Art of the Theatre*), and Adolphe Appia (*La Mise en scène du drame Wagnerian*).[13] Four years after his successful production of *To Damascus* I at Dramaten (19 November 1900), Grandinson was instrumental in bringing the French symbolist productions of Lugné-Poë (including both Strindberg's *Creditors* and Ibsen's *Rosmersholm*) to Scandinavia for the first time. At Dramaten, which was now run as an association of the actors themselves, he continued to explore new ways of expressing the internal values of such Strindberg plays as *Påsk* (*Easter*, 1900), *Brott och brott* (*Crimes and Crimes*, 1901), and *Karl XII* (1902). Above all, however, it was the auspicious *Damascus* premiere that stood out, in its author's words, as "something new and a masterpiece by way of direction."

Strindberg's underlying concept for his *Damascus* cycle was rooted from the start in his idea of achieving simplification by using projection effects to accommodate the rapid, dreamlike alternation of scenes, "provided the settings retain an abstract, shadowy, colorless tone, which is in keeping with the style of the play."[14] Even ten years before this, the dramatist's imagination had been fired by the prospect of replacing ordinary painted backdrops with projected pictures. In 1889, while an adaptation of his novel *Hemsöborna* (*The People of Hemsö*) was being staged at Djurgårdsteatern in Stockholm, he had occasion to write to August Lindberg about plans for a new play; "a semi-fairy tale dealing with the French Revolution, and using mainly a large magic lantern" as an evocative and economical means of depicting the episodes of history on the stage.[15] Later, like Lugné-Poë and many other symbolist artists of his day, he became captivated by the fleeting, dreamlike effects produced in the shadow plays he saw in Paris at Henri Rivière's famous cabaret theatre, the Chat Noir. This influence seems to have fueled his renewed interest in experimenting with projected scenery in his post-Inferno plays, in an effort to achieve a simpler, dematerialized atmosphere on the stage. "I don't want to use ordinary theatre decorations for my new plays," he told *Svenska Dagbladet* (21 January 1899) in an interview published to mark his fiftieth birthday. "All these old-fashioned theatrical rags must go! I only want a painted background representing a room, a forest, or whatever it may be, or perhaps a background could be produced by a shadow picture painted on glass and projected onto a white sheet."

In conjunction with the reduction of scenery, costumes, and props to their bare and meaningful essentials, Strindberg also advocated the adoption of a neutral platform stage ("something in the style of Shakespeare's time") to counterbalance the heavy photographic representation of parlors and kitchens on the naturalistic stage. "All this theatre nonsense that now overburdens the stage and weighs down the play without increasing believability must be eliminated," he maintained in his birthday interview. "It is the play itself, the dialogue, the plot that must capture the audience and create the illusion." In particular, the Shakespearean Stage created in Munich by Karl von Perfall and his associates in 1889 provided Strindberg with a favorite illustration of his own aims. This nineteenth-century version of an Elizabethan stage impressed him as a perfect theatrical model, to which he was to return many times in his continuous campaign for a new, simplified approach to stage illusion. In practice, however, substantive and revealing differences existed between the von Perfall experiment and the modification of it eventually adopted by Grandinson and Strindberg for the first production of *To Damascus* I.

By this time, the Shakespearean Stage in Munich had already attracted some interest in Scandinavia. One of the first and most detailed accounts of it was furnished by William Bloch, who had been sent to Bavaria in the summer of 1891 to study the new stage form and report his findings to the management of the Royal Theatre in Copenhagen.[16] Designed mainly to handle the rapid alternation of scenes in Shakespearean drama, von Perfall's reconstituted proscenium stage at the Hoftheater incorporated three distinct acting areas. A forestage or apron, from which five steps descended to the floor of the auditorium, was built out over the orchestra pit. Behind the proscenium arch was an unlocalized "middle stage," enclosed at the sides by stylized hangings painted in soft colors on ordinary canvas. The rear wall of this stage was a permanent curtained arch, a kind of second proscenium with openings at the top and sides to be used as windows, doors, or an upper gallery. Behind this structure lay an inner stage, described by Bloch as "a miniature theatre of its own, with its own settings, its own front curtain, and its own stage floor," raised three steps above the level of the main stage. Only this inner stage could be given "a real sense of localization, both with respect to furniture and props and with respect to scenery," the Danish director observes. A painted backcloth depicted the location of each scene, and a pair of side wings could be introduced to increase the illusion of place. Hence, when seen in conjunction with the middle stage, the setting in the background served to anchor the action in a particular location, be it a garden, a room,

a street, or whatever. In fact, Bloch is careful to note, the curtained opening to the inner stage was closed only "on those comparatively rare occasions when the spectator can have no doubt as to where a given scene is
taking place."

Thus, the Shakespearean Stage constructed by Karl Lautenschläger in
Munich emerges as a much more complex hybrid than Strindberg's idealized vision of a simple, naked platform might suggest. Nor could one
expect Scandinavia's foremost naturalistic director to share the playwright's view of such a stage as a model for the future. Seen through
Bloch's eyes, its chief advantage lay in the ease with which it overcame the
technical difficulties usually associated with multiple changes of scene,
thereby making it preferable both for plays written "before the advent of
modern staging principles" and for works "not conceived by their author
for performance." However, for modern plays "which for the most part
avail themselves of the full resources of contemporary stagecraft," he can
find no real use for von Perfall's method. "There can be no doubt," Bloch's
report concludes, "that it is distinctly inferior to the modern theatre when
it comes to scenic illusion, and that it in no way gives the actors the support they enjoy to such a great extent in a modern mise-en-scène."

By experimenting freely with new staging methods in the *Damascus*
production, however, Strindberg was determined to challenge the assumptions underlying this naturalistic line of reasoning. Divided into two parts,
the stage at Dramaten became in effect two stages – an inner and an outer
– joined by three connecting steps. The raised inner stage was framed by a
more austere version of the second proscenium in use in Munich, resembling "the crumbling wall of an ancient theatre, pierced by a wide, vaulted
opening. Above the wall one saw a piece of sky, where in the night scenes
a starry pattern was visible."[17] In contrast to the alternating playing areas
and in-depth figure compositions of von Perfall's Shakespearean Stage,
Grandinson's mise-en-scène transferred all of the action to the raised
stage-upon-the-stage defined by the vaulted, curtainless arch. In so doing,
he succeeded in projecting a convincing impression of unreality and distance. "The figures who appear here thus become smaller," observed the
critic for *Aftonbladet* (20 November 1900), "and in the half light, which
eliminates contours and often leaves the faces in shadow, it is easy to imagine oneself in an hallucinatory state induced by fever." In this way, it can
be argued, the spectators in the auditorium were themselves rendered
"dreamers" of the dream.[18]

Working in close collaboration, Grandinson and Strindberg also tried out the idea of projected pictures that would eliminate the use of painted scenery altogether. Although their attempts succeeded in producing a large and distinct pictorial background, however, it proved necessary to keep the area in front of the projection comparatively dark, making it impossible to see the faces of the actors clearly. Eventually the experiments had to be abandoned, and the traditionalist designer Carl Grabow was called upon to paint perspective backcloths depicting the shifting stations through which the Unknown must pass on his symbolic journey. For the most part, the seventeen changes of scene in the play were accomplished simply by the noiseless lowering and raising of these backdrops in the dark. By placing Grabow's otherwise representational scenery within the framework of the inner stage and by painting furniture and other requisite items on it, a stylized effect was achieved that obliterated any sense of naturalistic solidity. In the subdued, impressionistic lighting from colored overhead projectors, the characters in the drama seemed "to pop up and disappear as if by magic, thereby greatly strengthening the fantastical impression of these strange scenes."[19]

The ephemeral, dreamlike quality of the stage picture reached its height in the Asylum scene, the pivotal experience in the protagonist's ordeal. In the last analysis, the entire action of this play is a projection of the fantasies, memories, and dreams of the Unknown, but in the wholly hallucinatory Asylum episode he is brought face to face with a veritable chorus of doubles who represent "real" characters in his past life. To underscore the impression of the Unknown as the dreamer of this nightmare, Grandinson carried the metaphor of theatre-in-the-theatre one step further by erecting a yet smaller and more removed inner stage, bathed in blue light and framed by a smaller, vaulted arch that was a replica of the larger one. Behind this inner opening, seated at a long table that was illuminated by a greenish light, the spectral, soup-eating emanations of the dreamer's guilt appeared before him – the Lady (who knitted rather than ate), a jealous husband, grieving parents, a cruelly treated sister, an abandoned wife and children, a madman with an alarming resemblance to oneself, and others.

Juxtaposed with these phantasmagoric moments in *To Damascus* are quieter scenes like the moving reunion of the Unknown and the Lady ("By the Sea") in the fourth act – "a scene of great tenderness, closeness, desperation, and love," Ingmar Bergman has called it. In Bergman's production of

Plate 42 Photograph of the Asylum scene in the world premiere of *To Damascus* I
(Dramaten, 1900), with Tyra Dörum as the Abbess and August Palme as the Unknown.
The spectral "doubles" whom the protagonist encounters in this scene are seated in an
inner space formed by the vaulted arch in the picture – a replica of the larger arch (not
visible here) which Grandinson used to frame his stage.

the first two parts of the *Damascus* trilogy in 1974, this scene was performed
in a pool of light on an empty stage, utilizing only a back projection of
shining cloud formations that gradually took the form of shipmast crosses
in the closing moments. Although such was also the kind of solution
Strindberg himself had envisioned, he was obliged to content himself with
the style of staging captured in one of the surviving rehearsal photographs
from the world premiere, showing August Palme and Harriot Bosse standing on the raised platform stage in front of Grabow's painted seascape.
Missing in this photograph, however, is the framing arch that effectively
imparted both focus and distance to Grandinson's composition.

Although August Palme's Unknown was rich in lyrical warmth, some
critics felt that his portrayal lacked the sense of deep, suppressed suffering
that the role requires. In a review in *Stockholms-Tidningen* (20 November),

Plate 43 Rehearsal photograph from the world premiere of *To Damascus* I, showing the reunion of the Unknown and the Lady "by the sea." August Palme and Harriet Bosse are seen standing on the raised platform stage in front of Grabow's rather crude seascape. As in plate 42, the larger framing arch is missing in the photograph.

Alfred Lindkvist provided a more faceted description of Palme's psychological intensity: "Marked by an artistic realism, his facial expression and pantomime revealed both the somber melancholy of the thinker and the nervousness of the self-tormentor, agitated and strained to the point of madness. The haunted moods and fevered fantasies, the visions and premonitions that plague the penitent, all were delineated with compelling immediacy and intuitive strength." At the age of twenty-one Harriet Bosse, who had attracted critical attention earlier that season as Puck in *A Midsummer-Night's Dream*, gave a subdued and appealing performance as the Lady under whose spell the Unknown falls. The young actress also made a virtually mystical impression on the author himself, for whom life, dream, and drama were inextricably bound up. "It was great and beautiful," he wrote to her after the opening, "even though I had imagined the character somewhat lighter, with small traces of roguishness and with more expansiveness. A little of Puck – those were my first words to you! And they remain my last! A laugh in the midst of suffering indicates hope, and the situation certainly does not prove to be hopeless!" The Unknown's fateful encounter with the Lady in the opening scene of the play, and his

Plate 44 From Ingmar Bergman's 1974 production of *To Damascus* I–II at Dramaten: the reunion of the Unknown (Jan-Olof Strandberg) and the Lady (Helena Brodin) on an empty stage, accentuated only by Marik Vos' back projection.

own first encounter with Bosse during a rehearsal of that scene were, for Strindberg, interchangeable mirror images of one another. Six months later she became his third wife.

"Anything can happen; everything is possible and probable. Time and space do not exist; on a slight groundwork of reality, imagination spins and weaves new patterns made up of memories, experiences, unrelated fancies, absurdities, and improvisations." The exhortation implied in the familiar preamble to *A Dream Play*, the Strindberg play that above all others was to inspire the next generation of directors and designers in Scandinavia and Germany, went largely unheeded in the first production of this difficult masterpiece. To its author's chagrin, the play had its world premiere (17 April 1907) not at Dramaten but at Svenska teatern on Blasieholmen (formerly Nya teatern), where the precedent set by Grandinson's effective

Plate 45 The Growing Castle, its gilded roof rising above a forest of giant hollyhocks in bloom: design by Carl Grabow for the world premiere of *A Dream Play* (Svenska teatern, 1907).

staging of *To Damascus* was disregarded. Also overlooked were Strindberg's explicitly antirealistic stage directions, calling for "stylized murals suggesting at the same time space, architecture, and landscape" that were to remain at the sides throughout, supplemented only by changing backdrops. The playwright implored his director, Victor Castegren, to try to "transform the drama into visual representation without materializing it too much" (*LIT*, p. 293), and Castegren dutifully procured a sciopticon in Dresden, conducted some experiments with back projections, but quickly abandoned this possibility. When Albert Ranft, the business-minded theatre owner, also rejected the *Damascus* alternative of arches and backcloths, "the only thing left to do," as Strindberg puts it, "was to 'go to Grabow'" (*LIT*, p. 294).

Without the advantage of Grandinson's ingenuity, Carl Grabow's colorful but conventionally pictorial designs resulted in a heavily realistic scenography that was, in Strindberg's view, "too material for the dream." Awkward changes of scene and inept lighting techniques disrupted the play's mesmeric flow of fleeting, shifting images. What symbolism there was in the Castegren–Grabow endeavor seems to have been heavy-handed; the forestage was "transformed into a field of poppies, the symbol of sleep, while the stage behind it was framed by an arch, painted with garlands of poppies, within which the dream scenes appeared and dis-

Plate 46 Grabow's design for the Theatre Corridor in *A Dream Play*: to the right of the gate one sees the announcement board, the cloverleaf door, and the Billsticker's fishing net, exactly as Strindberg describes them.

appeared."[20] Generally rather baffled, the reviewers of the first production were inclined to address the play as a reading drama that defied adequate stage representation. "The task is so incredibly difficult that one hardly even has a right to make comments," Tor Hedberg wrote in *Svenska Dagbladet* (18 April 1907), but he and others went on to cite the absence of unity and coordination in the performance at Svenska teatern. In particular, the style of acting adopted by Castegren's ensemble wavered unsteadily between the conversational tone of naturalism and the symbolist declamation advocated by Lugné-Poë and his school. Only Harriet Bosse, now divorced from Strindberg, seems to have captured the spirit of the play fully. As Indra's Daughter, "her pure diction shone as always, and her soft, almost floating tread had just the right ethereal quality for the daughter of a divinity."[21]

On the whole, however, Strindberg was outspoken in his dismay at a production that "became a 'materialization phenomenon' instead of the intended dematerialization" (*LIT*, p. 294). During the years following the botched premiere of *A Dream Play*, he continued to grapple with a wide variety of schemes and plans for a simplified, stylized, even emblematic staging of it on the impossibly small stage at Intima teatern, which he and Falck founded in the autumn of 1907. These plans were never realized in practice, however, and thirty years would pass before Olof Molander's productions of this play finally succeeded in expressing the full power of its theatrical vision.

Although history plays and dream plays might seem an unlikely combination in a playwright, a parallel line of development leading out of the introspective Inferno crisis is defined by the body of plays in which Strindberg returned to the pageant of Swedish history for his inspiration. Between 1899 and 1900 he finished four full-length history plays in quick succession. *Folkungasagan* (*The Saga of the Folkungs*), *Gustav Vasa*, *Erik XIV*, and *Gustav Adolf* were then followed during the next decade by eight more histories, among them *Karl XII*, *Engelbrekt*, and *Kristina* (*Queen Christina*) in 1901, *Gustav III* in 1902, and, near the end, *Bjälbo-Jarlen* (*Earl Birger of Bjälbo*) in 1908. Strindberg's ambitious scheme, which originally called for a cycle of plays ranging over 700 years of his country's heritage, calls to mind the nationalistic cycle of fifty plays planned by Johannes Messenius three centuries earlier. In this sense, the plays of his cycle that Strindberg did complete reflect the abiding fascination with history that has characterized Swedish playwrights of almost every era. His dramatic method is, however, uniquely his own. Rather than concerning themselves with the actual events of history, his plays in this idiom interpret the inner lives of historical figures by focusing on moments, impressions, and themes which influence the complex tissue of the historical past. In the process, specifically Swedish history is transcended by the broader, elemental drama of human passions and weaknesses underlying it. "Even in the historical dramas," the playwright remarks, "the purely human is of major interest, and history the background: the inner struggle of souls awakens more sympathy than the combat of soldiers or the storming of walls; love and hate, and torn family ties, more than treaties and speeches from the throne" (*LIT*, p. 256).

For their dramatic compression and fluid, polyphonic structure, as well as for their layered characterizations of historical figures ("both in their greatness and their triviality"), these later history plays owe most to Shakespeare, whom Strindberg freely acknowledges as his "teacher." In the novels of Walter Scott, meanwhile, he also found a valuable storehouse of what he calls "ingredients, decorations, and stage properties" that could be used in his own plays to evoke historical atmosphere and make it concrete in the theatre. Strindberg's interest in Scott, the "great antiquarian," reflects an almost neoromantic fascination with the mood-evoking properties of historical pageantry, color, and detail. During the heyday of naturalism in the late 1890s, a work such as *Gustav Vasa* was brought to the stage with all the historical accuracy and theatrical swagger of a Meininger revival. The world premiere of this play at Svenska teatern on 17 October 1899 was spectacular in every respect, ultimately earning the worried Albert Ranft one of his biggest box-office successes. Carl Grabow's meticulously detailed naturalistic scenery was, in this case, seen to its best advantage in Harald Molander's lavish mise-en-scène. A gallery of vivid character portraits was created by the leading Swedish actors of the day, including Emil Hillberg as a majestic, Odin-like Gustav Vasa, Anders de Wahl as a vapid, nervously lyrical Crown Prince Erik, August Lindberg as an older, hardbitten Olaus Petri, and Tore Svennberg (the first Poet in *A Dream Play*) as a strong-willed and fiery Göran Persson, the royal adviser born to rule. "The Hanseatic office and the Blue Dove in *Gustav Vasa* were real museum pieces," Strindberg said of Grabow's scenography. "They were beautiful, but they would not have had to be so expensive" (*LIT*, p. 292).

By the time the playwright wrote this, in one of his memoranda to the members of the Intima company, he had reached the conclusion that a radically simplified, dematerialized style of staging was indeed as appropriate to the history plays as it was to the dream plays. A distinct change in popular taste had already taken place in this regard, he was convinced: "By the end of the century . . . the imaginative became active, the material gave way to the immaterial, the spoken word became the major thing on the stage" (*LIT*, pp. 289–90). Four months after the opening of Intima teatern, Strindberg had his faith in the power of simplification confirmed by August Falck's effectively stylized revival of *Queen Christina* (27 March 1908), in which Manda Björling played the troubled protagonist. In this production, the playwright maintained, one saw once and for all that scenery could be eliminated without rendering the performance itself either monotonous or shabby. The unadorned drapery stage adopted by Falck on this occasion was yet another offshoot of Strindberg's preoccupation with "the Shakespeare curtain" as a more flexible and less distracting alternative to realistic scenery. In this case, however, the tapestry-like hangings that enclosed von Perfall's Shakespearean Stage in Munich were replaced by a reddish-brown velvet backdrop and conventional side wings covered in the same material. As a result of Strindberg's study of seventeenth-century French theatre engravings, two low "barriers," or balustrades, were added at either side of the forestage, on which emblematic attributes could be placed to suggest changes of scene.[22]

For the first act of *Queen Christina*, which takes place in Riddarholm Church in Stockholm, all references to the actual place were cut and the action was presented simply as a gathering of people. The Treasury setting in the following act was symbolized by a pair of bookshelves in the Accountant's room – yet even these concessions to verisimilitude were regarded as superfluous by Strindberg, who likewise objected to the lavish period costumes imported by Falck from Berlin. Once changes of scene are eliminated, he reasoned, costume changes serve no purpose, whereas by allowing the actor to retain the same costume "the public will get to know him and will not mix him up with others, and the character will gain from this continuity."[23] It is in general the actor who, in his estimation, benefits most from simplified staging because it produces

> a mood of calm and reverence on stage that is extremely important to the performer . . . The open wings (three on each side) provided nuances of light and shadow, and made unnecessary all opening and closing of doors; entrances and exits were made without disturbance of any kind. With a soft carpet added, the artists at the Intima lived in a carefree, pleasant milieu, in which they felt at home and could create their roles undisturbed by the noise and commotion of the theatre and the stagehands' bustle which is otherwise part of it (*LIT*, p. 77).

In the wake of the innovative drapery–stage production of *Queen Christina*, Strindberg took to the proselytizing of this kind of staging as a universal solution for all plays. A letter written to Falck six weeks after the opening provides a revealing summary of his views on the subject:

> With simplicity one wins the solemn calm and quiet in which the artist can hear his own part. With simple decor the really important points became evident: the personality, the part itself, the speech, the action, and the facial expression . . . Yes, the spoken word is everything. You saw that in *Christina* in the artistic weaving together of destinies and wills. But the play can be acted anywhere, even in front of a Smyrna mat hung up in a cellar in the country.[24]

The Intima experiment

The final stage in Strindberg's lifelong campaign to redefine and reform the theatre is represented by the three brief but intensely active years

(1907–10) during which he and August Falck operated Scandinavia's best-known experiment theatre, Intima teatern. Like Hans Riber Hunderup twenty years earlier, Falck came to Strindberg as a young actor and enthusiast who was appearing in a touring production of *Miss Julie*. His proposal to establish a chamber theatre in Stockholm, along the lines of Max Reinhardt's new Kammerspiele in Berlin, immediately rekindled the playwright's own ambition to have a theatre of his own. It would, he wrote to Adolf Paul (6 January 1907), "be an intimate theatre for *Moderne Kunst*," and for it he set out to complete a quartet of chamber plays written in the style he considered suitable for the new stage: "intimate in form, a simple theme treated with thoroughness, few characters, vast perspectives, freely imaginative . . . Simple but not too simple, no huge apparatus, no superfluous minor parts." The basic criteria comprising this definition of the chamber-play form – the distillation of a single, unifying theme, its muted, unhistrionic expression in compressed and fluid form, and the suppression of all distracting effects and disturbingly ostentatious backgrounds – apply in broader terms to Strindberg's overall conception of the theatrical experience itself.

It is clear in retrospect that Intima teatern lacked the facilities necessary to realize Strindberg's complex vision to the fullest. Although initial plans for the project had called for a small art theatre of 400 to 500 seats, the structure ultimately acquired by Falck on Norra Bantorget, not far from Strindberg's new lodgings in the Blue Tower, imposed a much greater degree of intimacy than the partners had anticipated. The attractive auditorium, decorated in soft greens and yellows, held just 161 spectators, who were seated in close proximity to a minimalist stage measuring only six meters in width and four meters in depth. Within this severely constricted space, a total of twenty-four Strindberg plays were nevertheless performed during the three years the little theatre survived, ranging from the early romantic dramas and the naturalistic tragedies through *Queen Christina* and *To Damascus* to the chamber plays. Once the young company of eleven actors found its feet and evolved a suitably subdued, unaffected style of delivery, they fared best in such works as *Miss Julie*, *Easter*, and *Christina*. Least accessible and least popular were the difficult and elusive chamber plays, all four of which were attempted during the first months of the initial season.

Atmosphere ("a synonym for poetry," Strindberg says) is the very essence of *Pelikanen* (*The Pelican*), Opus IV of the chamber plays, with which

Intima teatern elected to open on 26 November 1907. A drawing of the set printed in *Dagens Nyheter* the next day depicts a room in typical Art Nouveau style – a cool and neatly aestheticized interior with stylized trees, pine cones in vases, a pair of white-painted bureaus, a rocking chair, and human figures in long, dark clothing. Strindberg had rescued his play at the last moment from the drab gray interior Falck had prepared for it ("Hide everything that can be hidden with curtains, portières, screens, plants, flowers in vases etc."), and he appears to have been satisfied with the end result. "There was something else in this room," he later observed, "there was atmosphere, a white fragrance of sickroom and nursery, with something green on a bureau as if placed there by an invisible hand. 'I'd like to live in that room,' I said, though one sensed the tragedy that would play its last act with classic tragedy's most horrible motif: innocently suffering children and the sham mother Medea" (*LIT*, pp. 296–7). Unfortunately, however, the young cast could not master the intricate musicality of this intense drama of human anguish and purgation, and the performance failed to draw.

In its plucky attempt to stage *Oväder* (*Storm Weather*) at the end of the following month, the Intima ensemble found it even more difficult to give adequate theatrical expression to this chamber play's atmospheric evocation of the twilight of summer and of life. The limited facilities of the cramped stage made it impossible to project the heightened reality of the Östermalm street scene in the first and third acts. On the other hand, the simplified, uncluttered interior created by the gifted young scene designer Knut Ström for the second act impressed the author with its "simple beauty." Here, at least, was the sense of mood he sought, evoked by "a room in which one could live and enjoy living; here was a home that was more comfortably homelike than any I had ever seen on stage" (*LIT*, p. 297). With Ström's cleanly stylized design, he adds, "we had left the Preface and *Miss Julie*" – in other words, the naturalistic conception of a detailed environment in the theatre.

The greatest challenge to be met was, of course, *Spöksonaten* (*The Ghost Sonata*), Opus III and the best known of the chamber plays. The proscenium of Intima teatern was, indeed, even decorated with two free renderings of Arnold Böcklin's *Die Toteninsel* (*The Island of the Dead*), the painting that appears as a backdrop for the final symbolic tableau in this play. Evidently as a kind of warning, *The Ghost Sonata* was furnished with the subtitle "A Fantasy" before its world premiere at Intima teatern on 21 January 1908.

However, its suggestive bonding of fantasy and reality seems for the most part to have eluded Falck and his charges. As a result, the performance created considerable confusion. "To discourse about food and servant problems in stylized, sepulchral tones and to be interrupted all the time by the evil one herself from the kitchen (wearing makeup fit for a student farce) is bound to end as utter parody," Bo Bergman reported tartly in *Dagens Nyheter* (22 January 1908). The affected diction and exaggerated makeup to which this critic and others objected were apparently adopted by the cast in order to add a "spooky," Maeterlinckian atmosphere to the proceedings. "Words were not spoken but aspirated laboriously, as if in terrifying visions, by actors painted chalk-white in order to look as emaciated as possible," observed *Stockholms-Tidningen* (22 January). Particularly grotesque were the automaton-like participants in the ritual of exhumation and psychic murder known as the "ghost supper," in which they struck reviewers as "mannequins," "wooden puppets," and "caricatures of humanity." Even the ghastly pale Arkenholz (Helge Wahlgren), the visionary student whose journey of discovery the play charts, intoned his lines and moved with the stiff walk and wooden gestures of a sleepwalker – or possibly (as Ingmar Bergman has later tried to portray this character) the dreamer of this dream play. In the role of the Young Lady, Anna Flygare's performance was conceded to be the most poetically effective; "a soulful, delicate, visually interesting portrait" of "the ailing human hyacinth."[25] In their crucial final confrontation, played not in the inner hyacinth room but in the same stylish *Jugendstil* salon used in the second act, she sat "in an elegant dress and fashionable coiffure, leaned back limply in one armchair, the Student in another, both of them making the play's dialogue into something almost obnoxiously spineless and languid."[26] Nor did any vision of Böcklin's Toteninsel materialize to signify the longed-for release of death. In its stead, a pair of doors opened at the back of the small stage to reveal an indeterminate "landscape with pines."

Two months after the problematic production of *The Ghost Sonata*, Falck's drapery–stage revival of *Queen Christina* fired Strindberg's enthusiasm for this style of neutral staging as the solution to all their difficulties – though it can hardly be said that it would have solved the more tangible problems of interpretation and direction that had beset the chamber plays. As his repudiation of naturalistic staging and acting grew to a virtual obsession, Strindberg proposed that even the realistically conceived environments in such plays as *The Father* and *Easter* should be replaced by an abstract framework of drapes. By performing *The Father* on the drapery stage used for *Christina*, he insisted, the play and its characters would be sublimated and raised above the level of everyday reality. Similarly staged "with curtains, door hangings, and a Brussels carpet," *Easter* should ideally appear "as if played in the clouds: but should be acted in the same way."[27] Falck stood his ground, however, and neither of these radical ideas was implemented. *Easter*, which became Intima teatern's most frequently performed play after its premiere at the end of the inaugural season, was presented without recourse to stylization, in a conventional, closed interior of light walls and glass doors that represented the glass veranda of a middle-class house in a small Swedish town. At the center of Strindberg's poignant family drama of atypical peace and consolation is the figure of the gentle, clairvoyant Eleonore, played in this instance by Anna Flygare with a shy, poetic intensity that gained her the greatest triumph of her career.

In one of his previous letters to Flygare (3 February 1908), Strindberg had offered detailed advice about the style of acting he preferred for such a role: "Take it broadly, like a singer, enjoy hearing your own voice, and even if the speed is increased maintain the legato . . . [B]e economical in your gestures and facial expressions; be graceful even in the less beautiful." This letter reveals more than the playwright's views on acting; it also illustrates the special nature of his relationship as artistic adviser to the Intima ensemble. Although lengthy periods of rehearsal were not unknown at this theatre (Falck mentions, for example, eighty rehearsals for their production of the two parts of *The Dance of Death*), the small acting company seems to have functioned largely without a director in the formal sense, relying instead upon mutual consultation and adjustment. As an actor who appeared regularly in these productions, however, Falck soon recognized the need for the objective guidance of a director. At the end of the first season, he accordingly asked Strindberg to assume this responsibility. "Not that we wanted to introduce a new style or transform our whole idea," he writes, "but only that we should have access to a judge and leader in connection with our artistic work. I thought that a director would be of great help with regard to rhythm and adjustment."[28] Although Strindberg consented and took this new task very seriously, he actually attended only four rehearsals of *The Father* and three rehearsals of *Svanevit* (*Swanwhite*), the first new productions of the 1908–9 season.[29] "The actors found their own way during rehearsals," he states, "adjusted themselves, with the help of the director, to each other's acting, and obtained good results . . . without my help" (*LIT*, p. 143). This implied faith in the collectivist method was rooted in his distrust of the director–autocrat who imposes a single point of view and thereby, in his words, "threshes the play to pieces." Neither excessive rehearsal nor directorial conceptualization must, he felt, be permitted to interfere with the actor's own imaginative response to the role and even his or her freedom to improvise.

Strindberg ultimately preferred the medium of written advice to the actors, and the principal result of his brief term as Intima's "director" is hence his very human and revealing *Open Letters to the Intimate Theatre*, which he published at the end of 1908. The letters are introduced by a so-called memorandum to the cast, signed "The Director," in which he endeavors to formulate his current views on the art of acting. As a poet of the theatre, Strindberg, like Yeats, regarded the beauty of language as the center of the theatrical experience, to which all other elements of the production must be subordinated. Like his great Irish contemporary, he extorted his actors to resist restless gestures and movements that only detract from the impact of the spoken word (it may be recalled that Yeats sometimes rehearsed his players in barrels). The actor in Strindberg's theatre must keep the audience in mind at all times, speaking clearly and slowly (legato) so that the words become a string of pearls, rather than adopting a staccato delivery that emulates a "wretched conversational tone of voice." Playing in this way, he reminds Flygare in his letter, "facial expressions and gestures are unnecessary for every word, for that is old-fashioned." At times his observations on grace and decorum call to mind the Rules for Actors formulated by Goethe (whom he admired, with reservations) more than a century earlier: "A lady should never snap or be cross even if her part involves conflict, but she should always be pleasing in moments of anger. This is an example of the beauty which is truth" (*LIT*, p. 140). It was, however, not a return to the ideals of Weimar classicism and *Schöne Wahrheit* that Strindberg sought, but rather a restoration of the modern actor's dissipated power of poetic and spiritual expressiveness. His ideas on the subject derived from many sources. One particular passage that seems to have stirred his imagination is underlined in his personal copy of Fuchs' *Die Schaubühne der Zukunft*:

> The Japanese actor does not shout, does not make noise; voices are hardly ever raised on the stage, hardly anything happens that goes beyond the polite tone of refined society. And yet the Japanese actor achieves dramatic effects of an intensity we have never known.[30]

As we know, the stylized expressiveness of oriental theatre appealed strongly to Fuchs, Yeats, Craig, and other modernists as an alternative to the naturalism they deplored – and Strindberg eagerly joined them in their struggle to displace the naturalistic mode of theatre he himself had helped to introduce in the 1880s.

Although he continued for a time to bombard Falck with plans, suggestions, and sketches for new methods of production, their partnership did not endure. Matters came to a head with Falck's restrained and very successful staging of Maeterlinck's *The Intruder* in the autumn of 1910. Although this play was ideally suited to the limited space and chamber tone of Intima teatern, its choice was taken by Strindberg as a deliberate affront. "You have *A Dream Play* and *To Damascus* (both with parts for your wife) and you have *Svarta handsken* [*The Black Glove*] which you have scornfully rejected," the irascible playwright wrote.[31] The breach could not be mended, and the last performances at the little theatre on Norra Bantorget were given on 11 December 1910, with *Queen Christina* at one-thirty, *The Father* at four-thirty, and *Miss Julie* at eight o'clock in the evening.

Strindberg's dream of a larger chamber theatre and an infinitely variable and flexible stage space remained unrealized. As significant as the brief history of the Intima is to the evolution of modern Scandinavian theatre, its audience appeal was small and its technical resources were severely limited. Six years after Strindberg's death in 1912, Pär Lagerkvist published a seminal reassessment of the stature and significance of this playwright's achievement. In this manifesto, called *Modern Theatre: Points of View and Attack*, Lagerkvist is outspokenly critical of the Intima experiment and its underlying assumptions. Many of Strindberg's works, he argues, "could be played to advantage on such a stage. But many, and among them the most important ones, could only lose by it. The fact cannot be avoided that a small stage implies, first and foremost, reduced possibilities. Such a stage is confined within a small space from beginning to end. When an effect built upon contrasts is necessary, it is hopeless and can do nothing. It has no possibility of expression through proportions, distance, and antitheses."[32] In other words, this spokesman for a new generation contends, the complex spatial and temporal dynamics of Strindberg's dramatic expressionism could not be adequately realized in performance before the more modern techniques of a new stagecraft were introduced to the Scandinavian theatre, during the period following the First World War. Once this eventually happened, however, the full range of this writer's dramatic production, from the earliest works of the romantic period to the naturalistic dramas, the dream plays, the histories, and the chamber plays, were eagerly taken up for reconsideration and revival by a generation of theatre artists intent upon a theatrical revolution. Ringing in their ears was Lagerkvist's affirmation of Strindberg's "newly created dramatic form" as the quintessence of the artistic instinct of the new age.

9 The modernist revolt

With its repudiation of the restricted "one-sidedness" of naturalism and "the typical Ibsen drama with its silent tramping on carpets through five long acts of words, words, words," Pär Lagerkvist's *Modern Theatre* (1918) signaled an important turning point in the development of the Scandinavian theatre. "The modern stage is a sorcerer's box full of a thousand possibilities," Lagerkvist urged his contemporaries, "and we make a mistake if we do not use them."[1] Yet in spite of Strindberg's progressive attitude and influence, the European revolt against stage naturalism led by such innovators as Appia, Gordon Craig, Meyerhold, and Copeau was comparatively late in reaching Scandinavia. Here, the naturalistic style so forcefully expressed in the productions of Bloch and August Lindberg was slow to disappear. At the Danish Royal Theatre, Bloch's spiritual home, the finely tuned ensemble playing that he perfected lived on in the work of his disciple Henri Nathansen, whose staging of his own play *Indenfor Murene* (*Inside the Walls*) in 1912 reaffirmed the emotional power of naturalism at its best. The lasting success of this genial, bittersweet slice of Jewish family life was due chiefly to the author–director's loving delineation of a richly particularized environment redolent with atmosphere. During the course of the following decades, the production became a tradition in itself, perpetuated in the performances of such leading players as Karl Mantzius, Sigrid Neiiendam, Johannes Poulsen, Holger Gabrielsen, Clara Pontoppidan, and Poul Reumert. As late as 1920, moreover, Nathansen himself gave an even more telling demonstration of his command of the Bloch method of mise-en-scène when he directed Strindberg's *The Dance of Death* at Dagmar Theatre. Audiences in Copenhagen had already seen this play acted by Intima teatern (on tour in 1913), but nothing in the performances of Manda Björling and August Falck would have prepared them for the savagery of the psychological battle waged by Bodil Ipsen's Alice and Poul Reumert's Captain Edgar. Typically, Reumert's approach to this role was a physically and psychologically detailed character study filled with "a grotesque, poignant truth and grandeur. His uncertain, march-like walk, his gruff, bristly demeanor, his haughty vulture's head, his open, drooping mouth, the forced, halting formality of his speech – all bespoke the weakness that tries desperately to brace itself up, the cowardice that conceals itself in a fancy uniform, the fabulist whose every intonation tells a lie."[2] In a comparable performance one year later at Nationalteatret in Oslo, Harald Stormoen ("as unsentimental as reality itself," thought Kristian Elster) combined the same realistically grounded psychological attack with a lighter, more sympathetic tone in his interpretation of Strindberg's bedeviled artillery captain.

Well before then, however, growing opposition to the naturalistic mode of theatre had begun to make itself felt in Scandinavia. A new generation of directors and designers had begun to emerge, attuned to the goals of simplification, stylization, and suggestion advocated by Craig and the adherents of the New Stagecraft. New concepts of stage design and new technical advances in lighting and staging – notably the introduction of the turntable stage, back projections, and the cyclorama – facilitated a more expressive approach to, for example, the surreal and visionary dramas of Strindberg's later period. In general, the renewal and "retheatricalization" of the Scandinavian theatre that occurred between the two world wars had a deep and lasting effect on the theatrical climate. A conjuncture of favorable conditions aided the modernist offensive. The status quo crystallized in Lagerkvist's revolutionary manifesto was ripe for change; for the creation of what he calls "a theatre which gives the imagination of both dramatist and actor greater freedom of movement and greater audacity, a simpler, more immediate and more expressive form."[3]

At the same time, a significant broadening of theatrical activity was also underway as new companies and theatres – large as well as small, commercial as well as experimental – sprang up in competition to the established national theatres in Copenhagen, Stockholm, and Oslo. Simlarly, regional theatres continued to grow in number and importance, and it was from this source that innovation and change sometimes stemmed. Perhaps the most remarkable "alternative" theatre of all was established when Det Norske Teatret in Oslo opened its doors in 1913 – an event that crowned the efforts of more than half a century to found a separate professional theatre for "Landsmaalet," the "new Norwegian" language based on peasant dialects and hence programatically independent of Danish. For its premiere, Det Norske Teatret chose Holberg's *Jeppe on the Hill* in a suitably contemporary New Norse translation. Although fierce debates over language reform soon ensued, the dialect theatre endured and gained a permanent place as the Norwegian capital's "other" national theatre.

Dozens of other new stages arose in the major Scandinavian cities during these years, some of them purely commercial and others with high artistic ambitions. Only three years after the founding of Nationaltheatret in 1899, Harald Otto's well-managed Central Theatre began to attract Oslo's theatregoers with a balanced repertory of popular entertainment and solidly acted productions of serious drama. In 1929, plans for a literary theatre devoted to the performance of new Norwegian drama were finally realized when Oslo's New Theatre, under the management of actor Ingolf Schanche, opened with an ambitious three-evening production of the Knut Hamsun trilogy *Ved Rikets Port* (*At the Gates of the Kingdom*), *Livets Spil* (*The Game of Life*), and *Aftenrøde* (*Evening Glow*). Copenhagen, too, supported a wide range of private theatres, both old and new. Casino and Folketeatret, the first theatres of this kind established in Denmark, were followed by Dagmar Theatre in 1883 and by the New Theatre in 1908. Under the leadership of actor–manager Thorkild Roose in the early twenties, Dagmar Theatre emerged as one of Scandinavia's most exciting theatres, and was proposed for a time in 1921 as a suitable second stage for the Royal Theatre. Its closest rival as Copenhagen's most progressive theatre was the company formed in 1917 by the veteran actress Betty Nansen, whose own strong, untraditional interpretations of such modern female protagonists as Ibsen's Mrs. Alving and Hedda Gabler, Strindberg's Laura (in *The Father*), and O'Neill's Anna Christie did much to fill the stalls of the playhouse that bore her name.

However, it was above all in Swedish theatre that the changes and developments of greatest consequence were occurring. Dramaten, inadequately housed since 1863 in Mindre teatern in Kungsträdgårdsgatan and reorganized in 1888 as a separate, privately owned share company, regained its officially "royal" status when it moved to permanent new quarters on Nybroplan in 1908, nine years after the Royal Opera had also acquired a new theatre of its own. Although the Royal Dramatic Theatre was now the most up-to-date of the three national theatres in architectural terms, it faced stiff competition from rival repertory companies in

Stockholm. The chain of theatres controlled by the actor–impresario Albert Ranft grew apace. Svenska teatern, which became the flagship of Ranft's fleet of playhouses, was regarded by many at this time as the capital's leading dramatic theatre. Although the Nya Intima started by writer–director Gustaf Collijn did not continue the traditions of the Strindberg–Falck era, it too acquired considerable significance during the second decade of the century with an ensemble dominated by Sweden's Strindberg actor *par excellence*, Lars Hanson. From very different points of view, both Collijn and Ranft prided themselves on their dedication to the production of new and older Swedish drama.[4] The most influential new Swedish theatre of the period appeared, however, not in Stockholm but in the thriving west-coast seaport of Gothenburg, where the ultramodern Lorensberg Theatre was opened in 1916. With the technical marvels of this superb facility at his disposal, the young director Per Lindberg was determined to put into practice the modernist aims and ideas to which he had been exposed during an apprenticeship with Max Reinhardt in Berlin. Chief among these aims was the creation of a new, nonillusionistic scenic art devoted to "expression rather than decoration."[5]

Director's theatre

Scandinavia's first glimpse of the new techniques and approaches that were reshaping twentieth-century European theatre was provided by the visits of Reinhardt and his smoothly disciplined company. In the eyes of the great German director, the theatre was neither a moral nor a literary institution. "The theatre belongs to the theatre," declared the 1911 foreword to the *Blätter des Deutschen Theaters*, which was issued by his office. "It has always been our aim to give it back to itself. Its fantastic richness of color, its limitless resources and variations, the blend of sound, words, color, line, and rhythm create the basis from which its profoundest effect stems."[6] Swedish audiences first encountered Reinhardt's new stage forms and expressive groupings in the Circus Schumann production of *Oedipus Rex*, with Alexander Moissi in the title role, which he transported to the Stockholm Circus in 1911. Four years later, Reinhardt's guest performances of Shakespeare at the Royal Opera stirred up a lively difference of opinion among the startled local critics. In *Twelfth Night*, his indispensable revolving stage caused the reviewer for *Stockholms-Tidningen* (11 November 1915) to lament the "earthquake in Illyria: we saw ships and houses dancing by." His staging of *A Midsummer-Night's Dream*, which had established his reputation as a director, was aptly described by *Dagens Nyheter* (14 November 1915) as a "symphony" of contrasting elements, "a masquerade, scenically lyrical and scenically grotesque, theatre in the theatre." In an interview published in the same newspaper six days before, Reinhardt had declared that "the whole decorative, sensual, pictorial line" in his work, which culminated in his *Dream*, had now "exhausted our resources," leaving the director far more interested in exploring "the mysteries of our inner life." This new line of inquiry soon bore fruit in his boldly expressionistic productions of Strindberg.

It was, understandably enough, these productions which had the greatest impact in Scandinavia and opened the eyes of receptive young innovators like Lindberg and Lagerkvist to the sensual, transcendental power of Strindberg's later dream plays. Especially influential was Reinhardt's grotesque and fantastical interpretation of *The Ghost Sonata*, which he brought to Stockholm and Gothenberg in 1917 with Paul Wegener as a ghastly, terrifying Hummel. ("With his shrunken, stony face and crumpled posture, as he sat there in his wheelchair banging his crutches and croaking in a hoarse voice, he left an impression as chilling as the barren coldness of a dead soul."[7]) When this "nightmare of marionettes," as critics called it, reached Copenhagen three years later, it made an indelible impact on Kjeld Abell at the outset of his playwriting career – not as a definitive interpretation of Strindberg's play, but as a revelation of a new way of experiencing theatre. "I ceased to think. During the brief moments in which the catastrophe took place, there was only time to feel. I felt with my eyes, my ears, my whole being," Abell later recalled. "For me, *The Ghost Sonata* was not an answer but a breath that filled the theatre's space and caused it to live, live in a question, caused me to live in that question."[8]

Reinhardt also returned to Stockholm and Gothenburg in 1920 with a production of *The Pelican* in which his skilled integration of theatrical effects created, to the astonishment of the young Olof Molander, "a scenic masterpiece which is not even suggested by a reading of this chamber play."[9] One year later, the Swedish-language production of *A Dream Play* directed by Reinhardt at Dramaten contributed even more provocatively to an overall vision of Strindberg in which, to borrow Siegfried Jacobsohn's words, "a shivering, desperate, shrieking humanity" struggles in an atmosphere "so distorted, so gloomy, so full of fantastic life and motion, that it might be Van Gogh's."[10] Aided by the experimental designs of the Austrian artist Alfred Roller, Reinhardt forged a dematerialized mise-en-scène that contrasted sharply with the conventionality and literalism of the play's first production at Svenska teatern fourteen years earlier. Not all critics agreed with an interpretation in which directorial prerogative was exercised to alter, among other things, the dramatist's conciliatory ending. In the closing scene, Reinhardt allowed Indra's Daughter to sink into the flames rather than enter the growing castle, from which the hopeful symbol of the flowering chrysanthemum was also removed. Critical disagreement notwithstanding, however, the seeds of theatrical revolution had now been sown. The advance of modernism in Scandinavia was now closely identified with the evolution of a scenic form capable of projecting the protean vision and complex visual dynamism of Strindberg's dream-play dramaturgy.

Although Reinhardt's famous 1911 production of the Hugo von Hofmannsthal adaptation of *Everyman* never visited Scandinavia, local versions of this medieval spectacle provided another early and important source of inspiration in the struggle for a new stagecraft and an open stage. Johannes Poulsen, already at the height of his career as an actor, made his debut as a director with a ritualized, Reinhardt-inspired production of *Everyman* at the Danish Royal Theatre in 1914. Poulsen, too, was determined that theatre must not be destroyed by a naturalism that channels it "from the vast, stormy sea of the imagination into an ever more narrow inlet" where it "now lies like a great fish, half-beached on the arid sands of reality and gasping for air."[11] In close collaboration with the Danish painter and scenographer Svend Gade, he created a purely presentational stage space comprised of three stylized spheres (Earth, Grave, and Heaven) interconnected by steps. The visual and symbolic focus of this rhythmic composition was a stairway to the heavenly realm that invoked Gordon Craig's own favorite image of a "flight of stairs leading up and leading down." Gade's projected, plastic lighting made use of a scale of symbolic color values, keyed to the various allegorical figures in the drama. Costumes were similarly expressive, patterned loosely on the style of the medieval frescoes found in rural Danish churches. As in his later attempt to stage the Danish miracle play known as the *Ludus de Sancto Canuto duce*, however, Poulsen's aim was not historical reconstruction but the evocation of a sensual atmosphere of medieval ritual and pageantry. At the epicenter of his *Everyman* experiment was his own grandiloquent performance in the title role – "a virtuoso presentation that passed like a magnificent storm," filled with "scenic pomp and spectacle – a mighty voice, powerful actions, sometimes a bit too superficial in manner."[12] For Craig, meanwhile, Poulsen's larger-than-life acting style mirrored an ideal – shaped in the image of Henry Irving – of immense theatrical force and virtuosity. "This is an actor – one who, on any stage and at any time, in Opera, Ballet, Farce, Tragedy, in all of it – can attain the chief thing, the essence, dramatic life – and who can speak to us by some few but powerful means," he wrote on the occasion of Poulsen's fiftieth birthday in 1931.[13]

Like Reinhardt's *Everyman*, the Poulsen spectacle aimed for and achieved broad popular appeal. Revived twice at the Royal Theatre (in 1921 and 1937) and a favorite of provincial audiences in Adam Poulsen's restaging, it eventually found its way to the Hollywood Bowl in 1936. The success of the endeavor also had swift repercussions in Stockholm, where the versatile critic, writer, director, and manager Tor Hedberg brought the Hofmannsthal *Everyman* to Dramaten in 1916. Having studied the Copenhagen production, Hedberg wanted a mise-en-scène that was independent of the Reinhardt–Poulsen pattern. Yet much seems to have remained the same. An open stage was built out over the orchestra pit, while in the background an imposing construction of steps led up to the heavenly gates. Conventional lighting techniques were discarded by the Swedish director in favor of "decorative and symbolic" area illumination provided by powerful frontal spots, the use of which his production introduced at Dramaten. In general, although this bold attempt at stylized theatre struck immediate responsive chords with the rising generation of reformers, it was far from perfectly realized. Pär Lagerkvist, who devoted a rare review to the production, reminded his readers that "the new stylistic austerity which is most forcefully exemplified in modern art has not yet to any degree inspired the art of the theatre." Although Hedberg's *Everyman* partially met his demands for simplicity, daring, and formal purity, he found the production marred by elaborate realistic touches and, in particular, by the highly embroidered, individualized acting of Anders de Wahl in the title role. This imposing, lyrical star from the nineties (whom Poulsen used in an outdoor revival of the play in Elsinore in 1926) seemed to the impatient young critic a "violently grimacing, gesticulating figure," miscast in a part that requires a medievalized acting style, "stiff, heavy, stringently stylized."[14]

In his own dramatic writing, in fact, Lagerkvist's preoccupation with the spare structure and style of medieval drama made itself felt from the beginning. In *Sista mänskan* (*The Last Man*), an early expressionistic work that stems from the same year as the *Everyman* controversy, he paints a stark picture of a frozen landscape, lit by a dying sun, in which the last survivors of a ruined city carry on a desperate struggle for existence. However, despite his efforts in the public debate that raged over the neglect of new writing at Dramaten, Lagerkvist failed to persuade Hedberg to give his play a hearing. Hjalmar Bergman, Lagerkvist's major contemporary in the new dramatic movement, fared scarcely better with his first two "marionette" plays, *Dödens Arlekin* (*Death's Harlequin*) and *En skugga* (*A Shadow*). Although these short experimental pieces were produced at Dramaten as a double bill early in 1917, their appointed director (Hedberg's brother) was so baffled by them that the result was a fiasco. In the end, it was not the work of these new playwrights but the efforts of a group of young directors and designers that ultimately brought about the breakthrough of modernism in the years following the First World War.

Per Lindberg, one of the brightest and most cosmopolitan of the new directors, also saw the *Everyman* production at Dramaten as an uneven but encouraging prelude to "a subsequent classical repertoire staged in accordance with modern principles."[15] Lindberg's own chance came in 1918 when he was attached to the new Lorensberg Theatre in Gothenburg, the ideal instrument for his art. This splendidly equipped regional theatre had been inaugurated two years earlier with an ambitious modernist revival of *A Dream Play*, directed by Mauritz Stiller and designed by Svend Gade in the same overtly symbolic style he had adopted in an earlier production of the play in Berlin. Masked by a permanent front scrim and framed by a huge oval enclosure, the stage in this complex experiment was a black velvet "dreamscape" illuminated in an oneiric, silvery gray light. However, such technical demands presented no problem at the Lorensberg Theatre, a totally modern 1,000-seat facility that incorporated a turntable stage, a cyclorama, and an advanced lighting board that permitted "so-called horizon lighting from seventy projectors to produce the candle-power of no fewer than 250,000 ordinary lights."[16] In addition to the technical wonders of the Lorensberg and its hospitable climate for experimentation, a third factor in Lindberg's favor was the selection of Knut Ström, who had worked for six years at the avant-garde Schauspielhaus in Düsseldorf, as his chief designer. Ström, who is justly regarded as Sweden's first modern stage designer, continued to exert a seminal influence in the theatre until the late 1950s; remaining in Gothenburg, he designed the stage and machinery for the ultramodern Gothenburg City Theatre, which in 1934

Plate 47 A purely symbolic design by Svend Gade for *A Dream Play*, staged at the Lorensberg Theatre, Gothenburg in 1916.

replaced the Lorensberg as one of the most technically advanced play-houses in Europe. It was, however, during the epoch-making years between 1919 and 1923 that Lindberg and Ström mounted a daring series of – mainly classical – productions that thrust the Lorensberg stage into the vanguard of the modernist movement, as the leading revolutionary force in Scandinavian theatre.

Well educated, articulate, and almost self-consciously aware of his art, Lindberg is an eloquent spokesman (first in "Some Words about Stage Direction," 1919) for a theory of directing that relates clearly to the ideas of Reinhardt and Meyerhold. The art of directing, he asserts, is "a scenic and personal amplification of the drama, so forceful that all the resources of the stage can be unified around the predominant directorial image for that particular play." For the actor, undividedly the focus of attention on Lindberg's stage, the chief prerequisites are physical freedom, elimination of strain, and vocal and muscular control. In this respect, he casts an envi-ous eye toward the "purely circus-like training" given the actor in the mod-ern Russian theatre. Plastic statuesqueness, an architectural rather than a painted stage, rhythmic linear movement, and a musical harmony of col-ors – these were for Lindberg, as they were for the other adherents of the

New Stagecraft, the basic ingredients of modern theatrical art. "Modern stage decor should be decorative, rhythmic, an outgrowth of the play . . . Why should it be enough for a stage picture to be imitated nature? Drama is rhythm. Why then should a setting be a dead copy?" he demands impatiently. His views on stage lighting reflect the theories of Appia and Craig. In addition to providing simple illumination and establishing an atmospheric rhythm, modern stage lighting must also become a means of creating accent, surrounding the characters with a plastic, sculptural lighting that will draw them closer to the audience. For herein, he insists, lies the key to the theatre's power: "to establish, by every means permissible, contact between stage and auditorium, to bring the actors and the audience closer to each other."[17]

The remarkable series of classical productions staged by Lindberg at the Lorensberg Theatre quickly and effectively put his revolutionary ideas into practice. *As You Like It*, presented at the end of the 1919/20 season, set the tone for the kind of experimentation with Shakespeare that was to follow. Lindberg's directorial image was rooted in the play's original festive occasion as a wedding celebration. Love shared the stage with melancholy in his buoyant conception, as the festivity of a stylized pastoral landscape contrasted with the darker, fresco-like court scenes. Every available means was used to draw the audience into the action; a built-out stage was fitted with broad steps leading down into the auditorium, where green-clad pages sounded a joyous fanfare to introduce the spectacle. The iconographic style of Lindberg and Ström eschewed the abstract or the purely mechanical, seeking instead an imaginative orchestration of line, rhythm, movement, and grouping that would crystallize the essential spirit of the production.

In his subsequent work with Shakespeare, Lindberg continued to experiment with a similarly expressive style of mise-en-scène. In October of the next season, his concept for *Hamlet* was based on "a fixed framework of blocks with a strong vertical accentuation, blocks whose rhythm and color can quickly and easily be transformed and changed during the nineteen tableaux."[18] Here one senses more than a passing resemblance to the famous Moscow *Hamlet* staged by Craig and Stanislavski. Much like Craig, Lindberg invariably visualized the successive movements of a play in terms of colors, as the essence of the mood and pulse of a given scene. The *Hamlet* production thus became a symphony in red and black ("the streaming blood and the eternal darkness"), and each of the nineteen "pictures" into

Plate 48 Watercolor sketch by Knut Ström for Shakespeare's *Romeo and Juliet* at the Lorensberg Theatre, 1922.

which the play was divided became a variation on this theme. Running from black through gray and dark brown into reddish brown, purple, and cerise, the structurally keyed color scheme was carried through both in the drapes and the costumes, culminating in the startlingly red dress worn by Gertrude. In subsequent productions of *King Lear* (February 1921) and *Othello* (October 1921), Lindberg continued to rely on simplified, expressive staging techniques, always in the service of what Meyerhold calls a "free composition" that uses only those architectural features that convey the essential spirit of the work. For *Lear*, which featured Lars Hanson in the title role, Ström's scenography combined flights of stairs and towering walls whose abstract patterns and textured surfaces suggested a rough-hewn, premedieval atmosphere. The visualization of *Othello* was likewise dominated by solid masses and dark, threatening shapes, including a drawbridge starkly accentuated against the sky for Othello's arrival on Cyprus. Lighter and more romantic in spirit was Ström's staging of *Romeo and Juliet* (February 1922), in which his stylized scenic composition of low, smooth walls, graceful arches, and spiked cypresses conveyed a subtle impression of Italian Renaissance art.

   Although newer drama played a less conspicuous role in the Lindberg – Ström collaboration, such modern works as Gunnar Heiberg's *King*

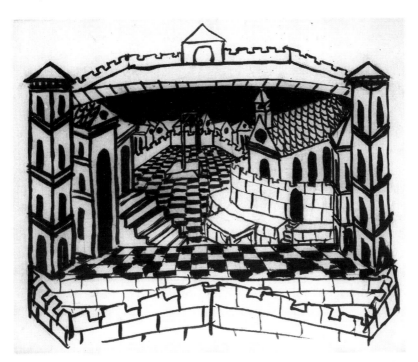

Plate 49   Design by Ström, in the spirit of a sixteenth-century woodcut, for Strindberg's
The Saga of the Folkungs at the Lorensberg Theatre, 1920.

Midas, Knut Hamsun's *Livet i vold* (*In the Throes of Life*), and Hjalmar
Bergman's *Lodolezzi sjunger* (*Lodolezzi Sings*) and *Herr Sleeman kommer* (*Mr.
Sleeman is Coming*) did gain a hearing. Considerable attention was also
devoted to Ibsen (*Peer Gynt, Ghosts, The Wild Duck*), but by far the most
prominent modern playwright in the Lorensberg repertory of this period
was Strindberg. Within the simplified, stylized, suggestive theatrical context advocated by Lindberg and Ström, Strindberg's poetic imagination
could achieve free rein. Light was rapidly becoming, for Lindberg, "the
theatre's palette. The deep stage with its dark perimeters, the bunched rays
of light between rolling or gliding planes and levels, this was a whole new,
independent, pathetic world. Where imagination and poetry belonged.
Where new settings could be created with the slightest possible change of
decor and without pauses."[19] In, for example, his 1920 production of the
poetic version of *Master Olof,* which for the first time included Strindberg's
bitter metatheatrical "afterpiece" depicting "the creation of the world and
its true meaning," Lindberg set aside once and for all the history-play
convention of pedantically "accurate" architecture, interiors, and

accessories. The strict simplicity of Ström's sets and costumes for this production set an example whose influence would continue to be felt for many years to come. "What can and is to be included of the historical milieu," wrote Axel Romdahl in *Svenska Dagbladet* (21 January 1920), "is decided solely according to the principle that nothing unnecessary must be shown, nothing false must be shown, and that, if anything beyond the unavoidable is shown, this must have a suggestive weight capable of underscoring and emphasizing the dramatic action."

The Saga of the Folkungs was attempted by Lindberg in the autumn of the same year, using an even more radically stylized Ström setting to accommodate this rarely performed historical drama. The raked, checkerboard stage, an asymmetrical and deliberately naive rendering of a Serlio-type city square, was intended to evoke the sense of a sixteenth-century woodcut. Lindberg's stage picture was painted with light, color, and expressive figure compositions. The first of the mass scenes in the square, when King Magnus is hailed by the jubilant multitude, seemed "quite simply without parallel" to the seasoned Stockholm critic August Brunius.

> We have never seen anything as magnificent on a Swedish stage as this immense altarpiece, in which every figure stands in clear, sculptural plasticity, wrapped in a dreamy mist and etched against a storm-blue horizon. Its beauty culminates in the Madwoman's pale silhouette against the sky – a Giotto fantasy as fascinating for the eye as for the mind, a picture and a revelation of equally striking power.[20]

Two years later, the Scandinavian premiere of *To Damascus* III at the Lorensberg carried the expressionistic staging of Strindberg to its most radical extreme. Directed by Ström and designed by his apprentice Sandro Malmquist (soon to become a major designer–director in his own right), this strongly acted performance took place on a virtually empty stage, the very bareness of which projected a sensation of great height and space. Strikingly akin to Appia's later projects for *Orpheus and Eurydice*, Malmquist's abstract landscape consisted of horizontal planes, steps, and geometrical forms. In this "rhythmic space," all recourse to representationalism was avoided, and hence significant objects or shapes projected on the cyclorama (the silhouette of a signpost outlined against the sky, for instance) took the place of constructed scenery.

Although the Lindberg–Ström campaign in Gothenburg in the early twenties remains the most striking indication of the breakthrough of the new modernism, it was by no means an isolated phenomenon. The revolution Lagerkvist had predicted was rapidly becoming a reality everywhere in Scandinavia. "Our time, in its lack of balance, its heterogeneity, and through the violent expansion of its conflicting forces, is baroque and fantastic, much more fantastic than naturalism is able to portray it," Lagerkvist writes.[21] An almost bewildering variety of theatrical experiments sought to lend expression to the new postwar spirit of unrest, of what Lagerkvist calls "the anguish we feel as life wells up against us." "Dionysus, grant us again a feast! Give us again a temple for intensified life!" exclaimed the Danish writer Svend Borberg in 1919. "We renounce science and all its deeds, the uniformity of time, place, and action, analysis, the logical construction, the false realism and the false psychology, 'parts' and 'points' – and we embrace instead only the unity of thought, the totality of atmosphere, the artistic composition. Grant us then the intoxication, the ecstacy, the great visions! Grant us again a place of revelation."[22] The road to the temple took many turns, but the basic rediscovery that theatre is, above all, theatre – neither staged literature nor imitated life – informed each new experiment.

Borberg's manifesto (entitled "The Decline of the Play") was essentially a denunciation of *literary* conservatism at the Danish national theatre, manifested in its indifference to new drama (including his own). It is, however, a mistake to assume a comparable resistance to new theatrical ideas, for such was not the case. In September of 1919, even as Lindberg was taking control of the Lorensberg Theatre, Johanne Dybwad's austere, Craig-inspired production of *Medea* at the Royal Theatre in Copenhagen, with the Norwegian star herself in the title role, was yet another example of the growing interest in the methods of the New Stagecraft. On this same stage only six months before, Johannes Poulsen's festive theatricalist revival of *Aladdin* had exemplified the "Reinhardt dimension" of the modernist approach – the art of mise-en-scène at its most sensual, colorful, and exuberant. Poulsen's lavish oriental paraphrase of Oehlenschläger's poetic fantasy divided the work into two full evening performances, each of which was given a limited run of fifteen consecutive nights. The first installment, entitled Thalia, was comprised of the lighter, more comedic episodes of the Aladdin tale; the second part, entitled Melpomene, was devoted to its darker, more tragic aspects. At times, the visual appeal of Gade's settings and Poulsen's mass scenes and processions was so great that, in the opinion of several reviewers, it overwhelmed Oehlenschläger's poetry. Nor was Carl Nielsen's symphonic score for the production entirely successful in blending its lyrical, balletic, and dramatic components into a coherent whole. Nevertheless, the overall effect of the *Aladdin* experiment was the revelation of a new and compelling style of theatre – "the old rag shop transformed into a golden and glittering treasure house," as Georg Brandes put it.[23] The governing force behind this new theatre art was the creative influence of the figure proclaimed by Olof Molander (who directed his first production at Dramaten in 1919) as "the regisseur of the future," the Craigian artist of the theatre who must present the text "filtered through his own spirit, stamped by his own individuality."[24]

When the noted modernist painter Isaac Grünewald was called upon to design the sets and costumes for a new production of Saint-Saens' *Samson and Delilah* at the Royal Opera in Stockholm in 1921, the flourishing theatrical revolution in Scandinavia took a distinctive new turn. When, for example, Reinhardt had invited Edvard Munch to provide the scenery for his famous Kammerspiele production of *Ghosts* in 1906, his choice was a repudiation of the older naturalistic conventions. By contrast, the decision by Harald André to engage Grünewald to design his production of *Samson and Delilah* was a more daring move, in that it proposed a defiantly two-dimensional, painted alternative to the three-dimensional use of mass and space advocated by Appia, Craig, and their followers. Accompanied by heated controversy and an unprecedented response at the box-office, Grünewald's bold, collage-style design concept opened the way for a new attitude toward theatrical decor as "decorative logic." Production problems were numerous, to be sure. Grünewald's eleven scene designs involved complicated set changes and even necessitated a partial reworking of Saint-Saens' opera. The orgiastically colorful, architectonically constructed costumes, meant to serve as a contrast to the manifest two-dimensionality of the scenery, proved in many cases almost impossible to sew, let alone wear. Not everyone understood the artist's intentions, and he himself recalls that he barely prevented the planting of "a photographically real moon" in his sky – "despite the velvet cactuses and shining silver trees, and despite the fact that my heavens were green."[25] Nevertheless, as this remark suggests, the finished result was a rare visual feast. In the first act, Samson encountered Delilah in a fantastical garden of palms that sprouted sunflowers, gleaming silver tree trunks, and cactuses that reached the sky. Delilah's seduction of the strongman in the second act took place in a surrealistic grotto setting painted in a rich range of red tones. In the water-

Plate 50 Scenography by the modernist painter Isaac Grünewald for Saint-Saens' *Samson and Delilah* (Royal Swedish Opera, 1921): the fantastical garden where Samson encountered Delilah in act 1.

color and gouache design for this scene, high cliffs resembling multifaceted basalt columns tower above the lovers, while gigantic suns are seen exploding in brilliant reds and yellows against an indigo sky. In Grünewald's effectively simple rendering of the prison in Gaza in the last act, the chained and blinded Samson is shown driving an enormous mill wheel whose size is accentuated by pale, focused lighting and a shadowy green-black background. In general, the aftermath of this seminal production was definitely a new appreciation of the creative force of scenography in the theatre. As well, the staggering bill submitted by Grünewald for services rendered provoked a sensational lawsuit that only heightened public interest in the figure of the theatre artist, whose work now began to command a separate section in the reviews of some drama critics.

During the same eventful year that saw Grünewald's staging of *Samson* at the Royal Opera and Reinhardt's production of *A Dream Play* at Dramaten, Stockholm audiences were exposed to yet another crucial development when Pär Lagerkvist's drama began to be staged for the first time. Although the first part of *Den svåra stunden* (*The Difficult Hour*), his cycle of three short plays about the moment of death, had been presented

Plate 51 Grünewald's surrealistic grotto setting for the seduction of Samson in act 2.

Plate 52 The prison at Gaza in the third act, defined simply by the solitary figure of the blinded strongman and the immense mill wheel at which he labors.

by Knut Ström at the Schauspielhaus in Düsseldorf in 1918, it was not until the Intima ensemble's production of *Himlens hemlighet* (*The Secret of Heaven*) in April of 1921 that Lagerkvist gained a hearing in his own country. The influential premiere of this minimalist drama, which featured Harriet Bosse in the principal role, was a very different but no less revolutionary manifestation of the modernist spirit. In this grim parable of the human condition, a collection of grotesque and hapless individuals live out their futile existence on "a huge, blue-black sphere" that is sharply illuminated by "a conical-shaped beam of light, verdigris-green in color." The visual effect created by this work in performance is obviously crucial, and it found full expression in the spatial concept created for the Intima production by Yngve Berg, another prominent painter and illustrator of the period. A spherical elevation over the stage floor was used to evoke an impression of the globe suspended in a vacant universe of blackness – an image unmistakably similar, in fact, to Gordon Craig's familiar design for the barren mound on which he placed Hjördis in the last act of his production of Ibsen's *The Vikings of Helgeland* in 1903. In this bleak space, suffused in an eerie violet light that pierced the encroaching darkness, the isolated figures in the drama carried out their absurd, disjunctive tasks. The Intima experiment had introduced a distinctive new voice in the theatre, and less than five months later Olof Molander boldly elected to open the 1921/2 season at Dramaten with another Lagerkvist one-acter, *The Difficult Hour* III, in which the rising young star Inga Tidblad was given the role of the small boy who makes his way through the frightening shadowland of death.

In his dramatic writing Lagerkvist was, in many ways, Strindberg's direct successor. Here, his commentary on the master's form also describes his own dramatic technique:

> Here, everything is directed to one purpose – the liberation of a single mood, a single feeling whose intensity grows and grows. Everything irrelevant is excluded even if it is rather important to the continuity or to the faithfulness of representation. Everything which occurs is meaningful and of equal weight. . . . And actually, no "persons" in the usual, accepted meaning, no analysis, no psychological apparatus, no drawing of "characters." And yet, no abstractions, but images of man when he is evil, when he is good, when in sorrow, and when joyful.[26]

Like Strindberg's plays, Lagerkvist's dramatic expressionism fired the imaginations of directors and designers alike. As a result, his plays contributed their share to the sweeping theatrical upheaval he himself had foreseen in *Modern Theatre*. His promising relationship with Molander ended in bitter disagreement over the latter's 1924 production of *Den osynlige* (*The Invisible One*), a deeply pessimistic allegory deploring mankind's miserable existence on "this cursed earth." Instead, it was Per Lindberg who eventually evolved a distinctive performance style for this playwright's mature works. Their long artistic collaboration, which lasted until Lindberg's death in 1944, profoundly influenced the evolution of Lagerkvist's dramaturgy and accounted in no small measure for the impact that performances of his plays often had in the Scandinavian theatre of the twenties and thirties.

The second transition

By 1921 the visits of Max Reinhardt, the Lindberg–Ström era in Gothenburg, and such diverse experiments as Poulsen's *Everyman* and *Aladdin*, Grünewald's *Samson and Delilah*, and the Intima's *Secret of Heaven* had begun to revolutionize Scandinavian theatre, and the second wave in this steady advance of modernism was at hand. A decisive turning point occurred when Lindberg, who left Gothenburg in 1924, mounted his ambitious theatrical assault on the capital during the 1926/7 season – not at one of the established theatres but in an unlikely partnership with Ernst Eklund, whose specialty was sophisticated drawing-room comedy, at Stockholm's newly completed Concert Hall. The formal, curtainless platform stage in this 2,000-seat house accorded well with Lindberg's egalitarian ideal of a flexible, classless "folk theatre" that would create a purely sensory experience involving everyone in the area of activity. "The illusionistic stage was a court theatre for the bourgeoisie – the chamber stage became a theatre for the intelligensia. What, then, shall we do for the people?" he demanded. The answer, in his opinion, was an open, neutral stage that corresponded to "the expressionistic vision of theatrical space as a unified whole . . . a flexible space in which stage arrangement, actors, and audience, united by the architecture of the place, share a common rhythm and emotion." His model at this point was Jacques Copeau's Vieux Columbier in Paris.[27]

The first of the seven plays Lindberg directed during his extraordinary Concert Hall season was *Antony and Cleopatra*, with Carl Ström and Harriet

Bosse in the title roles. Interestingly enough, he turned to Isaac Grünewald – whose style might seem the antithesis of the sculptural three-dimensionality required for his own open-stage concept – to design settings and costumes. The result was one of Grünewald's brightest achievements: a relatively neutral framework, light and airy in tone, within which a general's tent or a hoisted sail served to evoke a change of scene. The pulsing flow of the action was maintained by rhythmically shifting figure compositions on the open stage. The Egyptian–Roman dichotomy upon which Lindberg's directorial image rested was deftly visualized by Grünewald's rich and connotative color scheme, which adopted mainly orange and red tones for the Egyptians and cooler blues and whites for the Romans.

There was not, however, any sameness of style or predictability of approach in the various offerings of this crowded season. In presenting *The Bonds of Interest*, Lindberg adhered closely to Benavente's conception of his comedy as "a little play of puppets, impossible in nature, without any reality at all," in which the *commedia dell'arte* characters are "moved by plain and obvious strings, like men and women in the farces of our lives." The outcome was a festive, Grünewald-designed marionette comedy whose presentational style and playful *lazzi* recalled Vakhtangov's famous theatricalist production of *Turandot*, which had visited Stockholm in 1923.[28] In a darker and utterly different tone and style, the versatile Norwegian actor Ingolf Schanche also created an elegant and subtle Hamlet for the Concert Hall season. This and Lindberg's subsequent productions here – *Oedipus Rex*, Romain Rolland's Dreyfus play *The Wolves*, and Tor Hedberg's political drama *Johan Ulvestjerna* – were more or less eclipsed, meanwhile, by his provocative revival of *To Damascus* III. A purely expressionistic setting by John Jon-And conveyed a stylized impression of a mountain landscape made up of angular, abstract planes and contours and dominated by a strangely deformed cross. Although Harriet Bosse appeared as the Lady, the role Strindberg had created for her, the evening belonged mainly to Schanche, whose ironical portrayal of the Tempter stole the spotlight. Schanche's mocking and expressive countenance and his ability to combine irony and dread in his interpretations made him a fascinating Strindberg actor and an obvious choice for the part of the Unknown when Lindberg later directed his one-evening adaptation of all three parts of *To Damascus* at Nationaltheatret in Oslo in 1933. On this occasion, with "an inner absorption in the role, a human understanding of it, a surrender to the experience of it," he struggled with what Kristian

Plate 53 Preliminary design by John Jon-And for Olof Molander's experimental production of Racine's *Phèdre* at Dramaten, 1927. This sketch underwent some modifications in production.

Elster called "feverish virtuosity" to make emotional sense of the contradictory protagonist at the center of Lindberg's problematic experiment.[29]

The repercussions of the 1926/7 Concert Hall season were felt almost at once at Dramaten, where Olof Molander quickly responded to the implicit challenge with a modernist production of *A Midsummer-Night's Dream* in April. He, too, called upon the most sought-after designer of the day to dress his stage; Grünewald, who thus made his debut at the national theatre, responded with a colorful but somewhat more restrained design concept, consisting of a recognizable Athenian palace whose white columns and moss-green and red-violet walls were counterbalanced by the soft blues and greens of his seductive woodland decor. Early in the following season, influenced perhaps by the fact that Lindberg had now been hired by Dramaten, Molander's restless experimentation with form and style took a more daring turn with his controversial production of Racine's *Phèdre*. "If one wanted to be malicious, it could be said that Molander's *Phèdre* is Per Lindberg's greatest triumph to date," Agne Beijer observed drily in *Stockholms Dagblad* (6 October 1927). And there is, indeed, a Lindbergian ring to the rhetoric that accompanied the event. "With *Phèdre*

I have wished to realize a long-cherished dream, by being able to present what I would call synthetic theatre – that is, a synthesis of acting, music, color, and light," the director declared during rehearsals.[30] Transposed to a barbaric, prehistoric era, his interpretation of the drama literally revolved around an immense, megaphone-shaped column, much smaller at the base than at the capital, which provided the focal point in John Jon-And's expressionist stage design. This object was, in the minds of Molander and his designer, the symbol of the power and dominance of Thésée. Stage right, a pair of slender columns formed a stylized arch, decorated in deep red tones to signify Phèdre's passion. In a third "zone" at the opposite side of the stage, placed on a slightly higher elevation, a little temple suggested by three columns (not shown in Jon-And's design) stood for the chastity of Hippolyte, whose theme colors were white, light blue, and silver. Some critics cited the influence of Vakhtangov's *Turandot* on this exercise in stylization, while others noticed resemblances to the famous Tairov performance of this play in Moscow five years before. Either way, most found the "synthetic" concept superimposed or confusing. Racine survived the assault, however, thanks mainly to the magnetic Phèdre of Tora Teje, the role in which she emerged for the first time as one of this century's foremost tragic actresses. "Seldom if ever before has the artist achieved such harmony between intuition and conscious technique," Beijer remarked. "Her voice carried the verse as though it had been her natural language, soft, lyrical, full of passion. Even her plasticity possessed a purely musical beauty, free, expressive in the extreme, and yet controlled and majestic."

Less than three weeks after the *Phèdre* premiere, Lindberg opened a second front in the modernist assault with his inauguration of Dramaten's Club Theatre, the purpose of which was to present Saturday matinées of unperformed or rarely performed contemporary plays. This popular subscription program was closely tied to Lindberg's campaign for an egalitarian "people's theatre," affordable in price, democratic in principle, and attuned to the concerns of contemporary society and culture. Indeed, the most successful of the four programs put on by the Club Theatre during the 1927/8 season, Toller's *Hoppla! Wir leben*, seemed to Herbert Grevenius to make possible "the idea of literary folk theatre" which, had it endured, might have grown to become "the core of a folk theatre movement."[31] Particularly auspicious was the double bill with which Lindberg opened his experimental stage in October, consisting of Hjalmar Bergman's *Porten* (*The Gateway*) and Lagerkvist's *Tunneln* (*The Tunnel*), as the first play in his *Difficult Hour* trilogy came to be known. Both plays shared a simplified stage setting designed by Jon-And in the expressionistic mode: an abstract geometrical arrangement of blocks, planes, and triangles (the chaos of life) surrounded by a dark enclosure (the unseen forces about us). The minutely detailed description of the stage picture contained in Lagerkvist's text was deftly condensed by Lindberg into a supple chiaroscuro image of the moment of consciousness after death. As the Man in Tails, who has lost his life in a train crash, emerged from the tunnel with his sinister and indifferent companion, the Hunchback, the two figures were picked out of the darkness by colored follow spots. A sudden flash of brightness illuminated the stage to reveal, in the words of critic Erik Lindorm, "a setting of expressionistic torment and chaos," after which the scene was again plunged into a darkness "intersected by beams of white light."[32]

This innovative experiment was the beginning of a long and fruitful collaboration between Lagerkvist and Lindberg, who was quick to follow *The Tunnel* with an even more controversial full-scale production of *Han som fick leva om sitt liv* (*The Man Who Lived His Life Over*) in 1928. In this work, one of his best plays, Lagervist turns away from the more abstract symbolism of his earlier drama. Instead, he establishes a much more concrete framework for the internal conflict that rages within the title character, a shoemaker named Daniel who struggles without success to make his second life more meaningful than his first. One of the recurrent motifs in Lagerkvist's work finds expression here in Daniel's anguished existential cry for a chance to live his "real life," his "own life" in the face of a hostile and indifferent universe. In response to the play's subtle mingling of symbolism and heightened realism, Lindberg and his designer, Sandro Malmquist, created a stage space intended to reflect this idea: a scrupulous facsimile of a shoemaker's workshop surrounded by an abstract space crowded with shadows and accentuated by the silhouette of a cross.

Following his abrupt departure from Dramaten in 1929, Lindberg became more preoccupied than ever with the challenge of this writer's work. "Pär Lagerkvist continued toward the goal which he had set himself: 'The struggle for a new form must also be the struggle for a deeper personal vision,'" he wrote in a later essay on Lagerkvist's dramaturgy. "His drama is what drama was originally: a cultic action, an hypnotic festival for the moral edification of mankind."[33] The morally salutary "hypnotic festival" to which Lindberg refers is at the core of his vision of a "folk theatre," in which Lagerkvist would be seen as "a son and a poet of the people." Hjalmar Bergman, Lagerkvist's brother-in-law, had in fact already achieved this kind of broad popular following in a very different way, by exchanging the mordant disillusionment of his early plays for the good-natured humor of his later comedy successes, *Swedenhielms* (1925), *Patrasket* (*Rabble*, 1928), and his unsurpassed folk-comedy triumph, *The Markurells of Wadköping* (1929). On the other hand, the ethical seriousness and thematic density of Lagerkvist's drama could hardly be expected to achieve the same kind of popular appeal in the theatre, despite Lindberg's best efforts.

A notable exception was the production of *Bödeln* (*The Hangman*) that Lindberg mounted, in collaboration with the Norwegian director Hans Jacob Nilsen, at The National Stage in Bergen in 1934. *The Hangman*, adapted by Lagerkvist from his short novel of the same name, is an intense personal indictment of Fascism, and the enthusiastic response its performance elicited in Norway "almost grew to the proportions of a folk movement," according to Lindberg. Written to be presented without interruption, this play juxtaposes two moments in history; a dimly lighted medieval tavern filled with violent, beer-drinking workmen is suddenly transformed into a garishly illuminated nightclub patronized by frenzied Nazis whose bloodlust is even more frightening and senseless than that of their medieval forebears. Dominating both scenes is the brooding figure of the Hangman, a waiting, watching presence played with extraordinary force in Bergen by the veteran actor Kolbjørn Buøen. Lindberg and his designer, the young Per Schwab, used every means at their disposal to engage the audience directly in the emotional atmosphere of the drama. Film clips of trench warfare were used to link the two scenes; a thrust stage placed the savage Nazi orgy in the jazz club virtually in the audience's lap. Above the action, seated on a small platform of his own, Buøen's weary, blood-red executioner ("your Christ, with the hangman's mark on my forehead! Sent down to you!") bore silent witness to the unending ritual of violence.

When it was transferred to Vass teatern in Stockholm, however, Lindberg's production of *The Hangman* met with audience indifference, even with the formidable Gösta Ekman in the title role. Instead, it was with his touring production of *Mannen utan själ* (*The Man Without a Soul*) in 1937 that he at last succeeded, at least to some degree, in introducing a broad popular audience to Lagerkvist's writing and its appeal for pacifism. After a somewhat unpromising opening in Malmö, this Swedish National Touring Theatre production eventually attracted great popular interest in other regional centers – due perhaps in part to the fact that both playwright and director had renounced the strident expressionism of *The Hangman* in favor of a more recognizable framework of heightened, suggestive realism. At issue in the play is the inner struggle of a terrorist (The Man) who falls in love with The Woman, the wife of the man he has just killed. Unlike Alf Sjöberg's much starker staging of the play at Dramaten the following year, Lindberg's mise-en-scène relied on a concrete and importunate environment in which a crescendo of sound, light, and smoke effects suggested the war that rages during the play. The nameless protagonist, sensitively protrayed by Georg Rydeberg in the Lindberg production, must pass through a succession of Damascus-like stations in his quest for redemption, and each of these localities – a coffee bar, The Woman's room, a hospital ward, the cemetery, and the prison where he ends his life – was designed with vivid visual simplicity by Helge Refn, the able Danish scenographer who earned his first important success with this assignment. Refn's atmospheric coffee-bar set, bathed in green dusk and lit by red lamps, presented an effective contrast to his bare, cubistic design for the hospital room, which consisted only of glaring white walls, a central glass door, and the iron bed on which The Woman dies in childbirth. Disturbed by the melodramatic note sounded in the text by the "flood of radiance" through which The Man walks to his execution at the end, Lindberg strove for a sober open-endedness that eliminated all recourse to spurious religious symbolism.

Modernism reviled and revivified

The efforts of such modernists as Lindberg, Molander, Poulsen, and others notwithstanding, the aims and methods of the New Stagecraft did not go unopposed in the Scandinavian theatre. The turbulent 1927/8 season at Dramaten, to take one example, gave rise to a long and heated debate in the Swedish press over the issue of modern directing and the "dangers" it posed to the text, the actor, and even the social fabric. Violent controversy followed Molander's *Phèdre*, while Lindberg's riposte – a stunning expressionistic production of the Calderón masterpiece *Life's a Dream* – sparked off a veritable war of words. Far louder, however, were the howls of protest that awaited Edward Gordon Craig, the foremost spokesman for a New Theatre, when he came to Copenhagen in the autumn of 1926 to stage *The*

Pretenders at the Danish Royal Theatre. The occasion was the twenty-fifth anniversary of the acting debuts of Johannes and Adam Poulsen; as the sons of Emil Poulsen, the first Bishop Nikolas, it was only natural that they should be drawn to Ibsen's play as the perfect vehicle for their jubilee. Somewhat less clear is the exact nature of Craig's involvement. In an engagingly discursive letter (12 August 1926), Johannes Poulsen invited him to "draw the decorations and costumes for the performance. I myself am going to set the play up, but if you would come over here and set it up with me as interpreter, we shall be very pleased indeed. You will have a free hand in every respect."[34]

Craig came to the project with a supreme disregard for stage tradition and historical accuracy alike. "I have never been concerned in any attempt to show the spectators an exact view of some historical period of architecture," he later declared in the sumptuous portfolio of designs that he published to commemorate the production. "I always feel that the great plays have an order of architecture of their own, an architecture which is more or less theatrical, unreal as the play."[35] In *The Pretenders*, he told a Danish interviewer several weeks before the anxiously awaited premiere,

> we shall use Henrik Ibsen's dialogue and his characters but not his descriptions of the scenery. Local color is not something we will place very much emphasis upon – but then neither does Ibsen. We shall not try to represent the *church* or the *council chamber*, rather we shall represent *the spirit of the church, the spirit of the council chamber and the banquet* . . . In *The Pretenders*, as in *Hamlet*, a ghost appears – tell me to which historical period can one ascribe a ghost? No, drama is a product of our inner life, and we create on the stage a world for that inner life.[36]

In the light of such Craigish pronouncements as these, it is perhaps self-evident to add that his nonrepresentational approach to the play demonstrated an uncompromising repudiation of the traditional pictorialism of earlier productions of it. He did away entirely with the principle of successive decors, relying instead on a simple architectural device – a permanent structure of platforms that could be localized, in a symbolic manner, by means of projections, occasional hangings, the deployment of nonrepresentational set pieces and small screens, and the selective use of central objects expressive of the essential idea of a particular scene. A painted front curtain, decorated as an "old Norway map," could be closed at times to facilitate the more complicated changes of scene, without restoring the Reinhardt alternative of a turntable stage.

Perhaps the best scene in the Craig–Poulsen collaboration was the splendid opening of the play in the churchyard of Christ Church in Bergen, in which a crowd of warriors and citizens outside the church awaits the outcome of the ordeal with the white-hot iron that will confirm the birthright of Inga's son, Haakon Haakonsson. No traditional Norwegian stave church loomed in the background. Instead, Svend Borberg wrote in *Ekstra-Bladet* (15 November 1926), "the curtain rises and we see a forest of lances grow toward the sky, while behind them, projected on a cyclorama: a dream in yellow light and bluish shadow, a half-dematerialized cathedral." To others, it seemed as if the divine choice of Haakon was somehow "embodied by the stylized lines of light" that hover in the sky of Craig's well-known stage design. "We are at once removed from the usual theatre gothicism," Christian Gulmann concurred in *Berlingske Tidende* (15 November). "No painted church as a background for Meininger processions, but a beautifully effaced impression of high columns of light, and a forest of lances above the richly colorful warriors – a square in Florence rather than a picture of medieval Norway." The "Florentine" color harmonies to which many of the critics drew attention exemplify Craig's customary preoccupation with chromatic selection as the principal key to the expression of the inner essence of a text. In this case, Poulsen's promptbook for *The Pretenders* contains a shortlist of the four basic colors (selected from six possibilities) with which Craig sought to reveal the spirit of Ibsen's drama: gold, off-white, violet, and crimson.

All too often, however, the fleeting, impressionistic beauty of Craig's scenography seemed at odds with the prosaic physical reality of his actors – Johannes Poulsen as a grotesque, toothless Bishop Nikolas, his brother Adam as a sonorous Skule with no trace of the tragic essence of Ibsen's character, Eyvind Johan-Svendsen as a dark, inelegant, curiously antiheroic Haakon. Especially in some of the more intimate interior scenes of the play, the ponderous background of platforms and nonrepresentational gray set pieces seemed out of place. In the Bishop's death scene at the beginning of the third act, for example, it was difficult to reconcile the palpable convulsions and emotional vehemence of Poulsen's performance with the abstract symbolism of Craig's setting. Treated in Ibsen's stage directions and in most earlier productions of the play as a simple, closed interior that opens into a lighted chapel in the background, the episcopal

Plate 54 "A forest of lances grows toward the sky": the published version of Edward Gordon Craig's design for the opening scene of *The Pretenders*, produced at the Danish Royal Theatre in 1926.

residence in Oslo inspired Craig to envision a "mystical, religious, nocturnal atmosphere of horror." Wind machines were pressed into service to produce an undercurrent of "storm and wind in long, howling blasts." At the very front of the stage stood an upholstered armchair and an ornate couch with "new bolster"; behind these two solid pieces of furniture, one saw the entire depth of the large stage filled with twenty-odd of Craig's ubiquitous gray forms – "high, block-like shapes, some of them in a greenish light and one of them illuminated with blue," recorded one observer.[37] "The Bishop's chamber, resembling a warehouse cellar in the dockyards, filled with packing cases, robbed [Poulsen's performance] of all its mystique – despite a violet spotlight on one of the packing cases," the critic for *København* (15 November) observed sharply. "The strange blocks among which the Bishop dies" were classified by Valdemar Vedel as being among the most distracting elements in the scenography. Writing in *Dagens Nyheder* (15 November), Vedel added a general comment that goes straight to the root of the problem: "All such attempts at simplification will inevitably produce, at least at the outset, the opposite effect from that which is intended, in that the new way will always distract and seem much more obtrusive than that of natural custom."

The five-week rehearsal period for *The Pretenders* was fraught with disagreements and delays, and the actual extent of Craig's involvement in the process is still a matter of dispute. In the end, however, it was he who bore the brunt of the criticism of the production's stylistic inconsistencies and disregard for the Nordic tone and atmosphere of Ibsen's drama. "We have nothing against the stylization and simplification which Mr. Craig advocates, and we agree with him completely that all the old-fashioned theatre art is often offensively glossy," Viggo Cavling wrote in *Politiken* (15 November). He continued:

> But if one wants to stylize, one cannot stylize in general, but only within the framework and tone and milieu in which the play takes place – as Max Reinhardt and [Leopold] Jessner have done time and time again, with sublime results. And the Craigian method could undoubtedly have been applied with success here, if only the coldness of the North, the harshness of the Middle Ages, the darkness of Catholicism had been allowed to come through. Instead, we were given scenery composed of parti-colored blocks, Italian banners, French ribbon backdrops, Japanese lanterns, oriental gates, and so on.

Even an avid reformer like Borberg was obliged to admit that "this surely is not *Ibsen*! . . . This is an Irish tale, yes exactly Irish – undoubtedly Craig has Irish blood in his veins, as do all Englishmen with imagination, and this reminds us both in its ecstatic style and especially in its color harmonies of the miniatures of the Irish monks, of Yeats's *Countess Cathleen*, of red hair, green peasants' coats – wonderful, but why use it for Ibsen!" In other words, the demand in 1926 was not for a return to an outmoded pictorial illusionism. Craig's right to seek his inspiration in the tone and spirit of the play itself, rather than in the poet's stage directions, was not being challenged by the Danish critics – only his perceived inability to conceive a theatrical image that adequately served the tangible, localized Nordic world of Ibsen's drama ("that dreadfully difficult play for intellectuals," as Craig later called it).

Precisely in the terms in which Craig seemed to fail, Olof Molander succeeded in the cycle of Strindberg productions that he staged in Sweden during the mid-1930s. Imaginative in their application of the principles of the New Stagecraft yet solidly anchored in the concrete milieu and tone of

Strindberg's Stockholm, these seminal revivals marked the culmination of the modernist quest for theatrical renewal in Scandinavia. By then, his productions of *Phèdre* (1927), O'Neill's *Mourning Becomes Electra* (1933), and Euripides' *Medea* (1934) had established Molander as Dramaten's most resourceful director. As its chief from 1934 to 1938, he experimented freely with a fluid, supple scenic form that seemed more responsive than ever before to the associational, metamorphic nature of Strindberg's dramatic logic. As a devoted pupil of Craig's theories, he was convinced that a renaissance of the theatre would depend upon the ability of the director to master the three basic components of production – text, acting, and scene – and create "an harmonious synthesis of these elements, out of which the work of theatrical art will arise." For Molander, the modern stage "must not represent reality, it must bring forth an image of it, it must conjure up reality. When our imagination is activated by what we see on the stage, we boldly create a reality far more real than what can ever be represented on any stage."[38] Unmistakably Harald Molander's son in his feeling for concrete, pregnant detail, he combined painstaking directorial analysis with an acute sensibility that restored to Strindberg's plays a relevance and a Swedishness that conclusively set aside the approach taken by Reinhardt and his followers. The latter's "romantic expressionism" seemed, to Molander's mind, "completely alien to Strindberg's surrealistic dream-play dramaturgy. It is certainly true that nightmares are often its subject, but nightmares of everyday, of life as we live it, not a nightmare life in any higher sense, not caricature."[39]

In sharp contrast to Reinhardt's interpretation of *A Dream Play* fourteen years earlier, Molander's first production of it (25 October 1935) sustained a lucid undertone of resignation and consolation, a recognition of the humanity so often absent in the German *Schrei* versions of Strindberg's plays. There is no more eloquent witness to the power of Molander's conception than the young Ingmar Bergman, upon whose work this famous premiere was to leave a lasting impression:

> Molander has made us see the magic of Strindberg's dramaturgy. We have begun to understand that the strange fascination of the stage itself and the Strindbergian dialogue are compatible. Molander gives us Strindberg without embellishments or directorial visions, tunes in to the text, and leaves it at that. He makes us hear the poet's anxiety-driven fever pulse. It becomes a vision of toiling, weeping, evil-smitten

humanity. We listen to a strange, muted chamber music. And the
dream play emerges in all its grotesqueness, its terror, and its beauty.[40]

As this comment suggests, the spine of Molander's interpretation was its
identification of the Dreamer, in all three of his voices, with the playwright
himself. His presence was felt in the young, eternally expectant Officer, in
the mature Lawyer whose care-worn face bespoke the sufferings in which
he deals, and especially in the aging Poet who, actually made up to resemble Strindberg, sat at the feet of Indra's Daughter – his muse and his own
creation – to learn of the interchangeability of poetry and dream.

As the Daughter, Tora Teje was a majestic, melancholy figure in black
who often stood outside the action, as if watching a play-within-the-play
being enacted for her. As the lawyer, Gabriel Alw projected a furrowed,
agonized Christus image bent beneath the cross of the world's woes –
"and to Christ bearing his cross he was transformed before our very eyes,"
reported Herbert Grevenius, "when during the spectral Degree
Ceremony beneath the cathedral's mighty vault a crown of thorns, rather than the laurel wreath, was pressed down upon his head."[41] Watched
by Indra's Daughter, this moment was one of many instances in which
reality and dream seemed to merge into what some referred to as
Molander's surrealism. "Here one is in the midst of the dream, yet it seems
to us at the same time more real than reality, uglier, more unsettling, more
bitter, more beautiful. It is a condensed reality," observed Bo Bergman,
who had also reviewed the world premiere of this play three decades
earlier.[42]

In the opinion of many, the focal figure in the performance was the
irresistibly buoyant and hopeful Officer created by Lars Hanson – "in walk
and bearing a marionette of dreams, sorrow, and unhappiness, his face
frozen in an unforgettable mixture of eagerness and pained surprise," as
Frederick Schyberg saw him when the production visited the Royal
Theatre in Copenhagen later in the same season.[43] Particularly memorable
was the scene in which the Officer suddenly found himself seated on the
school bench again, obliged to relearn old forgotten lessons and repeat old
mistakes. Trapped in a nightmare of recurrence, he became both the
dreamer and the player in a dream sequence watched (dreamed?) by Indra's
Daughter. "In this scene Lars Hanson expressed a *wonderment* that came
from the depths of his spirit," another eyewitness recorded. "Surprise
became, all at once, uneasiness, fear, and touching helplessness. The lines

Plate 55a Work photograph from Molander's first production of *A Dream Play* at Dramaten, 1935. The divided stage at the beginning of the play used spotlights to isolate and juxtapose (*left*) the simple table at which the Officer sits inside the Castle and (*right*) the homely sitting room where he meets his parents.

Plate 55b Sven Erik Skawonius' more detailed setting for the Theatre Corridor invites comparison with Grabow's design for this scene in the original production of *A Dream Play*.

were spoken as if by a sleepwalker, seeking clarification because he is half aware that he is dreaming."[44]

Impressive as many of them were, meanwhile, the individual acting performances were in a sense eclipsed by the virtually mesmeric effect of Molander's mise-en-scène. Its basic style might well be called surrealistic. A rhythmic, oneiric flow of fragmentary settings designed by Sven Erik

Plate 56   Grünewald's festive design for a back projection of Fairhaven appeared on the cyclorama during the Foulstrand sequence in the 1935 production of *A Dream Play*.

Skawonius, each built up of selected bits of sharply etched reality, was collated with a succession of stylized back projections created by Isaac Grünewald. Each of Skawonius' dream images had its strongly lighted focus – a table and chair, an announcement board with hymn numbers in the cathedral scene, the omnipresent cloverleaf door in varying contexts, and so on. Beyond the minimal settings one saw at times only a background of impenetrable darkness. At other times, Grünewald's projected visions filled the cyclorama with suggestive glimpses of *fin de siècle* Stockholm – the red Horse Guard barracks that (according to Martin Lamm) inspired the play's growing castle, the old Royal Dramatic Theatre with Jacob's Church in the distance, and other allusions to a recognizable time and place. "This was precisely what was lacking in Reinhardt, and the resulting impression was therefore more chaotic and disconcerting than it ought to have been for Strindberg's own countrymen," Anders Österling argued in *Svenska Dagbladet* (26 October). "Now, Grünewald's imaginative projections provide us with the right reminder of the underlying reality of the scenes."

The dichotomic character of the scenography established an irony that suited Strindberg's purposes perfectly in, for example, the Fairhaven/Foulstrand sequences, where the language of disjuncture is the operative idiom. The oppressive confines of Foulstrand and its Quarantine Station were suggested very simply: a diagonal bit of tiled wall with an iron gate and an open tent with exotic exercise machines stood at either side of the stage on small revolving turntables. In the background, Grünewald's picture-postcard view of Fairhaven ("a vision of Swedish villas and greenery and sails on the water," as Österling described it) beckoned mockingly from across the strait. Then, with half a turn of the two revolves, the foreground became Fairhaven. The clapboard wall of the schoolroom and a corner of an open-air dance pavilion appeared in place of the tiled wall and the tent, while the sinister contours of Grünewald's Foulstrand – a barren, dying world of perpetual winter – loomed in the distance.

In the cheerless conclusion to Reinhardt's *Traumspiel*, the departure of Indra's Daughter had been followed by the sound and music of human misery and the appearance of a wall of pale human faces peering through the clouds of smoke from the burning castle. In Molander's consciously revisionist interpretation, the fire was no more than a hint of red back lighting that changed to pure blue as the flowering castle vanished and Indra's Daughter disappeared. Alone on a deserted stage, the Poet with Strindberg's face was left to watch as a jumbled photographic collage of faces filled the cyclorama. As if in benediction, a cross rose above the small altar on which the characters had laid their various emblems of human suffering; it bore the inscription that Strindberg had chosen for his own grave: "Ave crux spes unica" ("Hail, O Cross, our only hope"). Although a great deal changed in Molander's subsequent revivals of *A Dream Play*, the interpolation of religious mysticism was to remain a dominant aspect of all of them.

During 1937, the twenty-fifth anniversary of the playwright's death, the Strindberg renaissance fostered in part by Molander's work reached its height. Armed with the critical advice of Martin Lamm and with Skawonius' system of simplified sets and projections, he launched the Strindberg year at Dramaten with a new production of *To Damascus* I which again pursued a through-line based, as he put it, on "the autobiographical and the religious element" in the drama. "For the Unknown in this play is, to some extent, Strindberg himself."[45] Costumed and made up to convey a certain resemblance to the playwright, Lars Hanson evolved a very personal, unhistrionic reading of the main character that captured the difficult mixture of tragic anguish and irony in the play and its nameless protagonist. "With an intuition that is quite unique," wrote Sten Selander in *Svenska Dagbladet* (28 February 1937), "Lars Hanson has grasped and has allowed his infinitely revealing face to express what in some ways lies hidden at the very core of this role – a small, frightened, helpless young man with a bad conscience, unable even to comprehend why he is buffeted so hard by fate." In turn, this feeling of incomprehension established a more complex ironic perspective that often made the Unknown seem the bewildered spectator of his own life-dream. "Lars Hanson succeeded in making the character not only humanly believable but also humanly appealing," concluded Agne Beijer in his review. "One had the impression of a personal identification with the role that actually circumvents analysis, even though the characterization was, beyond any doubt, the product of an analysis that was, in its own way, no less penetrating or less precise than the research of literary criticism"[46]

In October of 1937, Molander undertook his third major excursion into Strindberg's post-Inferno period with his production of *The Saga of the Folkungs*, an ambitious experiment in which both the oneiric simplicity of *A Dream Play* and the moody introspection of *To Damascus* were replaced by sheer theatrical pageantry conceived on a colossal scale. Not unlike Lindberg's initial revival of this work seventeen years earlier, the Molander–Skawonius version of it was essentially a rich medieval tapestry of choreographed mass scenes and spectacular visual effects. Although Beijer and other critics expressed reservations about the interpretation of the play as simple historical extravaganza, Grevenius' vivid account in *Stockholms-Tidningen* (23 October 1937) suggests the powerful sensual impact of Molander's grandiose mise-en-scène:

> A gallows stands like a grim pointer toward eternity, and an immense iron chain stretches a meaningful greeting from a distant heaven to a desperate earth. Grotesque tumult and ceremonies, royal splendor and rage, drunken torchlight processions, Dominicans and Franciscans with flaming candles, the fever-red Plague Girl whirling about with her broom and chalking her crosses [on the doors of the doomed], the frenzied monotone dancing of the flagellants, with blood streaming down their backs, King Magnus groaning beneath his black penitential cross, the Madwoman on the roof shouting out: "There is blood on your crown, King Magnus." One is caught in the grip of these intense visual pictures.

The influence of these theatrical images on Bergman's 1956 film *The Seventh Seal* has often been noted.

During the following decades, Molander went on to direct a host of other important Strindberg revivals, including *The Ghost Sonata* (1942), *To*

Damascus II (1944), *The Great Highway* (1949), and others. When he was encouraged to leave Dramaten in 1963, following Bergman's appointment as the new head of the theatre, this veteran's defiant reply came in the form of back-to-back productions at the Stockholm City Theatre of O'Neill's *Mourning Becomes Electra* trilogy (1964) and his own collation of the complete *Damascus* trilogy (1965). None of his achievements held quite the same fascination for him and for his audiences, however, as his ongoing exploration of *A Dream Play*, the seventh and last production of which he presented at Det Norske Teatret in Oslo in 1965, the year before his death. For Molander, no production of this play was ever quite the ideal one. "I will never get the chance to mount *A Dream Play* in the way I would like," he told an interviewer in 1965. "The resources, not least on the acting level, which this Strindbergian masterpiece requires in order to, in my opinion, come even close to doing it justice are so colossal that no theatre has them at its disposal."[47]

Although the surrealism or "fantastic realism" he and his designer had introduced in the 1935 premiere remained the trademark of Molander's subsequent revivals, the character of this style varied considerably from one production of *A Dream Play* to another. His script for a Danish production of the play at the Royal Theatre in Copenhagen in 1940 indicates the adoption of a virtually operatic mode of musical accompaniment that involved an extremely complex pattern of musical cues. Most of the prologue in heaven was spoken to music from Ravel's *Daphnis et Chloé*, while during the remainder of the action one heard an almost continuous symphonic accompaniment, provided by an orchestral potpourri consisting of a Beethoven quartet, Chopin's "Funeral March," Ravel's *Daphnis* and his orchestral suite *Rapsodie espagnole*, Bach's *Toccata con Fuga* No. 10 (Strindberg's choice), a little Mozart, and much else. Both in the Copenhagen production and in a new revival at the enormous Malmö City Theatre in 1947, however, it seemed wise to Molander to discard the more obviously localized back projections of Strindberg's Stockholm. In Malmö these were replaced by evocative photographic images of neutral street scenes and summer villas in bleached grays and whites. In the controversial closing scene, as the characters came forward to place their offerings upon the altar, the gigantic silhouette of a heavy cross again rose slowly in the background, bearing the familiar Strindbergian epitaph.

Later in 1947 at the Gotheburg City Theatre, Molander's fourth approach to *A Dream Play* suddenly assumed a different, darker tone

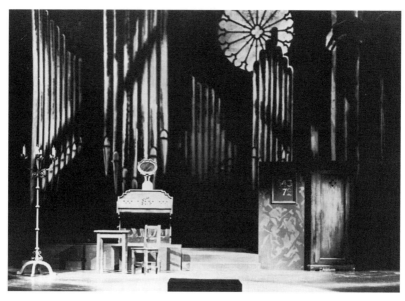

Plate 57 Arne Walentin's setting for the Cathedral in Molander's final production of *A Dream Play* (Det Norske Teatret, Oslo, 1965) was composed only of shadowy projections and selected set pieces.

permeated by defiance and despair. The driving force in this interpretation was now the psychologically intense and embittered Lawyer created by Anders Ek, whose crowning with thorns and symbolic crucifixion in the doctoral promotion scene became the drama's most harrowing experience. Projections were eliminated altogether, and Molander experimented instead with solid, plastic elements. The growing castle was thus a three-dimensional miniature of the Horse Guard barracks, resting on piles of straw and flanked by immense, multicolored hollyhocks. In the closing scene, flames licked at its roof but no faces appeared in the empty windows; as it sank noiselessly into the earth, a Molander cross again appeared in the background – this time, however, not the marker from Strindberg's grave but a high, slender silhouette against a fiery horizon, rising above the blackened ruins of a bombed-out city. In the foreground stood the solitary figure of the Poet, with his somber Strindberg countenance.

Although he was apparently dissatisfied that "only" forty-three rehearsals had been held for his last production of *A Dream Play* at Det Norske Teatret in Oslo in 1965, Molander later conceded in a radio interview that he regarded this version as his best. His collaborator on this occasion was Arne Walentin, one of Norway's most gifted stage designers.

In his preliminary correspondence with him, Molander asked the designer whether a more simplified and unified production concept could not be achieved by making "one composition out of all the sets, with a platform serving as mid-axis, around which chairs, tables, doors, wardrobe, etc. are placed?" His aim was "to clear away everything that is superfluous." Projections could serve to provide "a sustained backdrop, 'the description of the atmosphere in the atmosphere', so to speak. But what we place on the stage can be more ephemeral."[48] Walentin responded with scenography that made brilliant use of the limited stage facilities at his disposal and, in turn, stimulated Molander to approach the play in a new way, with (in the designer's words) "the reality of the dream-world" as his guide. A few key bits of scenery – notably an announcement board and the door with the cloverleaf pattern – were kept on the stage throughout the action. Other linking objects changed, as it were, from one thing to another, as when the lime tree that blooms and withers outside the theatre corridor became first a clothes rack in the Lawyer's office and then a candle-stand in the cathedral. A sense of place and atmosphere was evoked by Walentin's back projections, which ranged in style from a stark photographic image of decaying slums in the Lawyer's scenes to a shimmering vision of a rose window and organ pipes in the macabre degree ceremony.

Perhaps the most notable change in this production was the decision on Molander's part to eliminate the prologue in heaven. Rut Tellefsen, who played Indra's Daughter in the production, explained in an interview that "he found it more interesting and challenging to suggest the Daughter's divinity scene by scene than to state it clearly in advance." Her opening scene with the Glazier, played on a bare stage in front of a colorful, highly stylized flowering castle, was entirely dreamlike until, once having entered the castle, "they were considered to be in life-on-earth and their speech and movements ceased to be dreamlike and became realistic."[49] A correspondingly spare closing scene dispensed with the more overt religious and autobiographical allusions of the earlier productions. A blue door frame stood on an otherwise empty stage, framing the projected image of the flowering castle; through this doorway the characters passed in procession as they spoke their final lines. The castle projection turned a fiery red and then faded from the cyclorama, to be replaced by the sorrowful face of a woman whose image was repeated over and over until it filled the entire background. This one face, Molander was now persuaded, was enough to signify the suffering of all humanity.

Needless to say, by the mid-sixties both the theatrical and the political climate had altered drastically in Scandinavia. The Molander method – especially as reflected in his autobiographical approach to Strindberg – had now begun to seem, to some, "academic" and out of touch with contemporary realities. Indeed, Bergman's first stage production of *A Dream Play* in 1970 could be – and was – seen as a conscious refutation of the Molander "formula" for this play. Nevertheless, Molander's innovative interpretations of Strindberg, of O'Neill, and of the Greek classics had already changed the shape and direction of the Scandinavian theatre conclusively – as Bergman himself has repeatedly emphasized. The modernist ideas of directing and design so forcefully advocated by Lagerkvist, Lindberg, Poulsen, and others achieved full articulation in these productions. In itself, the remarkable history of Molander's voyage through *A Dream Play* exemplifies a broader course of events. For him and for others in the modern period, Strindberg's plays, like Shakespeare's, continued to be a rich and multifarious source of theatrical inspiration, stimulating fresh interpretations and the technical advances required to realize them.

Three new voices

During the turbulent decade preceding the outbreak of the Second World War, even as the popularity of Molander's classical revivals was reaching a peak, a new generation of playwrights arose, most notable among whom were Kaj Munk, Kjeld Abell, and Nordahl Grieg. Their writing reflected the invigorating influence of the new theatrical spirit, and it quickly came to form an integral part of the development of the modernist movement. All three were still in their thirties, and all were, in different ways, deeply preoccupied with a social and political situation that was growing more ominous every month.

Kaj Munk, the outspoken Danish poet–priest whose name became synonymous with the Resistance cause during the war years, made an unpromising debut as a playwright in 1928, when the Royal Theatre staged a heavily cut version of his unconventional historical drama *En Idealist* (translated as *Herod the King*). Three years later, however, this same theatre's production of *Cant*, a free-verse denunciation of sham piety and self-righteous hypocrisy, was a solid success with Johannes Poulsen as a splendidly gross and jovial Henry VIII and Anna Borg in a sensitive, unaffected portrayal of Anne Boleyn, whose rise and fall is the story of the play. In *Ordet* (*The Word*) Munk transposed the issues of faith, piety, and hypocrisy to a very different setting, the primitive society of a Danish country village. Especially in its controversial conclusion, in which Johannes, who imagines himself to be Christ, appears to raise his sister-in-law from the dead, this ambiguous "legend of today" seems a direct reply to Bjørnson's Pastor Sang, the "miracle priest" whose misguided zeal destroys his wife in *Beyond Human Power*. The outstanding productions of *The Word*, directed by Betty Nansen at her avant-garde playhouse in 1932 and by Johan Hauge at Det Norske Teatret the following year did much to secure Munk's position as this period's most incendiary new dramatist.

In *De Udvalgte* (*The Elect*), a biblical drama in "four chapters," Munk returned to his preferred mode, the historical spectacle drawn on a grand scale and seasoned with gleanings from Shakespeare and Oehlenschläger. Like Johannes in *The Word*, King David in this play is seen (as Munk explained in the program) as one of God's chosen ones, who may sin and err and fall and yet remain invulnerable because they retain something of "God" within them. In practice, the character of David lacks the conviction of this premise. The first production of the play at the Royal Theatre in November of 1933 effectively yoked Johannes Poulsen's operatic mise-en-scène with the fiery biblical splendor of Isaac Grünewald's scenery, but the weakness of the David figure became even more apparent in performance, when pitted against Poul Reumert's masterful portrayal of the cunning homosexual power broker Achitophel. On the other hand, the real power of Munk's ability to conjure up a gaudy and brutal world of history emerged in the Royal Theatre revival of *Herod the King* early in 1938, with Reumert as the pathological, power-crazed dictator who defies God and Clara Pontoppidan as his venomous, hunchbacked sister Salomé. Kierkegaard's familiar existentialist maxim, "Purity of heart lies in willing but one thing," is an apt epigraph not only for *Herod* but for Munk's dramaturgy as a whole. Its virtual intoxication with the notion of the single-minded historical strongman beyond good and evil, which for a time led the playwright to the brink of fascism, remains the chief source of dramatic interest in his work. Drama, this writer insisted, must bring back to the stage what Artaud would call the element of cruelty, the depiction of bold colors and violent scenes in an atmosphere that is dangerous and disturbing. "A new generation has grown up that does not go to the theatre to sit nicely and quietly, watching nice, quiet things," he writes in an article about the first production of *Herod*. Instead, this new audience seeks to "catch a glimpse of life . . . with all its flaming contradictions":

life from the world this new generation has grown up in, where one people rose up against another with their very existence at stake; where necessity knew no law, and there was no good or evil any longer because everyone thought only of himself and was his own God; while heads toppled, limbs were shattered, brains burst, and peace brought with it labor strife and fraud and callousness and poverty and pestilence. The new generation demands that this is the world in the very midst of which Art must stand.[50]

By the mid-thirties, imaginative psychological and social dramas by Carl Erik Soya and Leck Fischer had begun to add further substance to the contemporary dramatic renaissance started by Munk's work. However, until Munk's death at the hands of the Nazis in 1944, his closest competitor for popularity and critical acclaim was Kjeld Abell, whose playful verbal eloquence and innovative structural experiments represented the antithesis of Munk's "heroic" style. In general, astonishing technical virtuosity coupled with a prolific ability to devise new and provocative forms of theatre are the qualities that set Abell's contribution apart from that of any other playwright of his generation in Denmark or in Scandinavia as a whole.

"Why is there anything in the theatre called realism?" this iconoclast demanded in a seminal essay from the thirties.

Can theatre ever be realistic? Has "the human comedy" anything to do with everyday reality? Where should the sofa stand? Has the placement of the desk never anything to do with the position of the window? Must the actors always stand facing the audience? ... Who has decreed how reality should look? Does it always look like that?[51]

As Abell's art deepened, the questions multiplied, and their urgency seemed to increase. Underlying his restless quest for theatrical renewal was the fundamental purpose to which he incessantly returns in his theoretical writings: to restore the spectator, narcotized by the literal-mindedness of the naturalistic style, to his rightful place as "an active part of the endeavor." The audience is, for Abell,

the fully worthy opponent against whom the struggle must be taken up – with all the unreal theatrical devices and theatrical effects; victory must be won on both sides of the footlights – or rather, the barrier of the footlights should instead be felt to be eliminated – and in the midst of this battlefield of cardboard, painted cloth, and make-up, the true reality shall stand vigorously alive.[52]

After early work in what he called the "wordless theatre" of the ballet had taught him to control theatrical space and exploit nonverbal means of expression, Abell set about changing the shape of Scandinavian drama as he found it. *Melodien der blev væk* (*The Melody that Got Lost*), which launched Per Knutzon's influential avant-garde stage in Riddersalen Theatre on 6 September 1935, was a remarkable first play that combined the techniques of expressionism, film, and political cabaret in a fresh and original manner. Per Lindberg's production in Stockholm later that same season confirmed the work's extraordinary popular appeal. In its story of Larsen, a contemporary everyman who loses life's melody when he succumbs to the bourgeois pursuit of career and conventionality, audiences in London and Scandinavia alike seemed to find a perfect paradigm of "modern times." One year later, Holger Gabrielsen's elegant and witty production of *Eva aftjener sin Barnepligt* (*Eve Serves her Childhood*) at the Royal Theatre marked the decisive victory on the Danish national stage of the "unreal theatrical devices" Abell took such delight in. "He plays with theatre, using all its theatrical possibilities: visible scene changes and traps in the floor and tricks up the sleeve and monologues and asides," Schyberg wrote in *Berlingske Tidende* (9 December 1936) the next morning. "His world is the theatre's world of childish improbabilities and unrealities, of all its symbols – peopled with human beings, yet viewed with the foreshortening which is the theatre's."[53] In this freewheeling theatrical cartoon it is Eve, the mother of us all, whose plight one follows as she leaves her museum to experience the childhood years she never knew, only to find herself enmeshed in the prejudices and stereotypes of the respectable middle-class family into which she is born. Although these early social satires differ both in mood and tone from the political dramas and impressionistic fantasias Abell wrote in the forties and fifties, the overt theatricalism they employ remained the abiding characteristic of this theatre–poet's dramaturgy.

The strongly critical view of capitalistic society held by Nordahl Grieg, the third outstanding dramatist of the prewar period, was perhaps no more revolutionary than Abell's outlook, but the harsh, indignant tone of the young Norwegian playwright had little in common with the

Giraudoux-like irony of his Danish contemporary. Grieg's major plays are performance texts that draw freely on the documentary techniques of the agitprop theatre and "living newspapers" of the time: "Since real life, in all its grotesque brutality, is so much more powerful than anything a person can think up, it would have to be very stupid not to use archives and old newspapers," he told an interviewer.[54] *Vår ære og vår makt* (*Our Power and Our Glory*), which was written under the influence of his lengthy sojourn in Soviet Russia, is an uncompromising condemnation of the ruthless profiteering of Norwegian merchant ship owners during the First World War. In its rapid cross-cutting of short scenes – the juxtaposition, for example, of torpedoed sailors bailing a life raft and drunken profiteers boozing and womanizing back home – the play emulates the montage effect of films like Noel Coward's *Cavalcade*. In its skillful integration of sound, light, film clips, and other techniques of presentational staging, it also reveals both Grieg's strong affinity for the Russian experimental theatre of Meyerhold and his close collaboration with Hans Jacob Nilsen, the progressive director and manager who literally forced through its first production at The National Stage in Bergen on 4 May 1935. Less than a year later, the noted actress Bodil Ipsen made her directing debut at the Royal Theatre in Copenhagen with a rendering of the play that effectively avoided the mixed-media approach adopted by Nilsen. With the aid of Helge Refn's scenography, Ipsen exploited to the fullest the purely theatrical means of expression at her disposal – evocative figure compositions and movements, surging mass scenes, stirring music, and Refn's provocative visual images. The explicit, agitprop style of these images is best represented by the constructivist setting for the final episode: the surrealistic skeleton of a ship's hull stood center stage, flanked on one side by the cranes, factory stacks, and other emblems of the industrial worker, and on the other by the stylized portico of the Bourse, the stately pillars of which suddenly tilted to become twin cannons pointed at the audience.

Although Grieg's protest plays were roundly denounced in the conservative press as "communist infiltration," their popular appeal was undeniable. In *Nederlaget* (*The Defeat*), a sprawling masterpiece about the last stand of the Paris Commune against the National Guard in 1871, Grieg invoked a more distanced actuality to make his point. Like Brecht's *The Days of the Commune*, which is a free paraphrase of it, *The Defeat* mingles historical figures with invented bystanders whose views and attitudes reflect the political context for the Commune's fall. In a letter to the playwright, Hans Jacob Nilsen expressed special admiration for "a structure in which quiet moments alternate with the more violently agitated ones – a distribution of mass scenes and two-person scenes."[55] It was this rhythmic oscillation of moods that Nilsen sought to stress when he presented the play at The National Stage (20 April 1937), less than a month after its premiere at Nationaltheatret in Oslo. Balancing the bitterness and cynicism found in Grieg's vision of a brutalized world is a strain of hopefulness, affirmed by the opening notes of the choral ode from Beethoven's Ninth Symphony that Nilsen used as a leitmotif in his production. "Hope will come again on earth," says the fanatical believer Delescluze at the end of the play. "Those out there may scorch the grass with their grenades, but they can never kill the earth's ability to become green."

The Danish production of *The Defeat*, which was only partially successful in Svend Gade's overly naturalistic mise-en-scène, nonetheless made a strong impression on Kjeld Abell and his contemporaries. As the thirties passed and the decade's troubled economic situation was overshadowed by the reality of Nazi aggression, Abell's posture changed. Running through his wartime plays is a new attitude of defiance, engendered by the "bitter truth" Grieg's Delescluze says he has learned: "that good can only survive through force." If plays like Lagerkvist's *The Hangman* and Grieg's *The Defeat* echoed with the reverberations of a collapsing world, Abell's *Anna Sophie Hedvig*, which opened at the Royal Theatre on New Year's Day 1939, was an indictment of passivity and an exhortation to oppose aggression and tyranny. The strongly acted production, directed by Holger Gabrielsen and remembered for Clara Pontoppidan's moving portrayal of the title role, was in itself a significant factor in the wide popular acceptance of what remains Abell's best-known work. However, the full explanation of the play's appeal at the time is to be found in its underlying message of political resistance, couched in its ambiguous story of a quiet spinster schoolteacher who kills a power-mad school tyrant in order to protect her small world against the malicious and destructive actions of her enemy. "Must we not defend our small worlds? Do they not together make up the great world?" asks Anna Sophie Hedvig, who is depicted by Abell as the figurative comrade-in-arms of those who fought against fascism in the Spanish Civil War.

After the German invasion of Denmark and Norway in the early days of April 1940, the theatre was constrained but not silenced. Heavy losses

were sustained. Grieg, who immediately joined the Norwegian government in exile and enlisted in the armed forces, was killed in a bombing raid
over Berlin in December 1943. Munk was forty-five when he was murdered
by Gestapo thugs and dumped in a wayside ditch near Silkeborg in January
1944. Yet even in occupied Norway, where interference by the Nazis grew
to become intolerable, theatrical activity persisted. The Royal Theatre in
Copenhagen went on functioning under the firm leadership of Cai
Hegermann-Lindencrone, in spite of anonymous bomb threats, curfews
that sometimes forced performances to start at four in the afternoon, and
repeated warnings of demolition by the Germans because the playhouse
was known to be a Resistance arsenal of weapons and explosives. Caution
prevailed, meanwhile, and even the freer theatres of neutral Sweden displayed little appetite for stylistic innovation or renewal. Nevertheless, the
productions of Alf Sjöberg at Dramaten in the 1940s and the early work of
Ingmar Bergman, who made his directing debut at the small municipal
theatre in Hälsingborg during the last autumn of the war, were harbingers
of a fresh upsurge of theatrical creativity in the postwar era.

10 Tradition and experiment since 1945

During the second half of the twentieth century, Scandinavian theatre has been characterized by a wide diversity of experiments and styles, born of spiritual or political restlessness or of artistic discontent with the status quo. Throughout this period new directors, writers, actors, and designers have arisen in their turn to enrich, or disrupt, or modify the strong traditions of this theatre. In particular, the previous ascendancy of the three national stages has been challenged, more insistently than ever before, by large commercial rivals and alternative fringe groups alike. Here as elsewhere in Europe, the growth of small experimental theatres, the increasing significance of regional and touring companies, and the universality of television have all affected the perceived function and importance of theatre in the broader cultural matrix. Through it all, however, the redefinition of the modern Scandinavian theatre, a process which was set in motion during the formative period between the two world wars – the implementation of Lagerkvist's Strindberg-inspired vision of the stage as "a sorcerer's magical box" brimming with limitless possibilities – has remained an ongoing process. The productive interface of tradition and experiment has fostered what might be called a tradition *of* experiment, an attitude of extraordinary openness to new ideas, methods, and paradigms of theatre. It is an attitude inherent in Alf Sjöberg's passionate belief that we "must try with all the energy available to probe everything which we feel vibrates with human life, human revolt and protest, and that every concerted attempt to restrain this urge for freedom must be treated as a threat. In itself, many-sidedness is significant and indispensable."[1]

No one, in fact, exemplifies the range of experimentation in more recent Scandinavian theatre better than Sjöberg himself, whose career as a director spanned a fifty-year period at Dramaten that lasted until his death in 1980. For Sjöberg, the need to break new ground and find new ways of making theatre seems to have been virtually a moral imperative. "We cannot give up this searching, this unrest, any more than we can give up our freedom to choose, question, and try," he wrote in a seminal essay from 1950.[2] In the mid-forties, with more than fifty productions already to his credit, he enlisted Sweden's foremost visual artists to design a succession of productions representing some of the most exciting theatre in Europe at the time. In every case, detailed sketches contained in his own scripts leave no doubt about the extent to which his strong directorial concepts always impressed themselves visually on the stage design for a given production. For his staging of Garcia Lorca's *Blood Wedding* at Dramaten in 1944, Sven Erixson provided a starkly simplified stage space in whites, blacks, reds, and yellows, dominated by a rough-hewn stone stairway and house facade. The most revolutionary feature of Sjöberg's mise-en-scène, however, was the rhythm it derived from movement on changing planes and the integration of this rhythm into the tragic action. For Sjöberg's politically charged production of *The Flies* the following year, sculptor Eric Grate responded with a plastic, textured design concept that was, in itself, a surrealistic fusion of the ancient and modern associations which the director saw blended in Sartre's text. The most imposing of Grate's four designs for this play was his setting for the temple of Apollo in the last act, in which the climactic confrontation between Zeus and Orestes was acted at the feet of a towering Apollo figure of surrealistic shape and proportions, its arms uplifted in a warlike posture and its torso perforated with large circular holes.

With a cast that included such prominent actresses as Inga Tidblad as Viola, Viveca Lindfors as Olivia, and Mai Zetterling as Maria, it is not surprising that Sjöberg's *Twelfth Night* would remain the most popular of his many Shakespearean revivals. For its 1946 production, he called upon another gifted artist, Stellan Mörner, for an exquisitely suggestive, ethereal decor composed largely of impressionistic architectural screens and floating veils. It was a visual concept, Agne Beijer observed, "that gave the illusion that the comedy did not rest on any foundation at all but floated freely in a space that modulated from sky-blue to sulphur-yellow, against which were etched a succession of surrealistic forms, airy arabesques, and fragments of buildings that were completely impervious to static regulations governing normal, sensible building construction."[3] Here and there among these shapes gleamed crystal chandeliers, suspended without any visible support. The mood of ebullient theatricality that prevailed throughout obliterated any darker aspects the comedy may otherwise possess. Director and designer alike drew their inspiration from the figures and traditions of the *commedia dell'arte* – "something between Italian Renaissance and French rococo in style," Beijer thought, "lighter and brighter in tone, freer and more dancing in its choreographic patterns." Feste (Olof Widgren) was thus a wry Harlequin dressed in black and white, ironically thoughtful in his jests – a melodious Fool who sang Shakespeare's lyrics to Söderlundh's much-admired musical accompaniment. A final dance of celebration and the candlelight illumination of both stage and auditorium marked the end of the masquerade and the restoration of order to this untroubled Illyria.

Informing each of these productions was Sjöberg's determined rejection of the "elevators, turntables, buttons, and cues" he associated with the Germanic style of Max Reinhardt. "We want to create productions with no other resources than the simplest, the poorest," he insisted. "With the resources the actors have always possessed in their bodies, their limbs, their speech, their potential for ensemble playing. The only technical device which we cannot dispense with is light, with which we build rhythms and forms, dissolve and transform the thing."[4] However, while working within his ideal general pattern of a bare platform "stripped of every technical finesse," Sjöberg continued to seek new ways of incorporating this pattern in a given production. Not least in his work with Shakespeare, whose plays he often endowed with a strongly political ambience, Sjöberg adopted a wide range of styles, periods, and images with which to project his interpretation.

Richard III, which he staged in collaboration with Erixson in 1947, established both a production aesthetic and an interpretative stance that continued to color many of Sjöberg's major Shakespearean revivals of the 1950s and 1960s. In this instance, his approach was also strongly influenced by the recent war with Hitler. "In the play Richard rises up right after a war, on the rubble there arises this ludicrous being who with cold calculation seduces an entire people," he said in an interview some twenty years after the production. "He was not at all hard to recognize while Europe was still living in the rubble of the world war, while we watched great ideological conmen rise up all the time and try to seize power."[5] Seen in this way, the action of the play became an absurd and sinister clown show, dubbed by Sjöberg "The Fool Crowned." Lars Hanson's pale,

Plate 58 The expressionistically distorted unit setting created by Sven Erixson for Alf Sjöberg's production of Shakespeare's *Richard III* at Dramaten in 1947.

demonic Richard danced his grotesque mummery among the stern, baleful shapes of Erixson's expressionistically distorted setting. This simultaneous decor, which divided the stage space into large, neutral planes and levels, was transformed by changes in lighting and groupings and was decorated by a rich profusion of banners, tents, tapestries, and vividly colored and patterned costumes. The image Sjöberg sought to convey was of a world in ruins, pockmarked by openings into an underworld from which the ghosts of Richard's victims streamed.

In Hanson's performance, the power that Richard exerted over others was virtually mesmeric, born of calculated logic and a diabolical mastery of words. The majestic Tora Teje brought a new and quite unexpected tragic intensity to the bitter speeches and prophecies of Queen Margaret, a relatively minor character who, in Teje's hands, was transformed into the most powerful figure in the drama, apart from Richard himself. His final defeat is described by Sjöberg in a program article as "the death of the fool" – the destruction of the player of roles who is now frightened by the emptiness of his masks. "Without the possibility of finding himself, his own identity, among all the roles he has played, he dies in a climax that reveals both his clown nature and his anguish at never having been loved, not even by himself."[6]

In his production of *Romeo and Juliet* six years later, Sjöberg seems to have achieved his personal vision of a nonrepresentational setting for Shakespeare that would retain, in modernized terms, the spatial–dramaturgical relationships of the Elizabethan stage. In accordance with the director's instructions and sketches, Sven Erixson designed a setting dominated by a soaring, free-standing spiral staircase that formed the centrifugal force unifying the production. The crown of the spiral was Juliet's balcony, while a neutral space beneath the permanent structure served as a street, or a ballroom, or a tomb. As always, however, the real essence of Sjöberg's allusive composition was human interaction, expressed in terms of physical language and dynamic groupings. At the heart of this unconventional mise-en-scène was his attempt to express the union, separation, and reunion of Anita Björk's Juliet and Jarl Kulle's Romeo in terms of vertical moves up and down the dominant central axis formed by the stairs. "There stands Juliet on her balcony, ready to descend to the planet earth for her beloved's salvation," he writes in a memo entitled "The Play Spiral": "The exponent of the entire performance is a unifying spiral construction which, from the very outset, contains all the drama's points of rest and planes of action." Juliet's initial symbolic descent was counterbalanced at the end by the image of Romeo looking down from the balcony at his lover's grave. As he descended the staircase to join her, his "*new eyes,* his transformed gaze" beheld "this realm of death as an *arcade of light.*" In this way, Sjöberg's note concludes, "the drama reveals that the theatre's crude decor is only an illusory sign of an inner, other, spiritual reality. Thus, scenic illusion is conjoined with the image of the world as a theatre."[7]

In the nine major Shakespearean revivals that followed this production, Sjöberg's conception of a *theatrum mundi* underwent a variety of changes. In a finely acted production of *King John* in 1961, for example, he made a rough-hewn, emblematic platform stage designed by Lennart Mörk the ground for a living, dancing tapestry of systematic deception and political power games. Inspired in visual terms by the Bayeux Tapestry, this colorful medieval pageant began with an ironic dance of death in which characters in the drama exchanged masks under the watchful eye of a skeleton. Although these more "politicized" Shakespearean productions were sometimes criticized as overstated, the inherent openness of Sjöberg's method is readily apparent in a description of his "anti-Vietnam" *Troilus and Cressida* (1967) by playwright Per Olov Enquist, one of the important new voices in the ideological debate that arose in the sixties. "It is a performance filled with argument, details, themes, pictures, ideas, and conflicts, a synthesized multiplicity," Enquist observed at the time.

> One of the strengths of the production is its distinct suppleness, its multifaceted clarity. The play speaks of our time, of colonialism and aggression, yet Sjöberg has managed to avoid tying us too simply or tightly to, for example, Vietnam. . . . With a kind of gliding progression of images, he moves – and moves us – through epochs, through centuries of war, doing so with very modest and very simple means, without resorting to overexplicitness or a pat sense of engagement.[8]

Sjöberg's last Shakespearean effort, a production of *Antony and Cleopatra* presented in 1975 in the intimate studio space at Dramaten known as Målarsalen (The Paint Shop), was perhaps his most forceful reassertion of the determination to create a theatre for Shakespeare through the simplest, poorest means. This performance was *about* bareness and emptiness. Acted on a virtually naked oval platform furnished with only the most essential scenic elements, it reflected Sjöberg's vision of the play as "A Twilight Masquerade" – a contradictory pageant of outward splendor and inner disintegration in which all vestiges of pomp are at once undercut and reduced to shadows of themselves. The result became a ritual of unmasking in which the distinction between genuine emotion and role playing was constantly blurred. "At times the actors applaud one another's most passionate tirades, as if it were all a game of words and no difference existed between reality and pretense," Sjöberg wrote in a long program essay. "It is as if the play were being directed by an unseen master of ceremonies, a spoiler of games with an unmistakable desire to expose the masquerade and the emptiness of the grand phrases."[9] Seen from this existentialist, antiheroic point of view, the Antony of Anders Ek became a kind of suffering Strindbergian pilgrim on a painful journey of self-discovery in a spiritual landscape where no values are constant and reality changes shape with the illogic of a nightmare. Beneath her crude, cunning surface, Ulla Sjöblom's Cleopatra shared both Antony's existential soul-sickness and his alienation from the "new, cold, and realistic age" that Caesar, the archetypal puritan, represented. Played in a blaze of white light, the Monument scene was the pivotal moment in Sjöberg's pattern of suffering and redemption, when "the vulgar coquette at last assumes the role of [Dante's] Beatrice and raises up her Antony from the lowliness of the earth's surface to his final salvation." Their mystical union, in which she bestows upon Antony his longed-for release, bore a certain thematic resemblance to the apotheosis with which Sjöberg had ended his *Romeo and Juliet*. "Her fire burns away the last remains of his humiliation, and in her arms he finally recovers his lost identity," he writes in his program essay. Left without Antony, now "the human being in a void empty of all divine help," Cleopatra "yet finds strength to give the theme of freedom its final reiteration."[10]

Not, however, that Sjöberg's versatile and inquisitive imagination ever limited itself to classical or even generally familiar plays. In one of his most interesting experiments, he undertook to revive a pair of hitherto unnoticed works by the obscure nineteenth-century dramatist Carl Jonas Love Almqvist, both of them grotesque, scurrilous fantasies of staggering technical complexity. *Amorina*, which requires some sixty scene changes and nearly four hours of performance time, was staged by Sjöberg with the utmost simplicity and grace on Lilla scenen, Dramaten's smaller stage, in 1951. The metatheatrical setting designed by Yngve Larsson reminded the audience from the outset that they were watching a performance, enacted for them on a rude trestle stage-upon-the-stage. Almqvist himself appeared in flowing cape and slouch hat to act as master of ceremonies and narrator of his strange, kaleidoscopic theatre tale. The rapid progression of scenes was managed by Sjöberg through the use of lighting effects, back projections, and moveable screens. His reliance on mime play and scenes acted in silhouette added to the atmosphere of conscious theatricality he sought to evoke. Both in this production and in *Drottningens juvelsmycke* (*The Queen's Jewel*), which he presented on the same stage in 1957, the clash of divergent styles and emotional states produced a mood of discontinuity and disjuncture that Meyerhold (whose work Sjöberg knew well) terms "the grotesque." In the later production, Lennart Mörk's scenography made effective use of multiple areas on an open stage, the bareness of which was counterbalanced by vividly colored costumes and evocative set pieces. Here, moreover, the Brechtian character of Sjöberg's mise-en-scène came to the fore in his use of titles projected on a back screen. "The Almqvist productions were thus extremely important for those of us who had Brecht in mind," he later observed.[11] And indeed, apart from their interest as evidence of Sjöberg's ability to make the abstract concrete and to endow even the most baffling material with conceptual clarity, these experiments are primarily significant as preludes to the highly regarded series of Brecht productions staged by this director in the mid-sixties.

To Sjöberg, Brecht was quite simply "one of the most positive and vital figures to be encountered in the modern Western world. Because he believed that he could bring about a kind of change in the spectator."[12] The cycle of Brecht productions that Sjöberg staged at Dramaten redefined and reassessed this writer's position in the contemporary repertoire in Scandinavia. During the decade or so between 1963 and 1974, he directed no fewer than six Brecht plays: *Schweyk in the Second World War* (1963), *Mother Courage* (1965), *Herr Puntila and his Man Matti* (1966), the Lenz adaptation *The Tutor* (*Der Hofmeister* in 1967), *The Threepenny Opera* (1969), and finally *Galileo* (14 December 1974), perhaps the most important of his Brecht reinterpretations. All of these productions were conceived in conscious opposition to what he regarded as "the museum-like grayness which so often descends over a too slavishly orthodox Brecht performance."[13] Above all, his approach was shaped by his refusal to see this (or any) playwright as an "unchangeable, timeless, free-floating monument," for whom a performance tradition has already been inscribed in stone.

Brecht's personal association with the Scandinavian theatre had, in fact, been considerable. The first six years of his enforced exile (1933–9) had been spent in Denmark, where several productions of his plays – most notably Per Knutzon's staging of the world premiere of *Round Heads and Peaked Heads* in 1936 – had helped to strengthen his cause. Still more significant was the influence exerted on his writing by his exposure to the actors and acting traditions of Scandinavia. Of *Mother Courage*, for example, he declared in 1953: "I wrote this play for Scandinavia. In contrast to most other countries, theatre played a role in Scandinavia."[14] In particular, we know that Brecht's fascination with the protean abilities of Poul Reumert, the leading actor of his day in Denmark, influenced *Galileo* directly. Ruth Berlau states unequivocally that the part was written specifically for Reumert,[15] and there is evidence that an early version of *Leben des Galilei* may actually have been offered to him as early as 1937. Some sixteen years later Brecht asked again, but too much in the character, in the dramatist, and in his epic theories ran counter to Reumert's own convictions.

In Sjöberg's view, on the other hand, Brecht was not merely a professed and aggressive rationalist; he was also a theatrical magician whose plays contain a strong sensual appeal that is often overlooked (as it was by Reumert). In his own revivals, this director sought persistently to make this sensual element emphatic. If we are to reassert the relevance of Brecht's theatre, he argued, it is essential to activate and liberate the robust vigor and drive found in his plays – the element Sjöberg calls "the heathen appetite for life." The more we are able to share in this, he insisted, "the more strongly the political aspect will emerge."[16] Accordingly, he found the clue to a work like *Galileo* not in any impression of *Verfremdung* or apparent detachment in the playing style, but rather in the vigorous sense of contrast and discontinuity that characterizes the play's forward movement, governed as it is by Brecht's juxtaposition of disparate elements for the purpose of reflective irony. Sjöberg's version of *Galileo* consisted of fourteen scenes (scene 15 was cut, as it has usually been elsewhere), each of which was made to stand out as a separate entity. The scenic flow was fractured by the discreetly sardonic musical stanzas that introduced each unit. The machinery of the theatre stood exposed in Acke Oldenburg's setting, thereby letting the audience stand back and observe the process of shifting from one scene to the next. Brecht "dispenses with the idea of a continuous narrative and creates instead a series of transformations," Sjöberg later remarked. "He takes up a given subject and then sees to it that the next tableau breaks definitively with it, being intent on letting the audience notice the interruption."[17] The spectator was continually reminded in Sjöberg's production that he or she was in a theatre, not in medieval Tuscany or the Vatican. A few basic elements in the setting remained unchanged – notably the enclosing side screens and a segment of a gothic arch that hung suspended, at various heights, over the acting area. By utilizing these permanent pieces, Sjöberg counteracted any sense of diffuseness that might arise from the play's epic process, while at the same time suggesting – as Brecht requires – a certain historical flavor. On the generally bright stage, the figures of the actors in their vivid, textured costumes stood out against the calculated two-dimensionality of the painted background.

The ruling characteristic of Toivo Pawlo's performance as Galileo Galilei was its emphasis on the character's virtually animalistic power and vitality, his "unquenchable appetite for knowledge and food. His spontaneity. His childlike enthusiasm for his discoveries." This Galileo knew full well that his experiments undermined the established social

Plates 59 and 60 The juxtaposition of public and private scenes in Sjöberg's, production of *Galileo* (Dramaten, 1974) was visually accentuated in Acke Oldenburg's scenography. Here Galileo (Toivo Pawlo) presents his new invention to the Venetian republic, overlooked by a huge winged figure bearing a laurel wreath.

system, but this delighted him chiefly because it vindicated his own thesis. "He seems to possess no real social engagement; he is the perfect egocentric man of the Renaissance," Bengt Jahnsson wrote in *Dagens Nyheter* (15 December 1974). This dynamic and authoritative but also rather questionable genius delineated by Pawlo and his director was a man filled with humanity, with an inexhaustible, often ingratiating but far from admirable capacity for self-preservation. Sjöberg's critical attitude toward the character proceeded from his view of him as "a hedonist whose hedonism finds expression both in his enjoyment of life and in his enjoyment of his art." This is why he conceives of torture and physical pain as threats he cannot endure, the director noted. And for this reason as well, "his science threatens to become a purely physical passion. He becomes intoxicated with his art, just as the bad actor does with his absorption in his role. Both are caused by their virtuosity to lose sight of the whole."[18]

Hence, acute irony remained a ruling factor throughout Sjöberg's mise-en-scène. For example, the early scene in which Galileo presents his telescope to the Venetian republic was shaped by the director's emphasis

Later in the scientist's workroom, Galileo and his helper Sagredo (Erland Josephson) suddenly see their vision of a star-filled universe unfold before them.

on the fact that the so-called discovery is a hoax, copied from a Dutch original and used by Galileo only as a means of making money. The stage was opened to its full width to accommodate a grand and spacious decor that was, in itself, an ironic comment on the proceedings. Hovering overhead, a huge, winged figure hanging from the flies held a wreath with which to crown the scientist in his moment of triumph. Atop a stylized version of the traditional rough-hewn platform used by Renaissance mountebanks peddling their wares stood Galileo with his "highly saleable cylinder." Below him sat the figures of authority he so manifestly dominated, bunched together on a moveable fragment of an inquisitorial dais. Behind them, in a far corner of the composition, one saw Virginia, Galileo's young daughter, and Ludovico, both of whom know that the professed invention is a copy. Their silent, critical presence served to direct and control the audience's perception of the entire episode, rendering its ironic point graphically clear.

The multiplicity of perspective in this and other large public scenes was counterpointed in the more subdued and intimate episodes – the subsequent scene in Galileo's modest workroom in Padua, for example – with a virtually lyrical use of plastic light and space. In the scene in question, pools of cold lighting and heavy cloaks worn both by Galileo and Sagredo, his collaborator, signified the sense of chill and isolation that was associated at this point with the scientist, who "describes his fantastic revolutionary discoveries like someone who talks about the coldest mathematical facts."[19] Then, as the two men continued their work at the telescope, Galileo's great inner vision received stunning visual corroboration as a vast, star-flecked cosmos suddenly filled the cyclorama.

Ultimately, Sjöberg's layered interpretation of Brecht's most complex protagonist revealed neither a simple social criminal nor a hero of science suffering bravely for his convictions. All such easy, sweeping assumptions were systematically eliminated from this production concept, which seemed to reach the same dualistic, even ambivalent conclusion that the text itself invites. On the one hand, Galileo adopts the attitude of being the spokesman for scientific freedom, yet he also exemplifies the risks such freedom may entail. Sjöberg himself conceived of this production – the 129th of his career – as an "inducement," a starting point for a debate about the role of the scientist and the social responsibilities of science in the nuclear age. For Sjöberg, much as for Brecht, all art could be seen as "man's protest, his revolt against the conditions of life." Theatre, he often said, "is not a reflection of reality; theatre is a protest against reality."

An actor's theatre

During the mid-1950s audiences and critics in Scandinavia were also turning their attention increasingly to Malmö, the port city in southern Sweden where the stage productions of Ingmar Bergman had begun to attract widespread international recognition, not least because of the great popular success of such Bergman films as *Smiles of a Summer Night*, *The Seventh Seal*, and *Wild Strawberries*. Even by then, Bergman had begun to gather around him such "favorite" actors as Anders Ek and Gertrud Fridh. His six-year stay at the Malmö City Theatre as director and artistic adviser soon enabled him to build and train a veritable ensemble of performers – Bibi Andersson, Harriet Andersson, Ingrid Thulin, Gunnel Lindblom, Naima Wifstrand, Max von Sydow, and others – who were to appear with regularity both in his theatre work and in his major motion pictures. During the years of excitement and experiment between 1952 and 1958, he also began, for the first time, to devote himself in earnest to the imposing succession of classical revivals – of Ibsen, Molière, Goethe, Hjalmar Bergman, and especially Strindberg – that has become the keystone of his contribution to the modern theatre.

In a sense, Bergman can be taken as an interesting example of the significant influence of a strong regional theatre movement in Scandinavia. His professional theatre career began at the age of twenty-six, when he took over as the fourth artistic director of the Hälsingborg City Theatre in the autumn of 1944 – during the same period that his first original screen-play, *Hets* (*Torment*), was released under Alf Sjöberg's direction. During two vigorous seasons at this relatively small theatre, Bergman himself directed no fewer than nine productions, ranging from modern Swedish works to a pictorially expressive and politically engaged *Macbeth*. Although the technical facilities at Hälsingborg were minimal, Bergman's move to the larger and more prestigious Gothenburg City Theatre in 1946 taught him to master one of the most advanced physical stage facilities in Europe. In retrospect, one of the most exciting of his achievements during his three-season engagement here was Albert Camus' existential drama *Caligula*, the production that marked his debut as director on the demanding Gothenburg stage (29 November 1946). In this instance, an almost perfect coordination was achieved between Carl-Johan Ström's imaginative, carefully controlled stage design for an imperial Roman palace and the grotesque, surreal, at times even acrobatic concept of Camus' somewhat cerebral play that the young director presented to his startled audience. In the role of Caligula, the chiseled countenance of Anders Ek was, one critic remarked, not that of "the beautiful and familiar marble bust, but of an inwardly consumed individual with sleepless eyes and tense facial features." No one who has seen Ek's face as Frost, the tormented circus clown in Bergman's *The Naked Night* (*Sawdust and Tinsel*), could possibly forget its supple expressiveness. As for Bergman, who has always been ready to exploit the potentialities of the physical theatre to the fullest, his belief in the greater and more basic significance of the actor and the human face would continue to shape his vision of theatre, film, and their interaction.

Although Bergman had learned to handle the considerable complexity of the theatre machine at Gothenburg, the Malmö engagement faced him with a challenge of quite another magnitude. The vast open stage at Malmö had been completed in 1944 in response to Per Lindberg's call for a flexible, classless "folk theatre," but the result had been a curious hybrid. "The project manifested an insoluble collision between Per Lindberg's monumental people's theatre, with an arena stage and democratic seating, and Knut Ström's dream of visual theatre, created for scenographic visions in the spirit of Meyerhold and Reinhardt," Bergman says.[20] It took all his skill and determination to prove that the gargantuan complex that had resulted from this clash of ideas could, in fact, be used for normal dramatic performances. In turn, the special demands of this space exerted a profound influence on the maturation of the aims and methods of his scenic art. Perhaps paradoxically, the most important lesson the experience taught him was the preeminent value of simplicity and suggestion.

The art of the theatre, seen from Bergman's perspective, is at once a popular and a collective art, arising out of an intensely collaborative creative process. Even in the face of the severest technical challenges, he has remained steadfastly committed to a style cleansed of everything that could disrupt the influence of the living actor, who (as he put it) has "that wonderful ability to suggest directly."[21] Hence, by placing the actors in an ever more direct, more emphatic, and accordingly more hypnotic position in relation to the audience, he enables them to stimulate and ultimately control the spectator's emotional involvement. Step by step, as the actor in his theatre gradually became its undivided focus of attention, Bergman's elimination of obtrusive stage settings and effects grew steadily more pronounced.

Strindberg's darkly lyrical folk drama *Kronbruden* (*The Crown Bride*), with which Bergman established his technical mastery of the difficult main stage at Malmö in 1952, proved a crucial turning point in this development. In this production, he systematically removed the elements of folklore, fairy tale, and picturesque local color that had hitherto seemed indispensable to directors and critics of this ambiguous post-Inferno work. "Everyone went around in rehearsal clothes and we had only rehearsal lights," he later recalled. "It struck me that absolutely no more was needed, no lighting was needed, nothing was needed – nothing more than the performer ['*artiste*']. It is that simple"[22] However, the thrust of such extreme dematerialization and simplification is not toward abstraction or a "poor" theatre for its own sake. Rather, the intended goal is emotional concentration and emotional intensification, both on the part of the actor and on the part of the spectator. In the specific case of *The Crown Bride*, Bergman deliberately shifted the focus of interest from the external to the internal, from a potentially spectacular visual display to the inner drama of the play's protagonist, Kersti, and her Damascus pilgrimage toward penance, death, and an extremely equivocal salvation.

There is neither a predictability nor a sameness of style in Bergman's theatre work. During the Malmö years, he used both the 1,700-seat main theatre and an intimate studio stage to accommodate a broadly based repertory that ranged from older and more modern classics to full-scale popular renditions of Lehár's *The Merry Widow* (1954) and F. A. Dahlgren's much-loved national folk play *Värmlänningarna* (*The People of Värmland*), with which he concluded his Malmö stay in December 1958. During this period, moreover, film work and theatre work proceeded side by side. During 1957, the year of *So Close to Life* and the internationally acclaimed *Wild Strawberries*, Bergman found time to present two demanding productions on the big stage, Ibsen's *Peer Gynt* and Molière's *The Misanthrope*. Max von Sydow, fresh from his triumph in *The Seventh Seal*, acted both Peer and Alceste. Molière, a dramatist whose inherent theatricality has appealed strongly to Bergman over the years, was a particular source of inspiration in Malmö. In his first *Dom Juan*, staged in 1955 on a simple platform of rough boards against a naively painted backdrop, the audience became from the outset the initiated partner in the comic intrigue. In the opening sequence, a yawning, scratching, bare-legged, and decidedly unromantic Don Juan in a ludicrously short night-shirt was seen being dressed up in his seducer's outfit of silk and ruffles by his utterly illusionless servant, Sganarelle. "What was it that made us see right through Don Juan's noble exterior into his soul in all its corrupt tawdriness? Answer: those naked thighs," wrote Ebbe Linde in *Dagens Nyheter* (8 January 1955). The ritual of unmasking, which lay at the very core of Bergman's interpretation of this play, was communicated at once by this seriocomic pantomime with costume and wig, which made the spectator an informed partner, so to speak, in the comic intrigue. In the case of *The Misanthrope*, which he presented three seasons later, he used a very different theatrical strategy to forge a strong, almost confidential rapport between the audience and Gertrud Fridh's playful, quite innocently cynical Célimène and her rebellious Alceste. To stress the immediacy of the contact between stage and auditorium, Bergman and his designer, Kerstin Hedeby, actually brought the background forward almost to the proscenium line. Glimpsed in the dim, atmospheric lighting, Hedeby's glittering pastiche of a baroque theatre set seemed to extend beyond the checkerboard forestage to include the audience in the same continuous space.

Nowhere is the adaptability of Bergman's creative method more evident, however, than in his many and varied productions of Strindberg's plays. Among these *The Ghost Sonata*, which he directed in Malmö in 1954, has been a particular preoccupation of his. The intelligent amateur production of it that he staged in Stockholm in 1941 was evidently the first real revival of the play in Sweden since Reinhardt's touring production had startled Stockholm audiences twenty-four years before. Then, Bergman writes in the Malmö program, "came the great, totally shattering experience" – the first of Olof Molander's five major productions of the play, seen at Dramaten in October of 1942. For Molander, it had seemed vital to recognize in this and other Strindberg works the razor-sharp fragments of observed (specifically autobiographical) reality embedded in this writer's dramatic vision. As a result, the "facade of a new house on a city square" that is described in such close detail at the beginning of *The Ghost Sonata* was shown in his production as a virtually exact copy of Karlaplan 10, the stately mahogany-and-marble building in the Östermalm district of Stockholm where Strindberg resided (with an entrance at the less patrician address of Karlavägan 40, "around the corner") after his marriage to Harriet Bosse. Accordingly, when Bergman took up the play in Malmö, his own apparently realistic Östermalm street scene – complete with advertisement kiosk and drinking fountain, a projection of Oscar's Church, and the distant sound of church chimes and steamship bells from the Nybrovik docks – still seemed, at least at first glance, to bear the Molander trademark.

Looking more closely, however, critics and audiences found a wholly original vision of this perplexing classic. In essence, Bergman's approach charted a middle way between outright expressionism (the Reinhardt tradition) and the blend of naturalism and mysticism patented by Molander. The core of his concept was his structural image of the play as a dreamlike progression toward purification and a tenuous secular salvation – a progression measured here in three distinct scenic tempi, from the oneiric, film-gray "reality" of the first act to a much more stylized milieu of heavy drapes in the macabre universe of the ghost supper and, finally, to a completely simplified, overtly symbolic hyacinth room. Projections, lighting effects, and even a scrim suspended, like a barely visible veil, between the stage and the auditorium conspired to maintain an unbroken sense of the play as a dream. The dreamer in this production was Arkenholz (Folke Sundquist), the innocent student of life's pain who here seemed, in the words of *Morgon-Tidningen* (6 March 1954) "the last human being in a

Plate 61 Photograph of Marik Vos' setting (first scene) for the Bergman production of *The Ghost Sonata* (Dramaten, 1973). The high, concave screens were used for back projections.

dying world." Rather than resorting to the abstract metaphysical vision of Böcklin's *Island of the Dead* at the end, Bergman preferred a simple, purely human gesture of compassion on the Student's part as a final image. In this closing tableau, Arkenholz drew back the death screen once more and cradled the lifeless form of the Young Lady in his lap. Many critics found, however, that the lyrical and redemptive tone of the last scene seemed pale and unconvincing when juxtaposed with the harrowing emotional intensity of Benkt-Åke Bengtsson's performance as Hummel, the scheming "soul stealer."

The radically changed approach adopted by Bergman when he staged *The Ghost Sonata* at Dramaten nearly two decades later illustrates a tendency on his part to maintain an ongoing dialogue with certain plays and their problems. One basic objective of his 1973 revival was to perform the play on a virtually naked stage, stripped of every object and every item of scenery that might, in Bergman's words, "block the action and make it heavy." Apart from a bare minimum of significant objects – notably the marble statue of a young and attractive woman – most of the "scenery" designed by Marik Vos was suggested by means of lighting and projections on two high, concave screens and on the cyclorama visible behind them in the background. The result was an emphasis on human faces and figure compositions that exerted a pressure from the stage toward the auditorium and eliminated all sense of distance. A direct and unmitigated contact between the audience and the living actors was thereby achieved. Through the intricate rhythmic pattern of their movements, gestures, intonations, and tempo changes – supported by corresponding changes in the lighting and projections – they succeeded in materializing, in the intuitive imagination of the audience rather than in its conscious intellect, the *experience* of the dream. At the core of this suggestive process lies Bergman's reiterated conviction that any drama must always be played in two locations at once; on the stage among the actors and in the consciousness of every audience member.

At the center of the lattice of dynamic human interrelationships into which the director translated this particular Strindberg text was the twinning hinted at by the presence of the marble statue. This figure was an oblique image of the Mummy as she had once been in the past, just as she herself is now the grotesque image of what the Young Lady, her daughter and her alter ego, will eventually become. Both characters, if such they may be called, were played by the same actress, Gertrud Fridh. When the Student had walked away after his angry denunciation and virtual destruction of the Young Lady, Fridh reappeared in the guise of the Mummy to speak the final lines of consolation over "this child of the world of disappointments, guilt, suffering, and death" – an extraordinary benediction, in fact, over the corpse of her former self.

The redefinition of theatrical space and the camera-like sharpness of focus in Bergman's *Ghost Sonata* and in his subsequent production of *To Damascus* in 1974 were foreshadowed in the swiftly paced version of *A Dream Play* that he staged at Lilla scenen in 1970. Stripped down to fifteen compact scenes, with a total playing time of only an hour and forty-five minutes, this adaptation assumed the shape and style of a chamber play. In it, Bergman's emphasis on the creative partnership between actor and audience also acquired a new form of expression in his use of what might be called the strategy of the actor–spectator. His cast (twenty-four actors for the play's forty-three characters) emerged and simply took their places all around the periphery of the gray-black, curtainless stage, where they became, at one and the same time, characters waiting to be called into being by their creator – the meditative Poet seated at his desk – and actors awaiting their entrances. Lennart Mörk's minimalist design made no attempt to represent, in literal terms, the changing localities and stage effects described in the text. Instead, the only thing the audience saw and heard was the actors, who created the illusion that all these places were there before them. "No castle burns on the stage, no rhetoric flames in the dialogue," Bo Strömstedt wrote in *Expressen* the next day (15 March 1970). "Nor is it a biographical Strindberg Show in Molander fashion. Some wear masks in this production – but no one wears a Strindberg mask." The framework of religious mysticism was also largely excised, and the presence of a divine Indra and his Daughter was reduced to a somewhat absurd irrelevancy. The Daughter's final speech of leave-taking was assigned instead to the Poet (Georg Årlin) who, surrounded by the other characters, spoke it quietly and thoughtfully at the very edge of the stage. "Because all ornamentation has been eliminated, the words, the actor's voice, and the faces – so far forward on the stage that they appear as close-ups – succeed in engraving the Poet's visions on each spectator's imagination," observed the Norwegian critic for *Dagbladet* (Oslo). After the actors had left and the spotlight on the Poet's table was extinguished, the final image was neither Strindberg's flowering castle nor a Molander cross, but simply a glimpse of Malin Ek's young, vulnerable Agnes, the human side of Indra's Daughter, seated alone on the empty stage, her hand pressed convulsively to her face in speechless anxiety.

Although not the first modern director to question the necessity for the period settings and naturalistic trappings of Ibsen's prose plays, the revolutionary productions of Ibsen staged by Bergman at Dramaten during this period of his career literally changed the way the contemporary theatre regarded this playwright. "With Ibsen, you always have the feeling of limits – because Ibsen places them there himself. He was an architect, and he built," Bergman later said in an interview. "He always built his plays, and he knew exactly: I want this and I want that. He points the audience in the direction he wants it to go, closing doors, leaving no other alternatives."[23] Bergman's first production of *Hedda Gabler* in 1964 was a conscious attempt on his part to overcome these perceived limitations. His allusive distillation translated the play into a new theatrical dimension, as it were, by freeing it of its naturalistic mosaic of details – the thick carpets, the "indispensable" porcelain stove, and even the portentous portrait of Hedda's father, General Gabler. Using only seven simple rehearsal screens and a bare minimum of objects to denote the Tesman "parlor," the director and his designer (Mago) transformed the stage space into an immense, dark

Plate 62 Photograph of the Mago setting for Bergman's production of *Hedda Gabler* (Dramaten, 1964). The small, moveable screen that bisected the stage can be seen to the left of the prompter's box. The partially lowered house curtain conveyed its own sense of oppressiveness.

Plate 63 The Ekdal attic as it was conceived in the Bergman production of *The Wild Duck* (Dramaten, 1972). *Left to right*: Hjalmar Ekdal (Ernst-Hugo Järegård), Hedvig (Lena Nyman), Gregers Werle (Max von Sydow), Old Edkal (Holger Löwenadler), and Gina (Margareta Krook).

red, velvetlike enclosure that evoked the dominant mood of desolation and entrapment ("the odor of death" that Hedda tries to describe to Judge Brack), rather than illustrating it in a photographic manner. The aim of Bergman's various technical strategies was a close-up exposure of the inner reality of Hedda's situation. In the title role, Gertrud Fridh appeared as a restless, solitary presence, always visible on her own side of a moveable middle divider that bisected the stage into two equal and adjacent spheres of simultaneous action. To the audience's left, remorselessly exposed to view, was the unseen "inner room" of Ibsen's stage directions, the physical and psychic retreat where Hedda's piano and her father's pistols are kept. Even when not directly involved in the action, she seemed trapped before the audience, compelled to watch her own innermost spiritual agony dragged into the spotlight of public scrutiny. "One might have thought that Hedda was spying," Siegfried Melchinger wrote in an influential review in *Theater heute*, "but the impression produced was rather that the stage spied on her, that she was being dissected by it against her will."[24] In a production which, in Melchinger's words, "transformed the mathematical reality of the play into the workings of a dream," the outside world seemed distant and irrelevant. Illuminated in a uniformly cold light that tampered with contours and erased any secure sense of spatial dimensionality, all the characters in the drama appeared like figures suspended in an airless, time-stopped void.

In Bergman's production of *The Wild Duck* on the same stage in 1972, theatrical illusion was again defined by the presence of the actors, rather than by the traditional period settings, costumes, and accessories that had, for example, still figured prominently in Sjöberg's highly regarded revival of this play seventeen years earlier. As in his deconstructed *Hedda*, Bergman's use of exposed, close-up glimpses of peripheral or implied offstage action added a new and unexpected dimension to the audience's mode of perceiving the realistic action of Ibsen's drama. However, while Hedda's "inner room" had still been a place furnished with recognizable physical objects (her chair, a piano and stool, a mirror), the fateful and fleetingly perceived "interior loft" of the Ekdals, the abode of the wild duck and the location of Hedvig's offstage suicide, had no objective existence of its own. Its reality was suggested solely through the medium of the actor's art. Relocated at the very front of the stage, the fantasy world that Hjalmar and Old Ekdal have built up around themselves was created, before the eyes of the audience, by the facial expressions of the actors and the shadows of roof beams that appeared above and around the characters whenever they entered this kingdom of the imagination. "In other words, we on the stage are not the only ones who create the imaginary place – the imaginary attic. The audience, too, is asked to participate in the process," Max von Sydow, who played Gregers Werle, later observed in an interview. "So the spectator gets the attic he deserves, so to speak. If he refuses to visualize it, then there is no attic. But if he does his part, it will be a wonderful attic to behold."[25]

"You leave an opening to be filled by the audience's need to engage itself in the drama," Bergman told his cast during rehearsals for *Woyzeck* in 1969. "It is for this reason that the scene [of Marie's murder] has to be so simple and straightforward. It won't do to clog it with feelings. You must know what you are doing."[26] This finely acted production of Büchner's fragmentary tragedy, which featured Thommy Berggren in the title role and Gunnel Lindblom as Marie, represents a crucial turning point in Bergman's development, in two distinct respects. One is artistic. In its anti-illusionistic staging techniques, its use of a simple, open platform, its renewed emphasis on intense audience contract, and its resultant stress on the magnetic and revelatory power of the actor, it foreshadows the more strongly theatricalist approach adopted by Bergman in the 1970s and after. However, the *Woyzeck* production was also a response to the powerful societal changes that were occurring in the area of cultural politics. By this time, the turbulent wave of student uprisings, Vietnam protests, and resultant political activism that swept across Europe in the late sixties had begun to politicize and polarize theatrical activity, not only in Sweden but throughout Scandinavia. The prevailing antiestablishment sentiments of the new age clearly extended to an institution like Dramaten, which tried to respond with experiments such as the *Woyzeck* production. In this instance, lower ticket prices, two shows a night, a performance as brief as a movie, the abolition of an obligatory cloakroom, and "democratic" seating on two sides of a modified arena erected on the main stage were all innovations intended to entice a new, disaffected generation of theatregoers.

A published diary of the *Woyzeck* rehearsals makes it very clear that Bergman saw the experiment as his opportunity to repudiate "the theatre of circumstances" ("all this with a curtain, blackouts, illusion") as "a profound depravity." One of the most interesting practical initiatives to come of his concern with the audience's involvement in the creative process was his introduction of open public rehearsals for *Woyzeck*. "It is essential to undramatize the whole system of theatrical distribution, the hysteria surrounding dress rehearsal and opening," he explained when he first announced the idea. "I now believe that all this atmosphere of secrecy that surrounds us, and that I myself have enthusiastically endorsed, is finished."[27] In order to build a bridge between actor and spectator, the audience must be made to see "that there is no magic in our work, and that there is nevertheless magic in it," he says, echoing the sentiments also being expressed at this time by Peter Brook in *The Empty Space*. In order to recapture the attention of the audience and "compel its belief," Brook wrote in 1968, "we must prove that there will be no trickery, nothing hidden. We must open our empty hands and show that there really is nothing up our sleeves. Only then can we begin."[28]

If Bergman's *Woyzeck* can be viewed as an acknowledgment of the Lindbergian vision of an egalitarian folk theatre, then his three-year administration of Dramaten (1963–6) was a more mundane but no less useful exercise in theatrical democracy. He not only broadened the range of the repertory (as seen, for example, in Sjöberg's productions of Brecht and Gombrowicz), but also made it more generally accessible by lowering ticket prices. Turning a blind eye to budget restrictions (in the gentler days when such was still possible), he increased both the size of the theatre's acting company and the salaries of its members. These efforts to rejuvenate Sweden's national stage came, however, during an unsettled period when the opposition to "institutional" and "canonical" theatre was gaining momentum. The rhetoric of dissent may be sampled in a comment published at the time by the respected critic and editor Olof Lagercrantz. The writer is comparing Bergman's *Hedda* to a happening he attended, called "Picture–Poem–Sound":

> On Tuesday I saw *Hedda Gabler* at Dramaten. On Wednesday I witnessed lyric–dramatic games put on at the Modern Museum, created and performed by young poets. At Dramaten, a degenerate offshoot of an aged theatre tree. A piece written for eternity, but putrid with death. In contrast to this, the living images at the Modern Museum. Here nothing was meant to last, nothing was intended for eternity. For that reason it was alive.[29]

By the time Bergman left Sweden in 1976 to live and work in Munich, the revolutionary aims of the new radicalism had become part of the status quo. The political and cultural upheavals of the sixties and the proliferation of new forms of alternative theatre that derived from them had created a healthy pluralism in all three Scandinavian countries. The result was a theatrical climate that recognized no one ultimate principle or form to the exclusion of all others.

New stages for old

In the late 1940s, while Bergman was making his mark in Gothenburg and the productions of Sjöberg and Molander dominated the stage at Dramaten, Scandinavia's two other national theatres had occasion to celebrate jubilees commemorating proud pasts. Understandably, the fiftieth anniversary of the founding of Norway's Nationaltheatret in 1899 was somewhat eclipsed by the bicentennial celebrations of Scandinavia's oldest state theatre, the Danish Royal Theatre, in 1948. This propitious event was marked by an extraordinary display of theatrical riches that stretched the resources of the playhouse on Kongens Nytorv to the limit. The adjacent New Stage, which by 1957 became its regular second stage, was also pressed into service to accommodate the march-past of new and older productions. During the sixteen days between Holberg's birthday (3 December) and the actual anniversary (18 December), the festival program offered four ballets and no fewer than twenty plays, including three Holberg comedies, revivals of Gustav Wied, Ewald, Wessel, Oehlenschläger, Heiberg, Hertz, Hostrup, and Nathansen, five modern plays, Molander's Danish remake of his *Ghost Sonata*, and new productions of *Tartuffe*, *Othello*, and *The Wild Duck* staged by the able and versatile director John Price. The official eulogist on the birthday night was Kjeld Abell, whose *Ejendommen Matr. Nr. 267, Østre Kvarter* (*Lot 267, East District*) was a genial tribute in the form of a potpourri of familiar scenes and popular moments from the Royal Theatre repertory, designed by Helge Refn and acted by a once-in-a-lifetime cast headed by Poul Reumert and Bodil Ipsen (as the Master and the Lady of the House). Appropriately, Abell's charming poetic bagatelle was a fresh reminder of his vision of the theatre as "the free imagination's fantastic sanctuary" – a realm of infinite possibilities, created to incite the spectator to seek his or her own solutions. In a scene between the Dark Hostess (Melpomene) and the Light Hostess (Thalia), the latter tells a window washer who has found his way into this magical world: "They divided us up into two answers, a 'yes' and a 'no', two answers to life. But we are not answers! Only questions. We ask – you answer."

Private theatres were extremely popular in Copenhagen since the nineteenth century, and in the interim this commercial alternative to state-supported repertory theatre had prospered. Thus, by the 1950s both Folketeatret and the New Theatre were ready to celebrate their own anniversaries, as challengers to the representativeness of the "national" stage. Folketeatret, one of the oldest functioning private theatres in Scandinavia, observed its centennial in 1957 by restating, as it were, its claim to a prominent place in the theatrical establishment. An imposing round of congratulatory performances was presented by the national theatres of Finland, Sweden, Norway, and Iceland. During the long and palmy reign of Thorvald Larsen, the popular "folk theatre" tradition was broadened to embrace both the classical repertoire and productions of new works by writers such as Munk and Soya. Larsen's determination to break the Royal Theatre's (now virtually defunct) monopoly on the Danish classics was expressed in his choice of a vehicle for the actual anniversary production (18 September 1957): *The Political Tinker*, with which Holberg had launched Denmark's first vernacular theatre in 1722, was inventively cast on this occasion with the veteran revue entertainer Osvald Helmuth in the title role.

Although otherwise quite unrelated, the New Theatres of Oslo and Copenhagen shared a certain bond at this time as important rivals to their respective national theatres. Oslo's New Theatre, which regained financial stability in the postwar era thanks in large part to Lillebil Ibsen's prowess as a comedienne, became a subsidized municipal theatre in 1959. The New Theatre in Copenhagen, on the other hand, followed a different course. With a team of directors that included Sam Besekow and Edwin Tiemroth, and a superb ensemble led for some years by Mogens Wieth and Bodil Kjer, it was possible for Peer Gregaard to pursue an ambitious and demanding program of modern and classical works that earned his company its high reputation as "the national theatre's guilty conscience." Its style was exemplified by the finely balanced Besekow production of Anouilh's *La Valse de toréadors* in 1957, which embodied the period's ideal of poetic realism. As Ghislaine, impatient after waiting chastely for seventeen years to have her General, Bodil Kjer was an unpredictable caricature of a sentimental heroine – one who, once having thrown herself from a window in despair, would instantly be carried back in again. Mogens Wieth, the outstanding lyrical talent of his generation, brought to the mammoth role of General Saint-Pé a blend of bitter humor and deeply human, even tragic

Plate 64 Oliver Messel's stylized, mock-rococo setting for the Screen Scene (act 4) in *The School for Scandal*, designed for the Sam Besekow production of Sheridan's comedy at the New Theatre, Copenhagen, in 1958.

regret. When the time came to celebrate its fiftieth jubilee in 1958, the New Theatre moved in a different direction with its urbane and witty revival of Sheridan's *The School for Scandal*, directed by Besekow in a setting created by the British designer Oliver Messel. Messel's scenography was mock rococo, a bright and witty pastiche of the play's period and tone, complete with palpably real flowers in flat cardboard vases. A riot of color in his sets and costumes provided the perfect background for the escapades of Bodil Kjer's impetuous and wilful Lady Teazle.

By the time Peer Gregaard took over the management of the Royal Theatre, in 1966, sweeping changes in taste and attitude were already being felt by commercial operations such as the New Theatre. The inevitable crisis erupted in 1971, when a new and innovative revival of Holberg's *Jeppe on the Hill* sent the New Theatre into bankruptcy. Closure of the production was imminent, until the local authorities were persuaded to step in with a grant-in-aid – on the condition that a corresponding number of tickets were made available for free public distribution. Thus a politically acceptable formula for funding and ticket distribution was born. By 1975 the ex-commercial theatres of Copenhagen had been grouped together in a new bureaucratic entity called the Greater Metropolitan Regional Stage, a wholly subsidized "regional theatre" on an equal footing with the three provincial regional stages in Aarhus, Aalborg, and Odense. The political argument for funding such an arrangement was "audience development." To take the Danish model as a broad example, the practical underpinning of the system became a nationwide, computerized subscriber campaign designed to attract "new thousands" of citizens to the theatre by joining a state-run ticket bank known as Arte. Although the name seems to suggest "art," it is in fact an anagram derived from "*ar*bejder*te*ater," or "worker's theatre."

This thrust to replace the profit-and-loss considerations of private theatre with a fully funded, universally accessible theatre culture in Scandinavia has been especially evident in the growth and development of its extraordinary network of subsidized regional and municipal theatres. Some of these flourishing regional stages – notably Denmark's three municipal playhouses and Norway's National Stage in Bergen, Trøndelag Teater in Trondheim, and Rogaland Teater in Stavanger – have strong traditions that reach back to the previous century. Sweden's somewhat younger chain of fully supported city theatres is headed by the influential Gothenburg City Theatre and includes the playhouses in Hälsingborg, Malmö, Borås, Linkjöping, Norrköping, and Uppsala. The Stockholm City Theatre became part of this state-supported alliance in 1960, and seven years later a theatre in the northern outpost of Luleå was added to the organization. Northern Norway was likewise given a theatre of its own in 1971, when the collectivist Hålogaland Teater was established in Tromsø, one of the northernmost cities in the country. Since then, newer theatre centers have sprung up in Molde, Førde, Skien, and Mo i Rana. A further consequence of this conception of theatre as a cultural good to which the entire population has a right has been the creation of a National Touring Theatre (Riksteatern), active in Sweden since the 1930s and instituted in Norway, one of the largest but most thinly populated countries in Europe, in 1949. Journeying to hundreds of small communities throughout the year and often facing formidable obstacles, these institutions tour with a remarkable variety of professional productions. Det danske Teater

Plate 65a and b The Millhouse and "Castle rises on castle": two of Arne Walentin's most imaginative designs for the revolutionary *Peer Gynt* presented by Hans Jacob Nilsen at Det Norske Teatret in Oslo in 1948.

(The Danish Theatre), established in 1963, has less rugged geographical and climatic conditions to contend with, but its mission is basically the same as that of the two other national touring organizations: to foster and encourage a wider popular involvement in the experience of the living theatre.

From its founding in 1913, Det Norske Teatret in Oslo has been one of the true pioneers and supporters of such touring activity, as part of its unofficial mandate as Norway's "second" national theatre. Identified as it has been from its inception with the language and culture of rural Norway, this singular theatre is characterized by a stability of purpose that seems to have deflected much of the turbulence and soul-searching of the theatrical establishment as a whole in the sixties and after. On the other hand, neither its modest physical plant nor its Bjørnsonian pursuit of a rural ideality prevented Det Norske Teatret from emerging in the postwar period as one of the most avant-garde stages in Scandinavia. In 1948, Hans Jacob Nilsen directed and played the title role in a boldly antiromantic *Peer Gynt* that proved to be a milestone in the stage history of Ibsen's play. Determined to present this work not as a journey through Norway but as "a journey through a human mind," Nilsen put aside the incongruous nationalism and romanticism inherent in the famous Grieg music. Instead, the stark, dissonant tones of a new musical score by Harald Saeverud provided the director with the right unifying pattern of "musical–psychological development" in a production intended, as he put it, to send the audience from the theatre "shaken but fortified, more aware of the power the trolls have over us but better prepared to fight them."[30] The fulcrum of this revolutionary experiment was Arne Walentin's supple but by no means abstract design concept, which drew on the Reinhardt combination of a turntable stage and simplified, softly colored back projections, screened across the full width of a cyclorama. On the revolving stage stood stylized rock formations that were seen from a variety of angles as the action proceeded and the stage rotated. Otherwise, the only "scenery" consisted of simple, easily moveable set pieces. By utilizing the values of space, light, color, and form in varying permutations, Walentin and Nilsen succeeded in creating an atmosphere of dream and fantasy that would have been unthinkable with conventional painted scenery.

During the years around its fiftieth jubilee in 1963, both Ibsen and Brecht became key figures in the progressive repertory policy that Tormod Skagestad formulated for Det Norske Teatret. In the program for its first production of *Ghosts* in 1964, Skagestad declared his determination to render Ibsen's drama "relevant, alive, and contemporary for the generation living now." In this instance, the nature of the renewal was linguistic rather than scenographic; although Gerhard Knoop's mise-en-scène broke no new ground in theatrical terms, Skagestad's "adaptation" of the play to

Plate 66   Photograph of Walentin's set for the first scene of Brecht's *The Caucasian Chalk Circle*, directed by Peter Palitzsch at Det Norske Teatret in 1962.

colloquial New Norse thrust his theatre (once again) into the midst of a heated debate over language reform and classlessness in contemporary Norwegian society. The coming of Brecht, on the other hand, exposed the ensemble and its audience to a radically new style of performance. In contrast to Sjöberg's productions of Brecht at Dramaten, in which he largely ignored the thorny issue of epic acting and staging, the Norwegian company's performances of *The Caucasian Chalk Circle* (1962) and *Herr Puntila and his Man Matti* (1964) adopted a more faithful approach to Brechtian theory. Both plays were staged by the German director Peter Palitzsch, a veteran of the Berliner Ensemble who was encouraged by Skagestad to take three months of rehearsal to train the *Chalk Circle* cast properly in the techniques of epic theatre. The outcome was an encouraging success for the company and a great personal triumph for the young Liv Ullmann in the role of Grusche, the Brechtian image of "the seductive power of goodness" who risks her life to save and nurture an abandoned child. Ullmann's warmth, spirit, and humor provided a perfect counterbalance to Hans Stormoen's rough, full-bodied portrayal of the scoundrel judge Azdak, who decides the fate of Grusche and her child. "When this mountain of flesh and Liv Ullmann's slender, tough, maternal figure confronted one another, the performance rose to the pinnacle of art and the excitement hit the roof of Det Norske Teatret," wrote the Copenhagen critic Harald Engberg in *Politiken*.[31] Palitzsch's two Norwegian productions, his less successful staging of *Arturo Ui* at the Stockholm City Theatre (1966), and the Brecht productions of Ralf Långbacka in Gothenburg and Johan Bergenstråhle in Stockholm in the early 1970s all promoted a more orthodox Brechtian style as an alternative to Sjöberg's freer, more individualistic approach to the plays.

Seen in a broader perspective, however, it was not Brecht but O'Neill whose work best accommodated and exemplified the dominant style of psychologically motivated, naturalistically detailed acting that ruled the theatrical mainstream in Scandinavia at this time. *Long Day's Journey into Night*, O'Neill's posthumous autobiographical masterpiece, was the focus of particular interest in the fifties and early sixties. Productions of it at the Danish Royal Theatre and at Det Norske Teatret (where Tordis, Alfred, and Toralv Maurstad teamed up as Mary, James, and Edmund Tyrone) were highly acclaimed, but it was generally felt that no performance of the play could match the standard set by its legendary world premiere at Dramaten (10 February 1956). O'Neill had long been part of Dramaten's heritage. At the end of his life, he instructed his wife Carlotta to give his last works – with no royalties involved – to the Swedish national theatre, "in gratitude," as she wrote to *teaterchef* Karl Ragnar Gierow, "for the excellent performances they have given his plays over the years." During the playwright's lifetime, nine of his most demanding works had been produced there, including the European premieres of *Strange Interlude* (1928), *Mourning Becomes Electra* (1933), and *The Iceman Cometh* (1947). The 1956 production of *Long Day's Journey* was closely followed by world premieres of *A Touch of the Poet* (1957), *Hughie* (1959), and the Gierow reconstruction of *More Stately Mansions* (1962).

Above all, it was the exceptional group of actors assembled by the young director Bengt Ekerot that made the premiere of *Long Day's Journey* so remarkable. His production brought together Lars Hanson as a sodden but commanding James Tyrone, every inch an actor, Inga Tidblad as a desperately lonely, bird-light Mary Tyrone, Ulf Palme as the bitterly disillusioned alcoholic Jamie, and Jarl Kulle as Edmund, the fabulist spinning out his and his creator's longing for poetic expressiveness. As everyone writing about this production seemed to agree, its true strength lay not in its studied touches of verisimilitude but in the inner, psychological authenticity of the acting presentations themselves. "The acting, the overall unity of tone, the individual interpretations – all were as perfect as one can demand in an imperfect world," *Svenska Dagbladet* (11 February) wrote of this harrowing four-and-a-half-hour encounter with the four haunted

Tyrones. "*Ghosts* appears like an idyll in comparison," *Dagens Nyheter* added in its own rave review. "Strindberg's uninhibited self-exposure suddenly seems like a contrived arrangement in comparison to this long, naked, unbearably increasing cry of pain." In an interview after the opening, Ekerot himself declared that he could not imagine how naturalistic acting could ever be carried further – and most reviewers of the production readily agreed. What above all characterized this kind of approach was its elaboration of even the smallest nuance in the text. Spanning a broad range from a light, bantering, almost comedic tone in the opening act to the harshness of the bruising emotional confrontations that follow, Ekerot's mise-en-scène sought a gradation of moods and tones that lent it a strikingly musical quality. *Expressen* called the result "an ominously threatening chamber symphony." "The great art here lies in the weighting, the phrasing, the suggestiveness," *Aftonbladet* said of the fluid yet effectively concretized reality evoked by Ekerot's "invisible" direction of his actors.

The style of psychological acting so forcefully represented by this landmark production is eloquently explicated in the writings of the Danish actor Poul Reumert, one of its foremost exponents. "Acting is in its profoundest sense self-confession," Reumert wrote in one of his essays.

> Everything, every single feature of the character we watch and hear on the stage, carries the actor's own stamp, and there is nothing about it that is not his personal possession. Every emotion, thought, and all the qualities from the best to the worst have been discovered by the actor within himself – and all of them, artistically transformed, are used by him for his imaginary yet truly living creation.[32]

Reumert's own sixty-year career, which encompassed nearly four hundred different roles, showed his extraordinary versatility: Molière's Tartuffe, Argan, Arnolphe, and Mascarille; Shakespeare's Macbeth, Caesar, Polonius, and Jacques; Strindberg's Jean, Captain Edgar, Gustav Vasa, and the Father; and Ibsen's Peer Gynt, Manders, Daniel Hejre, and Solness are a random selection of his more familiar characters. After his French-language Tartuffe in Paris in the twenties and his acclaimed performances opposite Tora Teje in *The Dance of Death* at Dramaten in the thirties, his reputation became a genuinely international one. The strength of the influence he exerted on Scandinavian theatre as a whole was, in itself, a bastion of a performance tradition, the ideal of which was a conflation of the poetic and the concrete. The actor's "passionate, individualized search for naturalistic expression" was, in this aesthetic, always conjoined with "that which is called poetic style, and which some years ago was referred to as romanticism, as opposed to realism."[33] Yet Reumert played neither O'Neill nor Brecht, and he was convinced that both unmitigated psychological identification with a role and dogmatic critical detachment from it were equally hypothetical extremes which, in practice, must be seen by the actor in conjunction. "At times we notice that the one has taken over, at times the other, and occasionally they are united in a strange, complementary harmony, different from one individual to another. Secretly conditioned by the intellect's richness and the body's elasticity."[34]

However, by the time Reumert celebrated his sixtieth anniversary as an actor (16 February 1962) with a sprightly remastering of his Rolf Swedenhielm, the genially eccentric Nobel laureate at the center of Hjalmar Bergman's *Swedenhielms*, it was clear that an era was coming to an end. During the years that followed, the ranks of Scandinavia's leading actors were thinned by the deaths of such older stars as Bodil Ipsen (1964), Lars Hanson (1965), Reumert himself (1968), Tora Teje (1970), and Inga Tidblad (1975). Much more shocking was the loss incurred by the unexpected death of Mogens Wieth in London in 1962, shortly before his forty-third birthday, as he was preparing for a four-role guest engagement at the Old Vic that was to have culminated in his performance as Othello. Like Reumert, his great model, Wieth possessed both extraordinary versatility and a wide international reputation. During the years just before the Second World War, while still in his twenties, he rose to prominence as a robust, romantic, supremely lyrical Peer Gynt. After the war, during which he had trained as a paratrooper in the RAF, he returned to the Royal Theatre as Scandinavia's brightest new star. During the theatre's bicentennial in 1948 he enjoyed a remarkable triple success as a jovial but deeply tragic Hickey in *The Iceman Cometh*, an icy, fanatical Gregers Werle in *The Wild Duck*, and an unsentimental, controlled Othello, an innocent heart led into the darkness of suspicion by the evil hypocrisy of his surroundings. At every stage in his development – in his faceted interpretation of Torvald Helmer for Peter Ashmore's 1953 London production of *A Doll's House*, in his brilliant teamwork with Bodil Kjer at the New Theatre, and in his introspective portraits of the complex protagonists in Kjeld Abell's later plays – he drew upon a creative process that was rooted in the close, methodical analysis and accumulation of psychological detail. Often the results he achieved were attained in the face of extreme physical pain, caused by a chronic lung condition. "Intuition and inspiration were wrung from weeks of study at his desk and on the stage," Sam Besekow, frequently his director, wrote in his memorial tribute. "Artistic intention piled details upon details."[35]

Yet even by this time, as we have already had occasion to see, revolution was in the air. The traditional roles of actor, director, and playwright – even accepted definitions of what constitutes a theatrical event – were being questioned and hotly debated. Eugenio Barba, who started Odin Teatret in Oslo in 1964 and was invited to settle his Nordic Theatre Laboratory in the small Danish community of Holstebro two years later, led the assault on the "rich theatre" and its obsession with the twin chimeras of individual psychology and theatrical illusion. Inspired by the ideas of Jerzy Grotowski, Barba declared the theatre to be a ritualistic communal rite, dependent for its effect on a complete psychic and physical redisciplining of the "parochial" actor. Although his theories and experiments aroused their fair share of controversy, they very quickly provided a useful rallying point for the adherents of the new radicalism that arose out of the so-called "Youth Rebellion" of 1968.

Theatres of revolt

The phenomenon of free, experimental stages devoted to the exploration of new plays and new theatre forms is not a new one in Scandinavian theatrical history. Strindberg's ambitious but short-lived Scandinavian Experimental Theatre, thought of by him as Copenhagen's answer to Antoine's Théâtre Libre, is one example. Intima teatern in Stockholm is another. In the contemporary period, however, the need for smaller experimental stages – places where young actors and directors could test and develop new methods and styles – became more apparent. An important first step was taken in 1945 with the founding of the Studio Theatre in Oslo, created by a group of young theatre enthusiasts who had trained together during the war years and whose aim was (no less than) the renewal of Norwegian acting. Their model was Stanislavski; their emblem, the seagull of the Moscow Art Theatre. In many ways their goals and methods paralleled those of the new off-Broadway theatres that were springing up in New York around this time. Made up of an ensemble of nineteen actors, many of whom would go on to become leading figures in the established Nowegian theatre, the Studio was constituted as an actors' theatre devoted to the proposition that "the actor is the creative artist and must not, as happened in certain modern developments between the wars, become a pawn in the director's hand."[36] The consistently high standard of this company's productions set an example that had a lasting effect on the philosophy of actor training in Norway. Its repertoire was geared not to an intellectual elite but to a broad – and particularly a young – general audience. Most of the thirty-four plays it produced during its five-year existence were works by the leading modern writers of the period, including Wilder, Saroyan, Brecht, Chekhov, O'Neill, Maxwell Anderson, Anouilh, Williams, and others. In 1946 the ensemble took its production of Thornton Wilder's *Our Town*, with its rejection of the trappings of conventional realism, to Finmarken and other war-devastated regions of northern Norway, where it played under primitive conditions to audiences that had never before attended a theatre performance. Early in 1948 the Studio had one of its more controversial successes with its stage version of *Torment*, Ingmar Bergman's early filmscript about the destructive force of the malevolent schoolmaster Caligula. Bleak economic conditions ultimately put an end to the Studio Theatre in 1950, but not before it managed to stage its world premiere of Sean O'Casey's *Cock-a-Doodle Dandy*, a work whose ideology and experimental spirit were both in perfect accord with the aims of this young collective.

During the 1960s the number of autonomous chamber theatres multiplied rapidly, as a manifestation of the revolt against the canonical repertory and hierarchical structure of Scandinavia's institutionalized theatres, state-run and commercial alike. (It should be noted, however, that by the end of the decade all three of the national theatres were also running experimental stages of their own.) Among the first and most influential of the new mini-theatres was Fiolteatret, a tiny 80-seat backyard theatre that was established in the heart of the university quarter of Copenhagen early in 1962. Like most of the other intimate stages that arose at this time, Fiolteatret began as an expression of intellectual (rather than explicitly ideological) discontent – a response to a perceived need "for the theatre to break out of its traditional frame, to contact and seek inspiration from painters, composers, musicians, and poets, and to open new avenues of theatre by working directly with such people."[37] The early repertory of the new theatre was typical of its time and its absurdist pretensions – Beckett, early Albee and Pinter, Ionesco, and an occasional new Danish play for good measure. Many of the productions presented on its postage-stamp stage used the elements and traditions of revue and cabaret. Bodil Udsen, an accomplished revue comedienne, thus gave Fiolteatret its first popular success with her rich, engaging portrayal of Winnie in Beckett's *Happy Days*. Klaus Rifbjerg, the Danish satirical poet, emerged as its first new playwright of note with a plotless, cabaret-style piece called *Udviklinger* (*Developments*), "a play for four jazz musicians, four actors, and a small theatre." Rifbjerg's topical satire was directed with fine rhythmic sense by Carlo M. Pedersen in 1965 – though, in fact, it had first been produced two months earlier at Dramaten, where such experiments were typical of Bergman's expansive regime.

By the end of the sixties a new political consciousness and a new activism had begun to transform group-theatre activity throughout Scandinavia. Although their specific aims varied, group after group found itself drawn to a common conviction – that theatre could and should become a weapon in the class struggle. "The close of the sixties was the age of great discoveries," the feminist playwright and director Suzanne Osten observed. "We discovered the audience out in the daylight. We smashed our way out of the cellar darkness of avant-gardist convulsions. We discovered the causal connection between the injustices of the world and our own class structure. And we discovered children."[38] Given its shared goal of social change, the activist theatre movement sought to develop new means of engaging a "new" audience in the critical analysis and debate of social and political issues. Once liberated from the cellars and lofts of the intellectual avant garde, the political actor–commentator was free to interact as directly as possible with spectators "out in the daylight" of the real world where they lived and worked (or, in the case of children's theatre, played and went to school). By 1969 even Nationaltheatret itself began visiting schools and workplaces in the Oslo area with its own group-theatre dramatizations of social problems. Above all, the organizing principle of all such groups was defiantly collectivist. In itself, the equality of the collective structure, with its focus on the cooperative making of a useful work rather than on personal self-expression or talent, became the reflection of the better society advocated by the movement. Hålogaland Teater, the official regional stage established in Tromsø in 1971, quickly became Norway's most radical and controversial exponent of a democratic form of theatre "where the aim is not to enhance personal success, but to join in creating a good product serving a common goal."[39]

By the time Fiolteatret abandoned the university area in 1969 to relocate in a more spacious arena theatre on Halmtorvet, in the midst of one of

Copenhagen's least privileged and most crime-prone districts, its past as an outpost of intellectual avant-gardism was behind it. "Besides wanting to amuse and entertain audiences with a little social chastisement, it became increasingly clear to everyone in the ensemble that we also wanted to see theatre used in the struggle to change society in a socialist direction," the group declared in a policy statement issued in 1974.[40] Agitprop performances on urban streets and in local factories were added to the range of its activities. A significant part of its repertory was devoted to docu-dramas about the working-class issues and labor disputes of the day. For a group project about the exploitation of female textile workers, called *Kvinderne i Herning* (*The Women of Herning*, 1972), the designated writer of the script, Bente Hansen, and some of her actors actually took part-time jobs in the textile industry in order to confront the issues at first hand. Much like the smaller theatre later started in Torshov, an older working-class district of Oslo, by actors from Nationaltheatret, Fiolteatret sought to identify itself in solidarity with the people and concerns of the specific urban neighborhood in which it had settled.

The many other small groups making up what can be called a theatre of social purpose differed in a variety of respects, but most were patterned more or less directly on such high-profile alternative theatres as the Living Theatre of the Becks, Littlewood's Theatre Workshop, Chaikin's Open Theatre, the Bread and Puppet Theatre, and in particular Café La Mama. Especially in Sweden, the 1960s saw an explosion of small experimental stages, theatre collectives, and workshops devoted to a heady mixture of politics, poetry, music, and pornography. Stockholm-based groups such as the Free Pro Theatre, the Jester, the Arena Boat Theatre, the Pocket Theatre, the Pistol Theatre, and others put on an eclectic program of destruction happenings, street theatre, improvisations, houseboat theatre, political cabaret, guerilla theatre, agitprop revues, and a selection of more conventionally structured "underground" plays such as Shepard's *Chicago*. Most of the groups were itinerant in nature. The Free Pro Theatre regularly took to the road with its *lehrstücke* encouraging revolutionary socialism and the overthrow of capitalists and reformist trade unions alike. No less radical in its ideology, Narren (The Jester) was strongly influenced by the visit of the Café La Mama ensemble in 1967. Subsequently it emerged as one of the most provocative of the Swedish groups with its 1969 productions of *Flickan i Havana* (*The Girl in Havana*), which drew on the troupe's firsthand experiences in Cuba, and *Futz*, in which scenes of hardcore

sexuality nearly resulted in the laying of charges for gross public inde-
cency. Fickteatern (The Pocket Theatre), a breakaway faction of the Jester
group directed by Suzanne Osten, managed during its brief existence to
evolve a much more controlled and sophisticated style, inspired by the
techniques of the *commedia dell'arte*, for its own street and school performances of social satires and docudramas.

Like Nationaltheatret in Oslo, some major Swedish institutions such
as Dramaten and the Gothenburg City Theatre also began at this time to
develop group-theatre projects and in-house collectives of their own. A
landmark event in this process was *Flotten* (*The Raft*), a topical, highly idio-
matic satire of Swedish social democracy that was staged by Lennart
Hjulström and a group of actors from the Gothenburg City Theatre in
1967. Inspired by the collage and revue techniques so effectively employed
by Joan Littlewood and her Theatre Workshop in *Oh, What a Lovely War!*,
Hjulström's ensemble and the project's writers, Kent Andersson and Bengt
Bratt, worked closely together to develop their own biting, fast-paced allegory of Swedish society as a life-raft floating aimlessly across the sea of the
world toward an unknown destination. This extremely popular experiment was immediately followed by a cluster of sequels workshopped by
the same team of Gothenburg actors and writers. *Hemmet* (*The Home*, 1967)
scrutinized contemporary society through the prism of an old people's
home, while *Sandlåtan* (*The Sandbox*, 1968) saw it from a child's point of
view. Yet in each case, the underlying subject was the same – the intoler-
ance, injustice, and complacency fostered by the Swedish welfare state.
Nor did Danish audiences find any trouble recognizing themselves and
their own social problems in these plays when they were produced by
Preben Harris at his suburban Gladsaxe Theatre at the end of the sixties.

As the group-theatre movement became a more established fact of cultural life in Scandinavia, more groups began to associate themselves with
a particular township or municipality, as permanent, subsidized
"neighborhood" theatres. The fear that a conservative town council might
(and sometimes did) meddle in the collectivist management or the activist
repertory of its local group was generally outweighed by the greater
economic stability and physical rootedness afforded by such an arrangement. This phenomenon was especially evident in Denmark, where the
comparatively compact landscape became dotted in the 1970s and after
with a large number of resident group theatres.

Banden (The Troupe), which put down its tent poles in Odense, offers a prototypical picture of group-theatre activity in such a setting. A declaration of purpose published by the group in 1972, three years after its founding, proclaimed a charter of aims that were, by definition, common to this entire movement: "To make theatre *together* with the audience. To come to the audience. To create debate. To influence opinion."[41] From the outset, all ten members of the collective were paid the same and were expected to take part in the cooperative writing and preparation of shows – normally school productions for older classes, filled with acrobatic clowning and broad farce techniques meant to stimulate the young audience's awareness of social issues. Team Theatre, a somewhat older collective that settled in rural Herning (a leaisurely twenty-one miles from Barba's headquarters in Holstebro) in 1968, found both its subject matter and its justification in depictions of the lives, problems, and history of the inhabitants of the small Jutland farming community where it made its home. Typically, a children's play like *Det er bare noget vi spiller* (*It's Just a Game We're Playing*, 1978) was the outcome of direct consultation by the Team group and its writer, Kaj Nissen, with the schoolchildren for whom the piece was intended. At a usual performance of this play, the young audience would be seated on the floor of their school gym while the actors took places against the walls around them. Simple props, a conscious use of expressive movement, swift improvisations, and the potential of the neutral space itself all contributed to the enactment of the stereotypical games and dreams of the three sixth-graders in the play, themselves the unwitting products of their own social class. Even more obviously tailored to the specific audience that a group like Team had to seek out and retain were such larger-scale adult productions as *Et landmandsliv* (*A Farmer's Life*, 1981), a broad splash of total theatre in which the story of two young men grappling with the social and economic hardships of modern farming unfolded in a carnival atmosphere of country music, square dancing, and the rhetoric of a town-hall meeting. Across the water on the island of Fyn, Baggårdsteatret (The Yard Theatre) adopted a similar approach with its own Svendborg public in a work such as *Liv i fattiggården* (*Life in the Poorhouse*, 1982), a sprawling, open-air folk drama about "poverty down through the ages" that was actually performed in the town's former poorhouse, then a local museum.

Some companies which, like Fiolteatret, began life in the early sixties as "traditional" avant-garde stages also made the transition to subsidized neighborhood collectives. Svalegangen (The Gallery), which had been started as an experimental chamber theatre by young actors from Aarhus

Theatre in 1963, soon lost connection with its state-supported parent, which opened its own studio facility in 1968. During the 1970s, after reconstituting itself and its repertory, Svalegangen distinguished itself chiefly by commissioning new Danish plays, often documentary and political in nature and almost always created by young playwrights in collaboration with the performing members of the group. The work of the Jomfru Ane Theatre (named after the street where it is located), which became Aalborg's recognized neighborhood collective in 1980, reflected a more circumspect – if no less committed – position on the question of political theatre. This group, which was founded in 1967 as an experimental forum for the then new absurdist drama, eventually became known in later years for its forceful, professionally polished theatrical demonstrations against, for example, Denmark's use of nuclear power and its entry into the European Common Market. The special hallmark of these productions was their strategic use of rock music as a means of establishing an emotional rapport with the audience and intensifying its ideological response. Nevertheless, Jomfru Ane has remained adamant that its role in the political process is not "to formulate clear political goals," but instead to "sharpen the theatrical idiom in a political way." In a statement issued in 1977, the thirteen-member collective dissociated itself from the idea of "enacting the revolution on the stage, as so often happens in political theatre. People should not be bluffed into believing that the revolution will enact itself before their eyes, just like that. They must get out there themselves and make it happen."[42]

In an interview published in 1981, Eugenio Barba expressed his own views on the movement he had so strongly influenced and endorsed: "The political theatre has, right up until today, been a theatre that proclaims that Monday is Monday and Tuesday is Tuesday and no doubt about it – a theatre of the obvious."[43] This remark should not be seen as a repudiation of ideological theatre, however, but as an attempt to point out the main source of its potential stagnation. Without self-renewal and creative development, its ever-present snares remain redundancy and stereotype. What may once have seemed bold and provocative – the colorful street-theatre attacks by the radical social-action group Solvognen on NATO, commercialized Christmas, and the US bicentennial, for example – can glide imperceptibly into the limbo of historical phenomena, along with happenings, streakings, and Elvis. "It is the circumstances that determine whether the performance we give acquires political meaning," Barba continues. "I believe that the theatre is transformed into a political situation at the moment when the personal questions being asked compel the spectator to ask himself or herself the same questions. Suddenly the spectator recognizes them as existential: 'What am I really living for?'" This reconstitution of Brechtian theory found practical expression in Odin Theatre's 1980 production of *Brechts aske* (*Brecht's Ashes*). This montage-style reappraisal of Brecht, whom Barba regards as more than "the little, castrated saint we know from his plays," surveyed examples of his work "not as immutable books, but as his ashes: something which extenuates the meaning of a precise human experience that still radiates the ambiguity of life and action." Barba's Brecht was a man who paid a heavy personal price for the schism he imposed between rationality and emotion.

For a time after settling in Holstebro in 1966, Barba and his theatre laboratory conducted their experiments in relative isolation from the contemporary theatre scene in Scandinavia. Later in the 1970s the Odin ensemble turned outward in search of contact with new surroundings, notably in southern Italy and Peru. After 1980, however, Barba and his commune were firmly reestablished in their Holstebro setting, with the full support of the community. As such, his seminal methods of intensive work and demonstrations of vigorous actor training were able to provide a healthy counterbalance to the tendency on the part of the radical theatre movement to tolerate mediocrity (or worse) in the name of collectivist solidarity, and to discountenance individual talent as a manifestation of bourgeois elitism. On the other hand, Barba is the first to insist that, for him and his followers, theatre holds more significance as ideology and anthropology than as art. "All this about traditional quality means nothing for a group theatre," he says. "There are other qualities that matter here: human relations among the members, solidarity, organization." In a broader context, in terms of its influence on the future development of the Scandinavian theatre as a whole, it is undoubtedly too soon to assess the pros and cons of the effect exerted by the so-called Third Theatre advocated by Barba and the group-theatre movement, aloof from both the commercial theatre and the director-dominated, dramatist-oriented "art" theatre. One striking result, however, has been the substantial reallocation of public funding that has occurred in response to the growth in all three countries of noncommercial theatrical activity at the regional, municipal, and neighborhood levels.

Playwriting in transition

A noticeable absence of major new Scandinavian plays and playwrights became a matter of growing concern in the postwar years. Contrary to what one might have expected, the radical group theatres and their experiments did not seem to foster new dramatists of significance – as, for example, Chaikin's Open Theatre and Littlewood's Theatre Workshop had done. More often than not, the original writing produced by this movement in Scandinavia took the form of occasional pieces – documentaries, children's plays, or collectively scripted compositions tailored to a predetermined audience or event. When Odin Theatre actually did perform a version of Jens Bjørneboe's *Fulgeelskerne* (*The Bird Lovers*) in Oslo in 1966, the production (retitled *Ornitofilene,* or *The Ornithophiles*) left the Norwegian dramatist rather shaken. His Brechtian indictment of ex-Nazis who revisit Italy as affluent, bird-loving German tourists was subjected to a dissection so extreme that, he admits, "not even the torso of the text remained – only heart and lungs and brains were left." Instead, it was generally the less idiosyncratic productions of the established theatres that served the cause of emerging playwrights best. During the first decade or so after the war, a number of promising premieres at Dramaten attracted particular attention. With Alf Sjöberg's production of *Den dödsdömde* (*The Condemned*), the young Stig Dagerman won overnight fame with his disturbing existentialist parable of human injustice and despair. Ingmar Bergman made his directing debut at Dramaten in 1951 with a faithful and precise rendering of Björn-Erik Höijer's drama of life in northern Sweden, *Det lyser i kåken* (*Light in the Hovel*). Bengt Ekerot gave Lars Forssell's *Kröningen* (*The Coronation*) a brilliant modernist production in 1956, using masks, dance-like movements, and a sculptural setting of steel tubing to evoke the grotesque, disjunctive atmosphere of this mock-classical tragifarce about the death of Alcestis and the absurd terror of death shown by Admetus. After Dagerman's suicide two years earlier had put an end to his promising career, Forssell's debut at Dramaten was eagerly welcomed as a fresh sign of renewal in Swedish playwriting.

Among a generation of older dramatists that also included Denmark's Carl Erik Soya and Sweden's Vilhelm Moberg, the preeminent figure was still Kjeld Abell, whose plays have been widely performed throughout Scandinavia and whose death in 1961 left a gap not easily filled. As a playwright, Abell was to an unusual degree attuned to the demands and

Plate 67 Helge Refn's graceful expressionistic design for a temple in the sky in Abell's *Days on a Cloud* (Danish Royal Theatre, 1947).

possibilities of the practical theatre. More than a few of the leading roles in his plays mirror the personality and abilities of specific performers – in particular Clara Pontoppidan, Bodil Ipsen, and Bodil Kjer, three of the foremost Danish actresses of this century. In a comparable sense, the visionary, surrealistic imagery of Abell's later dramas met with a virtually ideal responsiveness in the evocative stage designs created for these plays by Erik Nordgreen and Helge Refn.

With Holger Gabrielsen's production of *Dage paa en Sky* (*Days on a Cloud*) in 1947, the Royal Theatre faced its public with one of the most unusual plays it has ever produced. This work represents a crucial turning point in Abell's dramaturgy, as the first in a series of associational, non-representational fantasias centering on the theme of self-destruction as an act of escape and (negative) isolation from the human condition. The action of this expressionistic fable takes place in the mind of its sole male character, a disillusioned scientist–physician called only He, during the split seconds between his suicidal plunge from an aircraft and his existential decision to choose life by releasing his parachute. These fleeting moments of Sartrean doubt and decision are expressed as days on a cloud in the heavenly regions through which the flyer falls – a cloud populated by goddesses of Greek mythology, who live a disconsolate existence

Plate 68 Design by Erik Nordgreen for Abell's *The Blue Pekinese*, in which the old-world café in the foreground dissolves into the brooding confines of Villa Gullcry. Danish Royal Theatre, 1954.

among ruined temples and toppled pillars, constantly at war with the death-bringing forces of the (unseen) male world of "Zeus and his gang." The crumbling, dusty symbol-world of the play was transfigured in a skeletal, ethereal stage setting by Helge Refn that was, in itself, a major factor in the success of this difficult production.

Four more major plays followed, each concerned with the problem of human isolation and alienation and each crucially dependent on strongly metaphysical stage imagery. In *Vetsera blomster ikke for enhver* (*Vetsera Does Not Bloom for Everyone*), a three-act chamber play first produced at the intimate Frederiksberg Theatre in 1950, Abell turned to the famous double suicide of crown prince Rudolph of Austria and his mistress Maria Vetsera for his inspiration. The actual historical event is used, however, only as an oblique, recurrent referent in a somber, Chekhovian indictment of a doomed civilization, effectively objectified in production by Refn's lushly decadent stage image of a festering, *Jugendstil* Villa Mayerling. In *Den blå*

Pekingeser (*The Blue Pekinese*), time and place intertwine and fluctuate in a freer and much more complex way, as living, dead, and as yet unborn characters mingle in an expressionistic concurrency of past, present, and future. The thematic tension in this play is again between the forces of isolation and death and the unrealized promises and demands of life, symbolized by the invisible presence of a bell-tinkling, horizon-blue pekinese called Dicky. In John Price's sensitive production of the play at the Royal Theatre in 1954, its evanescent, dream-play mood was perfectly articulated in Erik Nordgreen's design for the old-world Café Bern that dissolves before the eyes of the audience into the shadowy, unearthly precincts of Villa Gullcry, where the isolated Tordis Eck flirts with suicide. The action unfolds in the imagination of the central character, a detached observer of life called André, who at last succeeds in convincing both Tordis and an unborn child "to live, to be part of life." The performance of this elusive poetic experiment owed its impact in large measure to Abell's ability to shape roles around specific actors – in this case Bodil Kjer as the elegiac, moribund Tordis; Mogens Wieth as a visionary Orpheus who must coax her from the arms of death; and Clara Pontoppidan as Isabella de Creuth, the mysterious owner of the invisible blue pekinese.

Kjer and Wieth were together once again as the principals in *Kameliadamen* when it was produced at the New Theatre in 1959. The underlying text of this theatrical quotation is not the famous Dumas play but his lesser-known novel, also called *La dame aux camélias*. Abell's play begins after Marguerite's death and takes place in the shadowy study of Alexandre Dumas, who is both the narrator of the action and a major player in it. At issue here, however, is not a retelling of the threadbare tale of the consumptive courtesan, but a a deeply personal contemplation of the artist's relationship to his creation and his creativity. As such, this rather novelistic drama's universe is strongly linguocentric, defined more by a concern with language and the sound of language than by dramatic action in the usual sense. In *Skriget* (*The Scream*), which reached the Royal Theatre stage some eight months after Abell's death in 1961, this concern with voices, words, and the sound-sense they make became predominant in a play that is set in the belfry of a village church that is inhabited by an Aristophanic gallery of bird-characters. This kaleidoscopic fantasy moves on several interrelated levels at once – contemporary, biblical, anthropomorphic. The scream of the title, a piercing cry that interrupts the Sunday morning service in progress in the church below, has a spectrum of connotations, ranging from the sacrificial victim's scream of anguish to the mystical sense of exultation felt by those still sensitive enough to be affected by the sound. The bearing principles of the dramatic form – sequential logic, character development, a cumulative sense of inevitability – are discarded here once and for all. Abell's last poetic experiment seems virtually to postulate a new form of "theatre" – a mutational collage of voices and music, cries and whispers, disturbing sounds and disquieting silences that is perhaps irrevocably at odds with the demands and limitations of a stage performance. Harald Engberg mused in *Politiken* (3 November 1961) about the need for some "magical words that could transport this play to a stage and make it fly and reveal itself."

Although indisputably the foremost dramatist during the middle decades of this century in Scandinavia, Abell's singular style and complexity limited the reality of his influence on practical theatre. Other writers at the time chose a variety of directions, in search of a viable contemporary form. In his psychological drama *Thermopylae* (1958), the Danish novelist H. C. Branner wrestled in traditional Ibsenian terms with the issue of humanism in the war years. Ernst Bruun Olsen and his composer, Finn Savery, took Scandinavia by storm with *Teenagerlove*, a savage satire of the pop generation's music and mentality that was staged by the author himself at the Royal Theatre in 1962. New Norwegian plays became especially plentiful after the mid-1960s. Even a cursory overview indicates their diversity in terms of style and subject matter. Figures of recent history at odds with their restrictive societies provided the focus for such diverse plays as Jens Bjørneboe's *Semmelweiss* (1969), about the valiant efforts of the noted Hungarian physician to combat "childbed" fever, and Edvard Hoem's *Tusen fjordar, tusen fjell* (*A Thousand Fjords, A Thousand Mountains*), his 1977 drama about Ivar Aasen, the nineteenth-century creator of the New Norwegian language. Mythical figures ranging from the gods of Nordic mythology to Tarzan were subjects for ironic contemporary comment in (respectively) Peder W. Cappelen's *Loke* (1972) and Tor Åge Bringsværd's *Jungelens herre* (*Lord of the Jungle*, 1974). Strongly stylized – if very different – approaches to social criticism were adopted in Finn Cavling's symbolic zoo story *Gitrene* (*The Bars*, 1966) and Bringsværd's *Glasberget* (*The Glass Mountain*, 1975), a serio-farcical fable about capitalistic competition. Some of the cherished conventions of sixties realism were revisited in Knut Faldbakken's debut piece, *Tyren og Jomfruen* (*The Bull and the Virgin*), in 1976. In her similarly popular first play, *Et spil om fem kvinder* (*A Play about Five Women*, 1974), Bjørg Vik created an effective feminist drama out of the familiar situation of five former school chums meeting to celebrate their friendship and reveal their secrets. During this period of expansion in the 1970s, these and other Norwegian playwrights such as Klaus Hagerup, Pål Sundvor, and Sverre Udnæs all found strong support for their work both at Nationaltheatret and Det Norske Teatret.

The dramatist who followed most directly in Abell's footsteps at this time, however, was Lars Forssell, a versatile theatre poet whose rejection of the conventions of psychological realism in the theatre parallels the views expressed on this subject by both Abell and Lagerkvist. "How long will this terrible psychological drama – like some clumsy, unmusical bear with a chain around its leg – be permitted to go on dancing on the Swedish stage?" he demanded, as a young man of twenty-four, in 1953.[44] The production of *The Coronation* three years later served notice of the theatricalist experimentation that was to follow. *Söndagspromenaden* (*The Sunday Walk*, 1963) and *Galepannan* (*The Madcap*, 1964), both directed by Ekerot at Dramaten, were among the works that revealed significant new aspects of Forssell's emerging dramatic vision. In the first of these plays, his ironic view of his country's insularity and complacency takes the form of a wry retrospective of Swedish society and social mores around the turn of the century. *The Madcap*, the first of his three major history plays, uses Sweden's historical past in a different way to provide, in a Brechtian sense, a critical and dialectical perspective on moral issues. The title character and controlling consciousness of the play is the luckless Gustav IV Adolf, the Swedish king who was imprisoned and deposed by his officers as a result of his stubborn opposition to Napoleon in 1809. Forssell's retrospective chronicle of the exiled monarch's life of mistakes is almost Chaplinesque in character, emphasizing as it does the alienation and atonality of a tragicomic scapegoat figure struggling absurdly to maintain his dignity in a bewildering world – a character beset by irreconcilable inner contradictions, born in the wrong century and trapped in the kingly role that has been "forced" upon him.

The postmodernist tendency in this work is even more striking in Forssell's subsequent history plays. *Christina Alexandra* (1968) is apparently based on a commissioned filmscript that Bergman might have directed if funding for the project had not evaporated, and the play as it stands retains a certain cinematic quality. Its dream-play atmosphere of fluctuating, kaleidoscopic reality is shaped by the subjective perspective of the egoist-dreamer Christina, the Swedish queen who, after only five years on the throne, abdicated her crown in 1655, impulsively embraced Catholicism, and spent the last decades of her life in self-imposed exile in Rome. Forssell's oneiric chronicle of these events is concerned with the vacillating multiplicity and conflicting "faces" of Christina's character, from the innocence (and irresponsibility) of the child to the cruelty, coldness, and solitude of the old woman she becomes. Like Gustav Adolf, this frustrated, power-mad figure is seen by Forssell as another example of the "ideal role," composed of jagged, clashing polarities and ambiguities that reinforces his vision of an "atonal," genreless theatre in which an indeterminate feeling of uncertainty is the looked-for effect.

Characters from history, literature, and "life" mingle freely in *Värdshuset Haren och Vråken* (*At the Hare and the Hawk*, 1978), a more complex and diffuse work that focuses on the figure of Carl Michael Bellman, the genial lyric poet of the Swedish rococo. An intuitive recognition of such "real" Swedish personalities as Ulla Winblad and Fredman (from *Fredman's Epistles*, by Bellman), Jacob Guntlack (the notorious bandit–adventurer of the period), and above all Bellman himself is essential to the play's effectiveness as a theatrical "quotation" of the Gustavian era, to which the audience's critical scrutiny is directed. The bloodless coup in which Gustav III seized power on 19 August 1772 is the pivotal event which, although unseen, remains the ironic backdrop for this bitter historical "comedy" about power and powerlessness, might and right, and the double codes of justice and morality that appear to govern the actions of the oppressed and the oppressor – the hare and the hawk – in this world.

Both Forssell's Bellman play and Abell's Dumas play can be seen, each in its different way, as illustrations of a broader tradition of "famous artist" drama that has continued to flourish in Scandinavia. A more straightforward example of the type is Ernst Bruun Olsen's *Postbudet fra Arles* (*The Postman of Arles*, 1974), a well-crafted van Gogh dramatization in which the great painter – abetted by his interlocutor, the village postman – struggles with the justification of his art, the responsibility it entails, and the terrible burden of solitude it imposes. In a rather similar vein, Bruun Olsen's *Den poetiske raptus* (*A Fit of Poetry*), which reached the Royal Theatre stage in 1976, paints a good-humored portrait of Ludvig Holberg in the grip of the burst of creativity that resulted in his first comedies. A more demythologized image of Holberg emerges from the rough-and-tumble realism of Leif Petersen's *Rene ord for pengene* (*Plain Talk for Your Money*), which was performed on the Royal Theatre's intimate chamber stage in 1972 to mark the 250th anniversary of the founding of Grønnegadeteatret. Such iconoclastic treatment of Scandinavia's theatrical monuments became more pronounced in Per Olov Enquist's psychobiographical studies of such "sacrosanct" figures as Strindberg and Johanne Luise Heiberg. Enquist's *Tribadernas natt* (*The Night of the Tribades*), which was widely performed after Per Werner-Carlsson's fine first production at Dramaten in 1975, is a montage of Strindberg's writings that dissects the stormy relationship between the playwright and his first wife, Siri von Essen, whose allegedly lesbian attachment to Caroline Marie David is the main source of dramatic conflict. In *Från regnormarnas liv* (*From the Life of the Rainworms*, 1981), Enquist turns to Fru Heiberg as another example of an artist with "two languages." Beneath the public language of the great Danish actress's memoirs, carefully polished by her refined husband J. L. Heiberg, lies the forbidden and (purportedly) more authentic language of her squalid origins, the truth about which she reveals to Hans Christian Andersen, a kindred spirit in this regard, in a series of reminiscences from her past.

Although rather static and "literary" in character at first glance, many of these biographical "artist" plays were made memorable in performance through the very basic sense of recognition prompted by such miracles of theatrical transformation as Erik Mørk's Holberg personification in the Bruun Olsen play, Ernst-Hugo Järegård's suffering Strindberg persona in *Tribades*, and Jørgen Reenberg's virtual reincarnation of Andersen in the Danish world premiere of *Rainworms*. As for the role of Fru Heiberg herself, no one is likely to surpass the brutal emotional intensity of Christine Buchegger's perfect likeness in the German revival of the play directed by Ingmar Bergman at the Residenztheater in Munich in 1984, a year before his return to Sweden.

By and large, most of the new playwrights who thus emerged in the 1960s and 1970s have continued to remain active to the present day. They began to be joined in the mid-1980s, moreover, by a "second wave" of younger writers, among the most prolific and influential of whom has been Lars Norén, already one of Dramaten's most frequently performed modern dramatists. On the strength of these signs of growth and expansion, the feeling of crisis that had prevailed in the postwar years has gradually given way to a new sense that playwriting in Scandinavia may already be in the process of staging something very like a renaissance.

11 The plurality of postmodern theatre

The theatre in Scandinavia has undergone a sustained period of readjustment and change during the past fifteen years or so – and the cultural and political consequences of this process are still far from resolved. The social upheavals of the late 1960s and the sweeping changes in theatrical legislation and funding that followed in the 1970s affected – and continue to affect – every corner of theatrical activity in Denmark, Sweden, and Norway. Although the specific circumstances of this reorganization are complex and vary from one country to another, some broader general trends can be identified. For one thing, massive infusions of state subsidy have virtually eliminated the commercial element of profit and loss in theatre management – although it is often difficult to perceive any substantive difference between the populist repertoire of welfare-state subscription theatre and that of its much-maligned commercial counterpart. Moreover, the increased public involvement in the support of theatre arts soon brought with it both feverish political soul-searching and a certain amount of useful reassessment of the theatre's role in the cultural and social life of a nation. In general, the decentralization and "democratization" of theatrical activity that occurred in the 1970s has continued to foster a remarkable plurality – a view of theatre that recognizes no one ultimate principle or form to the exclusion of all others. A heightened political consciousness and an increased awareness of the theatre's power to influence society have contributed to a proliferation of new forms and styles of alternative theatre, aimed at reaching new audiences. Such endeavors as the anthropological experiments of Barba's Odin troupe, the Swedish performances presented in ethnological locations by Peter Oscarsson's ensemble at the regional Folkteatern in Gävleborg, and Morten Grunwald's innovative reuse of industrial space in his Gasworks

318

Theatre project illustrate a wider postmodern tendency to redefine and reconstitute not only the theatrical event but also the place where it encounters its audience. Typically, it was in the empty, flexible space of Grunwald's Gasworks Theatre that the *Mahabharata*, Peter Brook's most ambitious folk spectacle, made its successful Copenhagen appearance in 1988.

Regardless of how harmonious and frictionless the union of art and politics may seem, however, many have come to the sober realization that this bond will not, of itself, cause theatre to live and prosper. Only the presence of talent can accomplish that tricky miracle. Soon after his appointment as managing director of the Danish Royal Theatre in 1979, Henrik Bering Lisberg began to raise the objection that the available supply of capable actors and directors is an exhaustible resource that will not support unlimited expansion of a theatre system with any integrity left in it. "We have something like ten or fifteen more theatres now than we had in the sixties. Added to which come all the smaller groups that thrive and flourish and have a big following," he observed in an interview in 1982. "I once figured out that we have seven times more theatres per inhabitant than England does. And then I asked myself the question: 'Do we really have seven times as much available talent as England has?' I wouldn't like to answer that question! The real problem is maintaining a level of quality that is high enough."[1] When this capable administrator resigned his post in 1989, his rhetorical question was still unanswered.

The advent of adverse economic conditions in the early 1980s dealt an even more damaging blow to the expansionist vision of the previous decade. While this new economic reality has had permanent long-term effects on the smaller free groups and the larger institutional theatres alike, one of its most immediate and unfortunate results was the disruption of reconstruction plans for the Royal Theatre in Copenhagen and Nationaltheatret in Oslo. In the case of Scandinavia's oldest national theatre, an architectural competition concluded in 1979 was to have resulted in a badly-needed modern facility for dramatic productions, incorporating a flexible but fairly intimate main auditorium (750–800 seats) and a 175-seat experimental studio. In the face of shrinking appropriations however, only the venerable Old Stage – the 1,500-seat proscenium theatre that had risen on the site of the original Royal Theatre in 1874 – was fully renovated to house Denmark's thrivng national ballet and opera. After the theatre on Kongens Nytorv reopened in 1986, dramatic productions were confined largely to the so-called New Stage, actually an old 1,100-seat concert hall that had been taken over by the Royal Theatre as a permanent (if rather inadequate) second stage in 1957. To accommodate more experimental works, a new chamber theatre (Graabrødrescenen) was opened in 1981 as a replacement for Comediehuset, a smaller studio space founded in 1970. The closing of this facility in 1991 came as a particularly serious setback for younger writers and directors who had used it to advantage as a freer, less constrictive environment in which to try new methods and untested ideas.

Amfiscenen, a 250-seat circular amphitheatre created at Nationaltheatret in 1980, has enjoyed longer life as a flexible alternative space for Norwegian directors, actors, and playwrights. Moreover, when the main stage and backstage area at Nationaltheatret were destroyed by fire in the autumn of 1980, its chamber theatre became the chief venue for such major productions as Edith Roger's starkly simplified, expressively choreographed distillation of *When We Dead Awaken* (4 September 1981). Plans to renovate and improve the entire structure, which had stood unchanged since the inauguration of Nationaltheatret in 1899, had been made in the early 1970s, but the fire and the unfavorable economic climate in which it occurred placed the very existence of the institution in jeopardy. Two years passed before the Norwegian parliament approved even a modest appropriation for the necessary repairs, and it was not until the autumn of 1985 that the restored (but not enlarged) theatre finally reopened with a grandiose nationalistic revival of *Peer Gynt*, acted to the accompaniment of Grieg's rhapsodic music. Directed by Edith Roger, this unusual project was, in fact, conceived as a triptych of three productions of the play, each one beginning at a different point in Peer's life story and each showing the audience a different constellation of actors in the main roles. Although the heavy pictorialism of the stage design (by Tine Schwab) and the romantic interpretation implicit in Roger's concept met with critical disapproval, this spectacular revival was a popular success and hence an effective point of departure for the reopened theatre's vigorous campaign to reassert its historical position as "Ibsen's Own Theatre," devoted to a thoroughly contemporary but not an artificially rootless or "timeless" approach to the entire Ibsen canon. Even a less often performed work such as *When We Dead Awaken*, which Nationaltheatret acted for the first time in 1900 with Ibsen in the audience, has regularly been taken up for reinterpretation by a succession of its leading directors – in this case, Halfdan Christensen

(1934), Gerda Ring (1961), Edith Roger (1981), and Kjetil Bang-Hansen (1994). In itself, the sheer variety of the productions that made up Nationaltheatret's first Ibsen Stage Festival in 1990, which included among its offerings Ingmar Bergman's Swedish version of *A Doll's House* and John Barton's new adaptation of *Peer Gynt* for the Norwegian company, was intended to emphasize the breadth of the spectrum of practical responses and performance choices fostered by the challenge of Ibsen's plays.

The problem of theatrical subsidy in Norway is, of course, made no less complicated by the fact that the capital is the home of two distinct and competing "national" theatres, each with its own linguistic character. Almost simultaneously with the reopening of Nationaltheatret in 1985, Det Norske Teatret acquired an ultramodern new playhouse of its own. Equipped with state-of-the-art technology, this superb complex houses a 200-seat studio and a flexible 800-seat main auditorium that can be swiftly changed from a proscenium theatre to an arena. Despite increased financial difficulties and a greater emphasis on commercial entertainment (*Cats, Les Misérables*), the New Norse dialect theatre, in its new surroundings, continued to maintain its tradition of presenting bold and innovative productions. Peter Palitzsch returned in 1986, after a hiatus of more than twenty years, to direct his own robust, Walentin-designed version of Brecht's *Mother Courage*, featuring Liv Ullmann in the demanding title role. A year later, the veteran Danish director Sam Besekow undertook the mighty task of mounting the first complete stage production of *Kejser og Galilæer* (*Emperor and Galilean*), Ibsen's sprawling dramatization of the clash between Christianity and paganism in the reign of the Roman emperor Julian. Helge Hoff Monsen's nonrepresentational scenography located this rhetorical seven-hour performance in the simplest of settings – a bare, checkered stage, black chairs, and a large projected map of the Roman world of the fourth century – while his stylized costumes combined long, flowing caftans worn over black tuxedos. In 1989, this same designer chose a similarly abstract approach for Kjetil Bang-Hansen's new production of *The Pretenders*, in which heavy, padded costumes, menacing warriors in mesh masks, and a shadowy, geometrical set evoked an atmosphere of primitive violence and savagery underlying the struggle between Haakon and Skule for the Norwegian crown.

Among Scandinavia's major institutional theatres, it is Dramaten that has tended to predominate in recent years – due not least to Ingmar

Bergman's return in 1985. Under the leadership of Lars Löfgren, who became its artistic director in that same year, Sweden's national theatre has continued to enjoy the consistent state support necessary to retain its character as a "pure" repertory theatre with a frequently changing program and a strong, permanent ensemble. In addition, Löfgren's fleet of no fewer than five intimate experimental stages has been a key factor in the company's artistic development. "On the smaller stages there is always an element of productive uncertainty, which in turn arouses the interest of the audience," he told a Danish interviewer in 1991. "With a 100-seat house, it is easier both to survive a catastrophe and to experience something truly wonderful."[2] Much as the bicentennial of the Danish Royal Theatre had been a watershed in the theatre of the 1940s, Dramaten's own bicentenary celebrations in 1988 represented a similarly important occasion, both as a reaffirmation of tradition and as a demonstration of a commitment to fresh initiatives. Alongside major productions of Molière, Almqvist, Strindberg, and O'Neill on the main stage, ten new Swedish works were presented on the chamber stages during the jubilee season, written both by newcomers and by established dramatists such as Margareta Garpe and Staffen Westerberg. The cancellation of a new Lars Norén play, *Endagsvarelser* (*Creatures of a Day*), just before its premiere drew an angry public rebuke from Sweden's most prolific and controversial living dramatist, who denounced the "ideological vacuum" created at Dramaten by the influence of what he called "market forces and right-wing influences."[3] Nonetheless, it has often been this theatre's Strindberg-trained ensemble that has given Norén's harrowing domestic quartets of verbal and psychic violence their strongest performances, notably in such productions as *Nattvarden* (*Communion*, 1985), *Stillheten* (*The Silence*, 1988), and *Och ge oss skyggorna* (*And Give Us the Shadows*, 1991).

Apart from Norén's work, however, the appearance of important new plays has been limited in recent years to occasional exceptions like Svend Åge Madsen's *Nøgne masker* (*Naked Masks*), an ingenious Pirandello imitation first performed by Aarhus Theatre in 1987. Otherwise, in Scandinavia as elsewhere at this time, more creative energy and interest seem to be devoted to imaginative revivals, reinterpretations, and transpositions of both the older and more modern classics. Three different Strindberg revivals were included in Dramaten's jubilee season, the most ambitious of which was Lennart Hjulström's restaging of *Master Olof* (27 February 1988), a play which he first directed as a young radical at the Gothenburg

City Theatre in 1969. It was with the verse version of this sweeping historical chronicle that August Lindberg inaugurated Dramaten's new playhouse on Nybroplan in 1908, after which it was revived there both by Olof Molander (1933) and Alf Sjöberg (1951 and 1972). Hjulström joined this select group with a restrained, richly textured mise-en-scène that concentrated attention on the performances of Stellan Skarsgård as the vacillating idealist Olaus Petri (Master Olof) and Max von Sydow as the rugged embodiment of Gert Bookprinter, the fiery renegade in whom the spirit of revolt lives on after Olof's capitulation to the forces of authority.

Later in that same ambitious season at Dramaten, Bergman's acutely simplified rendering of *Long Day's Journey into Night* (16 April 1988) established an entirely different approach to a different kind of classic. The choice of this particular play was obviously influenced by the strength of the acting ensemble Bergman was able to bring together for this precisely balanced quartet of family sorrow. Jarl Kulle, who had played Edmund in the world premiere of O'Neill's play on the same stage thirty-two years previously, was a self-ironic and sympathetic James Tyrone, every inch an actor. Bibi Andersson's portrayal of Mary Tyrone made her the centripetal emotional force in the drama. As Edmund, the younger son and the playwright's alter ego, Peter Stormare depicted a deathly pale spiritual sufferer with burning eyes – a figure whose alienation bore an entirely different cast than that of the fiercely rebellious Hamlet he had created for Bergman the previous season. As the fourth member of the quartet, Thommy Berggren's portrait of the disillusioned elder son Jamie was regarded by some critics as the strongest acting performance of all, "a grinning but all too clear-sighted boozer on the brink of despair."[4] Reading the play almost as a conductor reads a musical score, Bergman succeeded in gathering these four distinctive voices and cadences together in a deliberately orchestrated chamber symphony of moods, contrasting tones, arias, and silences. His taut stage version, which cut more than an hour from the play's gruelling running time of four and a half hours, was a distillation calculated to stress what Bibi Andersson refers to in an interview as "the electric moments of life that come not when we're talking but in the moments of indirection and in the silences between us."[5]

As part of Bergman's total rejection of the conventions of psychological naturalism with which this play is almost always associated in performance, the cluttered interior described in O'Neill's stage directions was resolutely dismantled. Instead, the naked, unadorned setting designed by

Gunilla Palmstierna-Weiss was a place of limbo cut off from the outer world of familiar reality. On a small, lighted platform furnished with a scattering of significant objects and hemmed in by the encroaching darkness that surrounded it on all sides, the interlocked spiritual and psychological histories of the four Tyrones were enacted – or, perhaps, reenacted, if we see the play as the poet's dream. Nothing, in other words, was "true to life" here except the inner truth and torment of the human beings themselves. In this nonreferential space, unrelated to place or the passage of time, projected, obliquely angled images (a house facade, a window, a door, clouds, and, at last, a bare tree of silent promise) appeared and disappeared in the background like fleeting, dreamlike glimpses of a fractured reality. Thus, what the audience saw was a performance space for visions, dreams, and memories – above all, the memories of the poet Edmund with his black notebook, at once the captive and the observer of his life's bitter experiences. In a highly stylized mise-en-scène that revealed and commented on the concurrency of past and present, both Edmund and the others often only turned away from someone else's scene, rather than leaving the stage. At the end of the play, after the others had left the platform and had disappeared slowly into the wings, Edmund remained behind, picked up his notebook thoughtfully, and walked away. As he turned for a last look at the empty stage of his memories, the projection of a spreading, leafless tree, with its suggestion of renewed life, filled the background.

The sharpness of Bergman's directorial image of *Long Day's Journey* is, in fact, typical of virtually all the productions he has directed at Dramaten since 1984, when his bleak, strongly metatheatrical rendering of *King Lear* served notice of what was to follow. When he returned to Dramaten on a permanent basis the following year, after eight prolific years at the prestigious Residenztheater in Munich, he brought with him a profound regard for the emotional daring and intensity of German ensemble acting, together with a resolve to adopt new methods of work when he returned to Sweden. "I believe we have a great deal to learn from the best of German theatre," he said as he prepared to leave his Munich experience behind him. "It's not a question of going home and suddenly standing up and being a dictator. That's not the point. It's just that we can do more – we can always do more. The actors here teach you that all the time."[6] As such, rather like the stimulus provided by Reinhardt's guest performances seventy years ago, Bergman's (no less hotly debated) influence can be said to have opened a new window on the contemporary European theatre beyond

Plate 69 The final image in the Bergman production of O'Neill's *Long Day's Journey into Night* (Dramaten, 1988), with Peter Stormare as Edmund. Stage design by Gunilla Palmstierna-Weiss.

Scandinavia's borders. The change in his own attitude and approach has been clearly in evidence in the succession of "impossible" plays he has continued to attempt at Dramaten during this period – in the tough, defiant emotionality of his *Hamlet* (1986); in the clockwork precision of his ensemble in *Long Day's Journey into Night*; in the cool, shimmering formality of his *Madame de Sade* (1989); in the sheer ebullience of his reconstituted *Peer Gynt* (1991); and in the rich theatrical feast he made of *The Winter's Tale* (1994).

Of these productions, perhaps the best illustration of the blend of exactitude and emotional boldness in Bergman's method is his staging of the strange and potentially intransigent *Madame de Sade*, by the Japanese novelist–dramatist Yukio Mishima. Although no direct use was made of the Noh tradition with which this work is often associated, the orchestrated formalism and grace of Bergman's production at Lilla scenen (8 April 1989) carved out a style that was just as controlled and disciplined as the highly codified Noh form itself. Beneath a composed facade of elegant feminine gestures and rococo gowns, a virulent obsession seemed to grip the six women who calmly discuss the infamous exploits of the imprisoned de Sade. Where other directors of this impossibly disquisitory play have often failed, Bergman succeeded by translating Mishima's verbal rhetoric into a visual and choreographic rhetoric in which the slightest change in facial expression – a look, a smile, a raised eyebrow – carried significance. Under such tense conditions as these, the mere turn of a head or the snap of a fan that is opened or closed was capable of causing an emotional earthquake. Musicality, the musical arrangement of phrases and pauses, and emotional crescendos in language and movement patterns governed this performance from beginning to end. "With stylized refinement in each pose and gesture, the actors take their places on stage *en face* or in profile," one reviewer remarked. "They move as if to the measures of an inaudible music – flowing, rhythmical, and pleasantly melodious."[7] In this manner, the explicitness of the shocking images of brutality and sexual depravity that engulf Mishima's text were deliberately submerged beneath a ritualized surface of ceremony and elegance that served to intensify the audience's emotional responsiveness to the subtext of implicit violence and cruelty.

To strengthen the sense of proximity and actor–audience rapport that Bergman considers essential for this particular play, he and his designer, Charles Koroly, extended the stage of Dramaten's largest studio theatre out over the first five rows of the auditorium. A simple, symmetrical framework of deep-red columns and arches defined the open, semi-elliptical playing area. At the back of this fixed, neutral space, projected images created a shifting sequence of purely allusive visual motifs. At first, the delicate outline of a cherry tree was seen against a pastel background. This muted image gave way in the second act to the more disturbing impression of a raging fire. In the final act one saw what seemed to be a black sky filled with storm clouds. The aim here was obviously not to illustrate a concrete action in concrete terms, however, but rather to confront the audience with purely suggestive images of a state of mind – visual corollaries, as it were, to the process of spiritual disintegration which, to varying degrees, all six of de Sade's women undergo during their eighteen years of waiting for his release. This multifaceted process of collapse from within acquired – at least in this particular production – the emotional clarity and beauty of musical variations on a theme for six voices, scored in three distinctly phrased movements.

A further, more complex illustration of Bergman's use of mise-en-scène as the externalization of a play's inner crisis is his Swedish restaging of *A Doll's House* (17 November 1989). As in his other approaches to Ibsen, he again stripped away the play's traditional period setting and realistic conventions in an effort to lay bare its inner essence – the "despair, spiritual conflict, and dread" Ibsen describes in the memorandum he titled "Notes for a Modern Tragedy." In this production, however, Bergman adopted an even more overtly self-reflexive, metatheatrical style, which transposed the drama to a place where the illusion of reality played, so to speak, no part at all and the demarcation between past and present vanished along with it. Leif Zern described his impression of the experience as "chamber music for five voices," in which "the wide angle of the camera observes both time present and time gone by."[8] Glimpsed behind the action, enlarged images of other rooms from another time appeared like faded photographs from an old album. On a small, sparsely furnished platform in the midst of empty space, Pernilla Östergren's Nora played out (or, perhaps, replayed) her life's struggle surrounded by the four silent, shadowy presences who populate and define her world. Around the periphery of the low platform, waiting for their cues to step in upon it as actors in Nora's drama, sat Helmer, Mrs. Linde, Dr. Rank, and Krogstad. As in his Munich production of the same work at the Residenztheater eight years earlier, this visual device created an ironic double perspective that stressed Bergman's image of this play as a drama of destiny and entrapment, in which Nora is conscious from the outset of her frustration and her longing to break out of this unbreakable pattern of roles, masks, and games in which she finds herself confined. In his Stockholm version, Nora's final "escape" – in this case out through the auditorium – became much more deeply ambiguous, juxtaposed as it was with the silent presence of a little girl who, seen first at the outset with her doll (another significant silent player), now stood unnoticed in the background, watching her mother make her exit from the time-stopped world of the play.

In his production of *Peer Gynt* the following season (27 April 1991), Bergman took a new, buoyantly poetic approach to an Ibsen play he had directed very differently in Malmö thirty-four years earlier. In this grave and somber *Peer Gynt*, humor and even farce were never absent for very long; poetry was spoken without affectation, irony stressed without bitterness, deep emotional feeling expressed without the slightest sentimentality. Using a disciplined ensemble of thirty-five actors and extras, almost all of whom played at least two and usually three or more roles, the performance distilled Ibsen's expansive poetic drama into three tightly organized movements, with a total running time of just under four hours. Created specifically for Dramaten's small 160-seat studio, Målarsalen (The

Paint Shop), the spatial concept and setting (designed by Lennart Mörk) directly expressed Bergman's interpretation of the play as an inner journey through what he called "a world of Peer's imagination that we see created before us."

In essence, neither Peer nor the audience ever left the interior of Mother Aase's rough, wooden cottage, with its colored windows stuffed with rags and its slightly skewed walls covered with faded floral wallpaper. The fixed topography of this setting, which extended well into the auditorium of this little theatre, thus became the arena for Peer's monodrama, in which change took place with the swiftness of a poet's or a dreamer's thought. A simple, totally flexible rectangular platform capable of being raised or lowered or tilted on edge became, at will, a precipitous cliff or a banquet table, the forbidding wall of a madhouse or the pitching and rolling deck of a ship in a storm. In this dream of life, passing time, and death, anything was possible and likely in the eager, irrepressible, child-like imagination of the Peer created by Börje Ahlstedt. The reality of his long journey – to Haegstad, to the Ronde, to Morocco, to Cairo, and home again – was a purely theatrical reality enacted on the small stage-upon-the-stage that changed color for each movement, from red to white to somber black. The configurations of characters whom he met on his way were always drastically different in appearance and yet somehow always the same. The result was a system of mirrors, in which each experience or encounter was reflected in constantly changing and distorted guises. In this drama of analogous situations, the very act of repetition was, in itself, the essence of Peer's squandered life. At the end of the play, an observant spectator would have noticed that the grandfather clock, which could be heard continually ticking away the hours and the years, had stopped; its hands again indicated seven, the exact moment at which the performance had begun.

A theatre of alternatives

Although Bergman's remarkable series of introspective, emotionally charged distillations of the classics has had a profound effect on the development of Scandinavian theatre in recent years, it has by no means inhibited the proliferation of alternative and widely divergent performance choices and styles. Psychological and social relevance was, for example, the underlying objective of Wilhelm Carlsson's trenchant modern stage version of *Maria Stuart*, which played at Dramaten simultaneously with *Madame de Sade* in 1989. In this instance, Schiller's (purely imaginary) epic encounter between Queen Elizabeth and Mary Stuart became, in the respective performances of Gunnel Lindblom and Bibi Andersson, both an archetypal and a purely human power struggle between two women "taken down to an everyday plane where," as one critic put it, "they could as well be two middle-aged schoolteachers battling over a job as vice-principal."[9] Holberg, too, was furnished with a more "accessible" contemporaneity when Lars Knutzon staged his adaptation of *The Political Tinker* at the Danish Royal Theatre in 1991, with the versatile veteran Henning Moritzen as the would-be politician Herman von Bremen. Here, however, the director's concern was to transpose the play's "curlicued" language to a more colloquial and topical idiom that would, he argued, be better understood by a contemporary public. In a revealing program note, Moritzen also described his own sense of Holberg's dialogue as "a monument you must first work your way into and then find your way out of on the other side and act completely as if it were Neil Simon or Chekhov. Failing that, you will find yourself struck in the words . . . and the audience will not understand what you are saying." Much more radical means of stimulating renewed interest in a classical text were invoked in the Swedish director Staffan Valdemar Holm's unusual paraphrase of *Miss Julie*, which his New Scandinavian Experimental Theatre presented in Copenhagen in 1992. Intended, in Holm's words, to emphasize "the sexual ritual and the ritual of death" rather than the psychological motivation in Strindberg's drama, his antitragic quotation of it was, in essence, a kind of pornographic Punch-and-Judy show acted on a shallow, stylized relief stage in front of a white-tiled kitchen (or slaughterhouse or toilet) wall. Displayed in this harshly lit theatricalist setting and accompanied by a pounding tom-tom, the performance's hardcore sex sequences accentuated the brutal, animalistic nature of the struggle for dominance waged by Julie and Jean.

In contrast to productions such as Holm's *Julie* and Knutzon's *Political Tinker*, which paid no particular regard to authorial intentions, the reconstituted *Mourning Becomes Electra* directed by Jan Maagaard at the Danish Royal Theatre that same season (6 December 1991) took the emotional and psychological premises of O'Neill's tragedy as a basic point of departure for a fresh interpretation. In itself, Maagaard's tightly focused four-hour "condensation" of this monumental nine-act classical imitation could justly be compared to Molander's stage versions of Strindberg and O'Neill. Also Molander-like was the precision with which the mise-en-scène used stage space, sculptural lighting, and figure compositions in a simplified framework to suggest the essence of O'Neill's realistic/symbolic New England setting. Johannes Leiacker's expressive stage design for the Mannon house evoked an impression of "an immense mausoleum, a temple of death outlined against a fiery, blood-red evening sky."[10] Outside the house, where Lavinia (Electra) and her mother Christine (Clytemnestra) await the return of Ezra Mannon (Agamemnon), a simple, stylized portico composed of eight white steps and four towering, two-dimensional white columns created the effect of a masklike facade. Within the interior it concealed, where enlarged images of Mannon ancestors brooded, a criss-crossed network of steep, narrow stairways suggested a Piranesi prison world – or possibly, as Jens Kistrup was inclined to see it, "the Freudian subconscious made visible."[11] In this shadowy, nonrepresentational mind-space, small but effective changes in the lighting and the set moved the action swiftly from one "place" to the next. The crucial turning point when Lavinia discovers and swears to avenge Ezra's murder was, for example, a moment of elemental passion staged in the simplest terms, in a shaft of piercing light that turned the figures of father and daughter and the bed on which they sat into a blaze of light in the darkness. In general, the core of Maagaard's directorial concept was its crystallization of the trilogy's multiple psychological conflicts into the overriding emotional reality of the central, irreconcilable clash between the young, stern Lavinia of Benedickte Hansen ("a fire of ice behind a pair of watchful eyes burning with inhuman ideals," Kistrup thought) and the sensual, ruthless, desperate Christine created by Kirsten Olesen in the image of her previous roles as Ibsen's Rebecca West and Euripides' Electra.

At the farthest end of the spectrum from the style of empathetic emotional identification exemplified by Maagaard's *Electra* has been the rowdy iconoclasm of Peter Langdal, whose radical quotations and deconstructions of the classics have had a major impact on the Scandinavian theatre of the past decade. In 1984, at the age of twenty-seven, Langdal began to attract critical and popular attention with the antitraditionalist revival of *Erasmus Montanus* that he staged at Copenhagen's Betty Nansen Theatre, subsequently his principal base of operations. Although the ostensible occasion for the event was the tricentenary of Holberg's birth, the slangy, rough-and-tumble tone of Langdal's popularized version (retitled *The Return of Erasmus Montanus*) was anything but reverential. Designer Karin Betz, his regular collaborator, located the action in what was scarcely a

Plate 70 Johannes Leiacker's skeletal exterior for O'Neill's *Mourning Becomes Electra*, directed by Jan Maagaard at the Danish Royal Theatre, 1991. Orin Mannon (Mikael Birkkjær) is seen here flanked by his mother Christine (Kirsten Olesen, *left*) and his sister Lavinia (Benedikte Hansen).

room or even a "setting" at all – merely a neutral semicircle of rough boards that suggested a circus arena. Circus was, in general, a governing metaphor in the performance. The cast, most of whom were experienced revue comics, wore costumes and makeup that alluded to carnival or circus figures, while Erasmus himself was a bespectacled variant of a white-faced clown. The central paradox in Holberg's comedy – that the insufferable student is brought to renounce not only his folly but also the truth (that the earth is indeed round) – was given an added twist in an interpolated Langdal epilogue in which, after apparently having tunneled their way from the other side of the globe, two stage Chinamen emerged in bewilderment from a hole in the stage floor.

Although the claim has been made on Langdal's behalf that in, for example, his Holberg productions he attempts to restore the play to a style of theatre more akin to that of Holberg's own day, it seems more correct to say that his exuberant Artaudian anarchy shatters all ordered, academic concepts of "style." While it is still too soon to be certain where his jack-in-the-box theatre of gags and pratfalls will eventually lead, it has already undergone significant variations. An invitation from Morten Grunwald to open his new Gasworks Theatre with a production of *A Midsummer-Night's Dream* in 1986 prompted a different kind of Langdal–Betz experiment, tailored to the unusual requirements of the immense, dome-shaped interior of the Eastern Gasworks storage tank that Grunwald converted into one of Scandinavia's most interesting theatre spaces. In the midst of the sharply raked, three-sided auditorium, Betz erected an open, flexible setting that consisted solely of a bare, octagonal wooden floor and a small, curtained stage for musicians. Under the dome, above the audience, Oberon and his fairy realm held sway, an androgynous Puck flew, and even Helena could be seen wheeling a bicycle along one of the high catwalks in the old storage tank. In contrast to Peter Brook's brilliantly abstract *Dream*, which seems in some other respects to have served as a model, Langdal's production transposed the action to a more specific period framework, a fictive world of the 1950s. In his radical deconstruction of the play, any vestige of its poetic dimension was obliterated by the clown-show stunts of the rude mechanicals and the fairies, and by the unforeseen farcical improvisations of all concerned. Even before the play itself began, the audience encountered the actors in Grunwald's spacious lobby, where the entrance of the players took place – in true circus-clown fashion – in two old automobiles, one crammed with the mechanicals and the other carrying the four lovers and their courtly hosts, Theseus and Hippolyta (who, as in Brook's production, became Oberon and Titania in the fantastical woodland scenes).

Despite the fact that Langdal described his freewheeling paraphrase of *A Midsummer-Night's Dream* as "a demonstration of youth's potential for breaking through with its happiness in a pinstriped society," this and other of his early experiments were characterized chiefly by their ebullient eclecticism rather than their ideological intent. By the time he directed *The Threepenny Opera* at Dramaten in 1988, however, a more serious undertone of social indignation was apparent beneath the raucous surface of theatrical fun and games. Both in this production and in his subsequent Copenhagen revival of *Schweyk in the Second World War* (1993), Langdal attempted – with mixed results – to forge a fresh approach to Brecht's plays, cleansed of what he regards as the outdated conventions and didacticism of orthodox epic theatre. ("We wanted change, but we also wanted entertaining theatre – which is not the same thing as mindless theatre," he remarked before the premiere of *Schweyk*.[12]) In his more clearly focused reinterpretation of *The Threepenny Opera*, the customary Langdal blend of caricature, anachronism, broad farcical exaggeration, and close actor –

Plate 71 An unusually robust Polly (Inga-Lill Andersson) hammers her point home with a wooden mallet in Peter Langdal's rough-and-tumble interpretation of Brecht's *The Threepenny Opera*. Dramaten, 1988.

audience contact was used in a new way, as an unexpected means of reinforcing Brecht's trechant satire of a depraved social system ruled by greed and lust. In the process, Jens Kistrup observed in *Berlingske Tidende* (17 October 1988), he took the work back to its sources: "to the Berlin cabarets of the 1920s, the classical parodies of opera and operetta, and the film farces of the Chaplin era with their fist-fights, their wild chases, and their keystone cops." The flexible setting provided by Karin Betz placed the action in what seemed to be the interior of an old cinema, where an antiquated projector flashed Brecht's titles on a screen and a ten-man jazz orchestra from the twenties played Kurt Weill's familiar music. The end result was a dissonant mixture of sinister farce and mocking sentiment – an outlandish cinematographer's cartoon of reality, as it were, in which Peachum's beggars, Macheath's gangsters, and Jenny's whores stopped from time to time to watch and study the audience whose manners and morals they mimicked.

Two widely divergent views of theatre are represented in Langdal's extroverted quotations of the classics and Bergman's introspective, emotionally grounded transpositions of them. The essential theatricality of the theatre, the intimacy of the rapport between actor and spectator, and the banishment of all naturalistic conventions of staging are key principles common to the work of both directors – yet the result to which their application leads is sharply different in each case. The contrast between them is especially apparent in the respective productions of two seminal works they have both chosen to direct in recent years – *Peer Gynt* and *Hamlet*. The radical reworking of *Peer Gynt* that Langdal presented at his Betty Nansen Theatre (18 March 1989) was – not entirely unlike Bergman's version of the play two years later – a distillation that focused on the inner, imaginative journey of Ibsen's protagonist. The stage on which it was acted was a black, steeply raked slope that eliminated – as did Bergman's scenic concept – the representationalism of conventional scenery. Here, however, the similarities ended. Langdal's "activated lyrical reading" of the play divided itself into three compact "sets" ("just like a jazz concert or a tennis match," he noted), in each of which a different actor in the small ensemble played Peer. The action unfolded to the accompaniment of a new musical score played by Pierre Dørge and his New Jungle Orchestra – a mélange of jazz, rock, folk, and voodoo numbers designed ("just like film music") to evoke mental images of the various stations on Peer's pilgrimage through the world. As part of a deconstructive process that invited the audience's critical scrutiny without precluding its emotional response, Dørge's eight musicians also joined Langdal's six actors in performing the numerous speaking roles. The fractured protagonist who emerged from the "creative chaos" of Langdal's psychoanalytical exploration was neither a poet nor a dreamer, but rather a social misfit beset by the trolls of his own misguided egocentricity. His journey ended not, as in Bergman's production, in the arms of a redemptive Solveig but literally in a madhouse. Solveig's mountain hut, perched atop Betz's sloping stage, was painted on the bare wall of the theatre by Peer himself, watched by white-coated attendants and serenaded by an operatic Norwegian soprano's rendering of Grieg's rhapsodic closing song.

Disjuncture, the use of anachronism, and the dissonant clash of conflicting moods and images are techniques used by both Bergman and Langdal, but with different objectives and results. In the famous Bergman *Hamlet*, first staged in 1986 and subsequently seen on tour from Tokyo to Moscow, deliberate anachronisms, a jangling clash of styles, and an open defiance of the play's traditions all bespoke a more comprehensive sense of disorder and chaos in Hamlet's universe – a disjointedness so profound that any attempt to "set it right" inevitably seemed a futile and even absurd endeavor. In the scene of Polonius' brutal murder (and it was that in this production), the antiheroic Hamlet created by Peter Stormare even paused to scrawl the word "blood" in red chalk on the black background – an action that called attention both to the moral anarchy and violence of the world around him and to his own corruption at its hands. In a performance that began to the ironic accompaniment of *The Merry Widow* and ended in a roar of rock music and blazing machine guns as Fortinbras and his modern-day storm troopers came crashing through the rear wall to continue the casual slaughter, no room was left for catharsis. Horatio's recital of "carnal, bloody, and unnatural acts" found no hearers, as he was summarily dragged outside to be shot. Then, as the bodies of Gertrude and Claudius were roughly dumped into Ophelia's open grave, the corpse of Hamlet was placed on a high stage beneath an inferno of glaring lights, to be photographed and videotaped for posterity. Viewed in this harsh metatheatrical context, Hamlet's fall became, in the words of one commentator, "a death without hope, without consolation, without any mitigating circumstances – a crucifixion devoid of belief and without any resurrection."[13]

Langdal's *Hamlet* (3 October 1992) was, on the other hand, "antitragic" in an entirely different sense. Its overtly comedic tone approached broad farce in the antics of the Players and the Gravediggers (acted by Rosencrantz and Guildenstern). Built around a deliberately prosaic Hamlet (Søren Pilmark) who presented himself as the spectator's affable, commonplace contemporary, this production was essentially an ironic commentary on the "correct" response to the Hamlet myth and its familiar moments and passages – at least one of which, Horatio's "flights of angels" speech (v.ii) was only mouthed by the actor rather than actually being spoken. In general, this jarring paraphrase of Shakespeare's tragedy used every available means to challenge the audience's conventional expectations. The result was a *Hamlet* enacted on an imitation wing-and-border stage as "a super-exciting folk comedy, a shattering but touching thriller full of terror . . . but also full of humor and clowning that is by no means underplayed in this version."[14]

In many respects, Langdal's work has come to resemble that of such noted German directors as Peter Stein and Peter Zadek, whose radical quotations of the classics are designed to establish a critical distance that openly questions the underlying social and political assumptions of the text. In his invocation of creative anarchy, however, the young Danish director seems to hark back to Artaud's denunciation of "the idolatry of fixed masterpieces," based on his insistence that "we have the right to say what has been said and even what has not been said in a way that belongs to us, a way that is immediate and direct, corresponding to present modes of feeling and understandable to everyone."[15] Sometimes, in Langdal's case, the result is a purely idiosyncratic experiment that teeters on the brink of travesty. One such instance was his *Richard 3* (28 August 1994), an impressionistic 75-minute monologue conceived as a sarcastic rejoinder to a rather turgid full-dress revival of *Richard III* then being staged at the Royal Theatre by Jan Maagaard. Langdal's actionless meditation was played on a raised black arena stage erected by Karin Betz over the stalls of the Betty Nansen Theatre. Surrounded by the audience seated in the balcony, this open space conveyed the impression of a seedy hotel room, furnished with such predictable items as a red sofa-bed, a red telephone, a white washbasin, a black Bible, a mini-bar, and a television set. Alone except for a young woman who lay motionless on the bed, a tough, witty street fighter (Jesper Christensen) played the villain with gusto as he recounted (or, more likely, fabricated) the course of events and intrigues that brought him to the throne. To the dismay of some critics, no attempt whatsoever was made to create a believable portrait of Shakespeare's protagonist, "that foul defacer of God's handiwork." Instead, in the spirit of Artaud's credo that "a violent and concentrated action is a kind of lyricism," Langdal's intent was plainly to summon up a tactile, consciously disruptive image of the isolation and acute self-awareness that are Richard's chief characteristics in the original text.

Plate 72 Strindberg's remorseless opponents, Alice (Marie Göranzon) and her husband Captain Edgar (Jan Malmsjö) confront one another in Lars Norén's 1993 production of *The Dance of Death*, in a closed, windowless interior arranged by Charles Koroly in Dramaten's smallest stage space.

At Dramaten some months earlier an altogether different yet comparably expressive use of theatrical space and spectator proximity was demonstrated by Lars Norén in his widely discussed revival of *The Dance of Death* (13 November 1993). Norén's production, which marked his debut as a director, was conceived specifically for Fyran (The Furnace Room), the smallest of Dramaten's experimental stages, the minimalist proportions of which were the direct physical correlative of an underlying atmosphere of existential confinement and closure in which the characters in Strindberg's drama seemed trapped. Charles Koroly's semiabstract setting suggested a barren, windowless mausoleum of a room, sparsely furnished with a glass-top table and dilapidated tubular chairs that obscured any firm sense of period. Beyond an open double doorway, the wall of a mysterious inner chamber formed a shifting background that mirrored the changing moods in the implacable sexual struggle which rages between Captain Edgar (Jan Malmsjö) and his wife Alice (Marie Göranzon) on their silver wedding anniversary. There was no separate "auditorium" as such. Instead, the battleground for this relentless marital warfare was flanked on three sides by a single row of seats for fewer than fifty spectators, who thus found

Plate 73 The moving platform on which Leontes (Börje Ahlstedt), Hermione (Pernilla August), and Polixenes (Krister Henriksson, behind the masked child) were rolled in at the beginning of Bergman's version of Shakespeare's *The Winter's Tale* (Dramaten, 1994). Stage design by Lennart Mörk.

themselves literally in the midst of the harrowing psychic encounter. In a sense, this insistence on close involvement reflected Norén's determination in his own plays to implicate his audience as directly as possible in the ceremonies of domestic violence perpetrated by his characters. His choice of stage for *The Dance of Death* corresponded, Leif Zern observed in *Dagens Nyheter* (15 November), "to an interpretation of the play which accentuates the fact that it resembles a ritual, a form of spiritual journey. And for a ritual to take place, the observers must be transformed into participants. We are seated along three walls while the actors entice us to make the journey together."

On a wholly different scale, both the element of ritual and the realignment of the actor–spectator relationship were similarly essential features in the lavish production of *The Winter's Tale* directed by Ingmar Bergman on Dramaten's main stage later the same season (29 April 1994). Like *Fanny and Alexander*, his expansive farewell gesture as a filmmaker, Bergman's richly textured stage version of Shakespeare's romance was a fairy tale of life, in which the presence of that virulent and contagious human malice which has preoccupied his art was similarly overcome – by magic if not by logic. "A sad tale's best for winter," the young Mamillius tells his mother Hermione, and both his line and the toy theatre with which he played in the opening scene suggested the crux of Bergman's concept of the play as a performance within the performance, enacted by aristocratic dinner guests at a stately country home, set in the age of the Swedish poet Jonas Love Almqvist, whose haunting, bittersweet songs provided a running musical commentary on the action. When the real audience arrived, a performance seemed to be already in progress as elegant and laughing ladies and gentlemen in evening dress danced in a formal rotunda setting that recreated Dramaten's own marble foyer. When the time for the evening's "entertainment" came, some of the guests took places in the auditorium as spectators, while others prepared to play their parts in Shakespeare's drama. This mingling of "actors" and "spectators" was a dominant motif in a performance in which an ironic sense of metatheatricality was never absent – from the outset, when two masked children virtually identical to Fanny and Alexander dragged in a rolling platform on which Leontes, Hermione, and their guest Polixenes sat, to the conclusion of the drama, when living statues gathered in the rotunda to witness what amounted to the resurrection of Hermione from the bier on which she lay.

Within the permanent architectural setting designed by Lennart Mörk, moods, seasons, and locations changed by means of modulations in the lighting and the chromatic values of the costumes, the occasional introduction of simple screens and set pieces, and the evocative music and lyrics of Almqvist's songs. The outcome was a deeper, clearer perception of unity in this complicated, apparently bifurcated play, whose two halves were here shown to be mutually reinforcing counterparts of one another. The logic of the interpretation was, however, that of a dream or a fairy tale, in which probability was continually disrupted by the calculated improbability of Bergman's wry, anachronistic interpolations – the huge polar bear with flashing red eyes that pursued Antigonus to the accompaniment of silent-film piano music; the roaring motorbike on which Autolycus arrived to peddle his wares; the illuminated red devil who scampered across the stage to mock Leontes' repentance; and not least the wind-up alarm clock carried by Time, in this performance a stately marchioness in black crinoline. The only reality that mattered, in other words, was the intense human reality of the suffering and grievous divisions brought on by the violent, obsessive jealousy of Börje Ahlstedt's Leontes. Most painful of all was the trial and public himiliation of the shackled, anguished Hermione of Pernilla August, watched by the ever-present chorus of onlookers whose stylized, shifting patterns of movement recorded the violent emotional peripeties of the performance. "Events unfolded with the relentless logic of jealousy," one critic remarked. "It seemed for a moment that we left the world of the theatre behind and came face to face with the veritable passions themselves."[16]

In the end, the "lawful spell" cast by Bibi Andersson's indomitable Paulina ("It is required / You do awake your faith") precipitated not a trick but a miracle that absolved the penitent, nearly blind Leontes and restored his wronged queen to life. The rejoicing of the multiple reunions was muted, however, and Bergman's production gave the last line to a serving girl who returned the action to its original country-house frame by announcing that dinner was waiting. After everyone else had left, Time slowly rose from her place in the front row of the auditorium and remounted the stage. As she in turn departed, she placed her ticking clock on the stage floor, as a reminder of her sovereignty.

Taken together, these three recent classical reinterpretations by Bergman, Norén, and Langdal exemplify a plurality of approaches and alternatives that has remained characteristic of contemporary Scandinavian theatre at its best. In addition to the so-called institutionalized theatre represented by these productions, however, there is also the ever-changing constellation of independent, extra-institutional groups that furnish the Nordic countries with their exceptionally lively theatrical avant-garde. It is to these "free" groups that some Scandinavian critics now look for fresh innovation and change in the future. "The large institutions in the largest cities have based themselves primarily on a 'safe' audience" and hence on "a policy of 'safe' programming within a familiar repertoire and a familiar idiom," one observer of current Norwegian theatre asserts. "There has been little desire and need for experiment and active innovation."[17] By contrast, many of today's group theatres, disillusioned with the political utopianism of their forerunners in the sixties and seventies, have focused instead on specific projects involving radically new forms of performance text, based on the mutual collaboration of actors, dancers, musicians, and pictorial artists. The BAK Troupe, one of Norway's most notable project theatres of the present day, aptly describes itself as "seeking a means of expression based on different methods of dramatic composition," in which "the visual, textual, and musical images are of equal weight in the action on stage."[18] The climate of freer experimentation fostered by such activity has, in turn, enabled an emerging playwright like Cecile Løveid to evolve her own highly unconventional, imagistic style of dramaturgy. In an entirely different but comparable context, the Ung Klara (Young Klara) group organized in Stockholm by Suzanne Osten more than twenty years ago continues to furnish promising young playwrights like Barbro Smeds and Gunilla Linn Persson with the encouragement and training they need to develop their own work with the language and semiotics of theatre.

The future consequences of these and other challenges to the status quo remain to be seen. In a more general sense, however, theatre in Scandinavia seems always to be straining in revolt against being taken for granted, always searching out new ways of regenerating itself in the face of our changing and increasingly difficult times. At its most vital, as we have seen, it is often a self-reflexive theatre that insistently draws attention to its own theatrical nature, to the ironic proposition that a stage performance is, after all, a performance, implicating its audience in a direct manner that distinguishes it conclusively from the electronic media that threaten its existence. Many years ago, Kjeld Abell published a whimsical but thought-provoking dramatic sketch called "Night on Kongens Nytorv," in which the two bronze statues seated on the square outside the Danish national theatre conduct a nocturnal conversation. "There must be something to conquer, not just something to entertain," the statue of Holberg is thought to have told the statue of Oehlenschläger on this occasion. "The theatre is a fairy-tale world at war with the world outside." Such a theatre lives by continuing to demand more of its audience than the price of admission. Its healthy pluralism and its appetite for creative experimentation spring, as we have seen, from its long history of openness toward new and changing methods and styles of theatrical expression.

Notes

1 Early stages

1 Quoted in Torben Krogh, *Ældre dansk Teater: en teaterhistorisk Undersøgelse* (Copenhagen, 1940), p. 14. More recent scholarship on the Danish sources is found in *Dansk litteraturhistorie* (9 vols., Copenhagen, 1983–5), I, pp. 559–66 (Søren Kaspersen), II, pp. 195–257 (Janne Risum), and notes in IX. A discussion of the relationship between religious iconography and theatre is found in Søren Kaspersen, "Bildende Kunst, Theater und Volkstümlichkeit im mittelalterlichen Dänemark," *Popular Drama in Northern Europe in the Later Middle Ages: a Symposium*, eds. Flemming G. Andersen, et al. (Odense, 1988), pp. 201–50.

2 Quoted in Krogh, *Ældre dansk Teater*, p. 15.

3 Hans Jørgen Helms, *Næstved St. Peders Kloster* (Næstved, 1940), p. 339. Quoted in Kaspersen, *Popular Drama*, p. 205.

4 Quoted in Øyvind Anker, *Scenekunsten i Norge fra fortid til nutid* (Oslo, 1968), p. 6.

5 Cf. Krogh, *Ældre dansk Teater*, p. 300 and H. Wiers-Jensen, "De liturgiske Skuespil og deres sidste Udløbere i Norden i Stjernespillet," *Norvegia sacra*, I (Christiania, 1921), pp. 62f.

6 Quoted in Nils Personne, *Svenska teatern*, I (Stockholm, 1913), p. 16.

7 Quoted in Sophus Birket-Smith, *De tre ældste danske Skuespil* (Copenhagen, 1874), p. 12.

8 Martin Luther, *Tischreden*, IV (Berlin, 1848), p. 592.

9 Quoted in Personne, *Svenska teatern*, I, p. 17.

10 H. J. Huidtfeldt-Kass, *Christiania Theaterhistorie* (Copenhagen, 1876), p. 22.

11 Ibid., pp. 17–18.

12 Henrik Schück, *Messenius* (Stockholm, 1920), p. 91.

13 Cf. Klaus Neiiendam, *Renaissanceteatret i Danmark* (Copenhagen, 1988), pp. 74–5. *Karrig Niding* was also staged in Randers in 1606.

14 Personne, *Svenska teatern*, I, p. 29.

15 *Susanna*, ed. Aage Jørgensen (Copenhagen, 1972), p. 50 and note 181.

16 Ibid., p. 54 and note 152.

17 *Kong Salomons Hyldning*, ed. with commentary by Allan Karker (Copenhagen, 1973), p. 30. There is some question whether these lines refer to one mansion or two (Jerusalem and Zion).

2 Theatre at court

1 Quoted in Otto Andrup, "Hoffet og dets Fester," *Danmark i Fest og Glæde*, eds. J. Clausen and T. Krogh (Copenhagen, 1935), I, p. 316.

2 Quoted in Torben Krogh, "Optogsbilleder fra Christian IV's Kroningsfest," *Musik og Teater* (Copenhagen, 1955), p. 3.

3 Quoted in Torben Krogh, *Hofballetten under Christian IV og Frederik III* (Copenhagen, 1939), p. 19.

4 N. Slange, *Christian den Fierdes Historie* (Copenhagen, 1749), I, p. 33.

5 Cf. Neiiendam, *Renaissanceteatret i Danmark*, p. 142.

6 Quoted in Krogh, *Hofballetten*, p. 24.

7 Cf. Agne Beijer, "Le théâtre en Suède jusqu'à la mort de Gustave III," *Revue d'histoire du théâtre*, 2–3 (1956), p. 148.

8 Letter of 22 August 1655, quoted in R. Nyerup, *Efterretninger om Kong Frederik den Tredie og de mærkværdigste i Danmark og Norge under hans Regiering indtrufne Begivenheder* (Copenhagen, 1817), pp. 419–20.

9 Ibid., pp. 418–19.

10 Ibid., p. 421.

11 Krogh, *Hofballetten*, p. 90ff.

12 Program quoted ibid., pp. 98–100.

13 A comprehensive account of these seventeenth-century troupes in Sweden is found in Gunilla Dahlberg, *Komediantteatern i 1600-talets Stockholm* (Stockholm, 1992).

14 Ibid., p. 173.

15 Treu's list is discussed in detail in Krogh, "Københavns første teater," *Musik og Teater*, pp. 39–40.

16 Ibid., pp. 41–2.

17 Eiler Nystrøm, *Den danske Komedies Oprindelse* (Copenhagen, 1918), pp. 47–8.

18 Cf. Klaus Neiiendam, *Om iscenesættelsen på teatret i Lille Grønnegade* (Copenhagen, 1981), pp. 21–2. The floor plan of the theatre is printed here and discussed in detail.

3 Playhouses of the eighteenth century

1 Nystrøm, *Den danske Komedies Oprindelse*, p. 77n.

2 In "Just Justesens Betænkning" (i.e. Reflections), the preface to the first (unpaginated) edition of his comedies: *Comoedier / Sammenskrevne for / Den nye oprettede / Danske Skue-Plads / ved Hans Mikkelsen* (Copenhagen, 1723).

3 Nystrøm, *Den danske Komedies Oprindelse*, p. 101.

4 From the theatre's playbill, reproduced and commented in, e.g. Anne E. Jensen, *Teatret i Lille Grønnegade 1722–1728* (Copenhagen 1972), pp. 156, 158.

5 "Just Justesens Betænkninger over Comoedier," a 5.

6 Ibid., a 6.

7 The Danish actors had first commissioned Holberg's less successful fellow

dramatist, J. R. Paulli, whose intrigue comedy *Den seendes Blinde (The Blind Man's Vision)* had been acted in 1723, to write a play on the theme of the Christmas party and the masquerade, but Paulli's awkward attempt, called *Jule-Stuen og Maskarade,* failed to please Montaigu. It remained for Holberg to realize the subject matter's potential by reorganizing it into two separate "display comedies."

8 Quoted in Torben Krogh, *Studier over de sceniske Opførelser af Holbergs Komedier* (Copenhagen, 1929), p. 62, where the production is discussed in detail.

9 Personne, *Svenska teatern,* I, pp. 71–2.

10 The document is translated in *National Theater in Northern and Eastern Europe, 1746–1900,* ed. Laurence Senelick (Cambridge, 1991), p. 18.

11 L. Thura, *Hafnia Hodierna* (Copenhagen, 1749), p. 303; cf. Harald Langberg, *Kongens Teater: Komediehuset på Kongens Nytorv 1748–1774* (Copenhagen, 1974), p. 38.

12 Cf. Frederick J. Marker, *Hans Christian Andersen and the Romantic Theatre* (Toronto, 1971), p. 5. Considerable confusion about these matters arises in Bent Holm, "Fra pomp til pædagogik," *Dansk teaterhistorie: Kirkens og kongens teater,* eds. Kela Kvam, Janne Risum, and Jytte Wiingaard (Copenhagen, 1992), p. 116.

13 P. Rosenstand-Goiske, *Den dramatiske Journal,* ed. C. Behrens (Copenhagen, 1915–19), I, p. 4.

14 Torben Krogh, *Studier over Harlekinaden paa den danske Skueplads* (Copenhagen, 1931), pp. 81–2.

15 Ibid., p. 80.

16 Thomas Overskou, *Den danske Skueplads i dens Historie* II (Copenhagen, 1856), p. 309.

17 Rosenstand-Goiske, *Den dramatiske Journal,* I, p. 55.

18 Cf. Agne Beijer, *Drottningholms slottsteater på Lovisa Ulrikas och Gustaf IIIs tid* (Stockholm, 1981), pp. 21–2.

19 *Gustaviansk teater skildrad af Pehr Hilleström,* eds. Agne Beijer and G. Hilleström (Stockholm, 1947), p. 13.

20 Cf. Torben Krogh, *Christian VII's franske Hofaktører* (Copenhagen, 1947), p. 4 *passim.*

21 Clemens Tode, *Dramatiske Tillæg til Museum og Hertha: Kritik og Antikritik* (Copenhagen, 1784), p. 62.

22 A. M. Nagler, *A Source Book in Theatrical History* (New York, 1959), p. 296.

4 The Gustavian age

1 The petition is translated in Senelick, *National Theater in Northern and Eastern Europe,* pp. 66–7. Also in English, two new collections of conference papers have added substantially to the scholarship about this period. *Gustav III and the Swedish Stage: Opera, Theatre and Other Foibles,* ed. Bertil H.

Van Boer (Lewiston, N.Y., 1993) is devoted mainly to the music of Joseph Martin Kraus, but also contains useful essays on acting practices (Jacqueline Martin) and stage design (Barbro Stribolt). *Gustavian Opera: an Interdisciplinary Reader in Swedish Opera, Dance and Theatre 1771–1809*, ed. Inger Mattson (Uppsala, 1991) is a sumptuously illustrated compilation of symposium papers that discuss the intellectual climate, theatre architecture, stage design, operatic repertory, music, and ballet of the period.

2 Personne, *Svenska teatern*, 1, p. 89.

3 Cf. Kerstin Derkert, "Dramatiska teatern under den gustavianska tiden," *Den svenska nationalscenen: Tradition och reformer på Dramaten under 200 år*, ed. Claes Rosenqvist (Stockholm, 1988), p. 15.

4 Cf. Niklas Brunius, "'Alltid ny och alltid densamma': Lars Hjortsbergs spelstil," *Dramaten 175 År: Studier i svensk scenkonst*, eds. G. M. Bergman and Niklas Brunius (Stockholm, 1963), p. 127.

5 Letter dated 31 October 1788 (French spelling sic): *Bref rörande teatern under Gustaf III 1788–92*, ed. Eugène Lewenhaupt (Stockholm, 1894), p. 52.

6 See Clewberg's memoranda in Senelick, *National Theater in Northern and Eastern Europe*, p. 77.

7 Cf. Gösta M. Bergman, "Dramaten–från Bollhuset till Nybroplan," *Dramaten 175 År: Studier i svensk scenkonst*, p. 20.

5 The romantic theatre and its aftermath

1 Gösta M. Bergman argues the case for Lagerbjelke as an early "director" in *Regi och spelstil under Gustaf Lagerbjelkes tid vid Kungl. teatern* (Stockholm, 1946).

2 The production is reconstructed in detail in Torben Krogh's *Danske Teaterbilleder fra det 18de Aarhundrede* (Copenhagen, 1932), pp. 253–67.

3 August Bournonville, *My Theatre Life*, trans. Patricia N. McAndrew (Middletown, CT, 1979), p. 647.

4 *Svada*, ed. M. C. Bruun (1786), p. 179f.

5 Bournonville, *My Theatre Life*, p. 38.

6 Goethe's Rules for Actors in Nagler, *A Source Book in Theatrical History*, p. 429.

7 J. E. Rydqvist, *Heimdall*, 52 (1829), p. 206.

8 Quoted in Claes Hoogland and Gösta Kjellin, eds., *Bilder ur svensk teaterhistoria* (Stockholm, 1970), p. 146.

9 Overskou, *Den danske Skueplads*, iv (1862), p. 449.

10 "Fortegnelse paa Ombygninger, Forandringer og Forbedringer ved Det Kongelige Comediehus, 1825–50." Manuscript in the Royal Theatre library.

11 H. C. Andersen, *Mit Livs Eventyr*, ed. H. Topsøe-Jensen (Copenhagen, 1951), i, p. 99.

12 Translation by Peter Briton in *National Theater in Northern and Eastern Europe*, ed. Senelick, p. 39.

13 *Heimdall*, 15 (1831); cf. Kirsten Gram Holmström, "Kungliga teatern kring 1830 speglad genom *Heimdall*," *Den svenska nationalscenen*, ed. Rosenqvist, p. 79.

14 Karl Mantzius, *Skuespilkunstens Historie i det 19de Aarhundrede* (Copenhagen, 1922), p. 76.

15 Edvard Brandes, *Om teater*, ed. Harald Engberg (Copenhagen, 1947), p. 110.

16 Johanne Luise Heiberg, *Et Liv gjenoplevet i Erindringen*, 5th edn (Copenhagen, 1973–4), II, p. 227.

17 *Nord og Syd*, Ny Række, 2 (1857), p. 60.

18 *Fædrelandet*, 30 June 1861.

19 Edvard Brandes, *Dansk Skuespilkunst* (Copenhagen, 1880), p. 31.

20 Nathan David in *Kjøbenhavns Flyvende Post*, 64 (1830), II.

21 Heiberg, *Et Liv*, i, pp. 162, 157.

22 Quoted in Erik Aschengreen, *Fra Trine Rar til Maria Stuart: En studie i fru Heibergs kunst* (Copenhagen, 1961), p. 17.

23 Georg Brandes, *Samlede Skrifter* (Copenhagen, 1899), I, p. 452.

24 Søren Kierkegaard, *Crisis in the Life of an Actress*, trans. Stephen Crites (London, 1967), p. 87.

25 Heiberg, *Et Liv*, II, p. 70.

26 Clemens Petersen in *Fædrelandet*, 16 January 1860.

27 Heiberg, *Et Liv*, IV, p. 130.

28 P. Hansen, *Den danske Skueplads: Illustreret Theaterhistorie* (Copenhagen, 1889–96), III, p. 83.

29 Edvard Brandes, *Dansk Skuespilkunst*, p. 36.

30 Translation by Børge Gedsø Madsen, in *Playwrights on Playwriting*, ed. Toby Cole (New York, 1961), p. 17. Strindberg's essay, "On Modern Drama and Modern Theatre," dates from 1889, two years before the publication of *Et Liv* (for Fru Heiberg's remark, see IV, p. 99).

31 Harald Christensen, *Det Kongelige Teater i Aarene 1852–9* (Copenhagen, 1890), p. 246.

32 Bournonville, *My Theatre Life*, p. 351.

33 Quoted in Henning Fenger, *The Heibergs*, trans. and ed. Frederick J. Marker (New York, 1971), p. 168.

34 Quoted ibid., p. 169.

35 Heiberg, *Et Liv*, IV, p. 271.

36 Brandes, *Dansk Skuespilkunst*, pp. 342–3.

37 First published by Francis Bull in *Politiken*, 28 October 1949.

6 Ibsen's Norway

1 Tharald Høyerup Blanc, *Christiania Theaters historie 1827–77* (Christiania, 1899), p. 109.

2 *Morgenbladet*, 19 October 1851; translated by Peter Briton in *National Theater in Northern and Eastern Europe*, ed. Senelick, p. 150.

3 Øyvind Anker, *Den danske teatermaleren Troels Lund og Christiania Theater* (Oslo, 1962), pp. 46–7.

4 *Dansk Kunstblad*, 16 July 1836.

5 Quoted in Roderick Rudler, "Den første nasjonale scenograf i Norge," *St. Halvard* (1974), p. 69.

6 *Morgenbladet*, 9 December 1855.

7 Translation by Michael Meyer in *Henrik Ibsen: the Making of a Dramatist 1828–1864* (London, 1967), I, p. 140.

8 *Aftenbladet*, 28 April 1865.

9 See Blanc, *Christiania Theaters historie*, p. 195.

10 Translated by Peter Briton in *National Theater in Northern and Eastern Europe*, ed. Senelick, p. 156.

11 Quoted in Barrett H. Clark and George Freedley, eds. *A History of Modern Drama* (New York and London, 1947), p. 48.

12 *Christiania-Posten*, 28 September 1850; translated by Peter Briton in *National Theater*, ed. Senelick, p. 162.

13 Quoted in *The Oxford Ibsen*, ed. James Walter McFarlane, I (London, 1970), pp. 591–2.

14 Quoted ibid., pp. 600–3.

15 Quoted in Meyer, *Henrik Ibsen*, p. 168.

16 *Illustreret Nyhedsblad*, 13 December 1857.

17 Bent Lorentzen, *Det første norske teater* (Bergen, 1949), p. 102.

18 Quoted in Meyer, *Henrik Ibsen*, p. 113.

19 These and subsequent regulations are reprinted in Lorentzen, *Det første norske teater*, pp. 105–6.

20 Cf. Roderick Rudler, "Ibsens teatergjerning i Bergen" in *Drama och teater*, ed. Egil Törnqvist (Stockholm, 1968), p. 61.

21 *The Oxford Ibsen*, ed. McFarlane, I, pp. 373–4.

22 Cf. Rudler, "Ibsens teatergjerning," p. 66.

23 Max Grube, *The Story of the Meininger*, trans. Ann Marie Koller (Coral Gables, 1963), p. 81.

24 Georg Nordensvan, *Svensk teater och svenska skådespelare* (Stockholm, 1918), II, p. 363.

25 *Aftenposten*, 16 October 1900; quoted Rune Johansen, *Teatermaler Jens Wang: dekorasjonskunst og sceneteknikk* (Oslo, 1984), p. 126.

26 Cf. Johansen, *Teatermaler Jens Wang*, p. 127.

27 Georg Brandes, *Henrik Ibsen: a Critical Study* (London, 1899; reprinted 1964), p. 21.

28 Ludvig Jopsephson, "Om teater-regi" in *Perspektiv på teater*, eds. Ulf Gran and Ulla-Britta Lagerroth (Stockholm, 1971), p. 17.

29 *Aftenposten*, 25 February 1876.

30 Hellen Lindgren in *Ny ill. tidning*, 25 March 1885; quoted in Nordensvan, *Svensk teater*, II, p. 361.

7 Naturalism and the director

1 Edvard Brandes, "Et Vendepunkt i dansk Teaterhistorie," *Det nittende Aarhundrede* (1875), p. 95.

2 Edvard Brandes, *Fremmed Skuespilkunst* (Copenhagen, 1881), p. 279.

3 Brandes, *Dansk Skuespilkunst*, p. 36.

4 *Nationaltidende*, 17 October 1880.

5 George Brandes, *Kritikker og Portrætter* (Copenhagen, 1879), p. 210.

6 *Ude og Hjemme*, 4 May 1872.

7 Herman Bang, *Kritiske Studier* (Copenhagen, 1880), pp. 186–7.

8 *Ude og Hjemme*, 4 January 1880.

9 Herman Bang, *Masker og Mennesker* (Copenhagen, 1910), p. 223.

10 Brandes, *Om teater*, ed. Engberg, p. 110.

11 Ove Rode, "Et Teater i Forfald," *Verdens Gang*, 18 October 1882.

12 A small, black, undated *maskinmesterbog* (pp. 415–21) and the Royal Theatre's *Regieprotokol*, 18 October 1874 (pp. 115–16) provide what evidence we have concerning the staging of this production. (Royal Theatre Library).

13 Quoted in Robert Neiiendam, *Det kgl. Teaters Historie 1874–90*, IV (Copenhagen, 1927), p. 60.

14 *Ibsen: Letters and Speeches*, ed. Evert Sprinchorn (New York, 1964), p. 232.

15 *Ude og Hjemme*, 2 September 1883.

16 Nordensvan, *Svensk teater*, II, p. 351.

17 Archer's letter to his brother Charles about the Lindberg production was first published in *Edda*, 31 (1931), pp. 456–9; reprinted in *The Oxford Ibsen*, ed. McFarlane, V (London, 1961), p. 481.

18 Sven Lange, *Meninger om Teater* (Copenhagen, 1929), p. 246.

19 *Politiken*, 28 September 1922.

20 Henri Nathansen, *William Bloch* (Copenhagen, 1928), p. 86.

21 *Perspektiv på teater*, eds. Gran and Lagerroth, p. 28.

22 Ibid., p. 14.

23 Nathansen, *William Bloch*, p. 46.

24 Ibid., p. 75.

25 Letter to Edvard Fallesen, head of the Royal Theatre, dated 12 December 1882: *Ibsen: Letters and Speeches*, ed. Sprinchron, p. 215.

26 *Berlingske politiske og Advertissements Tidende*, 5 March 1883.

27 *Ude og Hjemme*, 11 November 1883.

28 Letter dated 14 November 1884, *Ibsen: Letters and Speeches*, ed. Sprinchorn, p. 242.

29 Gunnar Heiberg, *Ibsen og Bjørnson paa scenen* (Christiania, 1918). p. 47.

30 *Ibsen: Letters and Speeches*, ed. Sprinchorn, p. 243.

31 Quoted in Berit Erbe, *Bjørn Bjørnsons vej mod realismens teater* (Oslo, 1976), p. 176.

32 Nathansen, *William Bloch*, p. 48.
33 Bloch's holograph promptbook, signed by him on the title page, is bound together with the printed copy of the play submitted to the Royal Theatre on Ibsen's behalf: København: Gyldendalske Boghandels Forlag, 1884, pp. 244. (Royal Theatre Library)
34 *Intelligensbladene*, 12 January 1885, quoted in Erbe, *Bjørn Bjørnsons vej*, p. 198.
35 *Aftonbladet*, 31 January 1885.
36 *Dags-Telegrafen*, 24 February 1885.
37 *Regieprotokol*, 17 March 1881, p. 77. (Royal Theatre Library)
38 Quoted in Carl Rae Waal, *Johanne Dybwad, Norwegian Actress* (Oslo, 1967), p. 147.
39 Octavia Sperati, *Fra det gamle komediehus* (Christiania, 1916), pp. 195–6; translated by Peter Briton in *National Theater in Northern and Eastern Europe*, ed. Senelick, pp. 172–3.
40 *Morgenbladet* (Copenhagen), 24 February 1885.
41 William Bloch, "Nogle Bemærkninger om Skuespilkunst," *Tilskueren* (1896), p. 447.
42 *Berlingske politiske og Advertissements Tidende*, 23 February 1885.
43 *Politiken*, 24 February 1885; reprinted in Brandes, *Om teater*, ed. Engberg, p. 19.
44 Heiberg, *Ibsen og Bjørnson paa scenen*, p. 3.
45 *Ibsen: Letters and Speeches*, ed. Sprinchorn, p. 266.
46 *Illustreret Tidende*, February 1889.
47 *Aftenbladet*, 26 February 1891.
48 *København*, 7 April 1891.
49 *Teatret* (1901–2), p. 60.
50 *Berlingske Tidende*, 9 March 1893.
51 *Dannebrog*, 9 March 1893.
52 Heiberg, *Ibsen og Bjørnson paa scenen*, p. 65.
53 A. Lugné-Poë, *Ibsen* (Paris, 1936), p. 80.
54 *Vort Land*, 1 February 1897.
55 Cf. Johansen, *Teatermaler Jens Wang*, p. 77.
56 Ibid., p. 321.
57 A. Edmund Spender, *Two Winters in Norway* (London, 1902); quoted in *The Oxford Ibsen*, ed. McFarlane, VIII (London, 1977), p. 372.
58 *Aftenposten*, 6 February 1900.
59 *Dannebrog* (Copenhagen), 4 September 1899.
60 Edvard Brandes, *Holberg og hans Scene* (Copenhagen, 1898), p. 51.
61 Vilhelm Andersen in *Tilskueren* (1901), p. 509.
62 Lange, *Meninger om Teater*, p. 247.
63 Ny Kongelige Samling 4451, Regiebøger 6. (Royal Library, Copenhagen)
64 Ny Kongelige Samling, Regiebøger 3. (Royal Library)
65 *Verdens Gang*, 3 May 1906.

8 The Strindberg challenge

1 Quoted in Nordensvan, *Svensk teater*, II, p. 276.
2 *Open Letters to the Intimate Theatre*, trans. Walter Johnson (Seattle, 1967), pp. 289–90. Subsequent references in the text are identified as *LIT*.
3 In his autobiography *The Son of a Servant*, trans. Evert Sprinchorn (Garden City, NY, 1966), p. 6.
4 "On Modern Drama and Modern Theatre," trans. Børge Gedsø Madsen, *Playwrights on Playwriting*, ed. Cole, p. 17.
5 Letter dated 14 December 1887, published in *Politiken*, 18 December 1887.
6 Quoted in Gunnar Ollén, *Strindbergs dramatik* (Stockholm, 1961), p. 116.
7 Martin Lamm, *August Strindberg* (Stockholm, 1948), p. 178.
8 Letter to the members of the Intimate Theatre, 23 April 1908; cf. August Falck, *Fem år med Strindberg*, 2nd edn (Stockholm, 1935), p. 207.
9 Michael Meyer's translation of the preface is used here.
10 Quoted in Ollén, *Strindbergs dramatik*, p. 162.
11 In a letter to Bonniers dated 21 August 1888; cf. *August Strindbergs dramer*, ed. Carl Reinhold Smedmark, III (Stockholm, 1964), p. 363.
12 Quoted in Ollén, *Strindbergs dramatik*, p. 162.
13 Cf. Carl Öhman, *Strindberg and the Origins of Scenic Expressionism* (Michigan and Helsingfors, 1961).
14 Letter to Gustaf af Geijerstam, 17 October 1888: *Brev*, ed. Torsten Eklund, XIII (Stockholm, 1972), p. 19.
15 Letter dated 8 April 1889: *Brev*, ed. Eklund, VII (Stockholm, 1961), p. 308.
16 The holograph manuscript of Bloch's report, "Beretning om Shakespeare-scenen i München," is among his papers in the Royal Library, Copenhagen (UF 334, 1).
17 Tor Hedberg in *Svenska Dagbladet*, 20 November 1900.
18 Cf. Richard Bark, *Strindbergs drömspelteknink – i drama och teater* (Lund, 1981), p. 80.
19 John Nordling in *Idun*, 13 (1900), no. 47.
20 Rudolf Björkman in *Svensk kunst*, 6 (1907), p. 9.
21 Bo Bergman in *Dagens Nyheter*, 18 April 1907.
22 Cf. Gösta M. Bergman, *Den moderna teaterns genombrott 1890–1925* (Stockholm, 1966), pp. 291–2.
23 Falck, *Fem år med Strindberg*, p. 143.
24 Letter dated 9 May 1908: ibid., p. 192.
25 Sven Söderman in *Stockholms Dagblad*, 22 January 1908.
26 Vera von Kraemer in *Social-Demokraten*, 22 January 1908.
27 Falck, *Fem år med Strindberg*, p. 163.
28 Ibid., p. 193.
29 August Falck, "Strindberg som teaterägare och regissör," *Svenska scenen*, 2 (1916), nos. 29–30, p. 224.

30 Strindberg's marked, annotated copy of the Fuchs book is preserved among his papers in the Strindberg Museum, Stockholm.

31 Letter to Falck dated 14 September 1910: Falck, *Fem år med Strindberg*, pp. 317–18.

32 Pär Lagerkvist, *Modern Theatre: Seven Plays and an Essay*, trans. Thomas R. Buckman (Lincoln, NE, 1966), p. 31.

9 The modernist revolt

1 Lagerkvist, *Modern Theatre*, pp. 12–13.

2 Valdemar Vedel in *Nationaltidende*, 10 October 1920.

3 Lagerkvist, *Modern Theatre*, p. 38.

4 Cf. Freddie Rock, *Tradition och förnyelse: Svensk dramatik och teater från 1914–1922* (Stockholm, 1977), p. 38. This doctoral dissertation lists and analyzes the theatrical repertory of the period indicated.

5 *Göteborgs-Posten*, 30 March 1918.

6 Quoted in Bergman, *Den moderna teaterns genombrott*, p. 428.

7 *Nya Dagligt Allehanda*, 4 May 1917.

8 Kjeld Abell, *Teaterstrejf i Paaskevejr*, 2nd edn (Copenhagen, 1962), pp. 33, 37.

9 *Scenen* (1921), no. 1, p. 7.

10 Siegfried Jacobsohn, "Vignettes from Reinhardt's Productions" in *Max Reinhardt and His Theatre*, ed. Oliver M. Sayler (New York, 1924), p. 325.

11 Quoted in Kirsten Jacobsen, *Johannes Poulsen som iscenesætter* (Copenhagen, 1990), p. 16; this study contains a detailed reconstruction of the Poulsen *Everyman*.

12 Svend Leopold in *Vort Land*, 27 December 1914.

13 Letter to Haagen Falkenfleth, editor of *Nationaltidende*: see Frederick J. Marker and Lise-Lone Marker, *Edward Gordon Craig and "The Pretenders": a Production Revisited* (Carbondale, 1981), p. 31.

14 *Forum*, 12 February 1916, p. 83f.

15 *Acta Academica*, 1 (1916), p. 6.

16 Quoted in Bergman, *Den moderna teaterns genombrott*, p. 527.

17 "Några moderna teaterproblem," *Perspektiv på teater*, eds. Gran and Lagerroth, pp. 52–60.

18 Per Lindberg, *Regieproblem* (Stockholm, 1927), p. 53.

19 Per Lindberg, *Kring ridån* (Stockholm, 1932), p. 143.

20 *Svenska Dagbladet*, 21 November 1920.

21 Lagerkvist, *Modern Theatre*, p. 19.

22 Cf. Svend Erichsen, "Tredivernes nye Dramatiker" in *Teatret paa Kongens Nytorv 1748–1948*, eds. Alf Henriques, Torben Krogh, et al. (Copenhagen, 1948), p. 256.

23 Letter to Johannes Poulsen: Ulla Poulsen Skou, *Skuespilleren og Danserinden*

(Copenhagen, 1958), II, p. 20.

24 *Scenen* (1919), no. 13: Molander's early articles on directing are reproduced in his autobiography, *Detta är jäg*... (Stockholm, 1961), pp. 143ff.

25 *Scenen* (1923), quoted in Per Bjurström, *Teaterdekoration i Sverige* (Stockholm, 1964), p. 96.

26 Lagerkvist, *Modern Theatre*, p. 26.

27 Lindberg, *Kring ridån*, pp. 98, 146.

28 On the Russian guest performances in 1922/3, see Ulla-Britta Lagerroth, "Den modernistiska teaterns genombrott på nationalscenen," *Den svenska nationalscenen*, ed. Rosenqvist, pp. 295–8.

29 Kristian Elster, *Teater 1929–1939* (Oslo, 1941), p. 159.

30 *Svenska Dagbladet*, 24 September 1927.

31 Herbert Grevenius, "Den stora folkteatern," *En bok om Per Lindberg* (Stockholm, 1941), p. 126.

32 Quoted in Thomas R. Buckman, "Pär Lagerkvist and the Swedish Theatre," *Tulane Drama Review*, 6 (Winter 1961), p. 85.

33 "Några synspunkter på Pär Lagerkvists dramatik" (1940), reprinted in Per Lindberg, *Bakom masker* (Stockholm, 1949), pp.15–17.

34 See Marker and Marker, *Edward Gordon Craig and "The Pretenders"*, pp. 17–18 *et passim.*

35 Edward Gordon Craig, *A Production, Being Thirty-two Collotype Plates of Designs prepared and realized for The Pretenders of Henrik Ibsen and presented at the Royal Theatre, Copenhagen, 1926* (Oxford, 1930), p. 16.

36 "Gordon Craig om Teatret og Digterne," *Berlingske Aftenavis*, 27 October 1926. Craig's emphasis.

37 *Berlingske Tidende* (15 November 1926), in a separate article on the scenery and the audience that supplements Gulman's review.

38 "Regissören är teaterns tusenkonstnär" (interview), *Stockholms-Tidningen*, 10 December 1922.

39 "Möten med Strindberg," *Svenska Dagbladet*, 21 January 1949.

40 Program article for Bergman's production of *The Pelican* at the Malmö City Theatre, 25 November 1945; reprinted more fully in Lise-Lone Marker and Frederick J. Marker, *Ingmar Bergman: a Life in the Theatre* (Cambridge, 1992), p. 60.

41 *Stockholms-Tidningen*, 26 October 1935.

42 *Dagens Nyheter*, 26 October 1935.

43 *Berlingske Tidende*, 2 May 1956; reprinted in Frederik Schyberg, *Ti Aars Teater 1929–1939* (Copenhagen, 1939), p. 141.

44 Vagn Børge, *Strindbergs mystiske Teater* (Copenhagen, 1942), p. 283.

45 Preproduction interview in *Stockholms-Tidningen*, 26 February 1937.

46 *Göteborgs Handels- och Sjöfartstidning*, 2 March 1937; reprinted in Agne Beijer, *Teaterrecensioner 1925–1949* (Stockholm, 1954), pp. 245–6.

47 *Perspektiv på teater*, eds. Gran and Lagerroth, pp. 88–9.

48 Letter dated 29 October 1964, printed with other letters in Randolph Goodman, *From Script to Stage: Eight Modern Plays* (New York, 1971), p. 162.

49 Interview with Rut Tellefsen in Goodman, *From Script to Stage*, p. 163.

50 Kaj Munk, *Himmel og Jord* (Copenhagen, 1942), p. 221.

51 "Realisme – ?", *Forum* (October 1935), reprinted in Kjeld Abell, *Synskhedens gave*, ed. Elias Bredsdorff (Copenhagen, 1962), p. 189.

52 Ibid., p. 193.

53 Reprinted in Schyberg, *Ti Aars Teater*, p. 149.

54 Quoted by Harald Naess in *Five Scandinavian Plays* (New York, 1971), p. 294.

55 Quoted in Knut Nygaard and Eiliv Eide, *Den Nationale Scene 1931–1976* (Oslo, 1977), p. 102.

10 Tradition and experiment since 1945

1 *Prisma*, 3 (1950), nos. 5–6; reprinted in Alf Sjöberg, *Teater som besvärejlse*, eds. Sverker R. Ek et al. (Stockholm, 1982), pp.58–9.

2 Ibid., p. 57.

3 *Göteborgs Handels- och Sjöfartstidning*, 4 February 1946; reprinted in Beijer, *Teaterrecensioner*, p. 465.

4 Sjöberg, *Teater*, p. 63.

5 *Perspektiv på teater*, eds. Gran and Lagerroth, p. 111.

6 Sjöberg, *Teater*, p. 90.

7 Cf. Sverker R. Ek, "Den svenska nationalscenen förverkligad?", *Den svenska nationalscenen*, ed. Rosenqvist, p. 407.

8 *Kungliga dramatiska teatern 1788–1988*, eds. Erik Näslund and Elisabeth Sörenson (Stockholm, 1988), pp. 161, 165.

9 *Dramaten*, 50/1 (1975), reprinted in Sjöberg, *Teater*, p. 127.

10 Sjöberg, *Teater*, pp. 136, 138.

11 *Perspektiv på teater*, eds. Gran and Lagerroth, p. 115.

12 *Ord och bild* (1964), quoted in Sjöberg, *Teater*, p. 374.

13 Sjöberg, *Teater*, 162.

14 Quoted in Harald Engberg, *Brecht på Fyn* (Odense, 1966), II, p. 141.

15 Interview in *Information*, 20 January 1959.

16 Sjöberg, *Teater*, p. 162.

17 Ibid., p. 197.

18 Alf Sjöberg, "Brechts *Galilei*: en introduktion," *Dramaten*, 42 (1974/5), p. 6.

19 Sjöberg, *Teater*, p. 201.

20 Ingmar Bergman, *Laterna Magica* (Stockholm, 1987), p. 207.

21 Unless otherwise noted, observations by Bergman are taken from two interviews published in Lise-Lone Marker and Frederick J. Marker, *Ingmar Bergman: Four Decades in the Theatre* (Cambridge and New York, 1982).

22 Quoted in Henrik Sjögren, *Ingmar Bergman på teatern* (Stockholm, 1968), pp. 311–12.

23 Marker and Marker, *Ingmar Bergman: Four Decades*, p. 222.

24 *Theater heute*, 10 (1967), p. 8. Melchinger first saw the production when it was revived at Dramaten (and also visited Berlin) in 1967.

25 Frederick J. Marker and Lise-Lone Marker, "Bergman and the Actors: an Interview," *Theater*, 21 (Winter/Spring 1990), p. 77.

26 Henrik Sjögren, *Regi: Ingmar Bergman. Dagbok från Dramaten 1969* (Stockholm, 1969), p. 41.

27 Ibid., p. 14.

28 Peter Brook, *The Empty Space* (Harmondsworth, Middlesex, 1972), p. 109.

29 Quoted in P. G. Engel and Leif Janzon, *Sju decennier: Svensk teater under 1900-talet* (Stockholm, 1980), p. 143.

30 Hans Jacob Nilsen, *Peer Gynt: ett anti-romantisk verk* (Oslo, 1948), p. 37.

31 *Det Norske Teatret. femti år 1913–1963*, ed. Nils Sletbak (Oslo, 1963), p. 320.

32 Poul Reumert, *Om teater*, ed. Carl Bergstrøm-Nielsen (Copenhagen, 1971), p. 11.

33 Ibid., p. 100.

34 Ibid., pp. 99–100.

35 "Exeunt" in *Mogens Wieth*, ed. Knud Poulsen (Copenhagen, 1962), p. 62.

36 Jens Bolling in Studioteatret's first program, quoted in Anker, *Scenekunsten i Norge*, p. 55.

37 John Hahn Petersen and Preben Harris in Fiolteatret's program, 1963/4, quoted in Elin Rask, "Køb-og-smid-væk samfundet: Intimscenerne," *Dansk Teaterhistorie 2: Folkets teater*, eds. Kela Kvam, Janne Risum, and Jytte Wiingaard (Copenhagen, 1992), p. 210.

38 *Nya teatertidningen* (1977), no. 2, p. 34.

39 Klaus Hagerup in *Theatre in Norway 1979*, eds. Gunnar Alme et al. (Oslo, 1979), p. 47.

40 Quoted in Anton Fjeldstad, Aage Jørgensen, Margareta Wirmark, and Clas Zilliacus, *Gruppeteater i Norden* (Copenhagen, 1981), p. 69.

41 Quoted in ibid., p. 41.

42 Quoted in ibid., p. 108.

43 This and subsequent statements by Barba are from an interview published by Susanne Marko in *entré teatertidskrift* (1981), no. 3, pp. 4–10.

44 Quoted in Engel and Janzon, *Sju decennier*, p. 114.

11 The plurality of postmodern theatre

1 Interview quoted in Frederick J. Marker and Lise-Lone Marker, "Thalia in the Welfare State: Art and Politics in Contemporary Danish Theatre," *The Drama Review*, 16 (Fall 1982), p. 4.

2 Marianne Juhl, "Teater med vilje," *Weekendavisen* (Copenhagen), 15 March 1991.

3 Interview in *Dagens Nyheter*, 1 January 1988.

4 Lars Linder in *Dagens Nyheter*, 17 April 1988.

5 Frederick J. Marker and Lise-Lone Marker, "Bergman and the Actors," *Theater*, 21 (Spring 1990), p. 78.

6 Marker and Marker, *Ingmar Bergman: a Life in the Theatre*, p. 253.

7 Ingmar Björkstén in *Svenska Dagbladet*, 9 April 1989.

8 *Expressen*, 18 November 1989.

9 Hans Andersen in *Jyllands-Posten* (Aarhus), 15 April 1989.

10 Bettina Heltberg in *Politiken*, 8 December 1991.

11 *Berlingske Tidende*, 8 December 1991.

12 *Berlingske Tidende*, 12 March 1993.

13 Jens Kistrup in *Berlingske Tidende*, 21 December 1986.

14 Jens Kistrup in *Berlingske Tidende*, 5 December 1992.

15 Antonin Artaud, *The Theatre and Its Double*, trans. Mary Caroline Richard (New York, 1958), p. 74.

16 Ulf Sörenson in *Göteborgs-Posten*, 30 April 1994.

17 Jon Nygaard, "Why choose the worst and most costly, when the best is cheapest? On the Contrast between Action and Effect in the Norwegian Theatre," *Nordic Theatre Studies*, 4 (1991), p. 81.

18 Cf. Knut Ove Arntzen, "New Theatre in Norway: From Group Theatre to Project Theatre," *Scandinavica*, 31 (1992), p. 194.

Select bibliography

References to unpublished sources and to reviews and articles in newspapers and periodicals are normally found only in the notes.

General references

Artaud, Antonin. *The Theatre and Its Double*, trans. Mary Caroline Richard. New York, 1958

Barba, Eugenio. *The Floating Islands*. New York, 1978
Beyond the Floating Islands. New York, 1986

Bergman, Gösta M. *Den moderna teaterns genonbrott 1890–1925*. Stockholm, 1966

Brook, Peter. *The Empty Space*. Harmondsworth, Middlesex, 1972

Clark, Barrett H., and George Freedley, eds. *A History of Modern Drama*. New York and London, 1947

Cole, Toby, ed. *Playwrights on Playwriting*. New York, 1961

Fjeldstad, Anton, Aage Jørgensen et al. *Gruppeteater i Norden*. Copenhagen, 1981

Goodman, Randolph. *From Script to Stage: Eight Modern plays*. New York, 1971

Kindermann, Heinz. *Theatergeschichte Europas*. 10 vols. Salzburg, 1957–74

Marker, Frederick J. and Lise-Lone Marker. *Ibsen's Lively Art: a Performance Study of the Major Plays*. Cambridge and New York, 1989
The Scandinavian Theatre: A Short History. Oxford and Totowa, NJ 1975

Nagler, A. M. *A Source Book in Theatrical History*. New York, 1959

Senelick, Laurence, ed. *National Theater in Northern and Eastern Europe, 1746–1900*. Cambridge and New York, 1991

Denmark

Aarhus Teater 1900–1975. Aarhus, 1975

Abell, Kjeld. *Synskhedens gave*, ed. Elias Bredsdorff. Copenhagen 1962
Teaterstrejf i Paaskevejr, 2nd edn. Copenhagen, 1962

Andersen, Flemming G. et al., eds. *Popular Drama in Northern Europe in the Later Middle Ages: a Symposium*. Odense, 1988

Andersen, H. C. *Mit Livs Eventyr*, ed. H. Topsøe-Jensen. 2 vols. Copenhagen, 1951

Aschengreen, Erik. *Fra Trine Rar til Maria Stuart: En studie i fru Heibergs kunst*. Copenhagen, 1961

Aumont, Arthur and Edgar Collin. *Det danske Nationalteater 1748–1889: En statistisk Fremstilling*. 5 vols. Copenhagen, 1896–1900

Bang, Herman. *Kritiske Studier*. Copenhagen, 1880

Maskter og Mennesker. Copenhagen, 1910

Billeskov Jansen, F. J. *Danmarks digtekunst*, 2nd edn. 3 vols. Copenhagen, 1964

Birket-Smith, Sophus. *Studier paa det gamle danske Skuespils Omraade*. 2 vols.
　　Copenhagen, 1883–96

De tre ældste danske Skumespil. Copenhagen, 1874

Bojsen, Else. *Fra "Den Stundesløse" til "Gorm den Gamle": Maskinmesteroptegnelser
　　fra det Kgl. Teater 1782–1785*. Copenhagen, 1982

Borg, Mette. *Sceneinstruktøren Herman Bang*. Copenhagen, 1986

Borg, Mette, Kela Kvam, and Klaus Neiiendam, eds. *Holberg på scenen*.
　　Copenhagen, 1984

Bournonville, August. *Danske Theaterforhold*. Copenhagen, 1866

Mit Theaterliv. 3 vols. Copenhagen, 1848–77. (*My Theatre Life*, trans. Patricia
　　M. McAndrew. Middletown, CT, 1979)

Brandes, Edvard. *Dansk Skuespilkunst*. Copenhagen, 1880

Fremmed Skuespilkunst. Copenhagen, 1881

Om teater, ed. Harald Engberg. Copenhagen, 1947

Brandes, Georg. *Kritikker og Portrætter*. Copenhagen, 1879

Christensen, Einar. *Det kongelige Teaters Skæbnesaar 1931–1935*. Copenhagen, 1935

Christensen, Harald. *Det kongelige Teater i Aarene 1852–9*. Copenhagen, 1890

Clausen, Julius and Torben Krogh, eds. *Danmark i Fest og Glæde*. 6 vols.
　　Copenhagen, 1935–6

Craig, Edward Gordon. *A Production, Being Thirty-Two Collotype Plates of Designs
　　prepared and realized for The Pretenders of Henrik Ibsen and presented at the Royal
　　Theatre, Copenhagen, 1926*. Oxford, 1930

Davidsen, Elisabeth. *Henrik Ibsen og Det Kongelige Teater*. Copenhagen, 1980

Engberg, Harald. *Brecht på Fyn*. 2 vols. Odense, 1966

Teater 1945–1952. Copenhagen, 1952

Fabris, Jacopo. *Instruction in der theatralischen Architectur und Mechanique*, ed.
　　Torben Krogh. Copenhagen, 1930

Fenger, Henning. *The Heibergs*, trans. and ed. with an introduction by Frederick
　　J. Marker. New York, 1971

Friis, N. *Det kongelige Teater: Vor nationale scene i fortid og nutid*. Copenhagen,
　　1943

Friis, Oluf. *Den danske Litteraturs Historie*, 1. Copenhagen, 1945

Gade, Svend. *Mit Livs Drejescene*. Copenhagen, 1941

Gjelten, Bente Hatting. *H. C. Andersen som teaterconnaisseur*. Copenhagen, 1982

Hansen, Günther. *Das Nationaltheater in Odense: Ein Beitrag zur deutsch-dänischen
　　Theatergeschichte*. Emsdetten, 1963

Hansen, Peter. *Den danske Skueplads: Illustreret Theaterhistorie*. 3 vols.
　　Copenhagen, 1889–96

Heiberg, J. L. *Prosaiske Skrifter*. 11 vols. Copenhagen, 1861–2

Vaudeviller. 3 vols. Copenhagen, 1895

Heiberg, Johanne Luise. *Et Liv gjenoplevet i Erindringen.* 5th edn, by Niels Birger
    Warmberg. 4 vols. Copenhagen, 1973–4
Henriques, Alf. *Shakespeare og Danmark indtil 1840.* Copenhagen, 1941
Henriques, Alf, Torben Krogh et al. *Teatret paa Kongens Nytorv 1748–1948.*
    Copenhagen, 1948
Holberg, Ludvig. *Comoedierne,* ed. Carl Roos. 3 vols. Copenhagen and
    Christiania, 1922–4
    Epistler, ed. F. J. Billeskov Jansen. 8 vols. Copenhagen, 1944–54
Jacobsen, Kirsten. *Johannes Poulsen som iscenesætter.* Copenhagen, 1990
Jensen, Anne E. *Studier over europæisk drama i Danmark 1722–1770.* 2 vols.
    Copenhagen, 1968
    Teatret i Lille Grønnegade 1722–1728. Copenhagen, 1972
Jensen, Stig Jarl, Kela Kvam, and Ulla Strømberg, eds. *Dansk teater i 60erne og
    70erne.* Copenhagen, 1983
Kierkegaard, Søren. *Crisis in the Life of an Actress,* trans. Stephen Crites. London,
    1967
Kragh-Jacobsen, Svend and Torben Krogh. *Den kongelige danske Ballet.*
    Copenhagen, 1952
Krogh, Torben. *Christian VII's franske Hofaktører.* Copenhagen, 1947
    Danske Teaterbilleder fra det 18de Aarhundrede. Copenhagen, 1932. (Index by
        Ernst Bræmme and Klaus Neiiendam, Det Teatervidenskabelige Institut,
        1976)
    Hofballetten under Christian IV og Frederik III. Copenhagen, 1939
    Holberg i Det kgl. Teaters ældste Regieprotokoller. Copenhagen, 1943
    Musik og Teater. Copenhagen, 1955
    Oehlenschlägers Indførelse paa den danske Skueplads. Copenhagen, 1954
    Skuespilleren i det 18de Aarhundrede, belyst gennem danske Kilder. Copenhagen, 1948
    Studier over de sceniske Opførelser af Holbegs Komedier. Copenhagen, 1929
    Studier over Harlekinaden paa den danske Skueplads. Copenhagen, 1931
    Ældre dansk Teater: en teaterhistorisk Undersøgelse. Copenhagen, 1940
    (ed.) *Det kgl. Teaters ældste Regiejournal 1781–1787.* Copenhagen, 1927
    (ed.) *Komediehuset paa Kongens Nytorv 1748.* Copenhagen, 1948
Kvam, Kela, Janne Risum, and Jytte Wiingaard, eds. *Dansk teaterhistorie.* 2 vols.
    Copenhagen, 1992
Langberg, Harald. *Kongens Teater: Komediehuset på Kongens Nytorv 1748–1774.*
    Copenhagen, 1974
Lange, Sven. *Meninger om Teater.* Copenhagen, 1929
Leicht, Georg and Marianne Hallar. *Det kongelige Teaters repertoire 1889–1975.*
    Copenhagen, 1977
Mantzius, Karl. *Skuespilkunstens Historie: Klassicisme og Romantik.* Copenhagen, 1916
    Skuespilkunstens Historie i det 19de Aarhundrede. Copenhagen, 1922
Marker, Frederick J. *Hans Christian Andersen and the Romantic Theatre.* Toronto, 1971

Marker, Frederick J. and Lise-Lone Marker. *Edward Gordon Craig and "The Pretenders": a Production Revisited.* Carbondale, 1981

Mitchell, P. M. *A History of Danish Literature.* Copenhagen, 1957

Munk, Kaj. *Himmel og Jord.* Copenhagen, 1942. (First published 1938)

Nathansen, Henri. *Johannes Poulsen.* Copenhagen, 1946

  William Bloch. Copenhagen, 1928

Neiiendam, Karen. *Teatermaleren C. F. Christensens skitsebog fra Pariseroperaen 1839.* Copenhagen, 1989

Neiiendam, Klaus. *Middelalderteatret i Danmark.* Copenhagen, 1986

  Om iscenesættelse på teatret i Lille Grønnegade. Copenhagen, 1981

  Renaissanceteatret i Danmark. Copenhagen, 1988

Neiiendam, Robert. *Breve fra danske Skuespillere og Skuespillerinder 1748–1864.* 2 vols. Copenhagen, 1911–12

  Casinos Oprindelse og Historie i Omrids. Copenhagen, 1948

  De farende Folk: Træk af danske Provinsteatres Historie 1790–1864. Copenhagen, 1944

  Det kgl. Teaters Historie 1874–90. 5 vols. Copenhagen, 1921–30

  Det kgl. Teaters Historie 1890–92, ed. Klaus Neiiendam. Copenhagen, 1970

  Folketeatret 1845–1945. Copenhagen, 1945

  Gennem mange Aar. Copenhagen, 1950

  Mennesker bag Masker. Copenhagen, 1931

  Scenen drager. Copenhagen, 1915

Normann, Jacob Christian. *Holberg paa Scenen.* Copenhagen, 1919

  Teatret. Copenhagen, 1939

Nyerup. R. *Efterretninger om Kong Frederik den Tredie og de mærkværdigste i Danmark og Norge under hans Regiering indtrufne Begivenheder.* Copenhagen, 1817

Nystrøm, Eiler. *Den danske Komedies Oprindelse.* Copenhagen, 1918

Odense Teater 175 År, 1776–1971. Odense, 1971

Overskou, Thomas. *Den danske Skueplads i dens Historie.* 7 vols. Copenhagen, 1854–76

  Den danske Skueplads og Staten. Copenhagen, 1867

  Oplysninger om Theaterforhold 1849–1858. Copenhagen, 1858

Poulsen, Knud, ed. *Mogens Wieth.* Copenhagen, 1962

Rahbek, K. L. *Breve fra en gammel Skuespiller til hans Søn.* Copenhagen and Leipzig, 1782

  Om Skuespilkunsten. Copenhagen, 1809

Rask, Elin. *Det kritiske parterre: Det kgl. Teater og dets publikum omkring år 1800.* Copenhagen, 1972

  Trolden med de tre hoveder: Det kongelige Teater siden 1870, bygningshistorisk og kulturpolitisk. Copenhagen, 1980

Reumert, Poul. *Masker og mennesker,* 3rd edn. Copenhagen, 1963

  Om teater, ed. Carl Bergstrøm-Nielsen. Copenhagen, 1971

Rosenstand-Goiske, Peder. *Den dramatiske Journal*, ed. C. Behrens. 2 vols. and supplement. Copenhagen, 1915–19

Sandfeld, Gunnar. *Thalia i provinsen 1870–1920*. Copenhagen, 1969

Schyberg, Frederik. *Dansk teater i tjugonde århundrade*. Stockholm, 1942
   Dansk Teaterkritik indtil 1914. Copenhagen, 1937
   Teatret i Krig 1939–1948. Copenhagen, 1949
   Ti Aars Teater 1929–1939. Copenhagen, 1939

Skou, Ulla Poulsen. *Skuespilleren og Danserinden*. Copenhagen, 1958

Strømberg, Ulla, and Jytte Wiingaard, eds. *Den levende Ibsen*. Copenhagen, 1978

Swendsen, L. *De københavnske Privatteatres Repertoire 1847–1906*. Supplement 1907–1919. Copenhagen, 1919

Tode, Clemens. *Dramatiske Tillæg til Museum og Hertha: Kritik og Antikritik*. Copenhagen, 1784

Watson, Ian. *Towards a Third Theatre: Eugenio Barba and the Odin Teatret*. London and New York, 1993

Wiingaard, Jytte. *William Bloch og Holberg*. Copenhagen, 1966

Norway

Aarseth, Asbjørn. *Den Nationale Scene 1901–1931*. Bergen, 1968

Anker, Øyvind. *Christiania Theater repertoire 1827–99*. Oslo, 1956
   Den danske teatermaleren Troels Lund og Christiania Theater. Oslo, 1962
   Det Dramatiske Selskab i Christiania. Repertoire 1799–1844. Oslo, 1959
   Henrik Ibsens brevveksling med Christiania Theater 1878–1899. Oslo, 1965
   Kristiania norske teaters repertoire 1852–63. Oslo, 1956
   Scenekunsten i Norge fra fortid til nutid. Oslo, 1968

Ansteinsson, Eli. *Teater i Norge: Dansk scenekunst 1813–1863*. Oslo, 1968

Bjørnson, Bjørn. *Det gamle teater: Kunsten og menneskene*. Oslo, 1937

Bjørnson, Bjørnstjerne. *Artikler og taler*, eds. C. Collin and H. Eitrem. 2 vols. Christiania and Copenhagen, 1912–13

Blanc, Tharald Høyerup. *Christiania Theaters historie 1827–77*. Christiania, 1899
   Henrik Ibsen og Christiania Theater 1850–99. Christiania, 1906
   Norges første nationale scene (Bergen 1850–62): Et bidrag til den norske dramatiske kunsthistorie. Christiania, 1884

Brandes, Georg. *Henrik Ibsen: A Critical Study*. London, 1899

Brandes, Georg and Edvard. *Brevveksling med Bjørnson, Ibsen, Kielland, Elster, Garborg, Lie*, eds. Francis Bull and Morten Borup. Oslo, 1939–41

Bull, Francis. *Tradisjoner og minner*. Oslo, 1946

Bull, Marie. *Minder fra Bergens første nationale scene*, ed. H. Wiers-Jenssen. Bergen, 1905

Bødtker, Sigurd. *Kristiania-premierer gjennem 30 år*, eds. Einar Skavlan and Anton Rønneberg. 3 vols. Christiania, 1923–9

Dale, Johannes A. *Nynorsk dramatikk i hundre år*. Oslo, 1964

Elster, Kristian d. y. *Skuespillerinden Johanne Dybwad: Til belysning af realismen i skuespilkunsten*. Oslo, 1931

Teater 1929–1939, ed. Anton Rønneberg. Oslo, 1941

Erbe, Berit. *Bjørn Bjørnsons vej mod realismens teater*. Oslo, 1976

Fahlstrøm, Alma. *To norske skuespilleres liv*. Oslo, 1927

Frisvold, Øyvind. *Teatret i norsk kulturpolitik: Bakgrunn og tendenser fra 1850 til 1970-årene*. Oslo, 1980

Gjesdahl, Paul. *Centralteatrets historie*. Oslo, 1967

Premierer og portretter. Oslo, 1957

Haakonsen, Daniel. *Henrik Ibsen, mennesket og kunstneren*. Oslo, 1981

Heiberg, Gunnar. *Artikler om teater og dramatikk*, ed. Hans Heiberg. Oslo, 1972

Ibsen og Bjørnson paa scenen. Christiania, 1918

Norsk teater. Christiania, 1920

Huidtfeldt-Kass, H. J. *Christiania Theaterhistorie*. Copenhagen, 1876

Ibsen, Henrik. *Samlede verker* (Hundreårsutgave), eds. Francis Bull, Halvdan Koht, and Didrik Arup Seip. 21 vols. Oslo, 1928–57

Johansen, Rune. *Teatermaler Jens Wang: dekorasjonskunst og sceneteknikk*. Oslo, 1984

Josephson, Ludvig. *Ett och annat om Henrik Ibsen och Christiania Theater*. Stockholm, 1898

Just, Carl. *Litteratur om norsk teater. Bibliografi*. Oslo, 1953

Schrøder og Christiania Theater: Et bidrag til norsk teaterhistorie. Oslo, 1948

Koht, Halvdan. *Henrik Ibsen: Ett diktarliv*, 2 vols. Oslo, 1928–9; 2nd revised edn 1954. (*Life of Ibsen*, trans. and ed. Einar Haugen and A. E. Santaniello. New York, 1971)

Liche, Lise. *Norsk teaterhistorie*. Asker, 1992

Linder, Sten. *Ibsen, Strindberg och andra*. Stockholm, 1936

Lorentzen, Bernt. *Det første norske teater*. Bergen, 1949

Lund, Audhild. *Henrik Ibsen og det norske teater 1857–63*. Oslo, 1925

McFarlane, James Walter, ed. *The Cambridge Companion to Ibsen*. Cambridge and New York, 1994

The Oxford Ibsen. 8 vols. London, 1960–77. (Appendices provide rich source documentation.)

Meyer, Michael. *Henrik Ibsen*. 3 vols. London, 1967–71

Michelsen, J. A. *Det Dramatiske Selskab i Bergen 1794–1894*. Bergen, 1894

Midbøe, Hans. *Peer Gynt, teatret og tiden*. 2 vols. Oslo, 1976–8

Næss, Trine. *Arne Walentin, teatermålar og scenograf*. Oslo, 1978

Nationaltheatret i Kristiania: Festskrift i anledning af Nationaltheatrets aabning 1ste September 1899. Christinia, 1899

Nilsen, Hans Jacob. *Peer Gynt: ett anti-romantisk verk*. Oslo, 1948

Normann, Axel Otto. *Johanne Dybwad: Liv og Kunst*. 2nd edn. Oslo, 1950

Norsk Theaterliv, utgit av Norsk Skuespillerforbund. Bergen, 1923

Nygaard, Knut. *Gunnar Heiberg, teatermannen*. Oslo, 1975

Holbergs teaterarv. Bergen, 1984

Nygaard, Knut and Eiliv Eide. *Den Nationale Scene 1931–1976.* Oslo, 1977

Paulsen, John. *Samliv med Ibsen.* Copenhagen and Christiania, 1906

Paulson, Andreas. *Komediebakken og engen: Femti års teatererindringer.* Oslo, 1932

Reimers, Sophie. *Teaterminner fra Kristiania teater.* Christiania, 1917

Rønneberg, Anton. *Nationaltheatret gjennem femti år.* Oslo, 1949

Skavlan, Einar. *Norsk teater 1930–1953,* ed. Paul Gjesdahl. Oslo, 1960

Sletbak, Nils, ed. *Det Norske Teatret. Femti år 1913–1963.* Oslo, 1963

Sperati, Octavia. *Fra det gamle komediehus.* Christiania, 1916

    Theatererindringer. Christiania, 1911

Sprinchorn, Evert, ed. *Ibsen: Letters and Speeches.* New York, 1964

Steen, Ellisiv. *Det norske nasjonalhistoriske drama 1756–1974.* Oslo, 1976

Svendsen, Arnljot Strømme. *Den Nationale Scene: Det norske repertoire 1876–1974.*
    Bergen, 1975

Svendsen, Arnljot Strømme, Berit Erbe, and Kristen Broch, eds. *Ludvig Holberg,*
    en bergenser uten grenser. Bergen, 1984

Tennant, P. F. D. *Ibsen's Dramatic Technique.* Cambridge, 1948

Theatre in Norway 1979, eds. Gunnar Alme et al. Oslo, 1979

Waal, Carla Rae. *Johanne Dybwad, Norwegian Actress.* Oslo, 1967

Wiers-Jensen, Hans. *Billeder fra Bergens ældste teaterhistorie.* Bergen, 1921

    Nationaltheatret gjennem 25 år, 1899–1924. Christiania, 1924

Wiers-Jensen, Hans and J. Nordahl-Olsen, *Den Nationale Scene: De første 25 år.*
    Bergen, 1926

Wiesener, A. M. *Henrik Ibsen og "det norske Teater" i Bergen 1851–1857.* Bergen, 1928

Winter-Hjelm, K. A. *Af Christiania teaterliv i den seneste tid.* Christiania, 1875

Wolf, Lucie. *Fra Skuespillerinden Lucie Wolfs Livserindringer.* 3rd edn. Christiania,
    1898

Sweden

Arpe, Verner. *Das schwedische Theater von den Gauklern bis zum Happening.*
    Stockholm, 1969

Bark, Richard. *Strindbergs drömspelteknik – i drama och teater.* Lund, 1981

Baur-Heinhold, Margarete. *Baroque Theatre.* London, 1967

Beijer, Agne. *Dramatik och teater.* Lund, 1966

    Drottningholms slottsteater på Lovisa Ulrikas och Gustaf IIIs tid. Stockholm, 1981

    Slottsteatrarna på Drottningholm och Gripsholm. Malmö, 1957

    Teaterrecensioner 1925–1949. Stockholm, 1954

Bergman, Gösta M. *Den moderna teaterns genombrott 1890–1925.* Stockholm, 1966

    Pär Lagerkvists dramatik. Stockholm, 1928

    Regihistoriska studier. Stockholm, 1952

    Regi och spelstil under Gustaf Lagerbjelkes tid vid Kungl. teatern. Stockholm, 1946

    Svensk teater. Strukturförandringar och organisation, 1900–1970. Stockholm, 1970

Bergman, Gösta M. and Niklas Brunius, eds. *Dramaten 175 År: Studier i svensk scenkonst.* Stockholm, 1963

Bergman, Ingmar. *Laterna Magica.* Stockholm, 1987

Beyer, Nils. *Teaterkvällar 1940–1953.* Stockholm, 1953

Bjurström, Per. *Teaterdekoration i Sverige.* Stockholm, 1964

Brandell, Gunnar. *Svensk litteratur 1900–1950,* 2nd edn. Stockholm, 1967

Børge, Vagn. *Strindbergs mystiske teater.* Copenhagen, 1942

Cederblom, H. *Pehr Hilleström som kulturskildare.* Stockholm, 1929

Collijn, Gustaf. *Intimen: Historien om et teater.* Stockholm, 1943

Dahlberg, Gunilla. *Komediantteatern i 1600-talets Stockholm.* Stockholm, 1992

Dahlgren, F. A. *Förteckning öfver svenska skådespel uppförda på Stockholms theatrar 1737–1863.* Stockholm, 1866

Ek , Sverker R. *Spelplatsens magi: Alf Sjöbergs regikonst.* Stockholm, 1988

Engel, P. G. and Leif Janzon. *Sju decennier: Svensk teater under 1900-talet.* Stockholm, 1980

Erdman, Nils. *Ur rokokoens liv.* Stockholm, 1925

Falck, August. *Fem år med Strindberg.* 2nd edn. Stockholm, 1935

Flodmark, Johan. *Bollhusen och Lejonkulen i Stockholm.* Stockholm, 1897

Når dramatiske teatern grundades. Stockholm, 1914

Stenborgska skådebanorna: Bidrag til Stockholms teaterhistorie. Stockholm, 1893

Fredrikson, Gustaf. *Teaterminnen.* Stockholm, 1918

Grandinson, Emil. *Teatern vid Trädgårdsgatan.* Stockholm, 1902

Gran, Ulf and Ulla-Britta Lagerroth, eds. *Perspektiv på teater.* Stockholm, 1971

Gustaviansk teater skildrad af Pehr Hilleström, eds. Agne Beijer and Gustaf Hilleström. Stockholm, 1947

Hedberg, Frans. *Svenska skådespelare: Karakteristiker och porträtter.* Stockholm, 1884

Hedvall, Alfred. *Strindberg på Stockholmsscenen 1870–1922.* Stockholm, 1923

Hillberg, Olof. *Teater i Sverige utanför huvadstaden.* Stockholm, 1948

Hilleström, Gustaf. *Swedish Theatre during Five Decades.* Stockholm, 1962

Hoogland, Claes and Gösta Kjellin, eds. *Bilder ur svensk teaterhistoria.* Stockholm, 1970

Josephson, Ludvig. *Theater-Regie. Regissörskap och i-scen-sättningskonst.* Stockholm, 1892

Våra Teater-förhållanden. Stockholm, 1870

Josephson, Ragnar and Claes Hoogland. *Från Johanna til Amorina: Bilder och repliker från Dramatens spelår 1948–1951.* Stockholm, 1951

Klemming, G. E. *Sveriges dramatiska litteratur til och med 1875.* Stockholm, 1863–79

Kvam, Kela, ed. *Strindberg's Post-Inferno Plays.* Copenhagen, 1994

Lagerkvist, Pär. *Modern Theatre: Seven Plays and an Essay,* trans. Thomas R. Buckman. Lincoln, NE, 1966

Lagerroth, Ulla-Britta. *Regi i möte med drama och samhälle.* Stockholm, 1978

Lamm, Martin. *August Blanche som Stockholmsskildare.* 2nd edn. Stockholm, 1950

August Strindberg. Stockholm, 1948

Levertin, Oscar. *Gustaf III som dramatisk författare.* Samlade skrifter 18, 2nd edn.
Stockholm, 1911
Teater och drama under Gustaf III. Samlade skrifter 17, 2nd edn. Stockholm, 1911
Lewenhaupt, Eugene, *Bref rörande teatern under Gustaf III 1788–92.* Stockholm, 1894
Liljequist, Ann-Margret. *Sandro Malmquist och hans verksamhet som scenograf.*
Stockholm, 1985
Lindberg, August. *Barndoms- och ungdomsminnen.* Stockholm, 1915
Lindberg, Per. *August Lindberg, skådespelaren och människan.* Stockholm, 1943
Bakom masker. Stockholm, 1949
Kring ridån. Stockholm, 1932
Regiproblem. Stockholm, 1927
Linder, Erik H. *Fem decennier av 1900-talet.* 2 vols. Stockholm, 1967
Ljunggren, Gustaf. *Svenska dramat intill slutet af sjuttonde århundradet.* Lund and
Copenhagen, 1864
Marker, Lise-Lone, and Frederick J. Marker. *Ingmar Bergman: Four Decades in the
Theatre.* Cambridge and New York, 1982. (Revised and expanded in *Ingmar
Bergman: a Life in the Theatre.* Cambridge and New York, 1992.)
Mattson, Inger, ed. *Gustavian Opera: An Interdisciplinary Reader in Swedish Opera,
Dance and Theatre 1771–1809.* Uppsala, 1991
Molander, Olof, *Detta är jag . . .* Stockholm, 1961
Molin, Nils. *Shakespeare och Sverige intill 1800-talets mitt.* Göteborg, 1931
Näslund, Erik and Elisabeth Sörenson, eds. *Kungliga dramatiska teatern
1788–1988.* Stockholm, 1988
Nordensvan, Georg. *I rampljus.* Stockholm, 1900
Svensk teater och svenska skådespelare. 2 vols. Stockholm, 1917–18
Nya teaterhistoriska studier. Föreningen Drottningholmsteaterns Vänner 12.
Stockholm, 1967
Öhman, Carl. *Strindberg and the Origins of Scenic Expressionism.* Michigan and
Helsingfors, 1961
Ollén, Gunnar. *Strindbergs dramatik.* 4th revised edn. Stockholm, 1982
Personne, Nils. *Svenska teatern.* 8 vols. Stockholm, 1913–27
Ranft, Albert. *Memoirer.* Stockholm, 1928
Richardson, Gunnar. *Oscarisk teaterpolitik.* Stockholm, 1966
Ringby, Per. *Författarens dröm på scenen: Harald Molanders regi och författarskap.*
Stockholm, 1987
Robinson, Michael, ed. *Strindberg's Letters.* 2 vols. Chicago, 1992
Rock, Freddie. *Tradition och förnyelse: Svensk dramatik och teater från 1914–1922.*
Stockholm, 1977
Rosenqvist, Claes, ed. *Den svenska nationalscenen: Tradition och reformer på
Dramaten under 200 år.* Stockholm, 1988
Rydell, Gerda. *Adertonhundratalets historiska skådespel i Sverige före Strindberg.*
Stockholm, 1928
Schück, Henrik. *Messenius.* Stockholm, 1920

Silverstolpe, Carl. *Käller til svenska teaterns historia.* Stockholm, 1877
Svenska teaterns äldste öden. Stockholm, 1882
Sjöberg, Alf. *Teater som besvärejlse,* eds. Sverker R. Ek et al. Stockholm, 1982
Sjögren, Henrik. *Ingmar Bergman på teatern.* Stockholm, 1968
Regi Ingmar Bergman. Dagbok från Dramaten 1969. Stockholm, 1969
Stage and Society in Sweden: Aspects of Swedish Theatre since 1945. Stockholm, 1979
Smedmark, Carl Reinhold, ed. *August Strindbergs dramer.* 4 vols. Stockholm, 1962–70
Smith, Isak Fredrik. *Teater förr och nu.* Stockholm, 1896
Sprinchorn, Evert. *Strindberg as Dramatist.* New Haven and London, 1982
Stjernström, Edvard. *Några ord om teatern.* Stockholm, 1870
Stribolt, Barbro. *Stockholms 1800-talsteatrar-byggnadens utveckling.* Stockholm, 1982
Strindberg, August. *Brev,* ed. Torsten Eklund. 15 vols. Stockholm, 1948–76
Open Letters to the Intimate Theatre, trans. Walter Johnson. Seattle, 1967
Samlade otryckta skrifter, ed. Vilhelm Carlheim-Gyllensköld. 2 vols. Stockholm, 1918–19
Samlade skrifter, ed. John Landquist. 55 vols. Stockholm, 1912–20. (To be superceded by *Nationalupplagan av August Strindbergs samlade verk,* 68 vols. Stockholm, 1981–. Forty volumes of this edition are now in print or in press.)
The Son of a Servant, trans. Evert Sprinchron. Garden City, NY, 1966
Strindbergfejden, ed. Harry Järv. Solna, 1968
Sundler, Eva. *Isaac Grünewalds scenografi 1920–1930.* Uppsala, 1975
Svandberg, Johannes. *Kungl. teatrarne under ett halft sekel 1890–1910.* 2 vols. Stockholm, 1917–18
Teaterhistoriska studier. Föreningen Drottningholmsteaterns Vänner 2. Stockholm, 1940
Törnqvist, Egil. *Bergman och Strindberg: Spöksonaten – drama och iscensättning Dramaten 1973.* Stockholm, 1973
Törnqvist, Egil and Barry Jacobs. *Strindberg's Miss Julie: a Play and its Transpositions.* Norwich, 1988
Torsslow, Stig. *Dramatenaktörernas republik: Dramatiska teatern under associations-tiden 1888–1907.* Stockholm, 1975
Van Boer, Bertil, ed. *Gustav III and the Swedish Stage: Opera, Theatre and Other Foibles.* Lewiston, NY, 1993
Waal, Carla Rae. *Harriet Bosse, Strindberg's Muse and Interpreter.* Carbondale, 1990
Wahlund, Per Erik. *Avsidesrepliker: Teaterkritik 1961–1965.* Stockholm, 1966
Scenväxling: Teaterkritik 1954–1960. Stockholm, 1962
Wettergren, Erik and Ivar Lignell, eds. *Svensk scenkonst och film.* Stockholm, 1940
Widerström, C. H. *Minne af Kungl. dramatiska teatern.* Stockholm, 1825
Wiselgren, Oscar. *Bidrag till kännedomen om 1600-talsdramat i Sverige.* Stockholm, 1909

Wikland, Erik. *Elizabethan Players in Sweden 1591–92*, 3rd edn. Stockholm, 1977

Wollin, Nils G. *Desprez i Sverige: Louis Jean Desprez' verksamhet 1784–1804.*
    Stockholm, 1936

Special issues in English

The Drama Review, 26:3 (1982): Scandinavian Theatre

Nordic Theatre Studies, 6:1–2 (1993): Srindberg in Performance (published
    as supplement to *Theatre Research International*, 18 [1993])

Scandinavica, 31:2 (1992): Special Drama Issue

Index